USA TODAY bestselling author **Naima Simone**'s love of romance was first stirred by Mills & Boon books pilfered from her grandmother. Now she spends her days writing sizzling romances with a touch of humour and snark.

She is wife to her own real-life superhero and mother to two awesome kids. They live in perfect, domestically challenged bliss in the Southern United States.

USA TODAY bestselling author **Jules Bennett** has published over sixty books and never tires of writing happy endings. Writing strong heroines and alpha heroes is Jules's favourite way to spend her workdays. Jules hosts weekly contests on her Facebook fan page and loves chatting with readers on Twitter, Facebook and via email through her website. Stay up-to-date by signing up for her newsletter at julesbennett.com

BLACK TIE BILLIONAIRE

NAIMA SIMONE

CALIFORNIA SECRETS

JULES BENNETT

MILLS & BOON

First Published in Great Britain 2019
by Mills & Boon, an imprint of HarperCollinsPublishers,
1 London Bridge Street, London, SE1 9GF

Black Tie Billionaire © 2019 Naima Simone
California Secrets © 2019 Jules Bennett

ISBN: 978-0-263-27192-8

0919

MIX
Paper from
responsible sources
FSC® C007454

This book is produced from independently certified FSC™ paper to ensure responsible forest management.

For more information visit: www.harpercollins.co.uk/green

Printed and bound in Spain
by CPI, Barcelona

BLACK TIE BILLIONAIRE

NAIMA SIMONE

To Gary. 143.

One

She was beautiful.

Gideon Knight tuned out the man speaking to him as he studied the petite woman weaving a path through the crowded ballroom. Even wearing the white shirt, black bow tie and dark pants of the waitstaff, she stood out like the brightest jewel among the hundreds of guests at the Du Sable City Gala, the annual event of the Chicago social season, rendering those around her to mere cubic zirconia.

How was it that only *he* noticed the elegant length of her neck, the straight line of her back that tapered at the waist and flowed out in a gentle, sensual swell of hips? How did the other people in the room not ogle the particular way the light from the crystal chandeliers hit her bronze skin, causing it to gleam? How did they not stop and study the graceful stride that wouldn't have been out of place on the most exclusive catwalk?

Had he said beautiful? He meant exquisite.

And he hadn't even seen her face.

Yet.

"Excuse me." Gideon abruptly interrupted the prattling

of the older gentleman, not bothering with a polite explanation for walking away.

The other man's surprised sputtering should've dredged up a semblance of regret, especially since Gideon's mother had hammered better manners into him. But just ten years ago this gentleman wouldn't have deigned to acknowledge Gideon's existence. Then he'd been just another penniless, dream-filled, University of Chicago business student. He hadn't been *the* Gideon Knight, cofounder and CEO of Kay-Cee Corp, one of the hottest and most successful start-up companies to hit the market in the last five years. Now that he was a multibillionaire, this businessman, and people of his tax bracket and social sphere, damn near scraped their chins on the floor with all the bowing and kowtowing they directed Gideon's way.

Money and power had that peculiar effect.

Usually, he could dredge up more patience, but he despised events like this high society benefit gala. One thing he'd learned in his grueling battle to breach the inner sanctum zealously guarded by the obscenely wealthy one percent was that a good portion of business deals were landed at dinner tables, country club golf courses and social events like the Du Sable City Gala. So even though attending ranked only slightly higher than shopping with his sister or vacationing in one of Dante's nine levels of hell, he attended.

But for the first time that he could remember, he was distracted from networking. And again, for the first time, he welcomed the disruption.

He wound his way through the tuxedoed and gowned throng, pretending not to hear when his name was called, and uttering a "Pardon me" when more persistent individuals tried to halt him with a touch to his arm. Many articles written about him had mentioned his laser-sharp focus, and at this moment, it was trained on a certain server with black hair swept into a low knot at the back of her head, a body created for the sweetest sin and skin that had his fingertips itching with the need to touch...to caress.

That need—the unprecedented urgency of it—should've been a warning to proceed with caution. And if he'd paused, he might've analyzed why the impulse to approach her, to look into her face, raked at him like a tiger's sharp claws. He might've retreated, or placed distance between him and her. Discipline, control, focus—they were the daily refrains of his life, the blocks upon which he'd built his business, his success. That this unknown woman already threatened all three by just being in the room... Not even his ex-fiancée had stirred this kind of attraction in him. Which only underscored why he should walk away. It boded nothing good.

Yet he followed her with the determination of a predator stalking its unsuspecting prey.

How cliché, but damn, how true. Because every instinct in him growled to capture, cover, take...bite.

She would be his tonight.

As the strength and certainty of the thought echoed inside him, he neared her. Close enough to glimpse the delicate line of her jaw and the vulnerable nape of her neck. To inhale the heady, sensual musk that contained notes of roses, and warmer hints of cedarwood and amber...or maybe almond.

Tonight's mission would be to discover which one.

For yet another time this evening, he murmured, "Excuse me." But in this instance, he wasn't trying to escape someone. No, he wanted to snare her. Keep her.

At least for the next few hours.

Look at me. Turn around and look at me.

The plea rebounded off his skull, and the seconds seemed to slow as she shifted, lifting her head and meeting his gaze.

His gut clenched, desire slamming into him so hard he braced himself against the impact. But it still left him reeling. Left his body tense, hard.

A long fringe of black hair swept over her forehead and dark-rimmed glasses perched on her nose, but neither could hide the strong, regal lines of her face, the sharp cheekbones, the chocolate eyes or the lush siren's call of her mouth.

Damn, that mouth.

He dragged his fascinated gaze away from it with a strength that deserved a gold medal. But nothing, not even God Himself, could cleanse his mind of the acts those curves elicited. Acts that left him throbbing and greedy.

"Did you need a glass of champagne?" she asked, lowering her eyes to the tray she held.

No, keep your eyes on me.

The order rolled up his throat and hovered on his tongue, but he locked it down. Damn, with just a few words uttered in a silk-and-midnight voice, he'd devolved into a caveman.

Once more, a warning to walk away clanged inside him, but—like moments earlier—he ignored it. Nothing else mattered at the moment. Nothing but having that sex-and-sin voice stroke his ears. Having those hands slip under his clothes to caress his skin. And those oval-shaped eyes fixed on him.

"What's your name?" He delivered a question of his own, answering hers by picking up a glass flute full of pale wine.

If he hadn't been studying her so closely, he might've missed the slight stiffening of her shoulders, the minute hesitation before, head still bowed, she said, "I need to continue…"

She shifted away from him, preparing to escape into the crowd.

"Wait." He lifted his arm, instinct guiding him to grasp her elbow to prevent her departure. But at the last moment, he lowered his arm back to his side.

As much as he wanted to discover how she felt under his hand, he refused to touch her without her permission. Rich assholes accosting the waitstaff was as old a story as a boss chasing his secretary around the desk. Even though his palm itched with the lack of contact, he slid his free hand into his front pocket.

The aborted motion seemed to grab her attention. She raised her head, a frown drawing her eyebrows together.

"Gideon Knight," he said, offering her his name. "You have my name. Can I have yours?"

Again, that beat of hesitation. Then, with a small shake of her head, she murmured, "Camille."

"Camille," he repeated, savoring it as if it were one of the rich chocolate desserts that would follow the dinner course. "It's a lovely name. And it fits you."

Her eyes widened, an emotion he would've labeled panic flaring in their depths before she lowered her lashes, hiding her gaze from him. Again. "Thank you, Mr. Knight. If—"

"Gideon," he corrected. "For you, it's Gideon."

Her full lips firmed into a line seconds before she met his stare with one glinting in anger. How insane did it make him that he found the signs of her temper captivating... and sexy as hell?

"No offense, *Mr. Knight*—"

"In my experience, when someone starts a sentence with 'no offense,' they intend to offend," he drawled.

Once more he saw that flicker of anger, and an exhilaration that was usually reserved for fierce business negotiations surged in his chest. The exhilaration meant he was engaging with a worthy opponent.

"I'm going out on a limb and assuming your ego can

take the hit," she shot back. Then, as if she realized what she'd snapped—and who she'd snapped at—she winced, briefly squeezing her eyes shut. "I apologize—"

"Oh, don't disappoint me now by turning meek, Camille," he purred, arching an eyebrow.

In a distant corner of his mind, he marveled at who he'd become in this moment. Flirting, teasing, goddamn *purring*—they weren't him. His mouth either didn't know this information or didn't care. "I assure you, I can take it," he added.

Take whatever she wanted to give him, whether it was her gaze, her conversation or more. And God, he hungered for the *more*. Greedy bastard that he was, he'd claim whatever she chose to dole out.

"Mr. Knight," she began, defiance clipping his name, "I don't know if approaching the staff and toying with them is one of your usual forms of entertainment. But since you've invited me not to be *meek*, let me tell you this might be a game to you, but the waitstaff aren't toys to alleviate your boredom. This is a livelihood for workers who depend on a paycheck and not getting fired for fraternizing with the guests."

Shock vibrated through him like a plucked chord on his favorite Martin D-45 acoustic guitar.

Shock and…delight.

Other than his mother and family, no one had the balls to speak to him like she had, much less reprimand him. Excitement—something he hadn't experienced in so long he couldn't remember the last occurrence—tripped and stumbled down his spine.

"I don't play games," he said. "They're a waste of time. Why be coy when being honest achieves the goal faster?"

"And what's your goal here, Mr. Knight?" she challenged, not hiding her sneer.

If she understood how his pulse jumped and his body throbbed every time she stated "Mr. Knight" with a haughtiness worthy of royalty, she would probably swear a vow of silence.

"Cop a feel in a dark hallway? A little slap and tickle in a broom closet?" she asked.

"I'm too old to cop a feel. And I don't 'slap and tickle' either, whatever that is. I fuck."

Her head jerked back at his blunt statement, her eyes widening behind the dark frames. Even with the din of chatter and laughter flowing around them, he caught her sharp gasp.

A voice sounding suspiciously like that of Gray Chandler, his business partner and best friend—his only friend—hissed a curse at him. How many times had Gray warned him to temper his brusque, straightforward manner? Well, to be more accurate, his friend described Gideon as tactless. Pretty words weren't his forte; honesty was. Normally, he didn't regret his abruptness. Like he'd told her, he didn't indulge in games. But in this moment, he almost regretted it.

Especially if she walked away from him.

"Is that why you stopped me? To proposition me?" She dropped her gaze to the champagne glass in his hand, and with just that glance let him know she didn't buy his pretense of wanting the wine. He shrugged, setting it behind him on one of the high tables scattered around the ballroom.

"Why single me out?" she continued. "Because I'm so beautiful you couldn't help yourself?" she mocked. "Or because I'm a server, and you're a guest in a position of power? What happens if I say no? Will I suddenly find myself relieved of my job?"

Disgust and the first flicker of anger wormed its way through his veins. "Do I want to spend a night with you? Inside you? Yes," he stated, and again her eyes flared wide at his frankness before narrowing. "I told you, I don't lie. I don't play games. But if you decline, then no, you would still have a check and employment at the end of the evening. I don't need to blackmail women into my bed, Camille. Besides, a willing woman, a woman who wants my hands on her body, who pleads for what she knows I can give her, is far more arousing, more pleasurable. And any man worth his dick would value that over a woman who's coerced or forced into handing over something that should be offered or surrendered of her own free will."

She silently studied him, the fire fading from her stare, but something else flicked in those dark eyes. And that "something" had him easing a step closer, yet stopping short of invading her personal space.

"To answer your other question," he murmured. "Why did I single you out? Your first guess was correct. Because you are so beautiful I couldn't help following you around this over-the-top ballroom filled with people who possess more money than sense. The women here can't outshine you. They're like peacocks, spreading their plumage, desperate to be noticed, and here you are among them, like the moon. Bright, alone, above it all and eclipsing every one of them. What I don't understand is how no one else noticed before me. Why every man in this place isn't standing behind me in a line just for the chance to be near you."

Silence swelled around them like a bubble, muting the din of the gala. His words seemed to echo in the cocoon, and he marveled at them. Hadn't he sworn he didn't do pretty words? Yet it had been him talking about peacocks and moons.

What was she doing to him?

Even as the question echoed in his mind, her head tilted back and she stared at him, her lovely eyes darker...hotter. In that moment, he'd stand under a damn balcony and serenade her if she continued looking at him like that. He curled his fingers into his palm, reminding himself with the pain that he couldn't touch her. Still, the only sound that reached his ears was the quick, soft pants breaking on her pretty lips.

As ridiculous as it seemed, he swore each breath slid under his clothes, swept over his skin. He ached to have each moist puff dampen his shoulders, his chest as her fingernails twisted in his hair, dug into his muscles, clinging to him as he drove them both to the point of carnal madness.

The growl prowled up his throat and out of him before he could contain it.

"I—I need to go," she whispered, already shifting back and away from him. "I—" She didn't finish the thought, but turned and waded into the crowd, distancing herself from him.

He didn't follow; she hadn't said no, but she hadn't said yes, either. And though he'd caught the desire in her gaze— his stomach still ached from the gut punch of it—she had to come to him.

Or ask him to come for her.

Rooted where she'd left him, he tracked her movements.

Saw the moment she cleared the mass of people and strode in the direction of the double doors where more tray-bearing staff emerged and exited.

Saw when she paused, palm pressed to one of the panels.

Saw when she glanced over her shoulder in his direction.

Even across the distance of the ballroom, the electric shock of that look whipped through him, sizzled in his veins. Moments later, she disappeared from view. Didn't matter; his feet were already moving in her direction.

That glance, that look. It'd sealed her fate.

Sealed it for both of them.

Two

Shay Camille Neal pushed through the doors leading into the huge, industrial kitchen that wouldn't have been out of place in a Michelin-star restaurant. With a world-famous chef renowned for his temper as well as his magic with food, a sous chef and army of station and line cooks bustling around the stainless steel countertops and range stoves, the area hummed with activity.

Under ordinary circumstances, she would've been enthralled, attempting to soak up whatever knowledge she could from the professionals attending. But the current circumstances were as far from ordinary as chicken nuggets were from coq au vin.

First, as a member of one of the oldest, wealthiest and most influential families in Chicago, she usually attended the Du Sable City Gala as a guest, not a server. But when her best friend, Bridgette, called her earlier in the afternoon sounding like a foghorn had replaced her voice box, Shay had agreed to take Bridgette's place as a member of the catering staff. Though her friend owned and ran a fledgling food truck business, she still helped mitigate expenses and pay her personal bills with jobs on the side. The position with this particular catering company was one of her regulars, and Bridgette couldn't afford to lose the gig.

Shay had planned on skipping the gala, anyway. Facing a night at home with another binge of *House of Cards* on Netflix versus actually working in the periphery of a famous chef, the choice had been a no-brainer. Besides, Bridgette had assured Shay that most of her duties as an assistant to the line cooks would keep her in the kitchen.

Still, she'd donned a wig, dark brown contacts and glasses, as well as Bridgette's uniform. Because while she'd decided to skip out on the social event of the season, her older brother, Trevor, and his fiancée, Madison Reus—Senator Julian Reus's only daughter—were attending. Trevor already didn't approve of Shay's friendship with Bridgette. If he caught Shay doing anything less-than-becoming of the Neal name, especially because of her best friend, he would lose it. And Shay was pretty certain he would consider prepping vegetables and serving champagne cardinal sins.

In her defense, though, when the catering supervisor shoved a tray of sparkly wine at her and ordered her to make the rounds of the ballroom, she couldn't exactly say no.

Still, everything should've been fine—would've been fine—if not for one Gideon Knight.

Smoky desire coiled in her belly. She set the almost empty tray on one of the stations and pressed a fist to her navel. Not that the futile gesture extinguished the glowing embers.

Swallowing a groan, she strode toward the back of the kitchen and the employee break room. Shutting the door behind her, she entered the bathroom and twisted the faucets, thrusting her palms under the gushing water. Her quick version of a cold shower. Shaking her head at her foolishness, she finished washing her hands, but afterward, instead of returning to the kitchen, she stood in front of the mirror, staring at her reflection. But it wasn't her image she saw.

It was Gideon Knight.

They're like peacocks, spreading their plumage, desperate to be noticed, and here you are among them, like the moon. Bright, alone, above it all and eclipsing every one of them.

She exhaled slowly, the words spoken in that all-things-secret-and-sinful voice echoing in her head. In her chest. And lower. With any other man, she would've waved off the compliment as insincere flattery that tended to roll off men's tongues when they came across the heiress to one of the largest financial management conglomerates in the country. The compliments meant nothing, like dandelion fluff on a breeze. No substance and changing with the wind.

But not with Gideon Knight.

There had been a ring of truth in the blunt observation. As if his description of her wasn't an opinion but fact. She'd just met him, but she couldn't shake the sense that he didn't dole out flowery compliments often. As he'd stated so flatly, he didn't play games.

She believed him. But it only deepened her confusion over why he'd approached her of all people. To most of the attendees in the ballroom, she'd been invisible, inconsequential. Just another staff member there to serve them.

But not to him.

Even in a room full of Chicago's wealthiest and most glamorous people, he stood out. In the way a sleek, silent shark would stand out in a pool of clown fish.

God, she was officially losing it. And she laid the blame squarely at the feet of Gideon Knight.

Because, really, how could any woman stare into those midnight eyes and not forget everything but how she could willingly drown in them, even as he submerged her in a pleasure as dark and stunning as his gaze?

As soon as the illicit thought entered her head an image of him crouched over her, all that midnight-black hair loose from its knot and flowing over his shoulders, tumbling around them, flashed through her mind. Her heart thumped against her chest, and she exhaled an unsteady breath, that flame of unwanted desire dancing low in her belly again. With a mental shove, she thrust the hot image out of her mind, but the vision of how he'd looked just moments ago, when she turned for one last glance, refused to be evicted as easily.

His tailor, whoever he or she was, must've been in love with Gideon because his tuxedo traced his powerful but lean frame. From the wide shoulders and chest that tapered to a slim waist and down to long, muscular legs, he was the picture of urbane elegance and wealth. Strength. Beauty.

Imperial.

The word leaped into her head, and though she wanted to scoff at the description, she couldn't. It fit. With the beautiful eyes, the sharp slant of cheekbones, the arrogant nose, the wide, sensual, almost cruel curve of his mouth and the rock-hard jut of his jaw, he reminded her of a long-ago king from a mysterious Asian country, standing on a wall, an unseen wind teasing his long black hair as he surveyed the land he ruled. Hard, shrewd, somehow removed from the masses.

He would've been completely intimidating if not for the incongruity of all that hair pulled into a knot at the back of his head. Someone so polished, so sophisticated, so rigid in his appearance wearing a…man bun.

It was the rebellious flouting of the unspoken, constricting rules that governed their social realm that had stirred a curiosity she couldn't erase. Even now.

You're being ridiculous.

Shaking her head, she emitted a sound of self-directed disgust and yanked a brown paper towel from the dispensary. She quickly dried her hands, tossed the now damp towel in the trash and strode from the bathroom. With at least another three hours of work ahead of her, she couldn't afford to remain hiding back here any longer. More prep work awaited her, as dinner hadn't even been served yet—

The door to the break room swung open, and she barely managed to stifle her startled gasp.

The tall, imposing figure of Gideon Knight filled the doorway.

Her heart lodged in her throat. What the hell was he doing back here? But only seconds passed before the answer whispered through her skull.

You.

Denial, swift and firm, rose within her. But it couldn't extinguish the kindling of desire and traitorous, *foolish* hope.

"What are you doing here?" she demanded, swiping her already-dry palms down the sides of her pants. And when his gaze took in the nervous gesture, she cursed herself for betraying her agitation to this man.

"Looking for you."

Excitement fluttered in her before she could smother the reaction. Crossing her arms over her chest, she frowned. Fought the instinctive urge to retreat from the intense, sexual magnetism that seemed to pour off him and vibrate in the room.

"Well, I need to return to work." She pretended to glance down at the slim, gold-faced watch on her wrist. "So, if you'll excuse me…"

An emotion crossed his face, but was there and gone

before she could decipher it. Probably irritation at being told no. "I wanted to apol—"

But the rest of his explanation snapped off as the room plummeted into darkness.

Three

A cry slipped out of Shay, panic clawing at her throat.

The deep, thick dark pressed down on her chest like a weight, cutting off her breath.

What was going on? What happened? Why…?

"Camille." The sound of that calm voice carrying an undercurrent of steel snapped her out of the dizzying fall into hysteria. Hands wrapped around both her upper arms, the grip firm, steadying. His voice and his touch grounded her, although her pulse continued to thud and echo in her head like a hammer. "Easy." One of his hands slid up her arm, over her shoulder and slipped around the back of her neck. Squeezed. "Stay with me. Breathe."

She closed her eyes, as if that could block out the utter lack of light. Still, she latched on to him—his voice, his fresh yet earthy scent of wind and sandalwood, the solid density of the forearms she'd at some point clutched. Seconds, minutes—hell, it felt like hours—passed while she focused on calming her racing heart, on breathing. And soon, the sense of being buried alive started to lift.

His hold on her arm and neck never eased.

As the initial bite of panic slowly unhinged its jaws, the

weight of his touch—the security and comforting effect of it—penetrated her fear.

"—I'm sorry." Embarrassed, she heard a wobbly chuckle escape her. Belatedly, she loosened her grip on him and dropped her arms. "God, I don't... I'm not even afraid of the dark," she whispered.

"You have nothing to apologize for," he reassured her.

His hands abandoned her neck and arm, but one located and clasped her fingers. In the next instant, a pale blue glow appeared. A cell phone. The illumination barely pushed back the inky thickness surrounding them, but it highlighted his face, and relief weakened her knees. Only moments ago, she'd wanted to get as far away from him as possible. And now her eyes stung with gratefulness for his serene presence. For not being alone.

"I need to go see if I can find out what's going on. Here." Holding the cell out in front of him, he carefully guided her to the couch against the far wall. Still holding her hand, he lowered her to the cushion. "Will you be all right? I have to take my cell with me to try and either get a call or text out. I promise to return in a few minutes."

"Of course." She nodded, injecting a vein of steel into her voice. God, she was stronger than this. "I'll be fine here."

In the cell's minimal light, she caught his steady, measuring stare. "Good," he said after a few moments, returning her nod. "I'll be right back."

He disappeared, returning her to the dark. She focused on maintaining even breathing, reminding herself she hadn't been catapulted into a deep pit where terrifying, malformed things lurked, eager for the chance to take a bite out of her. She really shouldn't have watched Stephen King's *It* last night...

"Camille."

She jerked her head up, and once more that rush of relief washed over her as Gideon and his beautiful light appeared in front of her again.

"Hey," she said, unable to prevent the emotion from flooding her voice. "Were you able to find out anything?" Please let it be something fixable and short-lived, like the owner of this mansion had forgotten to pay his power bill.

"Blackout," he explained, tone grim, and her heart plummeted toward her stomach. "I wasn't able to get a call out, but I was able to send and receive a couple of texts to a contact on the police force. It's citywide. They're advising people to remain where they are, which," he continued, his full lips flattening for a brief second, "won't be an issue with us. I overheard security speaking to the chef and his staff. The tech guru who owns this overcompensating monstrosity of a home installed a so-called cutting-edge security system. And with the blackout, it's malfunctioned. We're all locked in for the foreseeable future."

She expelled a pent-up breath, pinching the bridge of her nose. Where was Trevor? Were he and Madison okay? What about Bridgette? Sick and in the dark? More than ever, Shay cursed leaving her phone in her car. Bridgette had warned her that her supervisor frowned on the staff having cells on them, so she'd stashed hers in her glove compartment, but now...

"We're going to be fine, Camille," Gideon said, his rough silk voice dragging her away from her worried thoughts. "Most likely, the blackout will only last several hours, and hopefully the boy genius will have his system worked out by them," he finished drily.

In spite of the anxiety over her brother and friend that still inundated her, she snorted. "Boy genius?"

Gideon arched a black eyebrow. "Have you seen him? He

can't be more than twenty-three. I swear, I can still smell the milk on his breath."

This time she snickered, belatedly palming her mouth to contain her amusement. "So you're what? The ripe old age of thirty? Thirty-three? And if you're here as a guest, then that means you must be at least wealthy or connected enough to have been invited. Which makes you what, Mr. Knight?" she asked, narrowing her eyes. "An idle man living off his family name and money? Or a successful businessman in his own right?"

She didn't know him, but he struck her as the latter. There was nothing about him that screamed idle. No, the sharklike intelligence that gleamed from his dark eyes belonged to a man who forged his own path, not one satisfied with walking the one others had paved for him.

He didn't immediately reply, but treated her to another of his intense gazes. He seemed to peer beneath skin and bone to the soul. To her secrets. With effort, she didn't shirk away from his scrutiny, instead notching her chin up and meeting his eyes without flinching.

Something glinted in his gaze, and the faint light from his phone tricked her into believing it might be admiration.

"I own and run a start-up that provides privately held companies with their equity needs. I suppose you can say we've been successful."

The vague and carefully constructed answer didn't stop recognition from rocking her. Start-up? As in KayCee Corp start-up? He couldn't possibly be *the* Gideon Knight, founder of the corporation that had taken the financial world by storm five years ago? If so, he was either exceedingly modest or being cagey with information.

Because KayCee Corp had been more than "successful." The electronic platform serviced major businesses, helping them track their shares with its top-of-the-line, unrivaled software. They'd recently announced their intentions to branch out and work with companies that were rolling out their initial public offerings. Though Trevor tried to keep Shay securely ensconced in the Social Development branch of RemingtonNeal Inc., their family business, she knew of KayCee Corp. Knew that Trevor desperately longed to acquire it.

Her wig, contacts and glasses concealed her true identity, but she still lifted her fingers to her cheek as if Gideon could see beneath the camouflage. Her throat tightened. Now would be a good time to come clean about who he sat with in the dark. But something held her back. Something, hell... She could identify it even without him searching her soul.

In that ballroom, Gideon Knight had gazed upon her with fascination, admiration...hunger. And he'd had no idea she was Shay Neal, heiress to a global financial empire. Not that she was an ugly duckling in a lake full of swans, but she bore no illusions. Her money, social status and connections were often just as much, if not more, of an allure than her appearance.

But not for him.

Even now, his dark stare roamed her face, lingering on her eyes before drifting over her cheekbones, her jaw, her mouth. Though it belied reason, she swore she could feel his gaze stroke over her skin. An illicit, mysterious, desire-stoking caress.

And here, in the isolated depths of this mansion, she wanted more.

Even if just for a little while.

The cloak of anonymity bestowed her with a gift of boldness—of freedom—she didn't ordinarily possess.

"I wonder what's going through your head right now?"

he murmured, drawing her from her thoughts. "And would you honestly tell me?"

That would be a no. "Careful, Mr. Knight," she drawled, tone dry. "You're beginning to sound a little too Edward Cullen-ish for my comfort."

"Last time I checked, I didn't sparkle in the sunlight or age out at eighteen years old. Although I do admit to a little biting. And liking it."

A blast of heat barreled through her, warring with surprise over his recognition of her *Twilight* reference. Curling her fingers into her palms, she willed the searing desire to abate, but it continued to burn a path along her veins.

"Still blunt, I see," she said, and no way could he miss the hoarseness rasping her voice. "You weren't lying when you claimed not to play games."

"Am I making you uncomfortable, Camille?" he asked, his head cocking to the side. His eyes narrowed on her, as if searching out the answer for himself.

She should say yes. Should order him to keep his straight-no-chaser compliments and need-stirring comments to himself.

Instead, she matched his head tilt. "And if I said you were?"

"Then I'd go out there in that kitchen and drag one of those chefs in here so you wouldn't be. Is that what you want?"

She shook her head, the denial almost immediate. "No," she said, although wisdom argued she should have him invite the whole crew into this small room. Protect her from herself. The self that couldn't help wondering if those stark angles softened with pleasure. Wondering if that hard-looking mouth became more pliable.

Wondering if that icy shield of control shattered under desire's flame?

A shiver danced over her skin. Waltzed along her nerve endings.

She was the moth dancing too close to those flames.

"What do you want?" he pressed, the deep timbre of his voice dipping lower.

He didn't move, didn't inch closer to her on the couch. But God, all that intensity crowded her, rubbed over her, slipped inside her. He wasn't a coy or playful man; he grasped the wealth of possibilities that question carried. And he offered her the choice of not addressing them...or taking all of them.

A lifetime of playing by the rules slowly unraveled beneath his heated stare. His question vibrated between them, a gauntlet thrown down. A red flag waved.

"Too many things to possibly number in the space of a blackout," she finally replied. Truth. And evasion. "But I'm fine with you here with me." She paused, and with her heart tapping an unsteady rhythm against her chest, added, "Only you."

A fierce approval and satisfaction flashed like diamonds in his eyes. "Good," he said, those same emotions reflected in the one word. "Because now we don't have to share this with anyone else." Reaching down, he picked up a plate and set it on the cushion between them. A grin curved her lips at the sight of the braised lamb, roasted vegetable medley and risotto piled on the fine china.

"Now, that's lovely," he murmured, his gaze not on the dinner but on her face.

She ducked her head, wishing the strands of the wig weren't tied back in a bun so they could hide the red stain creeping up her neck and flooding her face.

"You're certainly resourceful," she said, reaching for an asparagus tip. "Or sneaky."

His soft snort echoed between them. "I've been accused of both before. And both are just words. Whatever works to achieve my goal."

"Yes, I clearly remember your goal for this evening. You didn't mince words out there earlier. I guess you've achieved your aim. Spending the night with me."

Why had she brought up that conversation? What had possessed her to remind him of his claim to be with her—*inside* her? To see that glint of hunger again? To tempt him? God, she was flirting with danger. And doing so with a rashness that bordered on recklessness.

"Do you really want to dive into that discussion right now, Camille?" The question—a tease, a taunt—set her pulse off on a rapid tattoo.

Yes.

No.

"Not on an empty stomach," she whispered, retreating. From the faint quirk of his lips—the first hint of a smile she'd glimpsed on his austere face—he caught her withdrawal. "And you wouldn't happen to be hiding a bottle of wine over there, would you?"

The quirk deepened, and her heart stuttered. Actually skipped a couple beats at the beauty of that half smile. Jesus, he would be absolutely devastating if he ever truly let go. Her fingertips itched with the urge to trace those sensual lips. To curb the need, she brought her hands to her pants, intent on rubbing them down her thighs. But stopped herself, recalling they were damp from the food she'd just eaten.

"Take this." He reached inside his jacket and offered her a small white handkerchief.

Startled, she accepted it, again struck with how perceptive he seemed to be.

"Thank you," she murmured.

For the next half hour, they dined on the pilfered food, and as stellar and flavorful as the cuisine was, it didn't steal her attention like the man across from her. He...fascinated her. And after they finished, when he asked her if she would be fine with him turning off the phone's light to conserve the battery, she okayed it without hesitation.

Though he was basically a stranger to her, he emanated safety. Comfort. As if he would release all that barely leashed mercilessness on her behalf instead of against her. Maybe that made her fanciful, too. But in the dark, she could afford it.

Perhaps the blackness affected him in a similar fashion, because he opened up to her—well, as much as someone as controlled as Gideon Knight probably did. They spoke of mundane things. Hobbies. Worst dates. The best way to spend a perfect, lazy afternoon. All so simple, but she hung on every word. Enjoyed it. Enjoyed him.

Enjoyed the lack of sight that peeled away barriers.

Reveled in the desire that thrummed just below the surface like a drum keeping time, marching them forward to...what? She didn't know. And for the first time in longer than she could remember, she didn't weigh the effect of every word, the consequence of every action on the Neal family name.

Here, with him, she was just... Camille.

"We'll never see each other again once the lights come back on," she said. And it was true. They'd never see each other as Camille and Gideon, even if they happened to cross paths in the future. Because then, she would once more be Shay Neal of the Chicago Neals. "That almost makes me...

sad," she confessed, then scoffed, shaking her head, though he couldn't see the gesture. "Ridiculous, right?"

"Why?" he asked. "Honesty is never silly. It's too rare to be ridiculous."

A twinge of guilt pinged inside her chest. She was being dishonest about the most basic thing—her identity. "Because fantasies are for teenage girls, not for grown women who know better."

"And what do you believe you know, Camille?"

She turned toward him, toward the temptation of his voice. "That if not for a citywide blackout, a man like you wouldn't be with me..." She paused. "Talking."

"I don't know if I should be more offended that you're belittling me or yourself with that statement." A whisper of sound and then fingers—questing, gentle, but so damn sure—stroked across her jaw, her temple, the strangely callused tips abrading her skin. What did a man like him do to earn that hardened skin that spoke of hard labor, not crunching numbers? "Yes, I do. It annoys me more that you would demean yourself. A woman like you," he murmured. "Beautiful. Intelligent. Bold. Confident. What man wouldn't want to spend time with you? Only one too blind or stupid to see who stands right before his eyes. Read any financial blog or journal, Camille. I'm not a stupid man."

She snorted, trying to mask the flame licking at her from the inside out. Cover the yearning his words caused deep within her. "How did you manage to compliment yourself and reprimand me at the same time?"

But he ignored her attempt to inject levity into the thick, pulsing atmosphere. No, instead, he swept another caress over her skin. This time, brushing a barely there touch to the curve of her bottom lip. She trembled. And God, he had to sense it, to feel it. Because he repeated it.

"I don't date," he informed her, and the frankness of the

statement caught her off guard. Almost made her forget the long fingers still cradling her jaw.

Almost.

"Excuse me?" she breathed.

"I don't date," he repeated. "I know something, too, Camille. Relationships, commitments—they're lies we tell ourselves so we can justify using each other. Sex. Need. Passion—they're honest. The body can't lie. Lust is the great equalizer regardless of social status, race or tax bracket. So no, I rescind my earlier statement. If not for this blackout, it's very possible we wouldn't have passed these last couple of hours talking. But I don't care if we were in a ballroom or a boardroom, I would've noticed you. I would've wanted you. I would've done everything in my power to convince you to trust me with your body, your pleasure."

Oh damn.

She couldn't breathe. Couldn't move. Suspended by the hunger swamping her.

"Your turn, moonbeam," he said, his hand falling away from her face. And she immediately missed his touch, that firm grasp. Because he couldn't see her, she lifted her fingers to the skin that continued to tingle. "Tell me again what you know."

Moonbeam. The endearment reminded her of their conversation in the ballroom. Her brain argued that the word had nothing to do with love or sweetness and everything to do with hunger and darkness, and yet she jolted at the coiling in her lower belly.

"I know you're telling me you haven't changed your mind about wanting to spend the night with me. Inside me," she added, on a soft, almost hushed rush of breath.

"And have you changed yours?"

From the moment you called me your moon.

The truth reverberated against her skull, but she clenched her jaw, preventing it from escaping. Her defenses had started crumbling long before he'd come looking for her.

Did this make her a cliché? He wasn't the first man to profess he wanted her, but he was the first she longed to touch with a need that unnerved her. She'd never yearned for a man's hands on her body as much as she longed for Gideon Knight's big, elegant, long-fingered ones stroking over her breasts. Or gripping her hips, holding her steady for a deep, hot possession that had her sex spasming in anticipation...in preparation.

She exhaled a breath. Right, he still waited for her answer, and she suspected he wouldn't make a move, wouldn't feather another of those caresses over her until she gave it to him.

"Yes," she confessed, her heart thudding heavily against her rib cage.

"About what, Camille?" he pressed, relentless. "What have you decided? What do you want?"

He wasn't granting her a reprieve; he was making her say it. Making her lay herself bare.

Her sense of self-preservation launched a last-ditch effort to save her from who she'd become in the dark. Who she'd become in that ballroom. But desire crushed it, and she willingly surrendered to the irresistible lure of freedom...of him.

"You," she whispered. "I've decided on you."

She slid across the small space separating them and located his face. A soft groan rolled up her throat, and she didn't even try and trap it. Not when she curved her hand around the strong jut of his jaw, the faintest bristles of what would become a five o'clock shadow abrading her palm. Unable to stop, she stroked the pad of her thumb over the mouth she had been craving since she first noticed him.

Strong teeth sank into the flesh of her thumb, not hurting her but exerting enough pressure that she gasped. Then whimpered.

How had she gone twenty-five years without being aware that spot connected to her sex? That it would make her thighs clench on an ache so sweet, it maddened her?

Another gasp broke free of her, this one of surprise, as his fingers closed around her arms and abruptly dragged her to her feet. She swayed, but he didn't release her until she steadied. Then the sudden flare of light from his cell phone startled her again. After the dark, the pale glow seemed almost too bright. She blinked, glancing from the screen to the shadows it cast over Gideon's face.

"Why…" She waved toward the phone. "What about saving the battery?"

He shook his head, his features sharper, appearing to be hewn from flint. Except for those glittering, almost fevered eyes. *Oh wow…* Such intensity and…and greed there. It stirred her own hunger, stoking the fire inside her until she burned with it.

"I don't give a damn. I need to see you," he growled, shrugging out of his jacket and tossing it to the floor. Still controlled, but the movement carried an edge. And it thrilled her. "Take off your shirt, Camille. Show me what you've decided I can have."

With trembling fingers, she reached for the buttons of her white shirt. It required several attempts, but she managed to open it, and with his black gaze fixed on her, slipped it off. Warm air kissed her bared shoulders, the tops of her breasts and stomach.

A part of her argued that she should feel at least a modicum of modesty, and maybe Shay would. But not Camille.

As crazy as it seemed, here, with Gideon, she had become a different person. The flip side of the same coin.

Normally reserved, bound by expectations and family. But now... uninhibited, free to indulge in her own selfish desires.

"Gorgeous," he rasped. "So fucking gorgeous. Come here." He beckoned.

His almost growled compliment stole more of her breath.

"Your turn," she ordered, remaining in place, although her fingers already prickled to stroke the skin and muscle hidden beneath the thin veneer of civility presented by his tuxedo. "Show me what you promised me I can take."

His fingers tightened around the edges of his shirt, and for a moment, she feared—hoped—he would just rip it off. But once more, that control reemerged, and he removed his cuff links, tossing them carelessly on top of his jacket. Then, button by button, he revealed himself to her.

She stared at the male animal before her. Miles and miles of smooth flesh stretched taut over tight muscle and tendon. Wide shoulders, a deep chest. Narrowed waist. A corrugated ladder of abs. A thin, silky line of hair started just above a shadowed navel and traveled below, disappearing into the waistband of his suit pants. And darker swirls and shapes she couldn't make out spread over the left side of his ribs, emphasizing the hint of wildness, of fierceness he couldn't quite conceal.

Perfection.

He was utter perfection.

This time, he didn't need to demand she come to him. Shay covered the distance on her own, arms already extended. With a hum of pleasure, she settled her palms on him, smoothed them up to his shoulders, pushing the shirt down his arms. Then she returned to her exploration. Scraping her nails over small, flat nipples, mapping the thin network of veins under his skin, following the path of hair that started midchest. Dragging her fingertips down the delineated ridge of muscles covering his stomach. Tracing the black lines of his tattoo, wishing she could aim more light on it so she could decipher its shape.

He stood still, letting her tour him without interference, though he fairly hummed with intensity, with barely leashed power.

"Are you finished yet?" he growled, and she tilted her head back to meet his hooded gaze, her fingers settling on the band of his pants.

"Not even close," she breathed. "Kiss me."

Someone with his extraordinary sense of restraint most likely didn't take or obey orders from anyone. But with a flash in those eyes, he gripped the bun at the back of her head and tugged. She gave only a brief thought to the security of the wig before her neck arched. The next breath she took was his.

Her groan was ragged and so needy it should've embarrassed her. Maybe it would tomorrow in the harsh light of day. But tonight, with his tongue twisting and tangling with hers, she couldn't care. Not when he tasted like everything delicious but forbidden—chocolate-flavored wine, New York cheesecake, impropriety and wickedness. Not when he nipped at her bottom lip, then sucked it, soothing and enhancing the sting before returning to devour her mouth. As if she, too, was something he knew he shouldn't have but couldn't resist.

He lifted his head, taking that lovely mouth with him, and she cried out in disappointment. But he shushed her with hard, stinging kisses to the corner of her lips, along the line of her jaw, down her chin and neck…over the tops of her breasts. In seconds, he stripped her of her bra, baring her to him. His big hands lifted, cupping her, molding her to him. To his pleasure. And hers.

She grasped his shoulders, clung to him, her ability to

think, to move, to breathe a thing of the past as he lowered his head to her flesh. All she could do was stand there with increasingly wobbly knees and receive each lick, suckle and draw of those sensual lips and tongue. And enjoy them.

Unable not to touch the lure of his hair, she swept her fingers over his head, tunneling them under the knot containing the midnight strands. Eager to see him undone, she briefly wrestled with the thick locks, freeing the tie restraining them. The rough silk fell over her wrists, cool and dense, sliding through her fingers.

"Oh," she whispered, at a loss for words as the strands tumbled around his sharp cheekbones and strong jaw. They should've softened his features—should have. Instead, they only emphasized the stark planes of his face and his visceral sexuality.

"God, you're beautiful." The praise exited her mouth without her permission, but she couldn't regret the words. Not when they were the truth.

Pulling his mouth away from her breasts, he dragged a hot, wet path up her chest, her throat, until he recaptured her mouth. This kiss was hotter, wilder, as if the tether on his control had frayed, and suddenly, her one purpose was to see it snap completely.

With a small whimper, she trailed her hand over his shoulder, chest and torso, not stopping until she cupped his rigid length through his pants.

Damn. She shivered, both need and feminine anxiety tumbling in her belly and lower. He more than filled her palm. Reflexively, she squeezed his erection. God, he was so thick, hard…big.

A rumble emanated from his chest, and his larger hand covered hers, pressing her closer, clasping him tighter. His hips bucked against her palm in demand, and she gladly obeyed. Even as his mouth ravaged hers, she stroked him, loving the growl that rolled out of him. Wanting more.

Impatient, Shay attacked the clasp of his pants, jerking them open and tugging down the zipper in a haste that would later strike her as unseemly. But right now, she didn't give a damn. Nothing mattered but his bare, pulsing flesh in her hand. Touching him.

But just as she reached for him, an implacable grip circled her wrist, stilling her frantic movements.

"Not yet, moonbeam." He lifted one of her arms and placed an openmouthed kiss to the center of her palm, the resulting feeling radiating straight to her damp, quivering sex. With a quick crush of his lips to hers, he swiftly divested her of her remaining clothes and shoes, leaving her trembling and naked before him, except for the decidedly *un*sexy plain, black panties.

A burst of self-consciousness flared inside her chest, and she fought not to edge backward, away from the weak glow of the cell phone's light. But as if he'd read her intentions, Gideon cupped her hip, preempting any movement she might've made to hide.

"When a man stands before beauty like yours, there's only one position he's supposed to be in," he murmured. Slowly, he lowered himself to his knees, tipping his head back to continue to meet her gaze. "You deserve to be worshipped." He swept his lips across her stomach. "And pleasured." Another sweep, but over the top of her sex. Heat coiled tight, and her core clenched at the tantalizing caress. "Give me permission to give you that."

It might've emerged as an order, but he wouldn't continue without her go-ahead. She somehow knew that.

"Yes," she breathed, tunneling her fingers through his hair. Holding on tight.

With a deliberate pace that had her internally screaming,

he drew her underwear down her legs and helped her step free of them. Big, elegant hands brushed up her calves and thighs, and once more she wondered at the calluses adding a hint of roughness to the caress. But then she ceased thinking at all.

"Gideon," she cried out, fisting his hair, trying to pull him away or tug him closer—she didn't know. Couldn't decide. Not when pleasure unlike anything she'd ever experienced struck her with great bolts of lightning. Jesus, his lips, his tongue… They were voracious. Feasting on her, leaving no part of her unexplored, untouched. Long, luxurious swirls, decadent and wicked laps and sucks… He drove her insane with pleasure.

Just as he'd promised. Just as he'd assured her she deserved.

He spread her wider, hooking her leg over one of his wide shoulders, granting himself easier access. Like a ravenous beast, he growled against her sensitive, wet sex, and the vibration shoved her closer to the edge of release.

"You're so fucking sweet," he rasped, nuzzling her. "So fucking sweet and pure. A man could get addicted to you. But you have more to give me, don't you, baby? I'm a greedy bastard, and I want it all." He uttered the last words almost as if to himself, and with one palm molded to her behind, he dragged the other up the inside of her spread thighs.

Then he was filling her. Two fingers plunged inside her, and like a match struck to dry kindling, she sparked, flared, exploded into flames. Dimly, she caught his rough encouragement of "That's it, baby. That's it." She loosened a hand from his hair and clapped it over her lips, muffling her cries as she came against his mouth, her hips rolling and jerking.

Raw, dirty ecstasy, stripped to its barest essentials. That's who she'd become in this moment as he lapped up every evidence of her desire from her flesh, from the insides of her thighs.

"Please," she begged, weakly pushing his head away as he circled her with tender but relentless strokes. "I can't."

"That's nothing but a challenge to me, moonbeam," he rumbled, standing, his mouth damp. But when he lowered his head and took her lips in a torrid kiss that replicated how he'd just consumed her, she didn't back away from the flavor of herself on his lips and tongue. No, she opened wider to him, turned on so bright it ached.

Palming the back of her thighs, he hiked her in the air. On reflex she wound her legs around his waist. He crossed to the couch, and with each bump of her swollen, sensitive core against his stomach, that recently satiated heat flickered back to life, and she moaned with each caress.

Her back met the cushions, and Gideon towered over her, half his face cast in shadow. That obsidian gaze never left hers as he removed a thin wallet from his pants pocket and withdrew a condom. He tossed it down, next to her feet, and then she watched, enraptured, as he stripped off his clothes. Her breath snagged in her throat. *Jesus.* He'd been stunning in a perfectly tailored tuxedo. But naked, the trappings torn away, all that thick, midnight hair falling around his face and broad shoulders... He was *magnificent*. Long legs, powerful thighs... Good God, she'd felt him, but *seeing* him... Like the rest of him, his erection was proud, beautiful. Perfect.

As if of their own volition, her arms lifted, beckoning him to her. He tore open the foil square and sheathed himself then came to her, moving the cell phone to the floor next to them. His hard body covered hers, and a sigh escaped her at the contact. For a second, she couldn't smother the sense of never having felt so cherished, so protected.

"Ready, moonbeam?" he murmured, raising off her

slightly. Grasping her hand in his, he brought it between their bodies. As he'd done earlier, he wrapped her fingers around his thick length. "Show me," he ordered, planting his palms on either side of her head, granting her control.

Even if she harbored the smallest seed of doubt about this illicit encounter in the dark—which she didn't—his gesture would've eradicated it. Her chest tightened, her heart thudding against her rib cage. But her hand was steady as she guided him to her entrance. Shifting her palm to his taut behind, she pushed as she lifted her hips, taking him inside. Fully. Widening her thighs, she didn't stop until he was buried within her.

She gasped, a ripple rocking her body. God, he was *everywhere*. Over her, around her, inside her. So deep inside her. The weight and length of him stretched her, burned her, and she flexed against him, her flesh struggling to accommodate the sweet invasion.

His eyes closed, and he bowed his head, pressing his forehead to hers, his breath pulsing over her lips. Tension vibrated through him, strained the muscles in his arms, stilled his large frame. Long moments later, he lifted his head, and the effort to hold back was etched onto his features.

"Gideon," she whispered, waiting until he lifted his ridiculously dense lashes to meet her eyes. "Let go."

As if those two words sliced through the last threads of his restraint, he groaned and lost it.

On the tail of another of those sexy snarls, he dragged his erection free, lighting up nerve endings like an airport runway, before snapping his hips and thrusting back inside her. Driving her breath from her lungs and a wail of pleasure from her throat.

Oh God. She wasn't going to survive this.

Pleasure inundated her as he plunged into her body. Over

and over, relentlessly. He hooked an arm under her leg, tugging it higher and impossibly wider. With a choked cry, she wrapped her arms around his neck, holding on, a willing sacrifice to his possession. He rode her, wild and untethered, giving her no quarter. Not that she asked for any. She loved it. Every roll of his hips, every slap of flesh against flesh, every rake of his teeth over her shoulder.

In his arms, under his body, she transformed into a sexual creature who lived, breathed for him, for the ecstasy only he could give.

Electric pulses crackled down her back, sizzling at the base of her spine. Every thrust intensified the sensation. When he slid a hand between them and rubbed her, an avalanche of pleasure rushed toward her, burying her, stealing her consciousness. But not before Gideon stiffened above her, his deep, tortured groan echoing in her ear, rumbling against her chest.

"Camille," he whispered, and it sounded like a benediction, a prayer.

And as she tightened her arms around him before sinking under, she foolishly wished to be his answer.

Four

Gideon frowned, reaching out to shut off his alarm. Drowsiness still clung to him, a warm lassitude weighing down his muscles, and he wanted to savor it instead of drive it away. But that damn alarm.

"Damn it," he grumbled, but instead of hitting the digital clock on his bedside table, he slapped air. No table. No clock. Hell, no bed.

He sat up, groaning at the pull of muscle in his lower back. Tunneling his fingers through his hair, he dragged it back from his face, scanning the small room with a television, a long table against the far wall, a short row of gray metal lockers and the couch he was sprawled on.

The blackout.

Camille.

As if her name released a floodgate, the memories from the previous night poured forward. Serving Camille dinner. Talking with her. Kissing her. Being inside her. In response, his body stirred, hardening as image after image of her twisting and arching beneath him, taking him, flashed across his mind's screen like an HD movie.

He whipped around, scanning the room with new eyes,

searching for any sign of her. But only his clothes and the empty dinner plates littered the floor. No Camille.

Adrenaline streaked through his veins, and he snatched his pants from the floor, dragging them on. She couldn't have gotten far. Weak morning light trickled into the room through the high window, so it still had to be pretty early. And with the house still locked down...

No, not locked down. For the first time, the low drone of the small refrigerator in the far corner reached his ears. Power had returned, which meant the blackout had ended. Still, how much of a head start could she have? He had to find her.

Just as he swept his shirt off the floor a Queen song erupted into the stifling room. It'd been this that he'd initially mistaken for his alarm, but it was his mom's special ringtone. He strode the few steps required to recover the phone from beside the couch, arching his eyebrows in surprise that it still had power.

Only 3 percent, he noted, swiping a thumb across the screen.

"Hey, Mom," he said in greeting, fastening buttons as he spoke. "I have very little battery left, so I can't talk long. But I'm okay—"

"Gideon," she said, and her solemn tone cut him off. Anxiety and the first spike of fear speared his chest. He'd come to associate that particular note with one thing. And as she murmured, "It's Olivia," his guess proved correct.

Closing his eyes, he straightened his shoulders, bracing himself. "What happened?"

"She's in the hospital. I had to take her in last night." Her sigh echoed in his ear; the weariness and worry tore at him. "Gideon." She paused. "She saw the news about Trevor Neal's engagement."

A familiar anger awakened in his chest, stretching to life. "I'm on my way."

* * *

Gideon exited his sister's private room on the behavioral health floor of Mercy Hospital & Medical Center, quietly shutting the door behind him.

Behavioral health. Fancy words for psychiatric ward.

Scrubbing a hand down his face, he strode through the hall to the waiting area where his mother and her parents perched on chairs. The three of them zeroed in on him as soon as he entered the small space with the connected seating and mounted television. God, it reeked of sadness and exhaustion. The same emotions etched in his mother's and grandparents' faces.

"How is she?" his mom asked, rising.

Frustration, grief and anger choked him, and for a moment he couldn't speak. Instead he gathered his mother in his arms and hugged her close. Ai Knight had been his rock—his family's rock—since his dad died when Gideon was nine years old. Though his grandparents were here now, that hadn't always been the case. When she'd married Gideon's father, they'd disowned her. As immigrants from Kaiping who'd settled in Canada in the 1960s, they'd wanted their only daughter to marry a Chinese man from the "Four Counties," not a Caucasian from Chicago. But Ai had, and after she'd moved to the US with him, she and her parents hadn't spoken for almost ten years. But since then they'd reconciled, and his grandparents had even moved to Chicago to be closer to Ai and their grandchildren. Which Gideon was thankful for, since his father had been a foster child, and so his mother's parents were the only extended family he and his sister had.

"Gideon?" his mother prompted.

Sighing, he released her. God, he hated seeing her here in this room, the gravity of her daughter's illness weighing down her delicate but strong shoulders.

"Sleeping. They have her heavily sedated at the moment," he replied. Which wasn't much of an answer.

"How long will she be here?" his grandmother inquired, stretching her arm out and clasping her daughter's hand.

"I'm not sure, Po Po," he said, using the Taishanese term for maternal grandmother. His grandfather—his gung gung—remained silent, but settled a hand on his wife's thin knee. "The doctor said definitely the next seventy-two hours. Maybe more."

They remained there, silent but connected through physical touch. After several moments, he squeezed his mom's shoulder. "Can I talk to you out in the hall?"

She nodded, following him out of the waiting room— and out of earshot of his grandparents. They might be a tight family, but there were some things even they didn't know, and Gideon preferred to keep it that way when it came to his younger sister.

"What happened?" he demanded, softening the hard tone of his question by enfolding her hand in his.

"Since the announcement of Trevor's engagement, I've tried my best to keep her protected from the news. Even going on her computer and phone and blocking those society sites. But I knew that was only prolonging the inevitable. And last night, she found out. I heard her sobbing all the way from downstairs, Gideon," she whispered, the dark eyes she'd bequeathed to him liquid with tears. "I ran to her room and found her curled up in a ball on the floor of her bedroom, crying uncontrollably. Unable to stop. I was afraid. So I called the ambulance."

He ground his teeth together, an ache flaring along his jaw as he struggled to imprison the blistering stream of curses that would not only offend his mother but would be pointless.

Nothing he said could ease his sister's anguish. And no

amount of release could extinguish his hatred toward Trevor Neal, the bastard responsible for shattering the kind, loving, fragile woman who'd given him her heart. A heart Trevor had trampled, then tossed aside like trash.

It'd been a year ago, but to Olivia, Trevor's betrayal might as well as have been yesterday. She'd kept her love affair with the CEO of RemingtonNeal, Inc. from Gideon, because he and Trevor had no love lost between them; they'd been rivals and enemies for years. Gideon had never hidden his hatred toward the other man.

Which explained why Trevor had targeted her in the first place.

He'd romanced Olivia, manipulated her into falling in love with him, making promises of a future together. Then, out of the blue, he'd cruelly dumped her. But that hadn't been the worst of it. Olivia had been pregnant with his child. Trevor hadn't cared. He'd even ordered her to get an abortion, which she'd refused. But in the end, it hadn't mattered. She'd miscarried, and the loss had sunk her into a depression that had begun to lift only a couple months ago. Seeking to protect her from any further hurt, Gideon and his mother had kept the information about the engagement to themselves.

But now this had happened.

"I'm sorry." His mother interrupted his thoughts by cupping his cheek. "I know this has to be difficult for you, too. This whole engagement thing. How're you doing?"

He covered her hand with his and then pressed a kiss to her palm before lowering it. Schooling his features, he submerged the jagged knife of pain and humiliation beneath a sheet of ice. "I'm fine, Mom. I'm not the one who needs your worry today."

She didn't immediately reply, studying him. "I'm a mother. I have enough concern to spread around evenly," she said, and amusement whispered through him. "She was your fiancée, Gideon," she pointed out, as if he didn't know. "Cheating on you was hurtful enough, but this? And with him of all people?" She shook her head. "There's no way you can possibly be 'fine.'"

"Let it go, Mom," he murmured, sliding his hands into the front pockets of his pants and slightly turning away from her incisive gaze. "I have."

Lies.

He would never forget Madison Reus's betrayal. Or forgive it. Not when the man she'd cheated with had been Trevor.

The other man had made it his mission to bring Gideon down a peg. And this latest stunt—pursuing Madison, fucking her and now marrying her—had been a direct hit. Anger at his enemy and his ex swelled within him. Both were selfish, narcissistic and uncaring of who they destroyed.

Especially Trevor.

Gideon had been unable to protect his sister from him the first time. And now she still suffered from his cruelty. It sickened Gideon that he'd failed her, despite the fact that he hadn't known until it was too late. As her older brother, the man in the family, he should've been there. Should've asked questions. Should've…

Damn it. He ruthlessly scrubbed his hands down his face.

Never again. Trevor Neal wouldn't get away unscathed this time.

He would pay. Pay for them all.

Five

Shay approached the dining room entrance, pausing just outside, preparing herself for the first meal of the day. It was breakfast; it shouldn't be an event worthy of deep-breathing techniques. But depending on her brother's mood, it could go either way—calm and pleasant or tap dancing on her last damn nerve. Sighing, she straightened her shoulders and entered.

"Good morning," she said to Trevor, pulling out her chair to his left. As soon as she lowered herself into it, Jana, their maid, appeared at her elbow and set a plate with steaming hot food in front of her. "Thank you, Jana." She smiled at the other woman.

Trevor glanced up from the tablet next to his plate. "You're running late this morning," he said in lieu of a greeting.

"A little bit of a restless night," she explained.

Several restless nights, actually. But she kept that bit of information to herself, since there was no way she could tell her brother what—or rather *who*—had been interrupting her sleep lately.

"Are you okay?" His eyes, hazel like her own, narrowed on her face. "Feeling well?"

There were moments like this, when concern shone in his gaze, that made it hard to remember the increasingly cold and callous man her brother could be. Right now, he was the caring big brother from her childhood who'd affectionately teased her, who'd spent hours watching TV with her when she'd been sick with the flu and bored. That man had started to make rarer appearances over the last few years—since their father had fallen sick and died.

"I'm fine," she replied, cutting into her vegetable omelet. "What am I running late for?"

"The office. You have a meeting with the representative from the ASPCA. You can't afford to be late for that, not with the fund-raising gala for Grace Sanctuary just a few nights away. I'm counting on you to make this a success for not just RemingtonNeal but for Mom's memory," he reminded her.

No pressure. She swallowed the retort. Barely.

While she firmly believed Trevor had created her position and department specifically for her—vice president of Social Development—she did her best for it. Yes, it was an important job—anything bettering their city and the people living there was worthy—but it wasn't her passion. And it damn sure wasn't what she'd attended college and earned a BBA and MBA to do. She'd wanted to join her brother in running RemingtonNeal, but like their controlling, domineering father, he'd shot down that idea.

Usually, Trevor took no interest in her work unless a photo op happened to be attached to it. But Grace Sanctuary belonged to their mother—it had been her pet project before she died, when Shay was eleven and Trevor sixteen. Their father had continued its legacy until he passed, and now they did. The foundation funded various shelters throughout the city, as well as paid veterinarian, adoption and fostering fees for families taking in the animals. The fund-raising gala was important, as the donations from the attendees encompassed a large portion of the budget.

Still, Shay had headed the committee for the gala the past three years, and the last thing she needed was Trevor breathing down her neck or trying to micro-manage.

"Everything is going smoothly, and the benefit will be a success like it always has been," she said.

"I know it will. After all, it's in your hands," Trevor praised softly. "I'm sorry if I'm being overbearing, Shay. And if I haven't said it before, thank you. Believe me, I would be a lot more of a pain in the ass if you weren't in charge. I trust you to make this gala the best yet."

Warmth spread through her chest, and she swallowed past the lump of emotion lodged in her throat. Here was the big brother she knew and loved. The one whose approval she valued because it meant so much to her.

"Thank you," she murmured. Then, clearing her throat, she asked, "How's Madison?"

His fiancée had been joining them for breakfast more often lately. Actually, spending more time at the house, period. As if she were already preparing to be mistress of the home.

"She's fine." He picked up his napkin and dabbed at his mouth. "Just so you're aware, I gave her a key. She's dropping by later with an interior designer. There're some things she wants to change in the living and dining rooms, as I do most of my entertaining in those two places. And since she'll soon be living here…" He shrugged. "I didn't think you'd mind, so I told her to go forward with it."

Irritation twinged inside Shay's chest. As usual, Trevor didn't consult her about anything, even when it had to do with her home. Yes, Madison would soon be moving in as his wife, but it'd been Shay's home for twenty-five years.

Yet it hadn't occurred to him to ask her opinion, which didn't count for much with her older brother. Again, like their father.

The irony of it always struck her. Trevor and their father had had a...complicated relationship. He'd loved and revered Daniel Shay, constantly seeking his stingy approval, while at the same time, resenting his my-way-and-there's-no-such-thing-as-a-highway attitude when it came to running his company and his family. Especially when it came to raising his only son, who would one day inherit his financial kingdom. Yet, over the years, Trevor had become the reflection of their father. And the battle inside her—the warring factions of anger at his overbearing arrogance and protectiveness for the brother she loved—continued to wage.

But, as she was discovering, it was pointless to argue with Trevor regarding anything having to do with Madison Reus. Winning the hand of a senator's daughter had been a coup for him, and he spoiled her like a princess. And like royalty, Madison accepted it as her due.

That sounded catty even in her own head. *God.* Shay winced, sipping the coffee Jana had set before her.

Doesn't make it any less true, her inner bitch whispered.

"Of course not," she said evenly.

"Good." He nodded. "What're your plans for lunch? We could meet so you can give me an update on the benefit."

She shook her head. "I can't. I'm meeting Bridgette."

Trevor's mouth thinned into a flat, grim line.

Yes, she already got that he didn't like her friendship with the other woman. Bridgette's mother had worked for the Neal family when they were younger. Lonely, Shay had immediately bonded with the precocious, funny little girl who'd wanted a friend regardless of the difference in their families' tax brackets. Continuing that friendship had been one of Shay's very few rebellions against her father's and brother's edicts about being a Neal. She loved Bridgette like a sister, and Trevor's disapproval wouldn't make her give up her friend.

"Which reminds me," Shay continued, not giving him a chance to offer yet another opinion on her relationship with Bridgette. "I won't be able to make dinner tonight, either. I made other plans."

His gaze narrowed on her. "Dinner is with the senator, his wife and several of his friends."

"I'm aware, and I apologize for backing out at the last moment, but something came up that I can't reschedule."

She returned his stare, not offering an explanation about the "something" even though his eyes demanded one. The words actually shoved at the back of her throat, but she refused to soothe him, to cave just to keep the peace. Especially since he'd been the one to make the plans for this dinner without even checking to see if she was available. Sometimes her brother misinterpreted her silence for meekness. And sometimes she let his high-handedness go. But not when it mattered. And tonight mattered. To her.

"Shay," he murmured, leaning back in his chair, his mouth hardening even more. "I know I don't need to remind you how important the next few months are to me, to our family and, therefore, to RemingtonNeal. This wedding isn't just gearing up to be the social event of next year, but it's also only months before Senator Reus's campaign kicks off. We can't afford to have anything go wrong. We're Neals, with a name and reputation above reproach. Don't do anything to taint either."

Anger at his thinly veiled admonishment surged within her, and she fought down the barrage of words blistering her throat. The same throat that constricted as the noose of the Neal name tightened, suffocating her. She'd always been the dutiful daughter, the proper socialite and, except for in her head, had done it all without complaint. But lately, the constraints were chafing, leaving her raw and irritated. In emotional pain.

Well, you haven't been that *proper.*

The same snarky voice that had taunted her about Madison mocked her again, this time following it up with a parade of vivid, explicit images of the night she'd spent with Gideon Knight. Her belly clenched, a dark swirl of desire eddying far south of her navel. Flashes of those lust-drenched hours burst in her head like fireworks across a dark July night. Gideon kneeling before her, lips glistening with the evidence of the desire he'd coaxed out of her with that same talented mouth. Gideon leaning over her, midnight hair tumbling around them, his big body moving over hers…in hers.

Gideon sleeping as she quietly dressed in the murky morning light, the sharp angles and planes of his face not softened by slumber.

Heat rushed up her chest and throat and poured into her face. She ducked her head over her plate, concealing the flush that surely stained her cheekbones.

"Shay?"

She jerked her head up, freeing herself from thoughts of Gideon. Inhaling, she refocused on their conversation. "No, I don't need to be reminded. And missing one dinner isn't going to mar the Neal name or threaten the senator's campaign," she replied. Ignoring the narrowing of his eyes, she pushed her chair back and stood. "I need to get to the office. I'll see you later."

Leaning over, she brushed a kiss across his cheek, then left the room before he could attempt to dig into her reasons for not complying with his plans. As soon as she stepped over the threshold, she heaved a sigh. The tension that seemed to be more of a common occurrence when she was with Trevor eased from her shoulders.

Shoulders that were aching from carrying the heavy burden of her brother's expectations.

Six

Shay smiled up at her server as she accepted the black folder containing the check for the meal she'd just finished. Well, a little more than a meal. Her smile widened at the warm glow of satisfaction radiating inside her chest. A business meeting with the two women who had just left the restaurant, and one that had gone extremely well.

This had been her reason for ducking out on dinner with Trevor, Madison and her family. As much as Shay's job at RemingtonNeal bored the hell out of her, she was grateful for it. Without the six-figure salary, she wouldn't be able to finance her own secret company—an investment firm that funded innovative, promising start-ups—start-ups founded by women.

Shay made it possible for women to achieve their dreams, and with a percentage of the profits, she was able to continue growing her own business. Leida Investments—named after her mother—was hers alone, without any connection to her family. Even the incorporation documents weren't in her name. The anonymity—and the NDA she had all her clients sign—allowed her the freedom to use the degrees she'd earned without anyone trying to pigeonhole her. Yes, enduring the time she put in at her brother's company was well worth it when she could be her own boss.

If Trevor discovered her secret, he would do more than disapprove of it; he would sabotage it. As archaic as it sounded, he possessed firm ideas about her role in the family and the business. He might have created a lip service position for her at RemingtonNeal, but he intended for her to be a replica of their mother—wife, mother, philanthropist, socialite and the perfect hostess. The philanthropist part wasn't bad, but the rest of it? She mentally shuddered.

Tonight was a reminder of why she went to such measures to maintain her subterfuge. The excitement and joy that had lit Jennifer Ridland's and Marcia Brennan's faces as Shay slid an investment contract across the table had reinforced for her why her company must continue to thrive without any interference from her brother. The two women could revolutionize the travel industry, and she wanted to be the one who helped them do it.

Oh yes, this was well worth missing out on Trevor's dinner.

"Good evening, Ms. Neal. Do you mind if I join you?"

That voice. Shock blasted through her, and under it wound a current of something darker, sultrier. Her voice and breath crowded into her throat like an angry mob, strangling her for a long, panicked moment.

Even when Gideon Knight slid into the chair across from her, she remained speechless, frozen. It was as if her thoughts of him earlier that morning had conjured him. The bottomless onyx eyes no longer glittered with lust, but they held the same piercing intensity. It had her wavering between ducking her head and allowing him to pilfer her darkest secrets. The angular but beautiful face with its sharp angles and unsmiling, sinfully full lips... The tall, powerful body that seemed to dwarf the chair and table...

A shiver shuddered through her body, and she prayed he didn't notice. *What are you doing here?* almost tumbled from her lips before she hauled the words back. But recognition didn't shine in his eyes. Then, why would it? He'd spent a hot, sex-drenched night during a blackout with Camille, a member of the waitstaff. Across from him sat Shay Neal, composed heiress with long, dark brown hair instead of a wig, no glasses, hazel eyes instead of brown contacts and an eggplant-colored, long-sleeved cocktail dress instead of a uniform.

She bore no resemblance to the woman he'd known. Touched. Brought such immense pleasure.

"I'm afraid I'm just finishing up dinner, Mr..." She trailed off. God, she felt like such a hypocrite, a liar. Intentional deception wasn't her. But she couldn't confess how they knew one another, either. One, she'd lied to him about her identity. Two, if he discovered that she and Camille were the same person, he could use that to embarrass her family. If Trevor found out... She mentally shook her head. No, not an option.

"Gideon Knight," he said, setting a brown folder on the table. "And I promise not to take up too much of your time. But I believe you will want to hear what I have to say."

Though every instinct for self-preservation inside her screamed to run and run *now*, she remained seated. His almost emotionless tone didn't conceal the faint warning in his words.

And then there was the part of her—the part she struggled not to acknowledge—that trembled with desire from just being near Gideon. If she could just erase that night from her head...

"I'm sorry, Mr. Knight, but I don't know you." Not a

lie. Biblical knowledge didn't equate *knowing* someone. "Therefore, I don't believe there is anything we need to speak about. So if you'll excuse me…"

She set her napkin on the table and started to rise from her chair. Yes, she was being rude, but desperation trumped manners. She needed to get away from him before she did something foolish. Such as beg him for a repeat of a night that never should've happened.

"I know your secret, Ms. Neal."

Shay froze. Except for her heart. It pounded against her sternum like an anvil against steel. Hard. Deafening.

Slowly, she lowered herself to her seat, forcing her expression into one of calm disinterest. Hiding the fear that coursed through her like a rushing current.

He knew about the night of the blackout? What had she done to betray her identity? Oh God. *What did he intend to do with the information?*

"I'm afraid I have no idea what you're talking about," she replied.

His aloof, shuttered demeanor didn't alter as he cocked his head and studied her. "Is your brother aware of where you are tonight? Does he know about the meeting you concluded just minutes ago?"

Wait. What? "I'm sorry?" she asked.

"Does he know about Leida Investments?" he clarified, leaning back in his chair. "I must admit, I can't imagine Trevor Neal supporting his sister running a company that is outside of RemingtonNeal. More specifically, out from under his control."

Equal parts relief and unease swirled in her belly. Relief because he still hadn't equated her with Camille. But unease because how did he know about her business? Better question, why did he care?

"Forgive me for not seeing how it's any of your concern," she answered, ice in her voice.

"Forgiveness. Oh, we're so far past that," he murmured, and as she frowned at the cryptic words, he slid the brown folder across the table toward her.

That sense of unease morphed into dread as she stared at the banded file. She lifted her hand, but at the last moment, she froze, her fingers hovering above it as if it were a scorpion, ready to strike and poison her with its venom.

Yet she grasped it, then opened it.

Minutes later, her heart thudded against her chest wall like a hammer against stone. The pounding clang in her head deafened her. God, she wished it would blind her to what she was reading.

Report after report detailing shady business deals involving her brother, and even some with his future father-in-law, Senator Reus. Bribery for product placement, undercutting bidding contracts, predatory practices, procuring illegal campaign contributions on behalf of the senator. And these were just some of the accusations leveled against Trevor and RemingtonNeal.

"Why are you showing me these...these lies?" She dropped the stack back on the table as if it singed her fingertips. If it didn't betray weakness, she would've shoved her chair back from the table just to place more space between that file and her.

"Lies?" He arched a black eyebrow, the corner of his mouth lifting in the faintest of sneers. "Facts, Ms. Neal. Your determination to believe they're false doesn't make it so."

"And your determination to believe they're true doesn't make it so," she snapped, throwing his words back at him. "I don't know you, and I damn sure don't know the people who gathered this defamatory conjecture." She flicked a corner of the folder. "Let's face it, Mr. Knight. If any of this was provable in court, you wouldn't be sitting here across from me at a restaurant table. You would be meeting with the DA or SEC."

"That's where you're wrong," he said, cruel satisfaction glinting in his eyes. "It's amazing how the court of public opinion will try and convict someone much swifter than a court of law."

Her stomach rolled, bile churning before racing for the back of her throat. She hated to admit it, but he was right. Good God, if *any* of this information leaked, it would destroy Trevor's reputation, his engagement, and irreparably harm the family company. It wouldn't matter if the claims couldn't be proved; the speculation alone would be detrimental and the damage irreversible. Since their father died, Trevor's one goal—no, his obsession—had been to enlarge RemingtonNeal, to make it even more successful and powerful than what their father had done. None of that would be possible if even an iota of the data in this dossier was true.

Not that she believed it. She *couldn't*. Yes, Trevor could be merciless and cut-throat. She'd increasingly seen more and more evidence of this, personally and professionally, in the last few years. And it worried her. The glimpses of the brother she'd revered and adored as a child and teen were becoming further and further apart.

But it was those glimpses that gave her hope. That reminded her that underneath the often cold demeanor existed a good man. A man incapable of the things noted in that defaming file.

And bottom line… She loved him.

Love and loyalty demanded she believe in him.

"What do you want?" she asked, forcing a calm into her voice that was a farce. Questions, thoughts and *fear* whipped through her in a chaotic gale.

The man who'd fed her and provided her protection and
light in a blackout didn't sit across from her. No, this wasn't
the man who'd introduced her to such pleasure she still felt
the echo of it weeks later. This man… He was a stranger.
A cold, calculating, beautiful stranger.

"You."

The blunt announcement doused her in a frigid blast,
stunning her.

"Excuse me?" she rasped.

He couldn't mean…?

No. No way.

He didn't want her. He had to mean something else.

But God, her body was having one hell of a time getting
the message. *You.* Heat prickled at the base of her spine,
and desire wound through her veins like a molten stream.
A barrage of memories assaulted her—the sound of his
ragged breath in her ear as he thrust into her body, all that
dark, thick hair tumbling around his lust-tautened face, his
whispered "moonbeam" as he stroked her damn skin… Her
breath evaporated in her lungs, and she struggled to keep
any hint of arousal from her face.

"I want you." He leaned forward, his midnight gaze pin-
ning her to her chair. "More specifically, I want you to be
in love with me."

The images in her head splintered like glass, dousing
the passion-kindled flames inside her. She gaped at him.
Couldn't help it. After all, it wasn't every day that she sat
across from a lunatic.

"Are you crazy?" she demanded, clutching the edge of
the table as if it were the only thing keeping her from leap-
ing out of her chair. "I don't even *like* you. And we've never
met," she continued, ignoring the memory of skin pressed
to damp skin that flashed across her mind's eye. "How
could you believe you love me?"

He flicked a hand, the gesture impatient, dismissive. "Of course I don't love you. And I don't need your affection or professions of an emotion that is nothing but an excuse for fools and liars to behave badly."

Shay shook her head, confused. "But you just said—"

"Pretend," he interrupted. "You're going to pretend to be deeply enamored with me, and our whirlwind relationship will be as fake as that sentiment."

"You *are* crazy," she breathed. "That's ridiculous. Why would you even propose something like that?"

"Why?" he repeated, that damn eyebrow arching again. "Your brother."

She barked out a harsh crack of laughter. "My brother? Do you really think Trevor cares if I'm in a relationship with you?" Hell, he might be happy. Yes, he and Gideon were business rivals, and Trevor had been trying to acquire the other man's company for years, but her brother would probably consider it a coup for his sister to date such a successful and wealthy man.

But for the first time since sitting down across from her, Gideon smiled. The curling of his sensual lips was slow, deliberate…and menacing. "Oh yes. Your brother will care. And he'll understand."

"Another enigmatic message, Mr. Knight?" She waved a hand, frustrated. "I'm too old for games. Whatever your play is here, make it plain."

"I'll make this very plain, Shay," he said, using her given name even though she hadn't granted him permission to do so. His voice, as dark and sinful as his eyes, caressed her name like a long, luxurious stroke. It was damn near indecent.

"You can pretend to be my significant other, and convince your brother that you are mine. Or…" a steely edge that was both lethally sharp and smooth entered his voice

"...I can let the truth about Leida Investments drop into your brother's lap. Imagine his fury when he realizes the secrets his sister has been keeping. And then, while that little bomb detonates, I will release the information in that file to not just the SEC but to every news outlet and journalist I have access to. And believe me, the list is long. As would be the jail sentences your brother and his precious senator would face for everything they've been up to. What effect do you think the meltdown of your family name and company will have? How many people will want to accept funds from a woman associated with a man whose name will be synonymous with financial scandal and fraud? Even the desperate will think twice about that. So both of you would be ruined, if everything in that dossier leaks. That leaves us at an impasse, Shay."

He paused, and the import of his words—no, his *threat*—sank into her like the realization of a floundering person being swallowed by quicksand.

Slow but no escape.

"And the choice is yours."

Seven

Gideon inhaled as he entered his mother's Lincoln Park home, and the sense of calm that always settled on him when he was with his family wrapped around him like a warm embrace.

Though his mother and sister had lived in the six-bed-room, seven-bathroom home for only four years, it was home because they were there. It was as much his sanctuary as his own downtown Chicago condominium. As the sound of his mother and Pat Benatar singing about love being a battlefield on her ever-present radio reached him, he shook his head, amending his thought. No, it was *more* of a haven for him.

Because family was *everything*.

Striding past the formal living and dining rooms with their soaring twelve-foot ceilings, and the sweeping, curving staircase, he headed toward the rear of the house. His mother might have initially balked at him purchasing this home for her and Olivia in one of Chicago's wealthiest neighborhoods, but there'd never been any doubt about how much she adored the airy, state-of-the-art kitchen. With its wall of windows, restaurant-style ranges and cooktops, top-of-the-line appliances, large marble island and butcher block and dual workhorse sinks, Ai had instantly fallen in love. And it was in this room that he usually found her.

Like now.

Ai stood at the stove, still clothed in her professor outfit—elegant gray pantsuit with crimson blouse and hair in a loose bun at the nape of her neck—and barefoot. Her slim body swayed back and forth to the eighties' rock anthem, and Gideon stifled a snort as she perfectly executed an arm-and-hip dance move he recognized from the classic MTV video.

He gave her a slow clap.

She whirled around with a gasp, brandishing a tea strainer like a club. "*Gideon*," she scolded, splaying the fingers of her free hand over her chest. "Are you trying to give me a heart attack?" She replaced the strainer in the waiting cup of steaming water and shot him a look over her shoulder. "I warn you, if I go, all of my money has been left to your grandmother's Maltese puppy."

Chuckling, he crossed the room and pulled his mother into a hug. Her familiar scent of gardenias greeted him like a childhood friend. Only with his family could he be Gideon Jian Knight, the oldest son of Ai Knight, former cafeteria worker who busted her ass to provide for her children and earn her PhD in educational studies at the same time. With them, he could lower the guards he'd erected between him and the rest of the world, especially those who greedily grasped for money, connections, time or sex from Gideon Knight, CEO of KayCee Corp.

He jealously guarded his moments with his family.

Zealously protected *them*.

"That's fine," he assured her, with a quick kiss to her forehead. "I have the very best legal department, and they would be capable of breaking that will." He smiled as she swatted at him. But then he noted the two cups on the gleaming countertop, and his amusement faded. "How is she?" he murmured.

The light in his mother's eyes dimmed. "Better," she answered. She sighed, turning back to preparing the hot tea. "She's still sleeping more than I like and hasn't left the house since coming home from the hospital a week and a half ago. But…better." She checked the strainer in the second cup. "I was just about to take this up and sit with her for a while."

"I can do that, Mom. You obviously just arrived home." She didn't have to continue to work as a social sciences and history professor at the University of Chicago. He was more than willing to provide for her, as she'd done for him and Olivia. But Ai Knight wouldn't hear of it, and Gideon was proud to have one of the most loved professors at U of C as his mother. "Go upstairs, relax and I'll take care of Livvie."

"Thank you." She turned, smiling softly and extending her hands toward him. He enfolded hers in his, squeezing them. "But no, I want to spend some time with her before I grade papers. Although she always loves to hear you play. Maybe you could bring your guitar by sometime this week."

"I'll do that," he agreed.

His mother had been responsible for him first picking up the instrument. She'd found a battered acoustic Fender at a garage sale, and from the second he'd held it, he'd been enamored. Though extra money had been almost nonexistent during his childhood, she'd still found a way to pay for lessons. No one outside the family had ever heard him play, because it was for him. His peace. His way to lose himself and get away from the stresses of running a multimillion-dollar tech company.

Ai cupped his cheek, giving it an affectionate pat before

lowering her arm. "Now, not that I don't enjoy you dropping by, but is everything okay?"

"Yes. There's something I do need to speak with you about, though." He propped a hip against the island and crossed his arms over his chest.

She studied him, then nodded, copying his pose. "Okay. What's going on?"

"I had a…business meeting last night," he said. "With Shay Neal. Trevor Neal's sister."

Surprise widened his mother's eyes. "I didn't even know he had a sister," she whispered, then shook her head. "Why, Gideon? What could you possibly have to discuss with her?"

"Our common interest," he said. "Her brother."

"Gideon," she murmured, tilting her head to the side. "What did you do?"

Meeting his mother's gaze, he relayed his conversation with Shay, including his revelation of all he'd dug up on Trevor, the ultimatum he'd delivered and her refusal to give him an answer.

"What are you thinking, son?" she asked, worry crowding her gaze. "She's innocent in all this."

Innocent. His fingers curled around his biceps, tightening even as blood pumped hot and fast through his body. *Innocent* was one word he wouldn't have associated with Shay Neal.

He'd done his homework on her before ambushing her at the restaurant. Twenty-five years old. Graduated with honors from Loyola University's Quinlan School of Business with a bachelor's in finance and entrepreneurship and a master of business administration. A member of Women in Business and International Business Society. Currently worked as vice president of the Social Development department at RemingtonNeal. And from what he could tell, the position was nothing but a fancy term for event coordinator, and definitely underutilized the education she'd received. All this information could be found on her social network platforms or the company's website.

Only a deeper dive below the surface uncovered her ownership of Leida Investments. The degrees and obvious intelligence had made her interesting. But this—the company she owned in secrecy—fascinated him. This society princess who organized brunches and galas was a mystery wrapped in an enigma. And anything he couldn't dissect and analyze he mistrusted. Tack onto that her last name, and he wouldn't dare to blink around her, vigilant of the knife that might slide into his back in that flick of time.

Still…nothing, not his caution, his preparation or even the pictures included in his private investigator's file, could've prepared him for the impact of Shay Neal face-to-face.

His grandmother owned an antique locket that she'd brought with her from China. Inside was a black-and-white picture of her older sister, who'd died in childbirth. In the image, his great-aunt had been composed, stoic. But in her lovely features—in her eyes—there glimmered emotion, vitality. *Life.* It emanated through the aloof expression like dawn breaking through the last, clinging shadows of night.

And staring at Shay Neal had been like gazing upon that faded photo. Yes, she was gorgeous. No one could deny she was beautiful—the refined bone structure with high, proud cheekbones, the patrician nose with its flared nostrils, or the full curves of a mouth that belonged on a pin-up model and not a demure socialite. And he couldn't deny that just for a moment, his wayward, rebellious mind had wondered if her gleaming golden brown skin was as butter-soft as it appeared.

But it'd been none of those features that had drawn

him. Fueled an insane impulse to drag his chair closer and discover what scent rose from the corner where neck and shoulder met. Had his fingers itching to pluck the strings of his guitar and find the melody that would encapsulate her.

No, it was the intelligence, the spark, the *fire* in those arresting hazel eyes.

It made him mistrust her even more.

And then there was the niggling sense of familiarity that had hit him the moment he'd sat down at her table. As if they'd met before... But like he'd done last night, he dismissed the feeling. If he'd ever met Shay Neal, no way in hell he wouldn't remember.

"She's a Neal, Mom," he said, shoving thoughts of her—of the unsettling effect she had on him—away. "She doesn't have clean hands."

"That's probably the same logic Trevor employed when he went after your sister," she pointed out, and the words struck him in the chest, burrowing into his heart.

"I'm nothing like him," he ground out, lowering his arms and curling his fingers around the edge of the marble top. "He stalked Livvie, lied to her, used her, then tossed her aside like yesterday's trash. I've been completely upfront with Shay, laying my intentions out and offering her a choice. Trevor stole Livvie's choice from her." He broke off, tipping his head back and deliberately cooling his rising temper. "You might not agree with my methods, and I'm sorry for that. But I didn't do anything when he damn near broke my sister, because you both asked me not to. I can't let it go this time. I'm not going to allow Trevor Neal to continue mistreating women. By the time I'm finished with him, he will have nothing left, and no woman will fall victim to him again."

It was the guilt that drove him.

Because it was his fault Trevor had sought out Olivia in

the first place. If not for their mutual hatred and ongoing feud, she would've been safe.

"Gideon." His mother shifted forward, once more cupping his cheek. "You're right. I don't agree with your methods. I believe they will more than likely backfire, and not only will an innocent woman be hurt, but you will, too, son. If you have a conscience—which I know you do—there's no way you can't be affected by this path. And I wish you would end it now before this goes too far." She sighed, her gaze searching his. "But I also know you. And from the moment you refused to be born on your due date, I figured out you're stubborn. I'm not going to change your mind, I get that. So just...please. Be careful."

"Don't worry about me. I have everything under control," he assured her, hugging her close.

She didn't reply, instead squeezed him tighter.

He hated disappointing her, but nothing, *nothing* could dissuade him from his plans. Not her disapproval. Not Shay's reluctance and refusal to give him a decision.

He had one purpose. To bring down Trevor Neal.

And hell couldn't stop him from accomplishing it.

Eight

"Trevor, the gala is a wonderful success. You should be proud. I'm certain your parents would be," Senator Julian Reus praised, pumping his future son-in-law's hand.

I don't know how you can say that, since you never met either of them.

Shay mentally winced over the snarky comment echoing in her head. God, she really wanted to like the influential man who would soon be part of her family. But he was such a…politician. Charming. Affable.

And phony.

Good thing she never voted for him.

"Thank you, sir." Trevor smiled, then slid an arm around Shay's shoulders. "I wish I could take the credit, but it belongs to Shay. She's the reason we've already surpassed the donations from last year."

Pride glowed like an ember in her chest, and for the first time that evening, a genuine smile curled her lips.

"Thank you, Trev," she said, wrapping an arm around his waist and briefly squeezing.

"Next year, it'll be even more of a success, with Madison by your side. I'm sure she will be more than happy to step in and help organize this special event." Senator Reus announced his daughter's involvement in Grace Sanctuary as a foregone conclusion.

"Of course I will, Daddy," Madison agreed, tilting her head back expectantly, and Trevor obliged her with a soft, quick kiss on the lips. "Shay and I will make a wonderful team."

Madison turned that wide smile to Shay, and even though all the warmth that had filled her faded away, Shay returned it with one of her own.

Trevor's fiancée had been nothing but cordial to Shay, but again, there was something not quite genuine about her. Madison reminded Shay of the ice sculpture in the lobby outside the ballroom. Beautiful but cold. To stand too close would send a shiver through the body.

"Let's get through tonight first before thinking about next year," Shay said, not committing to anything. Trevor stiffened beside her, but she ignored the telltale sign of his irritation. Her mind jumped to that dark brown file Gideon Knight had slid across the table. She thought about how her brother donated significant funds to the senator's campaign. And she couldn't help but wonder if some of that money came from their mother's organization.

Stop it.

The sharp order ricocheted off her skull. Damn Gideon Knight. She hated that he'd infiltrated her head, and she couldn't evict him. Not his damn dossier or the man himself. It'd been four days since that meeting—no, ambush. Four days since she was supposed to give him her decision about his preposterous ultimatum.

Four nights of heated fantasies that left her twisting and aching in her bed.

What kind of sister did it make her that she woke up

shaking and hungry for the man who blackmailed her? Who threatened her brother's livelihood and freedom?

A sad excuse for one.

Smothering a sigh, she excused herself from their small group on the pretense of checking with the catering staff, and headed across the room. She'd taken only a dozen steps before tingles jangled up her bare arms and culminated at the nape of her neck.

She sucked in a breath and immediately scanned the crowded ballroom for the source of the unsettling, *exciting* feeling.

There. No...*there.*

Gideon Knight.

The unexpected sight of him glued her feet to the floor.

Unexpected? Really?

Okay, maybe not. As soon as that prickle had sizzled over her skin, a part of her had instinctively known who'd caused it. Only one man had ever had that kind of effect on her.

She stared at him, trapped in an instant of déjà vu. Seeing him in his black tuxedo, she was swept back to the first night they'd met. Once more he seemed like the imposing but regal warlord surveying his subjects, his armor traded for perfectly tailored formal wear, his hair emphasizing the stark but gorgeous lines of his face. The distance of the ballroom separated them, but she somehow sensed those black eyes on her, just like then.

Just like then, she fought the dual urges of fight or flight.

And by fight she meant the warring of their mouths and bodies for dominance.

Damn.

She balled her fist, forcing her feet to maintain a steady, unhurried pace forward. Even as her heart pounded a relentless rhythm against her sternum.

"How did you get in here?" she gritted out.

Conscious of any gazes that might be leveled on them, she kept her polite, social mask in place, when in truth she wanted to glare daggers at him.

His aloof expression didn't change...except for the arch of that damnable dark eyebrow. "I expect like everyone else. The front entrance. And paying the seven-thousand-dollar-a-plate fee."

"That's not possible," she snapped. "I looked over and approved the final guest list myself. Neither you nor your company's name was on it."

"Then you missed it. Maybe other matters distracted you," he added. A beat of charged silence vibrated between them. No need to name the "other matters." They both were well aware of what he referred to.

"Is that why you're here?" she demanded, and in spite of her resolve, her voice dropped to a heated whisper. "To pressure me for an answer?"

"It's been four days, Shay," he replied, and in that moment, she resented his carefully modulated composure.

The rash and admittedly foolish urge—no, *need*—to shatter his control swelled within her. She wanted the man from the blackout, the one who stared at her with flames of desire burning in his onyx eyes as he drove them both to impossible pleasure.

"I've given your four days longer than I'd usually grant anyone else."

"Well, I'm flattered."

"You should be."

She clenched her teeth so hard an ache rose along her jaw. "The answer is n—"

"Is this man bothering you, Shay?" Trevor appeared at her elbow, and both the venom in his question and his sudden, hard grasp elicited a gasp from her.

Gideon's gaze dropped to her arm, and anger narrowed his eyes.

"Get your hand off of her," he ordered. The volume of his voice didn't rise, but only a simpleton could miss the warning. "You're hurting her."

Scowling, Trevor glanced down at his fingers pinching her arm, then jerked his hand away. He lifted his regard to her face, and she glimpsed disgust, but also regret. She dipped her chin in a silent acknowledgment of his equally silent apology.

Turning back to Gideon, he snarled, "What are you doing here? You weren't invited. Leave. Now."

"I'm afraid that's not going to happen," Gideon said, with no hint of remorse. If anything, satisfaction rang loud and clear in those words. "I paid to attend just like everyone else here, and made a hefty donation on top of that. I'm staying."

"You can have your money back. We don't need it," Trevor spat, nearly trembling with rage as he edged closer to Gideon. "We both know why you're here. You lost. Get over it. It's not like it's the first time, and it damn sure won't be the last."

Fear spiked inside Shay's chest. *Good God.* She'd never seen her brother this angry. His reaction to Gideon's presence had to be more than a business rivalry. This was... personal.

"Trevor," she quietly pleaded, gently but firmly grasping his arm. "Please."

Gideon shifted his attention from her brother to her. And the same fury that twisted her brother's face lit his eyes like a glittering night sky. But as he studied her, some of the anger dimmed.

He retreated a step, his gaze still pinned on her.

Shock pummeled the breath from her lungs. Had he backed away...for her?

No. That was impossible. He didn't give a damn about her or her feelings.

Still…

"Have a nice evening. Both of you," he said, though his regard never wavered from her. "It was wonderful seeing you again, Shay," he murmured, then turned and headed farther into the room, not toward the exit as Trevor had demanded.

"What was he talking about, 'seeing you again'?" Trevor hissed as soon as Gideon was out of earshot. "When did you meet him?"

With Herculean effort, she tore her gaze from Gideon and met her brother's glare. Hurt and hints of betrayal lurked there. And guilt pricked her. For what, though? She'd done nothing wrong.

"A few nights ago when I had dinner with friends. He was at the same restaurant." She delivered the half-truth with aplomb. *God, when did I become such an accomplished liar?* "He just introduced himself, that was all. What in the world was that all about, Trevor?"

"Nothing," he snapped. Then, sighing, he dragged a hand over his closely cropped hair. "I'm sorry. I didn't mean to bark at you. Just…stay away from him, Shay. I don't want you to have anything to do with him. Do you understand?"

"I'm not a child, Trevor," she murmured, meeting his fierce stare. "And this isn't the proper place for this discussion, either. We have guests."

With that reminder, she turned and strode away from him and the disturbing scene that had just unfolded.

Oh yes, there was bad blood between him and Gideon. Now more than ever, she felt like a pawn in whatever twisted game the two of them were engaged in. And she hated it.

As the evening progressed, she couldn't uproot the bitterness. Maintaining her not-a-care-in-the-world socialite persona became a weightier burden, and by the time dinner was being cleared away, she was bone-deep exhausted. Peeking at the slim, gold watch on her wrist, she thanked God she had only about an hour more to do her hostess duty before she could escape.

"I noticed you talking to Gideon Knight earlier," Madison said, her tone low enough that Trevor, who was engrossed in conversation with Senator Reus, didn't overhear.

Surprised that she knew of him, Shay nodded. "Yes."

"Do you know him well?" she asked, and unease niggled at Shay. The air of nonchalance in Madison's seemingly innocent question seemed forced.

"Not really," Shay replied cautiously. "Though Trevor seems to."

"Oh, you don't know, do you?" Madison studied her, a gleam in her dark brown eyes. "Trevor didn't tell you?" she prodded before Shay could answer. "Gideon and I were… close before I met your brother."

"Close," Shay repeated, though the twisting in her stomach interpreted the coy choice of phrasing.

"Engaged, actually," Madison confessed, and this time, there was no mistaking the cat-that-ate-the-whole-damn-flock-of-canaries smile that curved her mouth. "We were engaged for a year before we ended our relationship. He wasn't happy about it." She chuckled, apparently amused at her understatement.

We both know why you're here. You lost. Get over it. It's not like it's the first time, and it damn sure won't be the last.

Trevor's accusation echoed in her head, and it now made sickening sense. As did Gideon's reason about why he'd proposed his ridiculous plan, that night at the restaurant.

Your brother, he'd said. All of this—hatred, blackmail, rivalry—was over a woman.

Her belly lurched, and she fisted her fingers, willing the coq au vin she'd just eaten not to make a reappearance.

"If I may have your attention, please?" Senator Reus stood, his booming politician's voice carrying through the ballroom and silencing the after-dinner chatter.

"Thank you. Now I know this evening is about Grace Sanctuary, and I speak on behalf of both the Reus and Neal families when I thank you for your generosity in both spirit and donations." Applause rose, and Julian Reus basked in it, his smile benevolent. No, the evening wasn't about him, but somehow, he'd managed to make it all about him.

"I'd just like to take this moment to recognize this wonderful charity, as well as Trevor Neal, who has spearheaded it since the passing of his dear parents. I'm so proud that I will be able to call him son in the very near future, as he and my beautiful daughter, Madison, embark on a journey together as man and wife. Trevor…" he accepted a glass of champagne from a waiter who suddenly appeared at his elbow, and lifted it high "…congratulations to you and my daughter. You are the son I wasn't blessed with, but am so fortunate to now have."

Around them, people hoisted their own wineglasses and echoed "To Trevor," as her brother stood and clasped the senator's hand, his huge grin so blinding, Shay had to glance away. The sight of him soaking up the senator's validation like water on parched earth caused pain to shudder through her.

Their father would've never praised him so publicly— or privately. Lincoln Neal had been a hard man, huge on demands and criticism, and stingy with compliments. She, more than anyone, understood how Trevor had craved his approval. And it'd been their father's refusal to give it that had changed Trevor. Their father had been dead for five years, and Trevor still drove himself to be the best…to be better than their father. This high regard from such an important man had to be like Christmas to Trevor. A thousand of them packed into one short toast.

Oh God. She dipped her head so no one could glimpse the sting of tears in her eyes.

She was going to cave to Gideon's ultimatum.

Family. Loyalty.

Those were the tenets that had been drilled into them from childhood. Definitely by their father, and even in one of the last conversations she'd had with her mother before she died. She'd stressed that Shay and Trevor always take care of one another.

Family loyalty wouldn't allow her to let Trevor lose everything. The family name. His company. His fiancée. His future father-in-law. There was no one left to protect him, except her. And until she could verify the truth of the information Gideon held—and she still doubted the veracity of it, especially given what she'd learned from Madison—she couldn't permit her brother to be ruined. Not when the kind but wounded boy she remembered still existed inside him.

He was her brother.

And to keep that happiness shining on her brother's face, she would make a deal with the devil.

And Gideon Knight was close enough.

It wasn't difficult to locate him in the crowded room. The entire evening she'd been aware of his presence, and when she glanced over her shoulder to the table several feet away, their gazes immediately locked. As if he'd only been waiting for her to look his way.

She gave him a small nod, and he returned it.

Exhaling, she turned her attention to the glass of red wine she'd barely touched throughout dinner. Now it, and about four more, seemed like a fabulous idea.

She would need all the courage she could get.

Nine

"When I agreed to meet you, I assumed we would go to another restaurant, not your home."

Gideon stepped down into the recessed living room of his downtown Chicago penthouse and slipped his hands into the pockets of his tuxedo pants. Shay hovered at the top of the two steps leading into the room.

He surveyed his home, attempting to view it through her eyes. The dual-level, four-bedroom, three-bath condominium was the epitome of luxury with its airy, open-floor plan, floor-to-ceiling windows, game and media rooms, indoor and outdoor kitchens and private rooftop lounge that boasted its own fireplace. But it'd been the stunning views of the Chicago River and Chicago skyline from every room that had sold him. It was like being a part of the elements while protected from them.

He'd left most of the simple, elegant decor to his interior designer, but scattered among the gray, white and black color scheme were pieces of him, if Shay cared to look close enough. Next to the god-awful piece of metallic abstract art on the fireplace mantel that he'd never gotten around to tossing stood a framed photo of him with his family, including his grandparents, at last year's Mid-Autumn Festival in Chinatown.

On top of the white baby grand piano where his sister sometimes plucked out "Mary Had a Little Lamb" sat the guitar pick he'd forgotten to put away the night before.

Peeking from between the couch pillows was the ear of a pair of Bluetooth headphones that he used to listen to music with while working from home.

Yes, if she paid attention, she might glimpse those hints into him. And part of him tensed with the need to go through the room and remove those clues from her sight. But the other half... That half wanted her to spy them, to ask questions. Which was bullshit, since their arrangement didn't require that kind of intimacy.

He shouldn't hunger for that—especially not from her. Not just sister to his enemy, but another beautiful woman who didn't want the real him. The last time he'd allowed a woman to enter into the space reserved for family, she'd betrayed that trust. Had left him so disillusioned, he'd vowed to never be that foolhardy, that reckless, again.

Only family could be trusted. Only family deserved his loyalty...his love.

Definitely not Trevor Neal's sister.

"This kind of conversation deserves more privacy than a crowded restaurant," he said, finally addressing her complaint. "Would you like a drink? Wine? Champagne? Water?"

"Champagne?" she scoffed, stepping down into the living room. "I guess this would be a victory celebration for you. But no. I'll take a Scotch. This situation calls for something strong that tastes worse than the deal I'm about to swallow."

Her acerbic retort had an inappropriate spurt of amusement curling in his chest. He squelched it, turning to fix her a finger of Scotch and a bourbon for him. Moments later, he handed the tumbler to her and silently watched as she sipped the potent liquor. Not even a flinch. His admiration grew.

When she lifted those beautiful hazel eyes to him, that niggling sense of familiarity tugged at him again. He cocked his head to the side, studying her. What was it…?

"Can we get this started, please?" she asked, setting the glass on the small table flanking the sofa. She rubbed her bare arms, and the sign of nerves pricked a conscience he'd believed to be impervious. "I'm sure you've already guessed that I'm going to agree to your ridiculous plan. Or let's just call it what it is. Extortion."

"You have a choice, Shay," he reminded her, sipping his bourbon.

"Yes," she agreed, bitterness coating the word. "Sacrifice myself or my brother to the beast. That's a hell of a choice."

He shrugged. "But one, nonetheless."

"You're not really this cold and unfeeling. I know you're not," she whispered, her green-and-amber gaze roaming his face as if trying to peer beneath the mask he chose to let her see.

Unbidden, the night of the blackout wavered in his mind. No. Those dark, hungry hours had proved he wasn't cold or unfeeling. For a rare instant, he'd lost the control he was much lauded for. But those circumstances had been extreme, and she wasn't a hardworking, passionate and fiery server named Camille. That woman had disappeared without a trace, filling in for another member of the waitstaff, and not leaving behind a hint of her identity. She'd seen the man he rarely let anyone see.

One Shay would never witness.

"If you need to make up an idea of who I am in order to

fulfill the pretense of falling in love with me, then go ahead. Whatever will allow you to deliver an award-winning performance for your brother and everyone else watching."

"Everyone else being Madison Reus."

The accusation punched him in the chest, and he braced himself against the impact. By sheer will he forced himself not to react. But inside…inside he snarled at the mention of *her*. The woman who'd taught him that love could be bought by the highest bidder. Who'd knowingly betrayed him with the one man he hated. Who'd shown him that placing his heart and trust in a person outside of family was a costly mistake—to his bank account and to his soul.

He would never repeat that particular mistake.

"You must have loved her very much to go to such lengths for your revenge," Shay continued when he remained silent. "That's what this is all about, right? How dare my brother date the woman you were once engaged to? You're punishing both of them by flaunting me in their faces?"

He caught the threads of hurt beneath that calm tone. And in spite of his resolve to maintain his distance, both emotionally and physically, he shifted forward. She didn't retreat, but instead tilted her head back to meet his gaze. Courageous. He hadn't been expecting that from her.

Just like he hadn't been expecting this inconvenient attraction. Even now, her scent—the fresh, wild lushness of rain right before a storm and roses in bloom—called to him like a siren's lure, urging him closer, until his hard, solid planes pressed against her soft, sensual curves.

Though all common sense railed at him not to touch, he ignored it and reached for the thick strands of hair that fell in a sleek glide behind her shoulders. Pinching a lock between his fingers, he lifted it, indulged himself and brushed it over his lips.

Never breaking his stare, he murmured, "You don't know what you're talking about."

He heard the slight catch of her breath. Noticed the erratic beat of her pulse at the base of her neck. From nerves? Desire? The hardening of his body telegraphed which one it voted for.

Step back. Remember the plan. Stick to the plan.

But he stayed. Playing with sin-wrapped-in-bronzed-skin fire.

"No?" she breathed, the corner of her mouth lifting in a sardonic smile. "Is this the part where I just blindly trust what you say because my lying eyes and lil' ol' brain can't possibly grasp the intricacies involved here?" She scoffed, jerking her head back, and he released her. "Please. I'm patted on the head and patronized every day, so forgive me if I call bullshit."

She turned away from him, and he ground his teeth together, his fingers curling into his palms to battle the urge to grab her and bring her back against him. She didn't understand. This wasn't about Madison; it was about another woman—his sister. And that bastard who'd abused her heart and shattered her mental state.

An eye for an eye. A sister for a sister.

But he couldn't admit any of that to her. Not when she would no doubt run back and tell Trevor everything.

"You're forgetting I know the secret about your job. And I don't mean that joke of a title at RemingtonNeal. I would be a fool to underestimate you, Shay."

She pivoted and something flashed in her hazel eyes, but before he could decipher it, she briefly closed them and pinched the bridge of her nose.

"Can we just get this over with?" she asked, weariness coating her voice. "Tell me what you need from me so you won't burn my brother's world to the ground."

"Like I told you at the restaurant. You and I will pretend to be a couple. A real couple, Shay. Which means convincing everyone that we're hopelessly in love." He couldn't prevent the bitter smile from curving his mouth. "I read that you took several drama classes in college. Time to dust off those old skills and bring them out of retirement. I'll require you to attend several events and dinners with me, and the same for you. The first time you try to twist out of this arrangement, it's off, and your brother's dirty dealings become public."

This time he clearly interpreted the emotion turning her gaze more green than brown. Anger. "Don't worry about me. I'll hold up my end of the bargain. But I won't carry this lie on indefinitely. You have a time limit of six months. That's all I'll agree to."

Six months would be more than enough time to carry out all he had planned. "Fine."

"And at the conclusion, you promise to destroy the report and all copies of it."

He nodded again, although he had no intention of doing that. Only a fool would reveal his hand. Did he feel a twinge of guilt for deceiving her? Yes, it didn't sit well. But he'd meant what he'd told his mother. His number one goal was to prevent Trevor from ever hurting another woman as he'd hurt Olivia. This arrangement with Shay was only one part of his plan.

"Okay, then." Shay inhaled a breath and tilted her chin up at a haughty angle, every inch the socialite. "One more thing. I'm not a whore. We might have to pretend affection for each other, but I won't have sex with you."

Irritation flashed inside him, and he took a step toward her before he drew to an abrupt halt. "I can promise you that when I take a woman to my bed, she wants to be there. I don't give a damn about love, because there's something much more honest—fucking. There are no lies when a woman is coming for me, and I don't want one in my bed who doesn't want to be there. If she can't give me the truth of her pleasure, then I don't want her under me. And any man who's satisfied with just getting a woman between the sheets, without giving a damn about her desire to be there, isn't a man."

Silence plummeted into the room, and that sense of déjà vu hit him again. He'd said something similar to Camille weeks ago when she'd accused him of using his position of power to screw her. He shook his head. He had to stop thinking about her. He couldn't afford to show any weakness or distraction around Shay.

"But you need to understand one thing, Shay, and come to terms with it." He moved forward again, lowering his head so their mouths were inches apart. So close he glimpsed the golden striations in her eyes and inhaled the heady scent of Scotch on her breath. "I'm not the other men you might have had dancing to your tune. For the next six months, you're mine. And while you might not be in my bed," he murmured, brushing the back of his finger over a sculpted cheekbone, "you'll act like you are. Which means you'll pretend to desire my touch, my hands on you. You'll behave as if you crave what I, and only I, can give you. Pleasure. Passion. A hunger so deep you don't know how you ever existed without me to take care of it for you. So, moonbeam, even if you loathe me, those beautiful eyes better convince everyone that I'm yours. And *you're mine*."

She wrenched away from him, stumbling backward, her panting audible testimony to the arousal that stained her cheeks and glinted in her eyes.

Fuck.

Need gripped his stomach, grinding and squeezing like a vise. He'd overplayed his hand. His aim had been to teach her a lesson, and he'd ended up the student with his knuckles rapped.

"Don't call me that," she ordered hoarsely. He frowned, at first not grasping what she meant. Then it hit him. Moonbeam.

Where had that come from? Why had he called her *that* name?

"Pet names, like we're something we're clearly not, aren't part of this, either." She tugged her shoulders back, and that delicate but stubborn chin went up again. "And for the record. I belong to *me*. Not my brother. Not RemingtonNeal. And definitely *not you*."

Shay spun around. Snatching up her coat, which he'd laid over the back of the foyer chair when they'd entered the penthouse, she strode out of his home.

He stood there, staring at the closed door, and a small smile played on his lips.

Whether she realized it or not, she'd just issued a challenge.

Accepted.

And he more than looked forward to winning.

Ten

Shay grimaced at the vibration of her cell phone in her back pocket as she served up an order of green papaya salad and tom yum to another hungry customer standing outside Bridgette's food truck. Her best friend's delicious Thai cuisine made hers one of the more popular trucks stationed at Hyde Park during the lunch hour.

Bridgette was a wonderful chef, and when she'd proposed starting a food truck business, Shay had insisted on investing. The love of food and cooking were just a couple things the two of them bonded over. And because they were such good friends, when Bridgette had called this morning, frantic because she'd been down a person, Shay had been more than willing to jump in and help. It hadn't been the first time she'd volunteered, and if Bridgette needed her, it wouldn't be the last. Just another reason Trevor resented her "lowbrow" relationship with Bridgette.

Good thing that she'd never told him about cooking and serving on her food truck.

Another insistent buzz of her cell, and she sighed. She knew who was calling her.

Gideon.

He'd left a message about joining him for lunch about a half hour after Bridgette's panicked call. She'd shot a text off to him, letting him know meeting wouldn't be possible. But had he accepted that? Hell no. Well, that fell under the category of His Problem.

Yes, she'd agreed to attend events with him, but she'd also meant it when she told him he didn't own her. She was more than willing to accompany him to dinners, lunches, parties, whatever. But she also needed notice, and not just a couple hours. She had a life and refused to hand it over to him.

She was already an indentured servant to the Neal name and reputation. He wouldn't become another master.

You're mine.

Those two words had played over and over in her head like a rabid hamster in a wheel. It'd been two days since she'd left his penthouse, and she hadn't been able to erase the declaration from her mind.

Or deny the spark of desire that had erupted into a conflagration inside her. Her thighs had clenched at the dark, sensual note so dominant in his voice. And in that moment, she swore she could feel the heavy, thrilling possession of his body taking hers, filling hers.

Claiming hers.

God, it wasn't fair. Not the words he uttered to her. Not the out-of-control reaction of her body to his.

She didn't have to pretend to know his touch. No, she had intimate knowledge of it.

Which was why she'd reacted so strongly—and unwisely—to the "moonbeam" he'd so carelessly tossed at her. That endearment had been special to her, meant for her alone. But it hadn't been. God only knew how many women he'd said it to.

She wasn't special.

And damn, that had hurt. More than it should've.

Another buzz, and she gritted her teeth. Probably a threatening message this time. The tenacity that had made him so successful as a businessman was working the hell out of her nerves.

Six months. She just had to hold on for six months. Then she would be free. From both this "agreement" with Gideon and from under the yoke of the Neal name.

Gideon didn't know the significance of her time limit. In that time, she would turn twenty-six and be in control of the trust funds from her mother and maternal grandmother. With that came financial independence. She wouldn't need her paychecks from RemingtonNeal to help finance Leida Investments. With the money from her trust funds, she would have more than enough capital, and while she wouldn't totally be able to escape the assumptions because of her last name, she would no longer be under the restrictions and expectations of her brother and her family reputation.

From birth, she'd been under a man's thumb: her father's, her brother's and now Gideon's.

In just six months, she would be liberated from them all.

"Here you go, babe." Bridgette handed her an order of pad thai, disrupting her thoughts of emancipation. "That's number 66."

"Thanks." Shay accepted it, bagged it and carried it to the window. "Here you go." She passed the food to the customer with a smile and turned to the next person in line. "Hi, how can I—"

Oh hell.

Gideon.

Her eyes widened as she stared at his cold, harsh expression. "What are you doing here?" she asked, and in spite of the "you don't own me" speech she'd just delivered to herself, apprehension quivered through her at the anger glittering in his gaze.

"Wasting my time hunting you down, apparently," he ground out. "You're already reneging on our arrangement, and it hasn't even been two days. I warned you about thinking I would dance—"

"Hey, man, order and move on. Some of us have to get back to work," someone yelled from in back of Gideon. And when several more grumbles of agreement followed, Gideon whipped his head around. Immediately, the mumbling ceased.

Good Lord. That was some superpower.

He returned his attention to her and in spite of his glare, she hiked her chin up. "I'm helping a friend out. She needed me today."

His gaze narrowed further, and he growled, "Open the door."

Before she could reply, he stalked off and disappeared. But seconds later, a hard rap at the side door echoed in the truck. From the grill, Bridgette tossed her a "what the hell?" look, and, bemused, Shay shrugged and unlocked it.

The door jerked open, and Gideon strode through it. His big body and intense presence seemed to shrink the interior to that of a toy truck.

Bridgette stared at him, openmouthed and struck silent. Which wasn't an easy feat. With sharp movements, he jerked off his coat and suit jacket and hung them on a wall hook. Then he rolled his sleeves up to his elbows and pinned both her and Bridgette with that dark glare.

"Well?" he snapped. "Where do you need me?"

Need him? What was happening?

Bridgette recovered first. "Can you cook?" At his abrupt nod, she handed him a knife. "You get an order of cashew chicken going, and I'll get the green curry."

Without a word, he crossed to the sink, washed his hands, then accepted the utensil and started chopping fresh vegetables and chicken like a pro. Bridgette again shot her a look, but Shay shrugged, still stunned and confused.

"You have customers waiting," Gideon reminded her, without turning around.

Now the man had eyes on the back of his head as well as cooking skills?

Again…*what the hell?*

Shaking her head, she returned to the window and the ever-growing line outside. For the next couple hours, the three of them worked like a well-oiled machine. Shay still couldn't quite grasp that Gideon Knight was there in the cramped quarters of a food truck, cooking Thai entrées like a professional.

She tried to imagine Trevor jumping in and helping out and couldn't. The image refused to solidify, because her brother would never have done it. Not many men of her acquaintance would've bothered getting their hands dirty. But then again, two hours ago she wouldn't have been able to picture Gideon getting his hands dirty, either. And especially not for her.

As Bridgette closed the serving window and hung the Closed sign, questions crowded into Shay's head. But before she could ask them, he turned, tugging down his sleeves and rebuttoning the cuffs.

"I'll be by to pick you up at seven tonight for a dinner party. This time, be there and ready," Gideon ordered, thrusting his arms into his jacket, then his coat, his tone warning her not to argue. And for once, she heeded it. "And don't keep me waiting."

With a brisk nod at Bridgette, he stalked out the door, leaving a weighty silence behind.

Bridgette was the first to break it.

"What in the hell just happened?" she yelled, voicing the same question that had been plaguing Shay since Gideon's sudden appearance.

And her answer was the same.

Damned if she knew.

Hours later, Shay stood in the foyer and stared at the front door as the ring of the doorbell echoed through her house.

Seven o'clock. Right on the dot.

Her pulse raced, and the roar of it filled her head, deafening her. Nerves. They waged war inside her, turning her belly into a churned-up battlefield. Any sane woman would be anxious about entering a charade and perpetrating a fraud on everyone she knew and cared about.

But she would be lying to herself if she attributed the lion's share of the nerves to their arrangement. No, that honor belonged to the man himself.

Who was Gideon Knight?

The attentive, protective and devastatingly sensual stranger from the night of the blackout? The aloof billionaire and brilliant CEO of a global tech company? The ruthless, revenge-driven ex-fiancé? The man who barged into a food truck, rolled up his sleeves and selflessly helped serve the Chicago masses?

Which one was real? And why did they all fascinate her?

Exhaling a breath, she rubbed her damp palms down her thighs. No fascination. Or curiosity. Both were hazardous and would only lead to a slippery, dangerous slope. One where she could convince herself that the tender, generous man was the true one, and the one who held her brother's future over her head was the aberration.

What had been one of her mother's favorite sayings? "When someone shows you who they are, believe them."

Well, Gideon had shown her he would go to any lengths, no matter how merciless, to achieve what he wanted. Even if it meant using and hurting other people in the process. She needed to believe this truth.

And accept it.

The doorbell rang again, and it unglued her feet, propelling her forward. She unlocked and opened the door, revealing her date for the evening. No, correction—the man she was madly in love with for the next six months.

Gideon stared down at her, his black eyes slowly traversing the curls and waves she'd opted for tonight, down the black cocktail dress with its sheer side cutouts and sleeves, to the stilettos that added four inches to her height. When his eyes met hers again, she barely caught herself before taking a step back from the heat there. It practically seared her skin.

Hazardous. Dangerous. She silently chanted the warnings to herself like a mantra.

He would set fire to her life and leave her covered in ashes.

"Seven o'clock," she rasped, before clearing her throat of the arousal thickening it. "Just as you requested."

"You're beautiful."

Struck speechless, she could only stare at him. His expression hadn't changed from the cool, distant mask, but those eyes, and now his voice... If his gaze made her tremble, the low, sensual throb in that dark velvet voice had her squeezing her thighs against the ache deep inside her.

"Where's your coat?" he asked, glancing past her into the house.

"I have it."

Get it together, she silently ordered herself as she briefly returned inside to grab her coat off the stand.

"Here. Let me." He stepped inside the foyer and took the cape from her, holding it up while she slipped into it.

Fastening it, she turned back to him, and her voice did another vanishing act when he offered her a crooked elbow. Her breathing shallow, she hesitated, then slid her arm through his and let him guide her out of the house and to his waiting Town Car. A driver stood at the rear door, but Gideon waved him away and opened the door for her himself.

God, she was too old for Cinderella-like fairy tales. If she'd ever had stars in her eyes, they'd been dimmed a long time ago. But here, sitting with Gideon Knight in the back of a car that was more elegant and luxurious than any limousine she'd ridden in, with the heat from his body and his earthy sandalwood scent invading her senses, she could almost understand why Cinderella had lost a beautiful shoe over a man.

"I didn't have a chance to tell you earlier, but…thank you. For stepping in and helping Bridgette this afternoon." She glanced at his sharply hewn profile. "How do you know how to cook? I wouldn't have expected it of…a man like you."

He turned to her, and even in the shadowed interior, his dark eyes gleamed. Dim light from the streetlamps passed over his face, highlighting then hiding his too-handsome features. She fought the urge to stroke her fingertips over those planes and angles, over the full curves of his mouth. Free those thick, silken strands and tangle her fingers in them…

"A man like me?" he repeated, the sardonic note relaying that he understood exactly what she meant. "I hate to tarnish your image of me, Shay, but my beginnings aren't as rarefied as yours and your brother's. My grandparents immigrated from China with nothing more than they could carry, and both of my parents worked barely above mini-mum-wage jobs when I was a kid. When my father died, Mom often worked two jobs to provide for us. And as soon as I was old enough, I took any kind of employment I could to help her. One of those happened to be as a short-order cook. If you ever need your yard landscaped or your gutters cleaned, I can do those, too."

Shame sidled through her in a slick, oily glide. She'd un-knowingly spoken from a lofty place of privilege, but her ignorance didn't excuse it. True, she didn't subscribe to the idle lives some of those in high society did—she believed in working hard and making a difference in the world—but she couldn't deny that she didn't know what it was to go without. To go to bed exhausted from menial labor or worried about how the next bill would be paid.

Gideon's mother, and even Gideon, obviously did.

"I'm sorry," she murmured. "I spoke out of turn." She paused, debated whether to say anything else, but ended up whispering, "Your mother must be proud of you."

He studied her for several silent, heavy moments. "She is. But then again, she would've been proud of me if I'd decided to remain a short-order cook in a fast-food res-taurant."

Shay digested that, turned it over and analyzed it again. Could she say the same for her parents? *No.* Her father would've easily disowned her. And as much as Shay adored her mother, Leida Neal wouldn't have been proud of or happy for her daughter if she had been anything less than what her name demanded—respectable, wealthy, connected and married to a man who fit those same qualifications.

The certainty in that knowledge saddened her. Did Gideon realize how fortunate he was?

"She sounds lovely," Shay said, ready to drop the un-settling subject. But then, because her mouth apparently had no allegiance to her, she blurted out, "I'm sorry about your father."

Another heartbeat of weighty silence.

"It was a long time ago."

"My mother died fourteen years ago. And I still miss her every day," she admitted softly.

Slowly, he nodded. "I remember," he finally said, surprising her. "Your brother and I went to high school together, and later attended the same college. But I recall when your mother died. The principal came for him in the middle of class and took him out."

"I didn't know you and Trevor went to school together." Shock whistled through her. "He never mentioned knowing you." Not that he mentioned Gideon at all unless it regarded acquiring his tech company. Or more recently, not unless a blue streak of unflattering adjectives followed his name.

His sensual mouth curved into a hard, faintly cruel smile. "Your brother and I have a long history. He was decent until that day. I was a scholarship student at an elite, private prep school. That already made me a target for most students there. But your brother wasn't one of them. Until after your mother died. Then he became one of the worst. That he and I were often head-to-head competitors in academics and athletics didn't help matters. Neither did the fact that I didn't take his or any of the other assholes' shit."

"He changed after Mother passed," Shay murmured, the dagger of pain stabbing her chest all too familiar when she thought about the boy who'd become a hardened man. "She was the…buffer between him and my father. My dad…" Shay shook her head, turning to stare at the passing scenery outside the car window, but seeing Lincoln Neal's disapproving, stern frown that was often directed at his children. But more so at his first-born child. "He was demanding, exacting and nearly impossible to please. And Trevor desperately wanted to please him. Which became impossible after our father died. Yet, even now..." Again she trailed off, feeling as if she betrayed her brother by revealing even that much.

"That doesn't excuse his behavior," Gideon replied, ice coating his voice.

"No," she agreed, more to herself than him. "But no one is created in a bubble. And no one is all bad or all good. Sometimes it helps to understand why people behave the way they do. And it helps us give them compassion and mercy."

Strong, firm fingers gripped her chin and turned her to face him. Gideon's touch reverberated through her, echoing in the taut tips of her breasts, low in her belly, and in the pulsing flesh between her thighs. He'd clutched her like this the night of the blackout, holding her in place, so he could watch her as she came. Now, like then, she couldn't tear her gaze away from his. Like then, her lips parted, but now, she swallowed down the whimper that clawed at the back of her throat.

"Your brother doesn't deserve compassion or mercy, Shay. So don't try to convince me differently with sad stories of his childhood." He swept the pad of his thumb over her bottom lip, and this time she lost the battle and released that small sound of need. His eyes narrowed on her mouth, then after several moments, lifted to meet hers. "Why does it feel like I've—" He frowned, but didn't remove his hand.

"Why does it feel like you've what?" she breathed, dread filtering into the desire. He'd heard her plead for him, for his touch, many times during the night they'd spent together. Had the sound she'd released just now triggered his memory?

God, in hindsight, she should've been up front with him

about her identity from the beginning. If she came clean now, he would only see her as a liar.

Maybe because you're lying by omission?

Shame crept in, mingling with the dread. She hated deception of any kind, and this didn't sit well with her. At all. But self-preservation trumped her conscience at this point. Her reasons for initially remaining quiet still stood. She didn't trust Gideon. Didn't know what he would do with the information that Shay Neal had masqueraded as waitstaff at one of the biggest social events of the year and then slept with him under false pretenses. Would he use it as another source of ammo in this war he waged with her brother, leaving her reputation and her company as casualties?

Possibly.

No, she couldn't afford to find out.

"Nothing." He dropped his hand from her face, his customary impassive expression falling firmly back in place. Turning from her, he picked up a small, rectangular box from the seat beside him. "Here. I have something for you."

She glanced down at the gift, then back up at him. After several moments, she returned her attention to the box and, with slightly trembling fingers, removed the lid. And gasped.

Delicate ruby-and-gold bangles nestled on black velvet. Tiny diamonds rimmed the bracelets, making the jewelry glitter in the dark.

They were beautiful. Just...beautiful.

"There're eight of them," he said, picking up the bangles when she didn't make a move toward them. "In Chinese culture, eight is a lucky number. Red is also lucky."

Gently grasping her hand, he slid the jewelry onto her wrist.

"Thank you," she whispered. In the past, she'd received earrings, necklaces and rings from men who hoped to win her over—or rather win over the Neal heiress. But none of them had been bought with thought or meaning. None of them had been for *her*, Shay. Whether he'd intended it or not, Gideon had given her a piece of himself, of his heritage. And for that alone, she'd accept. "They're gorgeous."

"You're welcome," he murmured, his fingers brushing over the tender skin on the inside of her wrist before withdrawing. For a moment, she caught a flicker of emotion in his eyes before he shut her out once again.

She felt the echo deep inside her.

And for some inexplicable reason—a reason she refused to explore—it hurt.

A charade, she reminded herself. They were both playing their parts, and gifts to his fake girlfriend were part of those roles.

As long as she kept that truth forefront in her mind, she wouldn't get caught up in the beautiful enigma that was Gideon Knight.

Eleven

"I feel like a zoo animal in a cage," Shay muttered, lifting a glass of white wine to her lips. "They could at least be subtler about the staring."

Gideon arched an eyebrow, scanning the large formal living room. Several pairs of eyes met, then slid away from his, caught ogling the newest couple in their midst. Satisfaction whispered through him. He'd accepted this particular dinner party invitation because of who would be in attendance. Not just business associates, but members of the social circle Shay was intricately a part of. Talk of their appearance together would rush through Chicago's society elite like a brush fire.

"They're wondering why you're with the beast," he said.

"Probably."

He snorted at her quick agreement, earning a dazzling smile from her. He had to hand it to her—Shay was a brilliant actress. As soon as they'd crossed the threshold into Janet and Donald's mansion, she'd immediately charmed his client and her husband. And though he knew the truth behind their arrangement, even he could almost believe Shay was smitten with him. Small, but intimate touches to his arm and chest. Gentle teasing. Special smiles. Yes, she deserved an award for her performance.

And as their hosts approached them, and she slid her arm through his, her soft breast pressing into side, he ordered his dick to stand down for about the fifty-fifth time... in two hours.

If he was a better man, he would insert some distance between them, not enjoy the sensual lure of her scent. Or savor each time he settled a palm at the small of her back—a back covered only by the same sheer material that "covered" her shoulders and arms. She was sex and class in this dress that skimmed every delicious curve.

Damn if the heat from her didn't seep into his palm and ignite every greedy need to stroke her skin, sift his fingers through the thick, dark strands of her hair...claim her saint-and-sinner body for his own.

The only woman to have stirred this unprecedented reaction in him had been Camille. It unsettled him. The mysterious waitress was no longer in his life. But Shay... Everything about her tested his control, his reason, his plans.

How he kept touching her when every rule of logic demanded he keep all displays of affection public to cement the facade of a happy, in-love couple. How she challenged him with those flashes of temper when no one except his best friend and business partner dared. How she surprised him with things like working in a food truck. How he couldn't jettison the sense that there was something familiar about her...

And then there was his jewelry on her wrist. The gold and rubies gleamed against her skin like sunlight and fire. And that fierce surge of possessiveness that had blindsided him in the car swelled within him again. He braced himself against it.

This wasn't the first time he'd bought a woman jewelry. Hell, the amount he'd bought Madison could have filled a store and still left enough diamonds to pay for a small city. He'd gone into the store this time intending to purchase a necklace or earrings, something that screamed wealth. But none of the pieces had felt…right. So he'd left, and instead had driven to a smaller jeweler. One where he'd bought his grandmother's birthday gift. And the bangles had been there, waiting. He hadn't intended to purchase something so personal to him, so…intimate, for what should've been just a flashy statement of ownership, with the sole purpose of making others take note. But he had. And unlike almost everything in his life, he didn't analyze it, instead going on impulse.

Because in that moment, as he'd handed his credit card over the counter, his need to see Shay wearing the pieces he'd personally chosen far outweighed caution.

And that need hadn't abated.

As he slid his hand up her spine and cupped the nape of her neck, the need deepened, sharpened.

"I should be annoyed with both of you," Janet Creighton said, her smile erasing the reproach from her words. Leaning forward, she dropped her voice to a conspiratorial whisper. "But the two of you outing yourselves as a couple tonight has made my little dinner party the social event of the season."

Shay smiled, glancing up at Gideon, and the warmth reflected in the gold-and-green depths of her eyes had his breath stumbling in his throat. "I told Gideon he should at least give you some warning of who his plus one would be, but…" She tipped her head to the side and murmured, "The rumors are true about that stubborn nature of his."

"I find myself giving in to you way too often, though. My reputation might not survive it," he replied, squeezing her neck and bringing her closer, brushing his lips over the side of her head.

Her fingernails bit into his arm, and he barely managed to fight back a groan. The tiny prick of pain echoed lower in his body, and he locked his jaw against asking her to do it again. But harder.

"You shouldn't let me know I'm a weakness," she teased, but only he caught the undercurrent of faint sarcasm. "I might be tempted to take advantage."

"I might be tempted to let you," he rejoined softly.

Silence thrummed between them, taut and tension-filled. Their gazes clashed, tangled, locked. The pretense seemed all too real. As did the desire that flared inside him, the excitement that flashed through him, as bright and hot as a bolt of lightning. What would she do if he lowered his head and took her soft mouth? Would she jerk away from him? Or would she use their act as an excuse to surrender, to let him taste her?

"Well, damn." Janet's awed, but amused whisper infiltrated the haze of arousal that had clouded him and his judgment. *Damn it,* he silently swore, returning his attention to his client. This was a facade, an act. One he'd set in motion. He couldn't afford to forget that. "Honey, I need you to take notes."

Beside Janet, her husband snorted lightly. "We've been married thirty-two years. My hand is cramped."

Shay's laughter drew more gazes in their direction, and Gideon smiled, both at the other couple and the pure delight in Shay's amusement.

"Dinner is almost ready," Janet said, shaking her head and throwing Donald a mock-irritated glance. "Let's go, you."

"That went well," Shay murmured, as soon as they were out of earshot. She slowly released his arm. "You can let go of me now."

Instead of obeying, he turned into her body, his hold on her drawing her closer until her breasts brushed his chest. He caught her sharp gasp, felt the puff against the base of his throat. Tiny flickers danced under his skin at that spot.

She stiffened, and he softly tsked, lowering his voice so it carried only as far as her ears. "You're supposed to enjoy my touch, Shay. Want more of it. But definitely not shy away from it." When she lifted her hands and settled them at his waist under his jacket, her fingernails digging into his skin through his shirt, he didn't hold back his low rumble of hunger. "I think you're intending to punish me, moonbeam," he growled above her mouth, pinching her chin with his free hand and tilting her head back. "But I don't mind a bit of pain with my pleasure. Would you sink those claws in deeper if I asked nicely?"

He expected her to wrench away from him; his muscles tightened in anticipation of controlling the reaction he purposefully coaxed from her.

But she sank her nails harder into his flesh, and the stings were a precursor of how she would scratch and grip him if they were stretched out on his bed. He tried to swallow his groan, but some sound escaped against his will. And the molten gold in her eyes almost eclipsed the brown and green.

She'd played him. Turned the tables so completely he ground his teeth together, imprisoning the words that would reveal she'd knocked him on his ass. Those words being *more, harder, please...*

"Gideon," she whispered.

"Well, don't you two look cozy," a new, all-too-familiar and despised voice drawled from behind them.

Gideon released Shay, shifting to her side and slipping an arm around her waist. He faced Madison and Julian Reus, careful to compose his features so they betrayed none of the disgust and hatred that burned in his chest for her, or the disdain he harbored for her father.

Underneath those emotions, satisfaction hummed through his veins. *Good.* He'd been waiting for their arrival. He'd expected Trevor to be with them, but since he wasn't glued to Madison's side, the other man must not be in attendance. That was a disappointment, but Gideon's cheating ex and her equally deceptive father were good enough.

He switched his attention to Madison. It stunned him that he'd once missed the avaricious, calculating gleam in her brown eyes. Given her long dark hair, sensuous features and curvaceous body, he couldn't deny her beauty, but it was hard, like a lacquer that distracted from the coldness beneath.

Love had truly been blind. No. It'd made him dumb and deaf, too.

"I must admit, when we heard the rumors of you being here with Gideon, Shay, we didn't believe it at first," Julian said, his tone as amicable as any good politician's. But his eyes blazed, yelling the things one would never want heard on an open lapel mic. "Your brother didn't mention you were attending tonight. Or that you were…" he paused deliberately "…seeing someone new. I'm sure he'll be interested to discover this turn of events."

If the senator had expected Shay to quail under his not-so-subtle condemnation, he'd sadly underestimated her. "Trevor is a wonderful brother, but he's just that—my brother. And I don't require his approval for who I choose to spend time with. Just as he didn't ask for mine with Madison." Shay smiled, and it could've cut glass. "Although I would've gladly offered it."

Julian blinked, his mouth hardening at the corners. "Your brother and I have much in common. We both admire honesty—and loyalty."

"You don't really want to go there, do you, Julian?" Gideon interjected, arching an eyebrow. He forced his voice to remain even, bored, but injected a thread of steel through it. He'd be damned if he'd let the man intimidate Shay or belittle her with his condescending bullshit. Especially not in front of him. "I'd be willing to discuss both with you. At length."

"Let's go, Daddy." Madison chuckled, the sound strained, her lovely features tight. Like her father's, her gaze ordered Gideon to do unnatural things with his own anatomy. "There are more people we need to speak with."

Shay waited until her soon-to-be sister-in-law and her father were out of earshot, then sighed. "God. This evening just became infinitely longer."

"I beg to disagree." He settled a hand on the small of her back again, guiding her forward. "The fun has just begun."

Shay breathed deeply as she washed her hands in the Creightons' bathroom. This moment alone, without the narrow-eyed glares from both Madison and the senator, or the microscopic attention of the other guests, was a mercy.

She hated being the subject of all that speculation. They'd reminded her of vultures, waiting to see who'd get their pick of carrion. Gideon seemed unfazed. But all those sidelong, greedy glances and not-so-quiet whispers... They'd crawled over her like ants attacking a picnic. By the time dinner concluded, she'd nearly raced to the bathroom. To be free. If only for a few moments.

"Can't stay in here forever," she said to her reflection.

That was the first sign of losing it, right? Talking to oneself. She smiled, shaking her head as she headed toward the restroom door. Her mother used to do the same, mumble to herself as she puttered around the kitchen when Dad wasn't there to catch her. God, Shay missed her. Missed her hugs, her quiet assurances, her confidence in Shay.

Well, one thing Leida Neal would've reprimanded her about was hiding like a coward in the bathroom during a dinner party. Snorting lightly, Shay exited the powder room…and nearly collided with Madison.

Damn.

"Hi, Madison." She greeted her brother's fiancée with a smile. "I'm sorry if you had to wait. The bathroom's all yours."

She shifted to the side, prepared to walk around the other woman, but the futile hope of avoiding a confrontation died a quick death when Madison stepped to the side as well, blocking Shay's escape. Madison smiled in turn, but it didn't reach her chilly brown eyes.

"No hurry, Shay. I was hoping to catch you alone for a few moments," she purred. "We have so much to catch up on, seeing as we apparently have more in common than I thought."

"I'm assuming you're referring to Gideon," Shay said, resigning herself to this conversation. It wasn't one she could've circumvented, but she hadn't anticipated having it outside of the guest restroom.

"You're a cool one, aren't you, Shay?" Madison asked, slowly shaking her head. "The other night you never mentioned you knew him. And when I told you about our past, you pretended to be dumb. It seems I underestimated you. I won't repeat the mistake."

Anger flickered to life, crackling like dry wood set ablaze. "I didn't pretend to be dumb, as you put it. Discussing my private life while you were at the table with my brother, your fiancé, didn't strike me as appropriate. And like I told your father, I don't need approval for my relationships," she said, working to keep the bite of rising irritation from her tone. After all, this was her future sister-in-law. Even if more and more she was beginning to question the wisdom of Trevor's choice. "Now, if I'd known you were attending this dinner party, I would've informed you so you weren't taken by surprise. But I wasn't aware."

Several silent moments passed, and a fury-filled tension thickened between them.

"Your brother always brags about how smart you are." Madison tsked softly. "Shay earned this degree. Shay graduated with honors from this program. So intelligent. And yet, when it comes to men, you're so naive." Her expression softened with a sympathy that was as false as her lashes. "What are the odds that *my ex* would turn around and fall for *my new fiancé's sister*? A little too coincidental, don't you think?" She chuckled, the sound taunting. "It's almost pathetic in its transparency. He's using you, Shay. Gideon still wants me, and you're caught up in his little plan to make me jealous."

Pain, serrated and ugly, slashed at her, the truth of Madison's words the razor-sharp knife. Why did it hurt? She'd gone into this charade knowing the reason behind it. Gideon hadn't tried to deny it. But reason had no place when humiliation and pain pumped out of her with every heartbeat.

Forcing her lips to move and her arm to lift, she waved away Madison's barb-tipped claims as if they were petty annoyances. "I don't see how any of this is your business, Madison. What is between Gideon and me is just that. *Between us.* Now if you'll excuse me…"

She moved forward again. If Madison chose to get in the way, this time she'd find her ass meeting the floor. Thankfully, Madison didn't try to block her, and Shay headed toward the dining room with a smothered sigh of relief.

"Ask him who broke it off with whom. He hasn't let go of me. If I wanted him back, Shay, he would be mine."

Madison's parting shot struck true. By sheer force of will, Shay kept walking.

But it was with a limp.

Twelve

"You ambushed me. Again."

Gideon turned from his silent—okay, brooding—study of the scenery passing by the car window to look at Shay. She'd been quiet since they'd left the Creightons' mansion ten minutes earlier. No, she'd been distant since returning to the dining room after dinner.

And Madison had followed a couple minutes behind her, wearing a sly grin. Personal experience had taught him his ex could be a malicious bitch. Had she said something to Shay? Had Madison hurt her? A wave of protectiveness had surged inside him, and he'd just managed to check the impulse to drag Shay onto his lap and demand answers. To ease the tension that had strung her shoulders tight. To assure her that if Madison had sharpened that dagger she called a tongue against Shay, he would fix it.

Instead, he'd remained sitting beside her at the table, continuing the charade until they could politely leave.

Disgust ate at him like a caustic acid. Disgust with himself. He'd led her into the lion's den and hadn't shielded her.

Every war has casualties.

He mentally repeated the reminder like a mantra. He'd

been aware when he'd included Shay as part of his plans that she might be wounded, but the end justified the means. He intentionally conjured an image of his sister lying on that hospital bed, black hair limp, skin pale as she stared listlessly out the window. Oh yes. The end justified the means. *Olivia*—her suffering, her brokenness, her loss— justified it.

"Am I supposed to know what that cryptic comment means, Shay?" he asked. "Because I can assure you, I don't."

She didn't flinch from his flat, indifferent tone or the dismissal in his question. "You knew Madison and the senator would be there tonight."

Gideon stared at her, not even debating whether to give her the truth or not. "Of course I did. Janet and Donald are business associates of Julian's."

"You didn't think to warn me?" She shook her head. "What if Trevor had been there?"

"And?" he asked, anger igniting inside him. "I hoped he would be. But it doesn't matter. Maybe him hearing about his sister dating his enemy from his future father-in-law or his fiancée might work out better than I intended."

"Do you care that your schemes and plans are hurting people?" she whispered.

The disappointment in her voice, as if he'd somehow let her down, raked over his skin. Burrowed beneath it.

He hated it.

Dipping his head, he leaned closer until only inches separated them. So close her breath ghosted over his lips. "Your brother?" He paused. "No."

"All this for her," she breathed, her gold-and-green eyes roaming his face. Summer on the verge of autumn. That's what they reminded him of. Shaking his head as if he could physically rid himself of the sentimental thought, he leaned away from her, turning back to the window. "Madison was right."

He stiffened, his suspicions confirmed.

Slowly, he straightened and shifted on the seat, meeting her gaze again.

"What did she say to you?" he growled.

"Nothing I didn't already know," she replied, her full bottom lip trembling before she seemed to catch the betraying sign. Her teeth sank into the sensual curve.

"What did she say to you, Shay?" he repeated, grounding out the question between clenched teeth.

"That you were using me to get back at her and Trevor. That she could have you back if she wanted. She…" Shay paused, and something flickered in her eyes. "She told me to ask you who broke up with whom. From that, I'm assuming she left you."

He didn't answer. Couldn't.

What did it matter if Shay knew the dirty details? Of how he'd walked in on her brother in Madison's bed. How the woman he'd believed he would spend the rest of his life with had told him she'd upgraded with Trevor.

None of it mattered now. Yet he couldn't shove the words past his throat.

Shay shook her head, chuckling softly. Except the sound contained no humor. "So is that your master plan? Was the file on my brother your way of ensuring I cooperated while you plotted to steal back your ex? That would show Trevor who the better man was, right? Teach him—"

"You don't know what you're talking about."

"That's another thing Madison accused me of being. Dumb. But I'm not. You're fighting over her like she's some ball you lost on the playground. And in the end, I'll look like the idiot she called me. But that doesn't matter to you, does it? Not as long as you win."

Her accusation struck too close to the doubts that had pricked at his conscience only moments before. That only stirred his anger.

He didn't give a damn if she knew the truth.

"Win?" He arched an eyebrow, not bothering to prevent his sneer. "Win what, exactly? A relationship based on lies and greed? A woman who would jump to the next dick as long as he was willing to pay handsomely for the privilege? Tell me, Shay, doesn't that sound like a terrible grand prize?"

She gaped at him, no doubt stunned by the ferocity of his reply. "What do you mean?" she asked, her gaze roaming his face, as if searching for the truth. As if she actually wanted the truth. "Do you mean she—"

"Cheated on me? Oh yes." He nodded, and the smile on his mouth felt savage. "We'd been together a year and a half, engaged to be married. Gorgeous, fun, witty, exciting—I didn't care who her father was or about her family name. All I wanted was her. And all she wanted was what I could give her. At least, until she found someone else who could give her more. Care to guess who that someone was?"

Her lips formed her brother's name, but no sound came out.

"Yes, Trevor. I came home early from a business trip and stopped by her place. I had the key, so I went in and found them together. In the bed I'd just made love to her in two days earlier. It hadn't been the first time they'd been together. The next day, when giving me back my ring, Madison informed me that it'd been going on for some time—six months. According to her, I might be rich, but Trevor had prestige, connections and a family name. She'd upgraded."

Shay's chin jerked up as if he'd delivered a verbal punch

to her jaw. Sorrow flashed in her eyes, and for a second, he resented her for it. He didn't want her pity; he wanted her to understand the kind of bastard she called brother.

"Your brother did it on purpose, Shay," he pressed. Just as he'd used Gideon's sister to get to him. "He went after Madison because she was my fiancée, and faithless bitch that she is, she had no problem sleeping with a man she knew I hated. She not only betrayed me with her body, but with her loyalty, her heart. So I don't need to prove to Trevor who the better man is. Because, Shay, your brother isn't a real one."

"Gideon," she whispered.

"No." He slashed a hand down between them, done with the topic. Done with laying out his stupidity before her. "And to address the second part of that statement, you're not dumb. Far from it. But you are blind." He narrowed his eyes on her. "Why are you so quick to believe the manipulative claims of a jealous woman?"

She blinked. "What do you mean?" She frowned. "Madison's not—"

"Jealous," he interrupted again. "Why is that so hard to accept?" He didn't wait for her to answer, but continued. "And this doesn't have anything to do with me. You're everything she wants to be. Respected. Admired not just for your beauty but for who you are—successful, brilliant, esteemed. She, like me, like Julian, watched as you charmed everyone around you tonight, and as they damn near competed to have a moment of your time. And that has nothing to do with your last name. That's all you. I'm the toy in this scenario, moonbeam," he murmured. The thought of being her plaything roughened his voice, tightened his gut. "And she wants me only because you—a woman she could never be—has me."

If he hadn't been watching her so closely, he might've

missed her flinch before she controlled it. "Why are you calling me that?" she rasped.

"The other women there tonight... They were like the sun—bright, obvious. Trying so hard to be noticed. But you, Shay, you don't have to try to grab someone's attention. Like the moon, you're distant, cool and beautiful. Men can't help but notice you. Be drawn to you, ready to beg for some of your light rather than be lost and alone in the dark."

Only the harsh grating of their breaths filled the back of the car. Part of him demanded he rescind those too-revealing words. But the other part—the greedy, desperate part—refused to, instead waiting to see what she would do with them.

"What game are you playing now, Gideon?" she whispered, her eyes wide...vulnerable. "I don't know how to play this one."

"Then set the rules," he said, just as softly. Unable not to touch her any longer, he cupped her deceptively delicate jaw, stroked the pad of his thumb over the elegant jut of her cheekbone. "Set the rules, and I'll follow them."

It was a dangerous allowance. In this "relationship" the balance of power couldn't shift; he couldn't hand her a weapon to use against him. Not when revenge for his sister's pain, his family's torment hung in the balance. But that knowledge didn't stop him from shifting closer to her, from tipping her head back and brushing a caress over her parted lips. From staring down into those beautiful eyes and letting her see the desire that hurtled through his veins.

"Just one. Make..." She paused, briefly closed her eyes, but then her lashes lifted. "Make me forget."

"Forget what, moonbeam?"

The answer was already yes. He'd surrender anything to her if she'd permit him to continue touching her.

But that same hunger to brand her vied with the need to

conquer what haunted her. He'd never considered himself some knight facing dragons, not for anyone, but for Shay, he'd forgo the armor and charge into the fire.

One hand rose to his wrist, the slender fingers wrapping around and hanging on to him. The other slipped inside his jacket and settled on his chest before sliding up to his neck, her thumb resting on his pulse.

"Forget that you're trying to destroy my brother, my world," she whispered. "Forget that you're going to break me. And I'm going to let you."

A vise gripped his chest and tightened until the barest of breaths passed through his lungs. If he was a good man, he would release her, promise not to touch her again. Walk away from this whole plan that already ensnared her like barbed wire. She was right; he would probably end up hurting her, and if he had a conscience, he would warn her to protect herself from him.

But he'd never claimed to be good.

Still, he could do what she asked. He could make her forget.

"Kiss me," he ordered in a low rumble. "Take what you want—what you need from me. And, moonbeam?" He lowered his head, pushing his thumb past the seam of her lips and into her mouth. Moist heat bathed the tip. "Don't be gentle," he growled.

She studied him, and as he watched her in turn, desire eclipsed the vulnerability that lingered in her gaze. He felt her teeth first, and the tiny sting arrowed straight to his lower body.

"Don't be gentle," he repeated, harder.

Her eyes still on him, she moved the hand on his neck so her fingers encircled the front. She squeezed just as her lips closed around his thumb, and she bit him.

"Fuck," he groaned, the sting arcing through him like a

sizzling bolt of electricity. "Baby." Her gaze darted to the side, toward the front of the car and his driver. "The divide is soundproof," he assured her, pulling his thumb free and rubbing the dampness over her bottom lip. Before repaying her with a nip of his own.

Another moan clawed free of him. Damn, he'd been aching—literally *aching*—to get his mouth on her. To taste her. Reaching for the console in front of the seat, he lifted the hood and hit a button, and another panel, this one smoke-tinted, slid across, concealing them.

"Are you good?" he asked. His dick throbbed, and he gritted his teeth.

He could wait until they reached their destination, but fuck if he *or* his dick wanted to. He needed to be inside her. From the moment he'd sat down across from her in that restaurant, he'd craved this. No, damn that. Longer. From the second he'd opened his private investigator's file and laid eyes on her picture. Even as he'd spun his plans of revenge, he'd envisioned those hazel eyes gleaming with the arousal he'd stirred. Pictured her sweet body bowing and twisting for him. Wondered if she would take him slow and easy, or hard and wild. God, he'd almost driven himself insane wondering that.

She nodded, but he shook his head. "Tell me, moonbeam. You good?"

"Yes," she breathed, giving his neck one last squeeze. She removed her hand, replacing it with her mouth, trailing a path up his throat, over his chin until she hovered over his lips. "I've set the rules," she reminded him, kneeling on the seat so she rose over him. "Now follow them like you promised."

She crushed her mouth to his.

The kiss wasn't patient, wasn't tentative. Her tongue thrust forward, parried with his, tangling and dueling. She took him as if she knew exactly what he liked, what he needed. It was…familiar. Something—a thought, a warning, maybe—tickled the back of his skull, but as she sucked on his tongue, drawing on him as if he were everything she needed to survive, that inkling winked out. Nothing mattered but the intoxicating, addictive taste of her. And in that instant, the question that had plagued him since he first gazed on her picture was answered: Shay would be hard and wild in bed. Or in the back of a Town Car.

"I want to…" She didn't finish her request, but reached behind him, removing the band holding back his hair.

The strands loosened, and her heavy sigh differed from the ones she'd been emitting during their kiss. This one? It matched the delight that softened her beautiful features as she drew his hair forward and up to her face. Tangling her fingers in the strands, she tugged on them, and the prickle across his scalp tripped down his spine, crackled at the base. He clutched her hips, digging his fingertips into the soft flesh.

"Beautiful," she whispered.

Only one other woman had ever called him that, and with that same note of awe coating the compliment. It'd shaken him then, and it did now. Once more that niggling sense of…something…teased him. But he shoved it away. Now, with his hands on Shay, with her storm-whipped rain and fresh roses scent embracing him, there wasn't room for thoughts of another woman. Especially one that was a ghost. Shay was sensual, golden-bronze flesh-and-bone. She was hot, pounding blood coursing through him. She was his insanity, his hunger brought to vivid life.

She was *here*.

For him.

With a growl, he skated his palms up the sides of her torso, and the zipper of her dress abraded his skin. Desperate to discover if his imagination matched reality, he impatiently tugged it down and wasted no time in pushing the material over her shoulders and down her arms. She obliged him, freeing his hair and joining him in getting rid of the clothing.

"No." The word escaped him before he could trap it.

"No?" she repeated, and he caught the hint of insecurity that crept into her voice. She started to lift her arms toward her torso, but he latched on to her wrists, lowering her arms back down before she could cross them.

"My imagination doesn't match reality. Doesn't even fucking compete." He cupped a breast and hissed at the delicious weight of her flesh filling his palm. Warm, soft, perfect. Reverently, he whisked his thumb over the nipple, watching in fascination as it beaded. No, she wasn't the first woman he'd touched like this, but none had been *her*. He tore his gaze from his hand on her to meet her eyes. "Nothing or no one could fucking compete."

Her lips parted, but no words emerged. Good. He was saying enough for both of them, and he needed to stop that before he took them somewhere they had no place being. Bending his head, he sucked a tip deep, flicking his tongue against her flesh before drawing hard. Shay shuddered, her hands cradling his head, holding him to her with a strength that telegraphed her passion. That and the nails pricking his scalp.

Switching breasts, he treated the other to the same devotion. She writhed against him, as if seeking to get closer. Cooperating, he fisted the hem of her dress and shoved it up her thighs. With a whimper, she straddled him, dropping down and pressing them sex to sex.

He growled around her flesh, suckling harder. And she rewarded his attention with a dirty grind of her hips that had him throwing his head back against the seat, eyes squeezed closed. Her panties and his pants and underwear separated them, but none of those inconsequential details mattered. Not when her hot, wet heat rode him. Not when each drag of her flesh over his cock shredded his control.

"Give me your mouth again," he ordered, in a voice so guttural he barely understood himself.

But she must've translated it, because she gave him what he asked for, her hips still working over him. She didn't stop, and the thrust of her tongue and pull of her lips mimicked each stroke below. Even as she yanked his jacket open and attacked his shirt, damn near ripping buttons loose to get her hands on his bare chest, she didn't lose him.

They groaned into each other when she touched him. Those slender, clever hands swept down his chest, lingering over his tattoos, tracing the ink with almost worshipful strokes.

"How is it possible that you just get more beautiful?" she whispered. He parted his lips to tell her she was the stunning one, not him, but she ripped away his ability to talk by brushing her fingertips over his nipples, rubbing them. His hips bucked into her. Live wires connected from her touch to the tip of his dick. He swelled, throbbing, *hurting*.

"I need to be inside you," he rasped against her mouth. He abandoned her breasts and burrowed his fingers in her hair, gripping it, holding her still so he could stare into those slumberous eyes. "Are you going to let me?"

"Yes," she breathed, trailing a route of fire over his clenched abs to the band of his pants.

"Are you going to take me like this?" he pressed, thrusting upward so she fully understood what he meant. "Take me like you own me?"

"Yes."

Almost too rough, he released her, reaching into his inner jacket pocket for his wallet. Quickly withdrawing a condom, he tossed the billfold to the floor. Within moments, he had his pants opened, his erection freed. Her swift intake of breath preceded the hot, tight clasp of her fist around him by seconds. His back bowed under the whip of pleasure, and his free hand wrapped around hers, so they pumped his flesh together. For several torturous and blissful moments, they stroked him, pushing closer to an ending that wouldn't include him balls-deep inside her.

"Enough," he muttered, and, removing their hands, tore open the small foil package and slid the protection over him. Above him, she fumbled under her dress, trying to push black lace panties down her hips. "Fuck that," he growled.

Shoving her dress higher until it encircled her waist like a band, he fisted the front of her underwear and jerked it to the side. For a couple seconds, he savored the vision of her bare, glistening sex and the erotic beauty of her silken thigh-high stockings against silkier skin. But then the lure of that feminine flesh proved too enticing, too much.

He slid his finger through the dark cleft, moaning at the wetness coating his skin. The sound dragged from her echoed his, and her head tipped back, shuddering when he circled her, applying minute pressure. Just enough to have her shaking like a leaf, but not enough to catapult her over the edge. That honor belonged to his dick.

Hands grasping his shoulders, she eased down his length, and though the drugging pleasure had his eyes nearly closing to savor the tight, smooth fit of her sex, he kept his attention on her. Because nothing—not the rippling clasp of her body, the quiver of her thighs, the sight of her taking him—could compare with the slight widening and darkening of those beautiful eyes. Those eyes conveyed how much she craved him, needed him.

Those eyes gave him all of her.

And greedy bastard that he was, he wanted it all.

Except for the very fine tremble of his tautly controlled muscles, he held completely still. Allowing her to claim him at her own pace. Even if each interminable second she took to inch down threatened to send him careening into insanity or orgasm—whichever came first. Finally, she sat on his thighs, and he was fully embedded inside her. And still he wouldn't free her from his gaze. Not when, in this moment, surrounded by her sweet flesh, everything clicked into place. He finally knew this gaze.

Knew *her*.

"Fuck me, moonbeam," he whispered. "And don't look away from me."

Sliding her hands over his shoulders and into his hair, she grabbed fistfuls of the strands and glided up his length. Air kissed his tip before she sank onto him again, swallowing him in the firmest, but softest heat. Again. And again. She released him, took him. Eased off him, claimed him.

She rode him, rising and falling over him, driving them both toward the rapidly crumbling edge of release. Her cries mixed with the litany of his own and still she continued to look at him. Letting him see what he did to her. Gifting him with that. Electric pulses zipped up and down his spine, crackling in the balls of his feet. He couldn't hold back much longer. He wasn't going to last.

He loosened a hand from her hair and tucked it between their undulating bodies and slicked it over the top of her sex. Once, twice. A third and a pinch.

She flew apart with a scream, stiffening, her sex gripping him, milking him. Daring him to dive into the abyss with her. Grabbing her hips, he slammed into her, plunging so deep he almost doubted he would ever find his way out of her.

She fucking leveled him.

Her arms closed around his shoulders, cradling him as he bowed his head, groaning out his release into her neck. He inhaled her thick, heady scent as his body calmed and his breathing evened. His senses gradually winked back online after pleasure short-circuited them.

Silence filled the interior of the car. Carefully, he withdrew from her, disposing of the condom and righting their clothes. Shay didn't look at him, paying undue attention to pulling down her dress and settling it around her thighs.

"Are you okay?" he asked, his voice seeming overly loud even to his own ears.

"Yes," she said, still not glancing in his direction.

Camille.

The name shivered on his tongue. He almost said it aloud just to see if she would respond. If her reaction would give her away. But he swallowed the name of the woman who'd haunted his thoughts since the night of the blackout.

The woman who was one and the same as Shay Neal.

It explained the nagging sense of familiarity. The feeling that they'd met before. Sinking into her body had sealed the knowledge for him. How had Shay thought she could continue to fool him once he was deep inside her? How could she believe he would ever forget the too-tight and utterly perfect fit of her?

She'd lied to him. All this time, she'd recognized him—how could she not?—but she'd kept the secret of her identity from him.

Why?

Several reasons entered his mind—embarrassment, protecting her reputation—but one kept blaring in his head, gaining validity.

Had meeting him at the Du Sable City Gala been a setup? Not the blackout, of course, but had she gone to the gala with a plan to meet him? To get close to him? Yes, he'd approached her, but what would've happened if he hadn't? Would she have found a way to get close to him? Found a way to get him to talk to her, to reveal information?

Had Trevor sent her to the gala with that purpose?

Minutes ago, Gideon would've said no. But with the haze of pleasure quickly evaporating and leaving him with a clearer mind, he couldn't know for sure. First and foremost, Shay was a Neal and her loyalty belonged to her brother. Hadn't she been willing to surrender to blackmail and sleep with the enemy—literally, now—to save Trevor? Gideon couldn't see her going so far as to fuck him in that dark break room for her brother. As she'd defiantly told him before, she didn't whore herself out for anyone. But... doing a little subterfuge on Trevor's behalf? Maybe that wasn't out of the question...

He studied her proud profile, waiting to see if she would tell him the truth now, after she'd allowed him back inside her body. Maybe she'd explain her reasons for deceiving him.

But she didn't.

Her silence was a punch-in-the-gut reminder of who she was—who they were to each other. She said she wanted to forget. But they never could. Especially when forgetting for even a moment meant letting his guard down and the enemy in.

And that's who she was.

The enemy.

Thirteen

Shay shrugged into her suit jacket, studying herself in her room's cheval mirror. The slim fit of the gray, pin-striped jacket and pencil skirt were flattering, emphasizing the curves of her waist and hips. The cream blouse with the throat-to-waist ruffle lent it a feminine flair. She'd gathered her hair into a loose bun and fastened a pair of her mother's favorite diamond studs to her ears. The whole look was professional, fashionable…

And armor.

Yes, she needed it today. Hopefully, no one looking at her would guess that the previous night she'd had hot, wild sex in the back seat of a car.

God. She closed her eyes, pinching the bridge of her nose. What had she been thinking? But that was just it. She hadn't been.

Groaning, she turned from the mirror. It would've been so easy to stay in bed today and burrow under the covers. Just pretend last night hadn't happened. After all, that was her forte lately. Pretend to be in a relationship. Pretend to be in love with Gideon Knight. Pretend she hadn't just thrown all common sense and family loyalty out the window and screwed the man who was blackmailing her.

Regret weighed down her chest, so she couldn't inhale without feeling its bulk. Not regret about the sex. It had been as cataclysmic as the first time, and though it'd been foolish to give in to him, she didn't have remorse over experiencing passion.

No, it was what happened after that earned her regret. For a time, she'd forgotten that Gideon hated everything and everyone associated with the Neal name. That he planned on taking down her brother if she didn't capitulate to blackmail. That they stood on opposite sides of a Hatfield-and-McCoy-esque feud.

But as soon as the pleasure ebbed from her body, he'd returned to his aloof, distant self. She'd practically felt the wall slamming up between them. He'd been gentle when he'd shifted her off his lap and adjusted her dress, but unlike the hands that had cupped her breasts, tangled in her hair and stroked between her legs, his touch had been cold, almost clinical.

Other than asking if she was okay and wishing her goodnight when he'd dropped her off at home, he hadn't spoken. And she'd never felt so vulnerable, so…alone. Not even after the night of the blackout.

And to think she'd been so close to telling him she was Camille. That would've gone over well. Not.

Well, lesson learned. Last night was a mistake she wouldn't repeat. She refused to let herself be vulnerable to him again. Get through the next six months. That was her goal. Protect Trevor from Gideon, come into her trust fund, then leave RemingtonNeal to concentrate on her own business.

The days of being under the thumb of the men in her life would come to an end.

To achieve the dream of independence, she could endure six more months of Gideon Knight.

With a sigh, she glanced at the clock on her bedside table. Well, no time for breakfast, and she could grab coffee at the office. If traffic cooperated, she would just make her nine o'clock meeting with the event planners for RemingtonNeal's huge annual holiday party.

Grabbing her coat and purse, she descended the steps, her mind already locked on the multiplying items on her to-do list today.

"Shay."

She halted at the front door, shooting Trevor a hurried smile as she set her purse on the foyer table to slip into her coat.

"Morning, Trevor. I'm sorry I don't have time for breakfast. I have a—"

"You'll need to make the time. I need to talk with you immediately. And it's too important to put off. I'll meet you in the study." He didn't wait for her agreement, but pivoted on his heel and strode toward the rear of the house.

Bemused, she stared after him. Removing her arm from her coat sleeve, she tossed the garment over her purse and followed her brother.

"Shut the door, please," he said, when she entered the room he considered his domain. As their father had done before him.

Trevor hadn't changed much in the room. Except for the dark chocolate office chair that sat behind the massive oak-and-glass desk, everything else was the same. The tall bookshelves that lined two of the walls, the heavy floor-to-ceiling drapes, the two armchairs flanking the big fireplace. She'd hated being called into this room when her father had been alive; it'd meant she'd somehow screwed up. And she didn't like it any better now with her brother.

"What's going on, Trevor?" she asked, crossing her arms over her chest. Another thing she hated. Feeling defensive.

"Why did I have to find out about you and Gideon Knight from Madison and her father?" he snapped, stalking around his desk. "Do you know how humiliating that was for me, receiving that phone call?"

Of course. How could she have forgotten about Madison and the senator?

Gideon, that's how. Gideon and sex in the back seat of his car.

"I'm sorry, Trevor," she said, truly remorseful. She'd fully intended to tell him about her and Gideon's "relationship" when she arrived home last night, but it'd slipped her mind. "I wanted you to hear about us from me first."

"Us?" he sneered, his hands closing on the back of the chair several feet from her. "There shouldn't even be an *us*. I told you to stay away from him," he reminded her with a narrowed glare. "Do you remember? It was when you told me you barely knew him and there was nothing going on between you two."

"Like I told Madison last night, the fund-raiser wasn't the place to discuss my personal life. Especially when you didn't try to hide your hostility toward him. I've been seeing Gideon for a while now, but because of who we are, we decided not to make our relationship public until we knew we were serious about it." Great. Now she was lying about her lie. "But like I also told the senator, I don't need to run my relationships by you for permission. I did intend to give you the *courtesy* of telling you about Gideon last night. So again, I apologize if you were embarrassed discovering it from someone else."

"Where's your loyalty, Shay?" he hissed. "Your duty to family first?"

Pain struck her like a fiery dart to the breast. It spread

through her until she vibrated with it. Reason whispered that he didn't know all she sacrificed—was still sacrificing—for him. But it didn't halt the hurt from his condemnation, his disgust.

"My loyalty is always to this family," she whispered. "Who I'm seeing socially should have nothing to do with you or my love for you."

"It does if you're screwing a man I hate. Have always hated," he snarled.

"Why?" she asked, lowering her arms and risking a step forward, closer to him. "Tell me why. Gideon told me you went to school together."

That hadn't been all he'd said, but even as shameful and horrible as her brother bullying him was, surely there had to be more to the story. Especially on Trevor's end. Yes, he was a snob, but she'd never seen him actively hate someone just because they came from humble beginnings.

"Yes, we went to school together, and he didn't know his place back then, either."

"Didn't know his place," she repeated slowly, not believing that he'd uttered those ugly, bigoted words. Yes, they were fortunate enough to be in that elevated percentage of wealthy Americans. But they were still black. They still endured racists who gave them the "you're not our kind, dear" looks when they dared enter some establishments. How dare *he*...

"Why? Because he's Chinese-American?" she rasped.

"No." He slashed a hand through the air. "I don't give a damn about that." The vise squeezing her chest eased a little, and relief coursed through her. "After Mom died, all I had left was Dad."

Oh God. "Trevor," she said, moving forward, holding a hand out toward him.

"No," he repeated, coupling it with another hand slash.

"I know you were there, but she was something different to me than to you. She was the shield, the…insulation between him and me. When she died, she left me exposed to him. To his expectations, his impossibly high standards, his disapproval. I didn't get time to grieve for her because I had Dad riding my ass, wanting to make a real Neal man out of me without my mother's babying. His words," he added, his tone as caustic as acid.

"I know," Shay murmured. "I saw how hard he was on you. But, Trevor?" She lifted her hands, palms up. "What did that have to do with Gideon? Dad didn't know Gideon."

"But he did," Trevor snarled. "Who do you think funded the scholarship that enabled Gideon to attend the prep school? One of RemingtonNeal's charities. And Dad never let me forget it. Sports, academics, even the damn debate team—Gideon and I were always head-to-head in everything, and when he beat me, Dad was always right there to remind me that a poor scholarship kid was better than me. That maybe he should hire him to run the family company because he was smarter, stronger, quicker, more clever. He constantly compared us, and it didn't end with high school, but continued in college and beyond, even following Gideon's career after he graduated. The one thing I'm grateful for is that he's not alive today to see you with him. He probably would claim him as his son, give him RemingtonNeal."

Shock pummeled her. She'd had no clue. But now his animosity toward Gideon made sense, because she knew her father. Knew how denigrating and belittling and cruel he could be. Especially toward Trevor. Lincoln Neal probably didn't even like Gideon, but using him as an emotional weapon against his son sounded like something he would do.

And Trevor… God, if her brother didn't let go of his bitterness, he would live trying to prove to their dead father that he was better than a man he might have counted as a friend once upon a time.

"Do you understand why you can't be with him, Shay? That man has been the source of my pain and unhappiness for over a decade. I won't allow him in my home or to eat at my table, much less date my sister." He shook his head. "End it."

I can't.

The words bounced off her skull, pounded in her chest. To call off her relationship with Gideon would be to destroy her brother. But even in an alternate universe where she and Gideon had met under normal circumstances without blackmail and revenge, she still wouldn't have broken up with him based on what her brother had shared. Trevor's antagonism for Gideon wasn't his fault—it was their father's. But with Lincoln Neal gone, Trevor had transferred all his resentment and pain to the one who was still alive.

"No, I won't end it with Gideon," she said. Sighing, she moved across the small distance separating them and covered his hand. "Trevor, I—"

He jerked away from her, taking several steps back and glaring at her. A muscle ticked along his clenched jaw. "You won't break this *thing* off with him?"

"No, Trevor, I won't." *I'm doing this for you*, she silently screamed. But the words remained trapped in her throat.

"I didn't want to do this, but you've left me with no other choice. Leida Investments, Shay."

For the second time in the space of minutes, shock robbed her of speech. Icy fingers of astonishment and dread trailed down her spine.

Trevor cocked his head to the side. "You believed I didn't know about your little company all this time? Nothing gets by me. And as long as you were discreet, I didn't see the harm in letting you dabble in business. It didn't interfere with your responsibilities to this family. But now, your actions are jeopardizing us. If you don't end it with Gideon, I'll ruin every business that has received money from you. And with my name and reputation, you know I could do it with just a whisper. Now, while you take some time to make your decision about who you're giving your loyalty to, I'm going to insist you step back from your job at RemingtonNeal. I've already asked Madison to take over some of your duties for the next few weeks. Consider it a leave of absence while you choose between a man you barely know and your family."

With that parting shot, he exited the room, not pausing to spare her a glance. Not even bothering to glimpse the devastation he'd left behind.

Not only had he dismissed her easily, replacing her with his fiancée, but he'd threatened her company, as well as the hard work and livelihoods of those she'd invested in.

He would cavalierly ruin others' lives to bring her to heel.

Forcing her feet to move, she left the study and retraced her steps to her room. There, she removed her suit and went to her closet for her suitcases. Forty minutes later, she once more descended the stairs, not knowing when she would return.

She couldn't stay here any longer.

Not when she wasn't sure who she was selling her soul to protect.

Fourteen

Gideon pulled up in front of the small brick house in the Humboldt Park neighborhood. With its white trim, meticulously manicured front lawn and currently empty flower boxes, the home was cute and obviously well taken care of.

But Shay still had no business being here.

Not when she had a home.

So why had she sent him a text informing him he'd need to pick her up here tonight, as she would be living in this place for the foreseeable future?

What the hell was going on?

The questions had burned in his head, then twisted his gut into knots. The need for answers had propelled him out of his mother's house, where he'd been visiting her and Olivia. He hadn't bothered replying to Shay's text but had entered the address in his GPS and driven directly there.

He shut off his car and walked up the tidy sidewalk to the postage-stamp-size porch. Maybe she'd heard him arrive, because before he could knock on the storm door, Shay appeared in the entrance, wrapped in a cashmere shawl and evening gown. She joined him on the porch, scanning his attire, her gaze running over his peacoat, down his black jeans to his boots, then back up.

"You're going to the ballet dressed like that?" she asked, frowning.

"No," he answered shortly. "Come on."

He'd offered her his hand before considering the gesture. They weren't in public, so the display of affection wasn't necessary. But when she wrapped her fingers around his, he only tightened his hold. And didn't think about why he did it.

Moments later, with her safe in the passenger's seat, the full skirt of her gown tucked around her legs, he started the car and drove away.

"What's going on, Shay?" he asked. "Whose house is that?"

"My best friend, Bridgette. You met her that day in the food truck," she replied, keeping her gaze straight ahead.

Impatient, Gideon pressed, "And? Why are you staying with her—how did you put it—for the foreseeable future?"

She sighed, and he steeled himself against the punch of that tired sound. "Because I left home. And I don't know when, or if, I'll return."

Surprise winged through him, and quick on its heels was fury. Cold, bright fury. "Did you leave or did Trevor kick you out?"

Another sigh, and when he glanced over at her she shook her head. "I left. We...had a disagreement, and I thought it best if I gave us both space."

"You're trying to make me drag it out of you, aren't you?" he growled.

"I'm not trying to make you do anything," she said, every inch of the society princess in that reply. "What's more, I don't *want* you to."

His fingers curled around the steering wheel, his hold

so tight the leather creaked. Part of him longed to jerk the car over three lanes to the side of the road and demand she confess everything to him, because he knew there was more to the story. And from those sighs and the tension in her slender frame, he sensed the "disagreement" with Trevor hadn't been pretty. It'd hurt her. And for that Gideon wished he could strangle the man.

But the other part… That part longed to pull over, too, but for a different reason. It wanted to park, release her seat belt and tug her onto his lap so he could hold her. Comfort her. Murmur into her ear that everything would be all right, that *she* would be all right.

Which was ridiculous. If there was a woman who didn't need comforting—didn't need *him*—it was Shay Neal.

Quiet settled in the car like a third passenger as he drove to his home. It wasn't until he pulled into the underground parking garage that she stirred.

"I can wait here or in the lobby while you change if you're not going to be long. The ballet starts in about thirty minutes," she said, straightening in the passenger's seat.

"Don't be ridiculous," he snapped, her obvious reluctance to be alone with him irritating him. Did she expect him to jump her? "I promise to keep my hands and dick to myself. Now can you please get out of the damn car?"

He didn't wait for her answer, but shoved the door open. But he still caught her grumbled, "Speaking of dicks…"

In spite of the anger and frustration churning in his chest, he couldn't suppress the quirk of his mouth. This woman gave as good as she got.

Minutes later, they entered his penthouse, and as he took her wrap to hang up, lust joined the cluster of emotions he was feeling. While the champagne-colored skirt of her dress flowed around her legs, the top clung to her shoulders, arms and torso—except for the deep V that dipped between her breasts and even lower in back. He briefly closed his eyes, turning away from the alluring sight of her. Immediately, images of the night in his Town Car skated over the back of his lids like a movie trailer. Him, cupping those breasts, drawing them into his mouth...

Cursing under his breath, he jerked open the closet door and, with more force than necessary, hung up her shawl and his coat.

How could she flaunt sex and sophistication at the same time?

"Would you like a glass of wine? Scotch?" he asked, stalking into the living room and toward the bar.

"Do we have time for that? If you don't hurry and dress, we're going to be late," she reminded him, following him, but halting on the top of the steps that led into the living room.

He removed the top of a crystal decanter and poured himself a finger of bourbon. Only after he'd downed a sip did he turn and face her. Staring at her golden skin and the inner curves of her breasts, he took another. He needed the fortification.

"We're not going to the ballet," he informed her.

She frowned. "What? Why not?" She stepped down into the room. "And why didn't you tell me you changed your mind at Bridgette's house?"

"Why?" he repeated, lifting the tumbler to his lips and staring at her over the rim as he sipped. "Because even though you won't admit it, you're hurting. Something more than a 'disagreement' had to have occurred to make you leave the only family you have left, as well as the only home you've known. I'm a self-confessed asshole, Shay, but even I wouldn't make you attend a social event and fake a happiness you're far from feeling. Especially when your brother might be in attendance." He swirled the amber liquor in his glass and arched an eyebrow. "And as for why I didn't tell you when I picked you up, that's simple. You wouldn't have come with me if I had. The last thing you need right now is to be alone. And since I know your friend supplements her food truck income with a part-time job, you would've been very much alone tonight. So that leaves me."

Her frown deepened. "It's a little creepy how you know so much about me and everyone I'm close to."

He shrugged, taking another taste of the bourbon. "Before going into battle, it's wise to be prepared and know everything you can about your enemy."

"Enemy," she breathed, then scoffed. "You just proved my point. We're not friends—far from it. So why do you care how I spend my night? I'm not your responsibility," she said softly.

"No," he agreed just as softly. "We're not friends. But can we call a truce and resume hostilities tomorrow?" He risked drawing nearer to her. "You're right, you're not my responsibility. But I am responsible. The argument was about me, wasn't it?" When she didn't reply, he gently pressed, "Shay?"

"Yes," she reluctantly admitted.

"Let me guess," he said, his anger rekindling. "Trevor wanted you to break it off with me and you refused."

"Correct again." She notched her chin up at a defiant angle, but he caught the slight tremble of her bottom lip. "But if I'd given in to his demand, then it would've meant destroying everything he cares about, destroying him. Still, it's not like I could share that with him. Instead, he threatened to dismantle my company, starting with ruining all the businesses I've invested in. Oh, and he fired me—or placed me on a temporary leave of absence. So those are my choices. End our relationship and destroy everything my brother loves. Or continue upholding our bargain and lose the company I love."

Fury blasted through him, and for a moment a red haze dropped over his vision. Trevor had threatened his own sister? Gideon grasped the tumbler so tightly the beveled edges dug into his flesh. He pictured that thick, brown file in his office safe, and had no regrets about his intentions to expose Trevor. A man like him deserved the hell Gideon planned to rain down on him.

"I won't let him do that," Gideon promised. Soon enough her brother would be too busy trying to pick up the flaming pieces of his life to worry about harming her company.

"It's not your concern." She waved a hand, dismissing his vow and the topic. "And you mentioned a truce? I accept." Moving forward, she extended her arm. "Should we shake on it?"

Gideon glanced down at her open palm before lifting his gaze to meet her eyes. Though his mind ordered him not to touch her, he wrapped his hand around hers. For several long moments, they stared at each other. An electric shock ran through him at lightning speed and jolted his body to attention. It would be an impossibility to be skin-to-skin with her and not respond. But he didn't pull her closer, didn't try to seduce with his words.

Space and sanctuary, that's what he'd promised her.

"Are you hungry?" he asked, lowering his arm to his side. "I can order in anything you'd like."

"I…" She hesitated, shrugged a shoulder and started again. "I can cook if you have something in the kitchen."

Since meeting Shay, he'd been surprised so many times, he should really stop being taken aback by her. But once more, she'd done the unexpected.

"You can cook?" Dubious, he scanned her beautiful hair, gown and shoes. "In that?"

She snorted. "You're not starting off this truce thing well. And yes, I can cook." If he hadn't been watching her so closely, he might've missed the flash of insecurity that was there and gone in an instant. "Show me to the kitchen? That is, if you don't mind me…?"

"No, this I have to see for myself," he assured her, and strode past her toward the room he rarely used. His housekeeper often prepared dinners for him that she left warming in the stove. So the pantry and refrigerator should both be stocked. "I'll even supply you with clothes so you don't get anything on your dress. See how accommodating I am?"

"Until tomorrow," she added from behind him.

"Until tomorrow," he agreed.

"I wouldn't have believed it if I hadn't tasted it for myself," Gideon exclaimed with wonder, staring down at his empty plate.

Shay shook her head, smothering a smile, although her cheeks hurt with the effort. Forking the last of the chicken carbonara to her mouth, she tried not to blush under his admiring scrutiny. She was twenty-five and an heiress—needless to say, she was used to compliments. But coming from this man… She returned her gaze to her plate, not wanting to analyze why it was different.

"Can I say something without breaking the tenuous bonds of our truce?" he asked, cocking his head to the side.

She wanted to duck her head and avoid his piercing contemplation. It cut deep. Exposing her. Even with the distance of the breakfast bar separating them, she had the sudden urge to lean back, insert more space between them.

But she remained seated and met his gaze. "Sure."

"I would've never pegged you for someone who enjoyed getting their hands dirty in a kitchen. I know you helped your friend out that day in the food truck, but I thought that was a fluke. What you did in there—" he dipped his head in the direction of the kitchen "—was skill. And spoke of someone who really enjoyed it. You're a walking contradiction."

"So your all-knowing file didn't include that information?" she mocked. Picking up her wineglass, she sipped the moscato, silently debating how much to tell him. Then, before she could make up her mind, her mouth was moving. "My mother loved to cook. We had a personal chef, but when Dad wasn't home, she'd commandeer the kitchen and cook for all of us. She would let me help, and some of my happiest memories are of the two of us preparing a pot of gumbo or baking a quiche. I learned to cook from her, but I also inherited my love of it from her."

God, where had all that come from? Embarrassment rose in her, swift and hot.

"Anyway, now your dossier is complete," she added flippantly. "I'll clean up."

She rose from her chair and, grabbing both their plates, circled the bar and headed toward the sink. As she set the dishes in it, a long-fingered hand settled over hers, stilling her movements.

"She would've been proud of you," Gideon murmured in her ear. Heat from his body pressed into her side, her shoulder. "Now, go relax. You did all the work, the least I can do is clean up."

Her first instinct with Gideon was always to defy his orders. She wasn't a puppy. But this time, she accepted his offer and slid from between him and the counter.

Coward.

Maybe.

Okay, definitely. But his unexpected displays of tenderness and the potent, dark sexuality that he emitted like pheromones combined to undermine every guard she'd erected since that night he'd so coldly rejected her after giving her devastating pleasure.

She went in search of the restroom, and after locating it and washing her hands, she continued her tour of his place. At least the downstairs. A formal dining room. A bedroom done in soft blues and cream. Maybe this was where his sister, Olivia, slept when she came over; he'd said the T-shirt and leggings he'd given Shay were hers. Until that moment, she hadn't even known he had a sister. But he didn't offer more information, and for the sake of their temporary cease-fire, she didn't ask.

Another bathroom. A study. A den.

She paused at the open door of that last room. With its two couches, love seat, numerous end tables, large coffee table, massive television screen mounted above the fireplace, this space appeared more lived-in than the rest of the penthouse.

She glanced behind her, but the hallway remained empty. *Just a peek*, she promised herself, then she'd leave. Moving into the room, she stroked a hand over the leather couch that bore a distinct imprint in the middle cushion.

Must be where Gideon sat the most. She could easily imagine the man she'd spent this evening with—in his black, long-sleeved, V-neck sweater, black jeans and bare feet—relaxing in this room. Feet up on the table, remote in hand, scanning through the no-doubt-numerous channels before deciding on...what? Funny. She knew how he had sex, but had no clue about his favorite TV shows or movies.

For some reason, that struck her as sad.

It also lit a hunger to discover more about him. Some things they'd shared in the blackout, but not nearly enough to satisfy her curiosity. What was his favorite color? His favorite band? Snack? Boo—

Oh God.

Breath trapped in her throat, she crossed the room toward the instrument that had captured her attention. No, *instruments*. Plural. A glossy black stand with padded interior cradled six guitars. She knew nothing of guitars, but she could tell the three acoustic and three thinner, sleeker electric guitars had to be expensive. And obviously well cared for.

A flutter tickled her stomach, launching into a full-out quake. She reached a slightly trembling hand toward the guitars.

"Do you play?"

She whipped around, guilt snaking through her. "I—I'm sorry," she stammered, backing away from the instruments. Damn, she was a sneak. And not even a good one. "I didn't mean to snoop, I…" She paused and inhaled a deep breath. "I was taking a self-guided tour of your house and saw the guitars. They're beautiful," she whispered. "I don't play, but obviously, you do…?"

He nodded, crossed the room on silent bare feet and halted next to the stand.

"For years," he said, brushing an affectionate stroke over the gleaming wood of an acoustic guitar. Her thighs tightened, the touch reminding her of how he'd caressed her skin. A lover's familiar caress. "We didn't have a lot of money when I was growing up. But when I showed an interest and aptitude for guitar, my mother somehow managed to scrape enough together for lessons. I didn't find out until I was a teenager, but my father played the guitar, too. I don't remember it, but I like to think I inherited my love of music from him, as you did cooking from your mother."

"Will you—" She broke off. God, she was pushing her luck. From his explanation, she sensed he didn't share this part of himself with many people. It didn't line up with the image of ruthless business tycoon. But in this moment, she wanted to see his clever, talented fingers fly over those strings. To witness him coax beautiful music from that instrument. To watch him lower that damnable shield and let her in. "Will you play for me?"

He stared at her, and her heart thudded against her rib cage. Finally, *finally*, he dipped his chin and reached for the acoustic guitar on the far end. He almost reverently lifted it off the stand and carried it to the love seat. She trailed behind him, not saying anything. Afraid if she uttered a word, he might change his mind. Once he perched on one end of the small love seat, she sank to the other.

Propping the instrument on his thighs, he plucked a few strings, turned the knobs at the top. Once he seemed satisfied, he cupped the neck, fingers at the ready there. And the other hand hovered over the big, rounded body.

Then he started to play.

And… *Jesus*.

She'd expected something classical, reserved. But no. Passion flowed from beneath his fingers. Passion, and anger, and joy and grief. So many emotions soared from the music, which sounded almost Spanish, but bluesy and a little bit of rock. It was fierce, soul-jarring and…and beautiful. So. Beautiful.

Pain swelled in her lungs, and she expelled a huge breath, just realizing she'd been holding it.

When his fingers stilled, and the music faded away, she remained speechless, breathless. Like she'd been transported to Oz and offered this rare peek behind the wizard's curtain. Only she didn't find a fraud, but a rare, wonderful truth about this man. One that few people were gifted with seeing.

He lifted his head, and those fathomless black eyes studied her. A faint frown creased his brow, and he reached for her, swiping his thumb under her eye.

"You're crying," he murmured.

"Am I?" she asked, shocked, wiping her fingers over her cheeks. Well, hell. She was. "I didn't notice."

"Was I that bad?" he teased, with a soft smile she'd never witnessed on him.

"You were—" *are* "—amazing," she whispered. "Thank you for sharing that with me."

The smile disappeared, but his midnight gaze glittered as if dozens of stars lay behind the black.

"I shouldn't want you." She blurted out the confession. "I shouldn't. But… Even knowing who we are… Even knowing this can only end one way, I still want to grab on to those moments when we're just Gideon and Shay, not someone's enemy or sister. When we're being honest with each other the only way we truly can."

Sex. Need. Passion—they're honest. The body can't lie. Lust is the great equalizer regardless of social status, race or tax bracket.

It was a risk saying those words to him, since he'd uttered them to Camille, not her. And from the gleam in his hooded gaze and the tightening of his sensual mouth, maybe he remembered giving them to another woman.

Honesty. Though her pulse slammed her ears, she had to drag her big-girl panties on and tell him the truth. She couldn't justify keeping it from him anymore, especially when he'd offered her the gift of playing for her.

"There's something you should know," she murmured. "I've been keeping something from you. The night of the blackout, Bridgette had come down with a bad cold and asked me to take her place at a job so she wouldn't lose it. Gideon, that was at the Du—"

"Shay, I already figured it out. You're Camille."

Her lips parted with a gasp. She blinked, staring at him. How had he…?

"Did you really believe I could be inside your body and not remember?" he murmured. "Not remember every detail of how tight and sweet you are? No, moonbeam." He shook his head. "I'd never forget that."

"Wait." It suddenly made sense now. His rejection afterward. "Is that why you were so cold to me? Because I hadn't told you?"

He studied her for a long, quiet moment. "It wasn't so much that you lied, but wondering *why* you were at the gala and why you kept the truth from me."

"Bridgette would've lost her job if she'd called in on such short notice, and with her business just getting off the ground, she can't afford that. And I had to use a disguise and a fake name. I've attended the gala in the past, and my brother also…" She trailed off, a dark inkling beginning to stir in her head. "My brother," she whispered. "Did you think I'd been there because of him? That I sought you out for him?"

After a slight hesitation, he nodded. "The thought occurred to me."

"Someone must have hurt you terribly for you to be so mistrusting and suspicious," she continued softly. And she had an idea about the identity of that "someone."

"Trevor had no clue I was there. There were only two people in that break room, Gideon—you and me. What happened between us was the scariest and most exhilarating, *freeing* thing I've ever done. That's what you make me feel. Terrified out of my mind because no one has ever affected me so viscerally I don't recognize myself. While at the same time, I'm excited because I like it…crave it."

As soon as the confession escaped her, she recognized that he could use it to his advantage. But she mentally shook her head. Gideon wasn't like her brother. He might utilize blackmail to gain her compliance, but never once had he tried to use her passion against her. He might be ruthless, but he possessed his own code of honor.

Sex. Desire. It was their Switzerland.

And she'd seek asylum there for a while before they found themselves on opposite sides of a war again. Because that was inevitable.

But for now...

She shifted closer to him, covered the hand that still rested on the body of the guitar. Lightly, she explored those fingers, amazed at how they could draw such magic out of the instrument and her. She wanted him to cradle, strum and play her.

She trailed a caress up his arm, over his shoulder and neck, until she reached his jaw. Cupping it, she mimicked the many times he'd held her in the same grip. She swept her thumb over his full bottom lip.

His gaze never leaving hers, Gideon carefully set the guitar on the table, then clasped her hand in his. He turned his head, placing a kiss in the center of her palm, then tracing a path to her wrist. His lips pressed there over her pulse, and her lashes fluttered down. But at the damp flick of his tongue, she gasped, eyes flying open. Liquid heat pooled between her legs, and she didn't even try to contain her whimper.

He rose, gently tugging her to her feet. Without releasing her hand, he led her out of the room, down the hallway and up the curving staircase. They entered a cavernous bedroom lit only by a single lamp on a nightstand. Not just any bedroom—his. The big king-size bed covered in a black spread and white pillows, two chairs flanking a large, freestanding fireplace, a couple glossy bedside tables, a rug—the almost austere decor was relieved by the breathtaking view of the Chicago River and city skyline through the three floor-to-ceiling windows, and the one wall that bore a black-and-white mural of a bare, leafless tree on a lonely plain. It was gorgeous. It was him.

Turning to her, he captured all her attention by cradling her face between his palms, tilting her head back and claiming her mouth. Slow, tender; raw and erotic. His tongue relayed all that he wanted to do to her—would do to her. And as she cocked her head to the side, granting him deeper access, she consented to it all.

"I've had you on a couch and in the back seat of my car. I want to take you on a bed," he muttered against her lips. "*My* bed."

As soon as her whispered "Please," passed her lips, he stripped her, haphazardly tossing her borrowed clothes to the floor. His clothes followed and, hiking her in his arms, he carried her to the bed. Her back hit the covers and his big, hot body pressed her into the mattress. He kissed her harder, wilder, more insistently, as if that leash on his control had unraveled. She dug her fingers into his hair, yanking off the band that corralled it and freeing the strands so they tumbled around both their faces. With a hot, low rumble, he kissed her again, then every inch of her received attention from his mouth, his fingers. By the time he tugged open the drawer on a bedside table and pulled a condom free, she shook with need, twisting and aching for him to fulfill his promise and take her.

Linking their fingers, he drew her arms up, their joined hands bracketing her head.

"Open for me, moonbeam," he murmured, desire burning hot in his dark eyes. The head of his erection nudged her entrance, and she willingly, eagerly widened her thighs and locked them around his slim hips. "Thank you, baby."

He groaned as he sank inside her, not stopping until her

sex fully sheathed him. She arched under him, grinding her head into the pillow. God, he stretched her, filled her. Branded her. When he started to move in long, hard thrusts that rocked her body and her soul, she felt claimed. And when her channel clenched around him, and she hurtled into an orgasm that threatened to break her apart, she shut her eyes and became a willing sacrifice to it.

Soon, the aftershocks rippling through her eased, and the fog of ecstasy started to fade. She tensed, waiting for him to roll away from her, to reject her. But when he drew her into his arms, his still-labored breathing bathing her neck, she slowly relaxed.

Right before she drifted away, his low, hoarse voice penetrated her heavy blanket of drowsiness.

"Don't let me break you, Shay. Protect yourself from me."

She didn't reply, but carried that warning with her into sleep.

Fifteen

Shay nabbed the slice of bread out of the toaster and spread avocado on it. She ate it leaning against the counter, alternating between sips of fresh coffee. Gideon had already left for the office, and with a glance at her wrist, she realized she didn't have long before she had to leave, too. Since she no longer had a position at RemingtonNeal, she'd scheduled a meeting with a potential client.

Staying the night hadn't been in the plan. But when he'd curled around her after he'd made her body sing its own special melody, she hadn't wanted to go anywhere. And then he'd woken her with a cup of steaming coffee, keys to one of his cars and a sweet but wicked kiss that left her toes curling into the mattress.

But those lovely gestures couldn't completely erase the kernel of apprehension that lingered at the edge of her consciousness.

Don't let me break you, Shay. Protect yourself from me.

His murmured warning stayed with her, and dread wormed its way through the warmth. He didn't caution her to be careful because he might hurt her, but because he would. And she would be foolish to ignore that truth. Real life was blackmail, revenge, vendettas and pain. Only in fairy tales did frogs turn to princes. Or wolves to heroes.

Cold seeped into her veins. Suddenly losing her appetite, she dumped the remains of her breakfast. She needed to get going and return to the real world outside this penthouse.

She was heading toward the closet to collect her wrap and dress when the front door opened. Startled, Shay stared as a woman who looked to be about her age entered. With wavy black hair that tumbled over her shoulders, smooth, unlined skin and a tall, slender frame wrapped in a camel cashmere coat, she was obviously too young to be the housekeeper Gideon mentioned last night. Jealousy, unbidden and bright, flared in Shay's chest. Whoever she was, she must be close to Gideon to have a key to his penthouse.

But then the other woman lifted her head, and the truth slammed into Shay. With those heavily lashed, beautiful onyx eyes, she had to be related to Gideon. And considering her age, she was most likely his sister.

"Oh, hi," Olivia said, arching a dark eyebrow in a manner so similar to Gideon's, it confirmed her identity. "I'm sorry. I didn't know Gideon had company. I can come back."

"No, you're fine," Shay objected, finding her voice as his sister half turned to grasp the doorknob. "Gideon's not home, and I was just leaving, too. You must be Olivia." Shay moved forward, her hand extended. Gideon's sister stepped away from the door with a smile, her arm lifting. "My name's Shay. Shay Neal."

Olivia froze, except for the arm falling woodenly back to her side. "Neal?" she repeated in a tremulous whisper. "Are you related to Trevor Neal?"

Unease crawled through her. "Yes. Do you know him?"

Olivia paled, her eyes widening. Visibly trembling fin-

gers lifted to her lips and pressed against them. "I didn't—
no, he wouldn't—"

Her fractured sentences made little sense to Shay, but
the woman's obvious distress amplified the dread until it
was full-out fear. "Olivia, are you okay?" she asked, risking moving closer.

Olivia jerked her head from side to side, tears glistening
in her eyes. "Why are you here?"

"Gideon and I are…" She paused, unsure of how much to
expose. "…seeing each other. Would you like to sit down?
Can I get you anything?"

Again, Olivia shook her head, the tears streaming down
her cheeks now. Unable to stand the woman's pain, Shay
reached for her, wrapping her in a hug. She half expected
Olivia to shove her away, but instead, the woman clung to
her, sobbing now.

God. Shay tightened her embrace, her own eyes stinging.
What kind of agony must Olivia be in to cause this kind of
reaction? It burrowed inside Shay, and she wanted to soothe
it, to take it from her. Gently, she guided the crying woman
to the living room and lowered them both to the couch. She
continued to hold Olivia, gently rocking her as her mother
used to do when Shay ran to her in need of comfort.

She didn't glance at her watch to see how long they sat
there. If Olivia needed her to remain the whole day, she
would. Anything so those awful, tearing sobs would stop.
Gradually, Olivia calmed, and only when she went silent
and the trembles eased did Shay slip her arms away. Her
shoulders twinged, but she ignored the slight ache. She left
for the bathroom. Minutes later, after a quick stop in the
kitchen, she returned with a box of tissues, a warm, damp
cloth and a bottle of water.

"Thank you," Olivia whispered, her voice hoarse from
her tears. "I—I'm sorry. I didn't mean to—"

"Please don't apologize. It's okay," Shay assured her. The woman's clear air of fragility stirred a sense of protectiveness in Shay. "I'm a stranger to you, and you don't have to talk if you don't want to, but I'm here. And whatever you say will stay between us."

For several moments, Olivia clutched the bottle between her hands. Though she'd wiped her face with the cloth, her eyes remained stark, her cheeks and lips pale. Shay waited, ready to listen if Olivia chose to confide in her, ready to just sit with her if she decided not to.

"I know your brother," Olivia finally said, haltingly at first. "I met him a year ago, and we...we fell in love. Or at least I did. I don't know if he ever did love me. But he told me so. And I believed him. I would've done anything for him—and I did. He asked me to keep our relationship a secret because he and Gideon were business rivals, and he didn't want any of that interfering with us. I'd heard Gideon mention Trevor before and knew he had no love for him, so I agreed. Also, I figured once he saw how much we loved each other, he would come around. Especially since I became pregnant."

Shay gasped, unable to contain her shock and dismay. At the sound, Olivia lifted her gaze from the water bottle. The grief and unadulterated pain there shook Shay, and she wanted to gather the other woman in her arms again. But she didn't, sensing Olivia needed to get this out, like lacerating a festering wound so it could heal faster.

"I thought he would be happy about the news. I was overjoyed. All I dreamed about was marrying him and starting a family. We would be doing it a little out of order, but I didn't care. But—but..." She paused, and a sob escaped her.

Shay grabbed her hand, offering her support, and Olivia went on. "When I told him about the pregnancy, he told me he didn't want me or the baby. To get rid of it because I was no longer useful to him. Then he walked away, like I was garbage he'd tossed out the window. He used me to get back at my brother. At the time, I worked at Gideon's company as his executive assistant. I was so naive, so snowed by Trevor, that when he asked me questions about Gideon's agenda, who he was meeting with, I gave him the information. He worded it to make it sound like he was only asking about my day, what I had on my plate, but he was pumping me for inside information. He never loved me, never had any intention of creating a family with me." She shook her head, her throat working, as if swallowing back another sob. "I refused to end the pregnancy, but it didn't matter. I miscarried and lost the baby."

Shay remained sitting next to Olivia, but inside she reeled, enraged screams slamming against her skull. Part of her longed to deny the story, to label Olivia a liar, but she couldn't. Not only could she not violate this woman all over again by not believing her, but deep inside her soul where only honesty existed, she knew Olivia wasn't lying. Her utter agony bore witness to it, and Shay believed her.

Grief assaulted Shay, welling up in her, and she silently wept. For Olivia. For her pain. For Shay's own pain. For Trevor's coldness, controlling behavior and dismissal of her hopes, dreams and needs. For her disillusionment about her brother. If Trevor could treat his own sister so callously as well as do something as despicable as take advantage of this woman for personal gain, then what else was he capable of? Maybe those things in Gideon's dossier?

Gideon. Was Olivia the reason behind his plans? The night in the restaurant, when he'd first showed her the incriminating file, he'd scoffed at her claim that Trevor wouldn't care who she was dating.

Oh yes. Your brother will care. And he'll understand.

Then, his assertion had been cryptic, but now, understanding dawned on her. No wonder he hated Trevor and had no qualms about blackmailing her. This was more than a business deal; Trevor had come after Gideon's family. If she'd harbored any fledgling hope after waking up in his bed this morning that maybe they could have something more than a truce, this knowledge obliterated it. She would always be a living reminder of the harm and damage her brother had inflicted on his sister, his family.

There was no forgiveness for that. Not for her brother. And not for her, being guilty by association.

Sixteen

"I still don't think this is a wise decision."

Shay stared out the rear window of Gideon's Town Car at the Gold Coast historic mansion lit up with a cheerful glow. A steady stream of people climbed the front stone steps of the place she'd called home for nearly twenty-six years, entering for Trevor and Madison's engagement party.

"You and Trevor might not be seeing eye to eye right now, but I'm sure he wouldn't want to celebrate his engagement without his sister," Gideon said from beside her.

She glanced at him, irritation and something deeper, sadder pressing against her breastbone like a large boulder. "You won't pass up an opportunity to turn the screw, will you?"

With his aloof mask firmly in place, he met her gaze, onyx eyes steady and unblinking. "No."

She faced the window again, that heaviness gaining weight. It'd been a week since she'd walked out of her childhood home. A week since her and Gideon's truce, which had stretched longer than the next morning. A week since she'd held Olivia as the woman broke down in her arms and revealed Trevor's betrayal.

Yes, now Shay understood the motives behind Gideon's blackmail. And a part of her couldn't blame him. But another part—the part that remembered the man who'd played guitar for her, the man who'd cuddled her close in his bed after tearing her apart with pleasure—longed for him to put all of this aside.

For her.

To want her more than revenge.

She shut her eyes, making sure to keep her head turned away so he couldn't glimpse the yearning that she was certain leaked into her expression. In spite of knowing it was the epitome of foolishness, she'd started to fall for Gideon.

No, that was a lie. The fall had started some time ago, at what moment, she couldn't pinpoint. Maybe when he'd revealed his own pain to her in the back seat of the car. Maybe when he'd raced to Bridgette's house and decided to place her comfort above putting on another episode of the Gideon and Shay Show at the ballet. Maybe when he'd sat on that couch with his guitar and revealed a part of himself that he didn't with most people.

Not that narrowing down the exact instant mattered.

The truth was she loved Gideon Knight.

His fierceness. His heart, which he tried to hide. His passion. His love for his family.

Yes, he was a hard man, a merciless man, but never a cruel one. And when she looked at him, gazed into those midnight-and-stars eyes, she dreamed. She stupidly dreamed that he could love her as he'd once adored Madison before she'd scarred him with her disloyalty and infidelity.

Maybe she did believe in fairy tales, after all.

The door to the car opened, and with a sigh, she climbed out, murmuring a thank-you to the valet who stood next to it. Seconds later, Gideon's body heat warmed her back, and his palm settled at the base of her spine. A spine she straightened.

No time for self-pity now.

She had the performance of a lifetime to give.

Because she was walking into the lion's den knowing her arrival on Gideon's arm would announce her decision to her brother—she'd chosen his enemy over family loyalty. That's how Trevor would see it.

And she wasn't naive; there would be consequences to her decision. No job at RemingtonNeal. She would most likely have to find a place to live because she couldn't stay with Bridgette forever. And, most importantly, Leida Investments and the businesses she'd invested in would be affected. Especially if Trevor followed through on his threat of tampering with the start-ups she'd funded. She had savings, and she could use most of it to provide capital. But the possibility of having to scale back or rebuild her company was very real without her salary.

The cost of loving Gideon was high.

And, God help her, she was willing to pay it.

Gideon walked silently beside her, but the tension rolled off him, and it ratcheted higher when they entered her home and handed their coats to a waiting servant.

She seamlessly fell back into the role of Chicago socialite and, pasting on a smile, mingled with the other guests. Many of whom didn't seem surprised to see her with Gideon, so the gossip about them as a couple must've made the rounds. Still, they were aware of the enmity between Gideon and Trevor as business rivals, and watched her and Gideon with an avid, greedy curiosity.

Especially when a path seemed to open, and they stood only feet away from Trevor, Madison and Senator Reus. Shay looked up, and her gaze connected with her brother's. Though he smiled for the benefit of those around them, fury blazed from his hazel eyes, so like hers. His glare shifted from her to Gideon, and a frightening rage hardened his expression before he controlled it.

"Stand tall, moonbeam," Gideon murmured in her ear. His big palm slid up her back and under her hair, curling around the nape of her neck. "He can't hurt you."

But you can. The words rang in her head, her chest. Tipping her head back, she said, "That's debatable. Cutting me off emotionally and financially and targeting my company definitely falls under the 'hurting me' category."

"Correction, then," he growled. "I won't let him hurt you."

That ship had sailed and was a faint glimmer on the horizon.

She straightened her shoulders and added a little more wattage to her smile. "We should go greet the happy couple."

"You mean, get it over with?" he retorted, dark eyebrow arched. She'd once detested the gesture, but now counted each one.

"That's what I said."

His low chuckle tripped over her bare arms. Inhaling a deep breath, she allowed him to guide her over to the trio who stoically watched their approach.

"Trevor, Madison, congratulations." She leaned forward and stiffly kissed Madison's cheek. Although she did return the feigned embrace, most likely for those closely observing them, Madison's rigid posture didn't relax. Straightening, Shay nodded to her brother's future father-in-law. "Senator."

"Shay," he murmured coldly.

"Your sister wanted to see you, wish you well," Gideon said to Trevor, his tone frigid, but she detected the undercurrent of anger. Of hatred. "She has a forgiving heart considering you put her out of her own house."

Oh God.

"She left by her own choice," Trevor snapped, the fury in his eyes leaking into his face. His lips twisted into an ugly snarl. "But come now, Gideon. We both know how trying *sisters* can be."

Nausea churned in her belly and raced for the back of her throat.

Dark waves of rage poured off Gideon, and he moved forward. Terrified, she latched on to his arm, fearful of what he might do to her brother. And she feared *for* Gideon, for the consequences he might suffer for his actions. She harbored no doubt that Trevor would enjoy pressing charges and using it against him.

"Gideon, no," she pleaded softly. "It's what he wants."

Trevor sneered. "Shay, I need to speak to you. Alone," he stressed.

"Fine," she agreed, more to separate Gideon from Trevor than to be amenable. "Gideon," she whispered. When he tore his still-frightening stare from her brother, she squeezed his arm. "I'll be right back."

"You don't have to do this," he reminded her, just as softly, but the fury still vibrated in his voice.

"Yes, I do," she returned. Rising onto her toes, she placed a kiss on his jaw. "They're not worth it." She waited for his abrupt nod before she turned back to her brother. "In the study, I assume."

Not waiting for his confirmation, she strode toward the rear of the house. Anger bristled under her skin, poking her like thousands of tiny needles. When she entered her brother's domain, she could barely look at him.

"How dare you bring that asshole into my house?" Trevor ground out through clenched teeth as soon as he closed the study door behind them.

"Your house?" She crossed her arms. "You were right

when you told Gideon that I chose to leave. Chose. Because this is *our* home, Trevor. I can bring whoever I want here, and you have no say. I don't need to ask your permission."

"I would've never thought you were a traitor," he snarled. "Mom and Dad wouldn't recognize you right now."

She absorbed the power of that blow and fought not to stagger from it. But the pain ebbed and flowed inside her.

Stand tall. He can't hurt you.

Inhaling a deep breath, she pushed past it.

"You're such a hypocrite," she said, surprised at her even tone. "So righteous and high-and-mighty. And to think I defended you. Believed in you. Trusted you. But you didn't deserve any of it."

"What the hell are you talking about, Shay?" he demanded. "I've done nothing but honor this family, the Neal name, *you*. You, baby sister, betrayed me."

"By thinking for myself, wanting something for myself? For daring to defy you? I'm not a sheep, Trevor. I have a mind. I have feelings. I have a heart, but there's only one Neal who can claim to possess the last two. Because somewhere along the way, you lost them to jealousy, pettiness and hate. No, *big brother*," she said, throwing his taunt back at him. "I've done nothing but stand by this family. I've protected it when you would've destroyed it with your greed and ambition."

"You need to stop right there," he warned in a dark growl, taking a step forward.

But he didn't intimidate her. Didn't control her. Not anymore. She didn't wait for him to advance, but marched forward and met him halfway.

"No, you stop. And listen. I know what you and your precious senator are up to," she said. "Insider information. Fixing contracts. Kickbacks. Illegal campaign contributions. And that's just the tip of it." When he rocked back in shock, his eyes flaring wide, she nodded. "Yes, Trevor, I know about it all. Because Gideon has a file on you, inches thick. I've seen it, read it. I'm aware of all your dirty dealings, which if made public could topple RemingtonNeal, ruin the Neal name and send you and Julian to jail."

"How long have you…?" His voice trailed off, but she understood his question.

"Weeks. Since before the Grace Sanctuary fund-raiser. I made a deal with the devil to save you. I agreed to pretend to be in a fake relationship with him so he wouldn't expose you. That's why I couldn't break things off with him. Because if I did, you would've been destroyed. But that's not all," she whispered, eliminating the small space between her and the man who wore her brother's face, but was a stranger. "He did all this because of Olivia. You remember her, don't you?" At his stony expression, she nodded again. "Of course you do. The woman you seduced, used to get back at her brother, impregnated, then tossed aside. All for your petty hatred and resentment. Now, who wouldn't Dad and Mom recognize?"

"You don't understand," he spat, but the anger in his eyes had been overshadowed by worry. By fear. Because he understood that his greatest enemy had the dirt on him, no doubt. "You could never understand…"

"Not understand what? How hard it is to live up to our name? To live under the yoke of it for so long that sometimes you feel like your back's going to break from the burden? Yes, Trevor, I do. The difference between you and me is that I'm choosing not to let it poison me until I make unconscionable decisions that hurt other people. I decided to help people rather than harm them. But just to get your way, you would steal that from me, too."

For too long, she'd allowed him and the duty of being a Neal to dictate her life, her behavior, her decisions. No longer. She might have been quiet, but she'd learned from the best.

Not him. Gideon.

"I love you, Trevor. For the brother and man you were, I'm giving you a choice now. Come after Leida Investments or any of the businesses I've invested in, or my trust fund, and Gideon won't have to leak any of that information to the press and SEC. I will. He gave me a copy of the file, and right now, it's tucked away safe. But if you dare touch anything that's mine—and when I say mine, that includes Gideon Knight and everything he loves—I'll take you down. And I won't lose sleep over it."

Trevor stared at her, shocked. But she didn't wait for his response. He couldn't say anything that would fix what he'd broken. She would just have to accept that some men changed for the worse instead of the better, and as much as it tore her heart apart, Trevor was one of them.

"I have to admit, Gideon, I never expected you to go to *these* lengths." Madison tsked, appearing at his side, her familiar scent teasing his nostrils.

At one time, he'd found the floral fragrance alluring. Now it was just cloying. She trailed fingertips down his arm and over the back of his hand. Tilting her head to the side, she offered him what she probably considered a coy smile. She didn't pull it off. Not when he knew the real woman behind the mask.

He shifted his arm, knocking her hand away. Foolish as hell of him to think he could slip unseen into the closed-off room that reminded him of his den. He'd needed space and time to walk off the killing rage that had consumed him when Trevor had alluded to Olivia.

If not for Shay, he would've put that bastard through the wall, his hands around his throat, and damn the consequences. But his name in that soft voice and the fear darkening her lovely eyes had stopped him. He'd put that hated emotion in her gaze, and he detested himself for it. Still, even with rage roiling inside him like a volcano set to blow, he would've accompanied her to that meeting with her brother. He hadn't wanted to leave her alone. That protective streak toward her had only widened and deepened in the time they'd spent together. Yet he also understood she needed to have it out with Trevor, to stand up to him on her own. And she couldn't do that with his life in imminent danger from Gideon.

But right after he marched into an empty room to cool off with a glass of bourbon from the bar, Madison had appeared.

Goddamn, he didn't have the patience to deal with her machinations right now.

"What lengths, Madison?" He lifted the tumbler to his lips, downing the last of the dark alcohol before setting the glass on the mantel. "I don't have time for your games."

"Time for me," she corrected, assuming a hurt expression. "That's what went wrong with us, you know? You spent so much time at the office or out of town at meetings, I felt neglected. I missed you and couldn't stand the loneliness."

He snorted. "Is this your way of trying to explain why I walked in on you sitting on Trevor's dick? Forget it, sweetheart. This guilt trip not only isn't going to work, but it's months too late. I don't give a fuck now."

"We both know that's not true, Gideon," she crooned, clutching his arm. He stiffened, hating her hands on him. It felt...wrong. There'd been a time when he'd enjoyed her teasing caresses, her heated strokes. But now? Now his skin prickled and crawled as if his very body rebelled against her. These days, he welcomed the touch of only one woman. Shay.

Again he shifted away, dislodging her touch.

"If you'd answered any of my phone calls this week, you'd know—"

"I didn't answer them because we have nothing to talk about," he said.

"So you're going to tell me that your love for me just died? Went away just like that?" She snapped her fingers, eyes flashing. "I don't believe it."

"Believe it," he growled. "You killed it. And you don't get a do-over. Get it through your head, sweetheart. I. Don't. Want. You."

Tired of this, he went to move around her, but she sidestepped, blocking him. Unless he wanted to grab her, pick her up and shift her out of the way, he couldn't pass. And at the moment, the thought of putting his hands on her caused his stomach to curdle.

"Then what was this whole…act with Shay about? You don't expect me, or anyone for that matter, to actually accept that you're madly in love with her? The sister of the man who stole the woman you love? You don't have to continue this silly pretense anymore, Gideon." She shoved into his personal space, so her perfume clogged his nose, crawled down his throat. He grabbed her shoulders to prevent her from coming any nearer. She flattened her palms on his chest. "I love you. I made a mistake leaving you for him. It's been you all along. And I know you still love me if you'll go to these lengths."

Screw this. He tightened his grip on her, prepared to move her. "Madison…" he growled.

"Yes, Gideon." She moaned, and shooting up on her toes, wrapped her arms around his neck and crushed her mouth to his.

Shock froze him. But just for a second. Bile scorched a

path to the back of his throat. Muttering a curse, he jerked his head back, circled her wrists and yanked her off him.

"Dammit," he snapped. But any more words died on his tongue.

Shay stood in the doorway to the den, her shuttered gaze on them.

"Oh, Shay," Madison cooed, panting lightly. "We didn't see you there." Perverse satisfaction threaded her tone.

"Shay," he breathed, already leaving the unfaithful bitch he'd almost married behind, forgotten, and moving toward the woman with the wounded eyes.

"I'm ready if you are," she said, her voice flat, hideously polite.

She turned on her heel and left, leaving a void in his gut.

Seventeen

Shay stared out the window of the Town Car, watching the landmarks that defined Chicago passing by in the distance. What she wouldn't give to be in one of those monuments right now. Just anywhere as long as it wasn't here, sitting in the back of this car, tension thick, her pain crushing her chest like an anvil.

Tonight had been a special hell. Between the confrontation and probable loss of her relationship with Trevor and walking in on Madison and Gideon kissing, she just wanted to hole up somewhere and wait out this pain. But how could she hide from it, when she embodied it, breathed it?

Next to her, Gideon was silent, brooding. She'd never seen him brood. Distant, yes. Taunting, yes. Passionate, God yes. But never this dark heaviness that seemed to reach out to her, wrap around her.

Hold on, she reminded herself. Just hold on until she could get out of the car and into her temporary home, where she could break down. But not now. Not in front of Gideon.

"Shay."

His deep, silken voice stroked over her skin even under her coat, and she flinched away from it.

"I didn't kiss her, Shay," he rasped.

She squeezed her eyes shut. As if she could block out the sight of Madison, her arms thrown around him, her mouth pressed to the one that she adored, needed. But that image would no doubt be branded onto her brain for all eternity. As well as the slashing pain on her heart.

Yet… "I know, Gideon."

A pause, and then an audible exhale. "You believe me," he stated.

She nodded. "Yes."

"Then, baby, look at me. Please." It was the "please" that had her turning her head and meeting that midnight gaze. "Then what's wrong? Why haven't you spoken to me, looked at me since leaving the party? Tell me what I've done and let me explain it."

"You haven't done anything," she said, scanning his features. Committing them to memory. "But I can't go through with this charade. Our agreement is over."

His head snapped back, his eyes narrowing on her face. "Why? Did your brother convince you to leave me?"

"Leave you?" She chuckled, and it grated her throat raw. "You once accused me of being blind, Gideon. It seems to be contagious. You can't see that I would do anything to stay with you. But not as a pretend girlfriend or a lover-for-now. I want the real thing. I *deserve* the real thing."

"Shay," he said, and her heart squeezed so hard, she placed her hand over her chest. "What are you saying?"

"I'm saying I love you. Desperately. Completely. Finally. There's no going back for me. There's no one else. And that's a problem, because you don't love me. You don't want me other than as a bed partner and a means to an end."

"That's not fair," he rumbled, the skin tautening over his cheekbones, anger diamond-bright in his eyes. "You mean more to me than a fuck. I've never treated you like that. I never would."

"No," she agreed. "You've been one of the few men in my life who saw past the socialite, the family name and money. You saw the business owner, the capable woman. When no one else respected me, you did…even as you used me to get back at my brother. And that's the problem. Because above all, the first thing you will always see is Trevor Neal's sister." She hesitated, but in the end, she had nothing to lose in laying it all out there. "I know about what he did to Olivia," she said.

Gideon transformed into living stone. Except for his eyes, which blazed with anger and another darker, more heartbreaking emotion.

"How did you find out? Surely *Trevor*," he spat her brother's name, "didn't confess his sins to you."

"No." She shook her head, hurting for him, for Olivia. Shame for Trevor's despicable actions coating her in grime even though she wasn't responsible for him. "I didn't tell you, but Olivia came by the morning after I moved out of my house. She broke down when she realized who I was, and she ended up revealing everything to me. She's the reason behind the file, the blackmail, the revenge, not Madison. Your hatred goes much deeper than him cheating with her."

"Yes," he confirmed, still cold, still impenetrable. "You saw for yourself what he did to Olivia. She's been emotionally fragile ever since he left her, and she lost the baby. The morning after the blackout, she'd found out about his engagement to Madison. And it sent her to the hospital. She's recovering, but she hasn't been the girl I remember since before your brother came along."

"And you'll never be able to get past that. Not that I blame you. He crossed an unforgivable line, and there's nothing that could justify it. But even realizing this, I can't waste one more day hoping you will let it go. Not one more day living a lie. It's time for me to live for me, to determine and shape my own future, and I can't do that with a man who insists on remaining in the past. A man for whom revenge is more important than love...than me."

"I didn't ask for your love," he snapped, and the tone, razor sharp, flayed her already wounded and bleeding heart. "I told you not to let me break you, Shay. I warned you."

"And I didn't ask for your permission to love you," she countered softly. "Don't feel guilty, Gideon. I'm used to not being enough for the men in my life. But the difference—what you've taught me—is I no longer give a damn. I'm enough for *me*."

At that moment, the car stopped in front of Bridgette's house. Shay didn't wait for the driver to come around and open her door. She unlocked it and did the honors herself. It was like a metaphor for her new life. She was tired of waiting on others. She was in control of her own fate; she could open her own doors.

And she would.

Starting now.

"Shay." Gideon's strong fingers grasped her wrist. "Please."

"Goodbye, Gideon," she whispered.

Then, pulling free, she stepped out of the car.

And didn't look back.

Eighteen

Gideon entered the numbers into the spreadsheet, then several seconds later swore under his breath and deleted them. *Dammit*. He'd been doing a repeat of this same thing for hours now.

Hours, hell. His fingers fisted on top of the keyboard. Days.

His concentration had been shot for five nights and six days. Since the five nights and six days ago when Shay got out of his car. When she'd announced she loved him, then walked away without looking back. As an image of her leaving him, spine ramrod straight, glide elegant and proud, wavered in his head, he squeezed his eyes shut. Bowing his head, he didn't will the mental picture away. No, he conjured it up over and over, punishing himself with the memory of the pain and soul-deep sadness that had darkened her eyes, of the words that had driven daggers into his chest.

Of the resolve and strength radiating from her that let him know if he didn't say something, *do* something to prevent her from exiting the car, he would never see her again. Never inhale her rain-and-roses scent. Never hear her husky voice. Never have her body pressed to his, fitting like a missing puzzle piece.

But he'd done nothing.

That grab at her wrist had been weak, and they'd both known it.

"Damn you, Shay," he whispered harshly. "Damn you."

Like he'd told her that night, he hadn't asked for her love. Didn't want it. He'd earned a PhD in how faithless love was. People threw that word around to abuse, betray and abandon others. Madison had claimed to love him. Trevor had vowed the same to his sister.

Love deceived, used and…died. It left pain and disillusionment and loss behind. It changed people for the worse, not the better. Intuition had warned him that if he allowed Shay in, if he risked opening to her, when she left—because experience had taught him the leaving was inevitable—the wreckage would be much worse than the damage Madison had inflicted. Shay would level him.

He refused to be played for the fool by *love* again. Ever.

With that "ever" ricocheting off his skull, he turned back to his computer screen and the report he'd been trying to finish for the past two hours.

His desk phone buzzed. "Mr. Knight, there's a Mr. Trevor Neal here to see you. He doesn't have an appointment—"

"Send him in," Gideon snapped.

What the hell was Trevor doing here? Scratch that. He didn't give a damn.

For the first two days after dropping Shay off, Gideon had tried to drown her out with alcohol. When that had failed, work had been his next attempt to erase her from his mind. Apparently, that wasn't succeeding, either. While meeting with Trevor was most likely a terrible idea, he was also spoiling for a fight. A grim smile stretched across his mouth. For the first time in days—six days and five nights, to be exact—he looked forward to something.

Seconds later, his office door opened, and the man he'd resented for thirteen years and actively hated since he'd harmed Olivia stalked inside. Harsh lines etched his forehead and bracketed his mouth, and his eyes, so like his sister's, blazed with anger. His hands curled into fists at his sides. Seemed like Gideon wasn't the only one looking for a fight.

His smile widened.

"Good afternoon, Trevor. I'd say it was nice to see you again, but we both know that would be bullshit. So we'll skip the pleasantries and get to what are you doing here." Gideon leaned back in his desk chair and templed his fingers beneath his chin.

"You son of a bitch," Trevor snarled.

"Well, that didn't take long," Gideon drawled with a sigh, his voice heavy with mock disappointment. Rising, he flattened his palms on the top of his desk. "What the fuck do you want?"

"Where's my sister?" Trevor demanded. "I checked with Bridgette. She's no longer staying there. So where is she?"

"I don't know," Gideon replied calmly. Though inside, alarm clanged in his head, his chest. As far as he'd known, she'd still been with her best friend. *Was she okay? Was she safe?* The questions barraged him, but he forced his focus back to the man across from him. "Why do you care? You let her leave the only home she ever knew because she wouldn't bend to your demands. Are you suddenly having an attack of conscience?"

Doubtful, since the man didn't have one.

"Not that it's any of your business, but I need to speak to her. Last time we spoke, she made some…irrational accusations and threats. We need to clear this up. As a *family*," he sneered.

Gideon arched an eyebrow. "Threats?" Pride and admiration warmed him. "There's an interesting turn of events."

"You would find it funny." Trevor scowled. "She wasn't like this before. I'm thinking it's the company she's been keeping."

"Thank you." Gideon dipped his head in acknowledgment. "And just for the record, your sister has always been strong. You were just too busy playing lord of the manor to recognize it. If you had, maybe you would've used her brilliance for the advantage of your *family* company instead of sticking her in some bullshit position. Then she might not have had to go form her own business, but could've helped yours grow."

"You know nothing about Shay," Trevor growled, shifting forward as if ready to leap over the desk. "Don't pretend that your *relationship*," he spat the word, "was real. She told me the truth about your blackmailing her into pretending you two were a couple. She also informed me about the file of lies you have on me."

Shock reverberated through him. When she'd claimed she wouldn't go one more day living a lie, had she been referring to confessing to her brother about their arrangement?

Flipping these new revelations over and over in his mind, Gideon returned his attention to Trevor. "You might have tried that argument with Shay, but don't bother with me. Everything listed in that file is the least of your crimes. We both know who you are, Trevor. We both know what you're capable of," he growled. "You used my sister, then tossed her aside like she was something beneath your shoe. No, I take that back. You would've at least paused and scraped something off the bottom of your precious loafers. You didn't even give her that courtesy. And for what? A grudge against me from high school? You broke her, and for you it was business as usual."

"Like you broke my sister?" Trevor accused. "Eye for an eye? Don't stand there and preach to me like you're so self-righteous, when you turned around and did the same thing to Shay. You used her to get back at me. That doesn't make you the hero in this story."

"You're right."

Trevor's mouth snapped closed, his eyes flaring in surprise at Gideon's quick agreement, before narrowing. He was probably wondering what Gideon's game was now. But there wasn't any game. There wasn't any trickery to slide another point home as if this was a contest to be won.

He'd used Shay. Oh yes, he'd justified it as righting a wrong against Olivia, as protecting future women from being hurt by Trevor. But the truth couldn't be denied any longer. His actions hadn't been noble—they'd been selfish, vengeful…and reprehensible. Maybe unforgivable.

Not because of Trevor. He still had zero fucks to give about Trevor. But because he'd dragged an innocent into it. As blameless as Olivia had been in Trevor's schemes, Shay had been just as blameless. His mother's warning haunted him, ringing in his head like a premonition that had come to pass. He *had* ended up hurting others. And the most important person he'd hurt was Shay. No, he wasn't Trevor—could never deliberately deceive and devastate someone, then walk away from a child he'd created—but he'd also blackmailed, hurt, then turned his back on the woman he loved.

God. He loved her.

The force of the revelation struck him with the blow of a mallet to the chest. He sank to his chair, staring blindly ahead.

He loved Shay.

Somehow, despite every wall, every barrier and shield he'd thrown up, she'd wedged herself into his heart, his soul. No wonder he'd felt so empty these past days. The one who'd given him life again was gone. Because, yes, she'd resuscitated him, jolting his heart so it beat again. She'd given him more than work to be excited about—she'd given him her quiet humor, her defiance, her wit, her loyalty, her body…her love.

And what had he done? Thrown it back at her like it meant nothing.

Don't feel guilty, Gideon. I'm used to not being enough for the men in my life.

Pain, razor sharp and searing hot, razed his chest. He gasped at the agony of it. Nothing—absolutely nothing—could be further from the truth. She was more than enough. She was *everything.* But he'd been willing to throw away a future with her for revenge.

"Gideon," Trevor snapped, hauling Gideon out of the hell he'd plummeted into.

He jerked his head up, blinking. God, he'd forgotten all about this man standing in his office. And now he didn't have time for him or the vendetta that had brought both of them low. Urgency spiraling through him, Gideon shot to his feet and strode across the room. Removing a large picture from the wall, he revealed the safe behind it and quickly punched in the code to open it. He withdrew the thick, brown file inside, then slammed the safe door shut, not bothering to replace the painting.

"Here." He marched over to Trevor and shoved the dossier containing all his damning information into the other man's chest. "Take it. There aren't any more copies other than the one I gave your sister."

"What?" Trevor gasped. He clutched the folder, glancing at it before his gaze whipped back to Gideon. "What's your angle now? You can't seriously just hand this over to me without wanting something in return."

Gideon stepped back, shaking his head. "No angle. No ulterior motive. But you're right. I do want something in return. Or rather, someone. I want Shay. More than that file or revenge against you. But that's for me to fix, not you."

How he'd go about doing that, he had no clue. Hell, by all rights, she shouldn't forgive him. But he needed her. He loved her.

And he'd fight to have her. Harder than he'd ever fought to pay back Trevor.

Because winning Shay was more important than any battle he'd ever faced.

Nineteen

"Order up, babe."

Shay turned around and rushed across the minimal space inside the food truck to grab the two cartons of larb served over thin noodles. Snatching up napkins and plastic utensils, she placed everything in a bag and handed it to the waiting customers through the window. Smiling and thanking them, she turned to the next person and took his order for green papaya salad.

Bridgette had called that morning, asking if she would help her out on the truck again. Though Shay suspected her friend had arranged this sudden lack of help to keep her busy and her mind off a certain person, she'd jumped at the chance to get out of her newly leased, empty Edgewater apartment. More specifically, she'd been eager to get out of her head.

In the almost two weeks since she'd walked away from Gideon, she'd found an apartment—despite Bridgette's argument that she could stay with her as long as she wanted—located a small office space for Leida Investments, officially resigned from RemingtonNeal, opened a safe deposit box for the damning file on her brother and done more research on start-up companies that she could invest in.

Yes, her family and love life had exploded, but she refused to stop living. A gaping hole existed where her heart had once been, but that didn't mean she would roll over and give in. She'd meant every word she'd uttered to Gideon.

This was her time. Her life. And no one but she was in control of it.

She might have lost the man she loved because he wanted revenge and hate rather than her, but for the first time in longer than she could remember, she loved herself. She *valued* herself. And she was demanding it from everyone in her life.

As Bridgette had put it, Shay was a boss.

Dammit, yeah, she was.

She'd learned something in the last couple weeks. She would've loved having Gideon in her life. But he *wasn't* her life.

And she was okay with that.

"Have another order for the larb, but by itself, without the noodles," she called out to Bridgette over her shoulder before returning her attention to the window and the next customer. "Hi, how can I..." She trailed off, the sudden lurch of her heart to her throat preventing the rest of the words from escaping.

No.

No.

She stared into midnight eyes with stars and the scream inside her head increased in volume. It wasn't fair. What the hell was he doing here? Telling him she loved him and having him reject her had been agonizing, humiliating. How did he not know that? Was he a sadist getting pleasure from her pain?

Well, *screw that.*

She schooled her features into the cool, polite mask she'd mastered since she'd been old enough to sit at the adult table. He wouldn't get anything else from her. She didn't have it in her to give.

"What are you doing here, Gideon?" she asked, proud when not so much as a tremor shook her voice.

Behind her, Bridgette appeared next to her elbow like a bodyguard. "What the hell is this?" she demanded, spatula still in hand.

"I got this," Shay murmured to her friend. "We're busy, as you can tell," she said to Gideon. "And you and I don't have anything left to say to each other."

Again, she sounded calm even to her own ears. Sounded as if her fingertips didn't tingle with the need to touch him.

But inside...

Inside she quaked. Love, hurt, yearning, desire—they all coalesced and swirled in her chest, leaving almost no room for air. She dragged in what little she could and waited.

"You don't have to say anything, moonbeam. All I ask is for you to listen."

"Don't call me that," she snapped, and silently cursed herself for betraying that much emotion. She shouldn't care if he murmured that endearment. It shouldn't affect her.

"Two minutes, Shay." His dark gaze searched hers. "Please."

Please.

Like before, it gave her pause.

"Two minutes. That's it," she agreed.

"Thank you," he said, then hesitating, he dragged his hands over his head. Taken aback by the uncharacteristically nervous gesture, Shay narrowed her eyes on him. Noting for the first time the faint smudges under his eyes, the two-minutes-past-five-o'clock shadow that darkened his jaw. Where was the clean-cut, reserved man she'd known?

He gave a rough, abrupt chuckle. "Now that I'm here, I don't know where to begin." Sighing, he dropped his arm. "First, I should apologize. And I am sorry, Shay. I used you. There's no getting around that fact. I rationalized and defended my actions by claiming I wanted justice for Olivia. That your brother had gotten away with hurting people long enough, and if no one else would make him pay, then I would. But what I didn't want to admit is that I blamed myself.

"I hated myself as much as, if not more than, him. It was my job to protect my sister, and I failed. If I'd been a better brother, she would've felt free to tell me about the relationship with Trevor instead of keeping it a secret. And most of all, if not for me, she wouldn't have even been on his radar. Me. It all came back to me, and I couldn't bear the guilt, the shame and, God, yes, the anger. It was that anger that led me to do what I had judged him for—ruthlessly using you to get to him. I convinced myself I was more honorable than him, but in my rage, I'd *become* him. And worst of all, I hurt you. That, I will never forgive myself for."

Soul-deep shock robbed her of speech. Even the long line of people behind him had stopped grumbling and were quiet. A few even had their phones out. She mentally winced. Gideon wouldn't be happy to know he was probably live-streaming on social media.

"Gideon, you don't have to—" she began, only to be cut off.

"Yes, I do. I'm desperate, Shay. I don't have any pride left. Not when it comes to you. And I don't want it. Don't need it. Not when it kept me from telling you how important you are. God, baby, you're *vital*. Nothing is the same without you in my world. Before you, work, family, money, success—those were priorities. Hell, they were everything. But since you walked away from me, I still have all of those, and aside from my mother and sister, they don't fulfill me anymore.

"I can't concentrate at work because I'm wondering where you are, what you're doing…if you're thinking about me. I could escape into all the things wealth buys, I could travel to the most exotic places on this earth, but I'd see nothing, appreciate nothing, because you wouldn't be there with me. Success?" He held up his hands, palms out. "Until you, I measured success by how many clients I had, the profits, how many doors opened for me. But now? Success is how many times I can make you smile. How many times I can hear you say I love you. How many nights I can fall asleep beside you. How many ways I can prove to you that you're loved. So far, I've been damn unsuccessful."

"Wow," Bridgette whispered beside her. Shay shot her friend a look, and she shrugged, smiling sheepishly. "I mean, bastard."

Shaking her head, Shay returned her gaze to the man who'd captured her attention and that of an increasingly growing lunch crowd in Hyde Park. She blinked back the tears stinging her eyes, and her heart pounded thickly against her rib cage. Hope tried to rear its foolish head, but she slapped it back down. She'd been stupid enough to spin impossible dreams around this man once, even though he'd never made promises to her. And that was just it. She could no longer afford to pin nebulous hopes on a man who refused to put her first. No matter how lovely his speech.

"Thank you for the apology, Gideon. I really do appreciate it. But I can't risk taking a chance on you. How long before you realize you're sleeping with the enemy—literally—and resent me for it? I can't live waiting for that day to happen."

"You don't get it, moonbeam," he said, moving closer to the service window. And in spite of her resolve, she leaned forward, a part of her—the part that woke up aching for him every night, the part that refused to stop believing in fairy tales—desperate to hear what she didn't get. "I love you. I don't know when it happened. When I sat down across from you in that restaurant and you essentially told me to go to hell? When you refused to answer my phone call and cater to me because you were helping a friend? When I played my guitar for you? Maybe…" He hesitated, swallowed hard. Then whispered, "Maybe the first time I saw you as Camille."

"Saw you as Camille? What kind of kink are y'all into?" Bridgette muttered from behind her.

Shay ignored her, latched on to every word falling from Gideon's lips. Ensnared by those onyx eyes that she couldn't tear herself away from.

"I don't deserve you. But there's no man on this earth who does. But that won't stop me from fighting for you. From fighting for *us*. From begging you to not throw me away, even though I almost did. Moonbeam, you complete me in a way revenge never could. Without you as my conscience, my lover, my friend, I'm empty. I want to be full. I want to be found. Please, don't leave me out there again. I love you, Shay Neal. Desperately. Completely. Finally. There's no going back for me. There's no one else."

He gifted her with the words she'd given him. Only this time, he was the one standing on the ledge, hoping she would grasp his hand and pull him back to safety, to love. He'd pushed her over that night. And now, she could do the same. Pay him back. Turn away to a future that he wouldn't be in, but would still be good. Or she could reach across, risk her heart again and jump off the edge, trusting him to catch her. And hold her forever.

There was no choice.

Running, she barreled out of the truck, but before she

could round it, she crashed into Gideon. He hadn't waited, but met her halfway. That's what they would always do—meet each other. Never fail to be there for one another.

Dimly, she heard a roar of applause and cheers, but as his arms closed around her, and she wrapped hers around his neck, everything else ceased to exist. He captured her mouth in a kiss that stole her breath and sent heat roaring through her. But most of all, it shattered every remnant of fear and doubt, promising her with the thrust of his tongue, the molding of his lips, that he would love her, cherish her, worship her. And she returned the vow.

"I love you," she whispered, peppering his mouth, jaw and chin with kisses. "I love you so much."

"I thought I'd never hear you say that again," he rasped, pressing his forehead to hers.

"I promise you I'll never stop telling you." She took his mouth this time, leaving them shaking against each other. "I love you."

"Forever?"

"Forever."

Epilogue

One Year Later

"Mrs. Knight, your husband's here to see you."

Shay smiled, pressing the speaker button on her desk phone. God, she never tired of being called that. "Please send him in, Jackie." Seconds later, her executive assistant opened the door, grinning as Gideon strode past her. Leida Investments was still small, but now Shay could afford a staff. Even if that staff was just Jackie. Still, the business was steadily growing, and Shay couldn't be happier.

Well, she took that back, her smile warming as Gideon crossed the room and took her into his arms. With the news she'd just received not minutes ago, she could indeed be happier. And she was.

Her lips parted under his, and as always, his kiss kindled the desire that only he could stir within her. She tilted her head back farther, opened her mouth wider, and he dived deeper. By the time he lifted his head, their rough breaths echoed in the office.

"I'm supposed to be taking you to lunch," he reminded her with a sensual smile that was reflected in his eyes.

"But with you kissing me like that, hell, moonbeam, you might *be* lunch."

She chuckled. "You're bad. And I refuse to keep your mother and sister waiting. I had to twist Bridgette's arm to let me have Olivia for an afternoon, so nope, not missing lunch."

Gideon's eyes brightened at hearing his sister's name. And no wonder. Olivia had come a long way in a year. After hearing the whole story about what Trevor had done to her, Bridgette had decided to take her under her wing. And Olivia hadn't had much of a choice. Bridgette had bulldozed her way into Olivia's world, and assumed the role of big sister, as Shay had. Soon, she had Olivia in the food truck, working beside her, and to Olivia's surprise, she'd enjoyed it and was wonderful with people and the business side of it. Bridgette had taken her on as a partner, and now the two of them were planning to buy another truck.

And Trevor... A sliver of sadness wormed its way into Shay's happiness. It happened whenever she thought of him. She hadn't shared the file she had on him; he was her brother, and no matter what he'd done, she couldn't destroy him. But things like that had a way of exposing themselves. He and the senator were in trouble with the law and SEC now. Soon, Trevor would lose not only his wife, the family business and reputation, but also his freedom. He'd caused a lot of pain and loss to people both emotionally and financially, and now he faced the consequences of his actions. She loved him, but she also hadn't seen him since the night of his engagement party.

"Are you sure about lunch?" Gideon asked, cupping her chin and tipping her head back for another press of his lips to hers. "I'm sure Mom and Olivia would understand."

"Yes." Shay laughed, then cradled his cheeks between

her palms. "I'm hungry." She paused. "And especially since I'm eating for two now."

Shock blanked his features. Slowly, understanding dawned, and his black eyes glittered.

"What?" he rasped. "Are you telling me that we're... that you're..."

"Pregnant," she finished with a wide grin, slipping her arms around his neck again. "We're going to have a baby."

"Moonbeam," he whispered, awed. With a reverence that brought tears to her eyes, he stepped back, and her arms fell to her sides. He knelt in front of her, his big hands spreading over her still-flat abdomen. "Jesus, Moonbeam. How can you continue making me the happiest, richest, most loved man in the world?" He dipped his head, brushed his mouth over her belly. Rising to his feet, he pulled her into a tight, hard embrace and buried his face in her neck. "I love you, Shay. I love you so much."

"I love you, too. Forever."

* * * * *

CALIFORNIA
SECRETS

JULES BENNETT

To my sister, Angel.
You're always willing to drop your
workload to help me with mine.
Love you more than cake!

One

The red bikini never failed to arouse him…and the damn thing was just hanging there on the heated towel bar in his en suite.

When Harper Williams donned that collection of triangles and strings, he always enjoyed peeling the flimsy material from her curvy body. As much as he always wanted to tear it off, he enjoyed this sexy suit way too much to destroy it.

Ethan Michaels slid on a gray T-shirt and stepped back into the bedroom of his penthouse at Mirage. The adults-only resort was beyond luxurious and grand. In addition to all the amenities that made this five-star resort so sought out, the breathtaking property sat in the middle of Sunset Cove, a private island off the southern coast of California, making this resort a most magnificent destination.

While waiting out his time until he orchestrated an epic surprise reunion with his bastard of a stepfather, Ethan had started a fling with the owner of that tempting red bikini. He'd always been a sucker for red…and the lush body beneath didn't hurt, either.

The one-night stand had turned into nearly a month of passion and R-rated sleepovers. Even with the time that had passed, he and Harper had kept things casual, simple—just the way he preferred his temporary arrangements, and she seemed more than okay with how their fling was going.

Ethan had no clue what brought Harper as a single guest to Mirage—and he had no intention of asking. She'd been alone like him, and they'd just gravitated toward each other, as most people who came to the adults-only resort were couples.

He and Harper had fallen into a perfect routine of meeting in his room for dinner in the evening. He'd always make sure the chef prepared something special just for them and the waitstaff always accommodated every need—Ethan would remember each loyal employee when he took the resort back into his name.

There was never a set time for Harper showing up in the evening, but Ethan always made sure something was ready for her. During the day, though, they did their own thing and went their own ways. Occasionally he'd see her on the beach and take her a drink, but they never so much as touched outside his penthouse.

Watching her parade around on the beach seemed to be the ultimate foreplay.

But he couldn't get too distracted—he still had a

job to do, a vendetta to secure. His time here wasn't all about play. Harper was just an enjoyable by-product. He didn't care one bit that she seemed to be using him to pass her time, as well. He did wonder what she was biding her time for, but again, he didn't want to pry, because anything personal was out of the question.

All it would take would be one quick message to his assistant to have any answer he wanted about Harper, but that would imply that he wanted to know her beyond the bedroom. Some may call him cold, and they might be right, but Ethan had his reasons for the distance, and they were nobody else's concern.

Besides, he never started a fling if the woman wasn't on board for something casual and fun or if he thought for a second she was husband shopping. He'd never lead a woman on or pretend he could offer anything more than his body and a small portion of his time.

So, while some may think he was a coldhearted bastard, the only person who was hurt at the end of the day was himself. It was that pain that kept him focused on why he sought revenge, why vindication was so important. Using women was never his plan, but using his own body was.

Ethan grabbed his cell from the nightstand and checked his emails as he stepped onto the balcony. That fresh salt water and the ocean breeze never got old. He was meant for the beach, while his twin brother, Dane, was meant for the mountains. They were so alike, yet so different.

Nothing too pressing on the email front, so Ethan sent a text to his investigator to make sure the timeline for Robert Anderson's arrival was still correct. His dear ol' stepfather had been due at Mirage three weeks ago, but for some reason or another—likely illegal—the man was running very late. People like Robert flittered around from one spot to the next without a real plan or too much of a schedule.

But Ethan was patient. He'd waited nearly twenty years to get retribution…a few more days wouldn't matter.

He pocketed his phone and glanced down to the beach. White canopies draped over the two-person cabanas. Staff roamed around with trays of drinks. The calming water rolled up against the shoreline, only to roll back out again. Yeah, he could easily stay right here and wait on Robert because passing his time at a posh luxury resort while enjoying passionate nights with Harper was sure as hell better than anything else he could be doing for work or otherwise. He used his days to maintain and work on growing his night clubs across the country, and he couldn't think of a better temporary office to work from.

Mirage—the beautiful resort his mother had created, which had been wrenched away from her sons after her death—was always meant to be his. This place felt like home, and soon, so very soon, he'd be in charge just like his mother had always intended.

With the twentieth anniversary of her death approaching, Ethan knew it was well past time to make Lara Anderson's dream a reality. Sticking Robert Anderson in some hellhole where he belonged would just be icing on the proverbial cake.

As Ethan turned back toward the living area, his cell vibrated in his pocket. He pulled it out to see Harper's name light up the screen.

Strange. They never texted or called. They kept this arrangement strictly superficial.

Where are you?

He hesitated but ultimately replied that he was in his penthouse. She'd only been gone from his bed a few hours. Since she'd left, he'd gotten in a full work-out and managed to touch base with each of his managers for his nightclubs across the country. He was in the middle of branching out globally and hoped a deal in France would close soon.

Time zones were often a bitch to work around, but he had a dedicated staff and couldn't run his company without such trusted members. Ethan demanded loyalty and, in turn, compensated his crew nicely.

He already had a master plan of who he'd bring on to Mirage to help with a smooth transition, though he fully intended on keeping the bulk of the resort's staff, so long as they proved themselves worthy. He expected nothing but the best, especially where his mother's legacy was concerned.

Ethan glanced back to his phone again, but Harper hadn't replied. He had no clue what she wanted, but he needed to touch base with his brother. They might have drifted apart when their mother died, they might have dealt with her death in their own ways and closed out the world and each other, but Dane was all Ethan had left. No matter their past grief, Ethan always knew he could count on his twin.

They'd forged together to make a solid plan in reclaiming their mother's pair of properties. Dane had acquired his resort in the mountains of Montana—now it was Ethan's turn.

Mirage in Montana had been seized by Robert, but with a bad gambling move, he'd lost the place. Dane had gone in with a plan of charming the new owner's daughter. He'd succeeded in acquiring the property, but somehow, he'd managed to fall in love and was planning a wedding.

Ethan would just take the property. Hold the wife.

He'd just pulled up Dane's texts when the penthouse elevator whooshed open. Ethan shifted his focus from the phone to Harper.

As much as he appreciated her in, and out, of that red bikini, he had to admit those lush curves were killer in her strapless emerald green sundress. All that dark skin on display…damn, he couldn't wait until tonight. Maybe she'd still have that dress on, because that thing sure as hell would provide easy access.

Her jet-black curls spiraled down her back with random strands draped over her shoulders. There was nothing about this woman he didn't find sexy and appealing. Had she come here because she couldn't wait for tonight?

No. That wasn't desire staring back at him. There was a look in her rich brown eyes that had him stilling, his heart clenching…not in a good way. She crossed the spacious suite, her wide gaze never wavering from his. The only sign that she was nervous or upset was the way she toyed with the delicate gold bracelet she always wore.

"What happened?" he asked, knowing she wouldn't be here with that panicked look in her eyes nor would she have texted him unless something was wrong.

"We have to talk."

Ethan let those words sink in before he let out a bark of laughter. "That sounds like the precursor to a breakup."

Which didn't make sense, considering they weren't an actual couple. There was nothing to break up.

Her worried look didn't even crack. "That's not why I'm here."

"Then what has you looking like your world has come to an end?"

Harper took in a deep breath, and for the first time since they'd met a month ago, she didn't seem like the confident, poised woman he'd come to know.

"I'm pregnant."

Saying those two words out loud didn't make this situation seem any more real or any less terrifying. Since taking the test this morning, she'd been in a fog, wondering how to tell Ethan, worried how he'd react, scared for her own future and how she'd provide a child with a stable home. But Harper had never backed down from a problem or a confrontation. She'd overcome so much heartache and tragedy, she couldn't look at this like a mistake or a setback.

Harper firmly believed everything happened for a

reason…even if she didn't understand and the timing was less than ideal.

Her entire life since Ethan approached her on the beach had been a series of firsts—the red bikini, the one-night stand, the continuation of that one night into an ongoing fling with a virtual stranger, the shower sex, the balcony sex in the middle of the night and now the two blue lines.

She'd had one serious relationship, but that had ended just before her sister died. Harper wasn't looking for any other commitment that would inevitably bring on more pain. But the fear of this situation settled heavy between them.

"Say something," she demanded after the yawning silence only added to her ever growing worry.

Ethan's bright eyes locked onto her. "You're serious."

Harper let out a mock laugh. "Do you think this is something I'd joke about?"

After another moment of awkward, tension-filled silence, Ethan muttered a curse and shook his head.

"No, but I don't know what to think." He raked a hand through his messy hair before shifting his attention back to her. "I won't ask how you know it's mine. I may not know much about you, but I know you haven't shared anyone else's bed."

"You're the first man I've been with in nearly a year."

Harper smoothed a hand over her queasy belly. She was more nervous about this conversation than she was nauseated from the pregnancy. But she hadn't been with a man in so long, which would explain part of the reason why she'd found Ethan so charming and irresistible. The other reason was because she was still trying to find her footing with her late sister's company, and Harper had used sex with Ethan as a much-needed means of escape.

She also kept hearing her sister's nagging in the back of her mind. Her fun-loving, life-of-the-party sister who always had encouraged Harper to step out of her comfort zone. Coming to this resort alone, wearing that bikini in a size fourteen, faking a confidence she didn't feel…all of these things were firsts for her.

"I didn't want to keep this from you," she went on, then paced to the double doors leading to the balcony. "I just found out this morning. I realize we barely know each other, but I'm not the type of person to lie or mislead anyone."

Life was too short, her goals too big to play games with anyone. She'd seen him, wondered what a fling would be like since she'd never had one, then decided to take charge of her life and seize the moment. She'd been trying to do more living in the moment since Carmen passed.

She'd brought the red bikini with her because her sister had always accused her of being too boring, too vanilla, and Harper had wanted to put herself out there with a bold confidence.

Now look where that landed her.

"You seem calm."

Harper glanced over her shoulder and collected her thoughts. "Calm? I'm scared to death, I'm stunned, I'm worried how I'll juggle it all. Getting hysterical won't change a thing or help me sort out these feelings. So, maybe I am calm, but it's not because I'm comfortable, it's because I'm shocked."

Those piercing eyes usually held so much desire and passion, but now...

Harper turned her attention back to the breathtaking view of the turquoise water and white sand. She didn't want to witness his worry, his doubts... She had her own to deal with. This was the last thing she wanted to confront him about, but he deserved to know. This temporary fling had now resulted in a lifetime connection to Ethan Michaels. As if she didn't have enough going on in her life already.

Coming to Mirage had been the first step she'd taken in moving her and her sister's design business into the next phase. Harper had every intention of making Two Sisters Design the go-to for every business, every home owner, everyone who wanted a change in their office or house or hotel.

Carmen had always had a grand vision of their business. Harper had been reluctant at first when Carmen asked for her help, worried she wouldn't measure up to her sister's amazing talents, despite Carmen's high praise on small projects.

But after her sister was killed in a robbery six months ago, Harper knew she had to step up and take over. It's what her sister would've wanted. Carmen would've had faith in Harper. Harper just needed to have faith in herself...which was how she landed at Mirage.

She'd decided to start here because her father owned the adults-only resort. He wanted to do an overhaul and, though she'd first met the man when she was twenty, she was trying to have a relationship with him. Trying…and somewhat succeeding.

Robert Anderson was a man who traveled and worked all over the world. Seemed business was more important to him than family, but what did she expect? He hadn't even known she'd existed for two decades, so she shouldn't have expected him to jump into the role of doting daddy. Yet she had expected just that.

Her sister was all she'd truly had in life, and now that she was gone, Harper craved any semblance of family. Her free-spirited mother gallivanting around the globe didn't count.

Harper wasn't sure what all her father did for a living, but she knew he was in real estate. And he'd been willing to give her a chance with one of his most prestigious properties. Having Mirage in her portfolio would seriously help boost her business.

And she would carry out her duties to prove to her father, to herself and to her sister that she was capable…despite starting a family much sooner than she'd ever planned.

"What's going through your mind?"

Ethan's sincere question filled the room, and she turned to face him. She couldn't help but laugh as she fiddled with the gold bracelet at her wrist.

"I have no idea," she told him. "I have so many thoughts, but I do want you to know that I don't expect anything from you. I won't make you do anything you're not ready for. I'm a big girl—I can handle anything thrown at me."

Wow. Her little speech sounded strong, though she

felt anything but. Yet, despite her anxiety, she couldn't let the fear win, because that's not what Carmen would've wanted. One tragic event after another had made her steely when it came to pain and reactions, but she wasn't about to let Ethan into her past, into her mind and all the reasons why she wasn't flipping out right now.

"Listen," she began, shoving her wayward curls over her shoulders. "This is a lot to think about. We'll just take some time to process and then talk later. I know we haven't gotten too personal with our information, but I will be here for at least another month, probably longer. And even then, I'll be coming and going quite a bit."

She'd never told him her reason for being here. Their physical relationship left no room for small talk or the get-to-know-you phase. Everything would change now. They'd have to dig into each other's lives, because now they were bonded forever.

When Ethan continued to stare at her across the room, Harper figured she should go and leave him alone with his thoughts. She wasn't sure what to say right now. Her purpose for coming to his room had been to tell him the truth, but she hadn't thought much beyond that.

Harper pulled in a shaky breath and started across the penthouse. The moment she stepped by him, Ethan's arm snaked out and caught her around the waist, his hand curling around her arm. Sliding his thumb over the inside of her elbow, he stopped her with that one simple, arousing gesture.

Her body responded, just as it always did to his tantalizing touch and heavy-lidded stare. Ethan Michaels was a potent man, and now she had to figure out how to shift from looking at him as a fling to seeing him as the father of her child…which wasn't going to be easy, considering she didn't know basic things like his middle name or even where he was from.

"You're not leaving," he told her. "We may not figure out all the answers now, but I know one thing for certain."

Why did his tone sound like a promising threat?

Ethan's eyes held her as breath caught in her throat. "You're not doing this alone. I *will* be part of this baby's life…and yours."

Two

Ethan might not know how to handle this situation, but he sure as hell knew he wasn't about to walk away from responsibility. This was a child…*his* child. His family life may be uncertain and in shreds, but deep down, at the end of the day, family mattered more to him than anything in this world.

Wasn't that why he was here to begin with? Every action he'd taken over the past twenty years had led him to this moment, all for the sake of his late mother and her wishes.

No matter what might come of him and Harper, that child was his future, and he would provide and be part of his or her life.

"I don't want a relationship just because I'm pregnant," she stated with a defiant tilt of her chin.

Ethan released her arm but didn't back away. She was quite adamant about this whole casual, uncommitted relationship status, which was perfectly fine with him, but each time it had been mentioned or hinted at, Harper had a flash of hurt in her eyes.

Who had hurt her? What had she gone through to bring her to this point? More importantly, why did he care to make it his business? He'd known about this baby for all of five minutes, and already his mind was playing with him. He had his own past hurts to focus on. Not that he wanted Harper to be in pain—he'd never want that—but he couldn't afford to get swept into her world and risk losing sight of his goals.

"I never said anything about a relationship," he countered. "But we're bonded together whether we like it or not."

Beneath that steely look in her dark eyes there was a hint of vulnerability and fear. She wasn't quite as calm as she led him to believe, but he'd be more worried if she wasn't scared. Hell, he was terrified, but there was nothing that would pull him away from his child or the woman carrying it.

His mother had been a hardworking, single mom. Ethan couldn't ignore the parallels here.

He would have Robert Anderson out of the picture and this resort back in his possession before his baby was born. Timing and persistence were everything right now.

"How long are you staying?" she asked. "We probably should dig a little deeper into each other since, well…"

She was more than welcome to go ahead and dig, but he would only feed her enough information to pacify her curiosities until he had his personal life all straightened out. No need to involve her in his family affair, which he was quite certain would get messy.

"I have no set plans." Partial truth, but all he was willing to give. "I'm here for as long as I want to be."

Harper's brows drew in. "You're so vague. Please tell me you're not married or running from the law."

Ethan laughed. "I'm not running from the law, and isn't it a little late to ask about a wife?"

"I assumed you didn't have one before we hooked up, but now I feel I should know the truth."

Ethan shook his head. "No wife, no girlfriend. I have a twin brother in Montana, and that's all the family I have. Well, he's getting married soon, so I guess I'll have a sister."

Harper's gaze darted down to her clasped hands, and he thought he saw that flash of hurt again, but maybe not. Maybe he just couldn't read her well enough quite yet. He knew exactly how to read her in the bedroom, but now, well…this was completely new territory. Trying to get a bead on women emotionally had always been foreign to him.

"What about you?" he asked.

Harper shifted her attention back to him. "I have a father that I met when I was twenty. My mother is a little eccentric and floats from one spot on the globe to the next. I'm not sure what hemisphere she's in half the time. I had a sister, but she passed away six months

ago. She was…everything to me. I'm still trying to figure out how to do life without her."

Well, damn. Not what he thought she'd say. He'd
pegged her for someone with several siblings, doting
parents that all gathered around a big table for each
holiday. He figured she was here as a loner to get away
and have some time for herself.

But instead, she was alone. Like him.

Oh, he had Dane, but since their mother's death,
nothing had been the same. For nearly twenty years, an
invisible wedge had separated them, and Ethan was hoping that by getting their mother's resorts back, maybe
they'd find closure and get back that relationship they'd
once had.

So, his twin was getting a wife and Ethan was getting a child. Not at all what he'd envisioned when they'd
started this journey.

"Sounds like we have something in common besides physical attraction," he told her. "Loss of family
is… It's rough."

Harper tucked a dark curl behind her ear and nodded. "I'm keeping this baby."

She laid claim like she dared him to argue. He had to
admire a woman who wasn't afraid to say exactly what
she wanted and made no apologies about it.

"I assumed," Ethan replied. "If you hadn't wanted
to, I would have tried to change your mind. Family is
everything to me."

Harper pursed her lips then blew out a sigh. She
stepped back from him and headed toward the patio
doors once again, only this time she opened them and

stepped on out into the sunshine. Ethan followed her, having no clue what to say or do. For the first time in his life, his confidence, his control slipped.

No, that wasn't true. His control had slipped when his mother died and Robert stole everything from him and Dane. Ethan had vowed to never feel helpless again—which was why he was taking this revenge head-on.

Ethan moved in beside Harper and rested his arm on the railing. The ocean breeze lifted her curls from her shoulders and sent them dancing in the wind. His body responded, immediately recalling how those strands glided over his bare skin.

Damn it. He shouldn't be lusting after her now, but, well…he couldn't help himself. Knowing she was carrying his child made her even sexier, and he hadn't thought that was possible.

"It's clear that you want to be involved, but I need you to know that I really don't expect you to be there every minute."

"Duly noted."

She turned her attention to him for a brief moment, but then she glanced back to the ocean. "So what now?"

"I'll bring a doctor to the resort to make sure you and the baby are healthy." Damn. He was a selfish idiot. He hadn't even asked the obvious question. "Are you feeling okay?"

Harper nodded. "Tired and nervous, but that's all."

"Don't worry. I'm going to take care of you both. I'll have the doctor here by the end of the day," he stated.

Harper laughed as she jerked her gaze back to him.

"Do people normally just jump when you snap your fingers?"

"Yes."

Shaking her head, she turned away from him and crossed to the chaise. "Well, I have my own doctor, and I'll call her to see what to do."

She took a seat and stretched out, lacing her fingers over her abdomen. He immediately envisioned her in a few months with their child growing. Emotions flooded him—anticipation, worry, uncertainty, excitement.

"I meant what about us now?" she asked. "We're not exactly a couple, and this certainly changes things between us."

"Nothing about this attraction has changed," he replied.

Ethan had to force himself to remain still, to not cross the balcony and take a seat on the chaise and pull her into his lap. They had never been alone this long without touching. The ache inside him grew with each passing minute, but they both needed to process this life-altering moment, and Harper needed space. Hell, so did he, but he still wanted to use sex as a distraction…just like he'd always done.

Only this time that default mode wasn't going to be the best option. He had to care, had to put himself out there, at least a little, because he was going to be a father.

The idea nearly had his weak knees buckling. What did he know about parenting? His mother had been a saint putting up with twin boys, but she'd suffered a fatal stroke when they'd been teens. The only father figure he'd had around was Robert Anderson, and that had just been for a handful of years and had ended when the bastard stole everything from Dane and Ethan. So this was going to be one area he had to learn all on his own…a vulnerable spot to find himself in.

Harper swung her legs over the side of the chaise and came to her feet.

"Listen, I have some things I need to do today," she told him. "We both should take some time to process, and I will contact my own doctor."

"I will—"

Harper held up her hands. "I don't deal well with anyone trying to control me—that's going to be the first personal thing about me you need to understand. I can take care of getting my own health care. I promise not to leave you out."

Ethan didn't like it, but he understood her need to be in charge of her own body. Now he didn't stop himself from crossing the patio. He did, however, use all his willpower to prevent himself from reaching for her.

"Come back tonight," he told her. "Eight. I'll have dinner ready."

Her dark eyes leveled his. "You don't seriously want to keep this up."

Ethan took another step until their bodies lined up perfectly, then he framed her face with his hands and covered her lips with his. She arched against him and let out a little moan, the same moan that always drove him out of his mind. This time was no different.

Just as quickly as he'd started the kiss, Ethan released her and took a step back.

"I'll see you at eight."

Ethan moved back into the penthouse and headed toward the bedroom. As dramatic exits went, that wasn't the best. But, considering they were in his suite, he couldn't exactly leave.

He waited until he heard the elevator chime her departure before he sank onto the edge of the bed. What the hell had he gotten himself into?

He'd always prided himself on keeping all emotions and people out. That was how he'd lived for the last twenty years, but he was going to have a hell of a time continuing on that path. Harper needed him, and so did their child. That slap of reality had Ethan more afraid than anything. Was he even capable of opening up? Could he be what a child even needed?

Money was one thing—he had plenty of that and could offer everything Harper and a child could ever want. But he wasn't going to be a hands-off dad…he just had no clue how to open his heart just enough for his baby and not get hurt.

After being shut down for so long, Ethan wondered if any of this was even possible.

Three

Harper clutched the notepad and pen as she circled the open ballroom once more. She would've already had all the last-minute notes she needed had her mind not been preoccupied volleying back and forth between redecorating Mirage and decorating a nursery.

Focus.

She had to remain true to her sister's dream and to this job. Yes, her life had taken a complete twist from what she'd planned, but she wasn't going to get off course. She had a job to do, and what type of mother would she be if she just gave up on her commitments whenever life got difficult or scary?

There. See? She was already thinking like a parent... not that she knew much about that role. The closest thing she'd had, her one and only life support, Carmen, had been taken much too soon. Harper would give anything to have her sister/parent/best friend here to offer advice or a hug. Harper could definitely use a consoling hug right about now.

Tears pricked her eyes, and she cursed as she blinked them away. Getting upset wouldn't change a thing, which was why she needed to focus and stay on track.

Harper jotted down a few more last-minute notes as she slowly made her way around the open space once again. This room was currently closed off from the rest of the resort. From what Harper could gather, when Mirage first opened, there had been quite a few extravagant dances and receptions here. She wanted to bring this room back to life and compete with the newer resorts that had opened recently.

The resort was beautiful; the location demanded nothing less. But there were areas that had been overlooked and neglected for a few years, and she was overly excited, if a bit nervous, to revamp the entire place and polish those hidden gems back to a new sparkle.

She'd already done all of her designs and had everything ready to go. But the nervous worker inside her wouldn't let her rest. She wanted to look at each room, making sure there were things she hadn't forgotten.

This would undoubtedly be the most pivotal project she may ever take on. Perfect timing considering she was also taking on the most important role of her life...mother.

Harper glanced to her notes and realized in all her wanderings over the past couple of hours, she'd managed to doodle a baby rattle on the paper.

She'd always been one to leave random drawings on her work, but she truly had no idea she'd done this on her sketches and notes about the ballroom.

Good thing she was the only one who would see these, right?

Just as Harper started to leave the grand ballroom, her cell vibrated in her dress pocket. With her free hand, she pulled it out and stared at the text from her doctor's office confirming her appointment.

She'd make a quick day trip to LA and be back here and on the job, hopefully before her father arrived. She really wished he'd get here, because there was only so much she could do without getting his approval. Oh, she'd love to have free rein, but he wanted to give one final okay to everything before she was let loose with the funding to start tearing up all the old to replace with new.

Sliding the cell back in her pocket, Harper made a mental note to tell Ethan about the appointment when she met up with him later. And that was just absurd. Going back to his penthouse for dinner like they'd been doing, like they were just going to continue this fling as if nothing had changed.

Talk. That's all they could do tonight. There would be no sex. In fact, she'd find the ugliest thing she'd packed and wear it. Granny panties, too. Nothing sexy at all was going into that penthouse suite.

Actually, Harper should probably tell him they'd have dinner in one of the main restaurants. That would be best all around. They needed to curtail their desires. They'd had sex—amazing, toe-curling sex—but now it was time to move on and figure out what was best for all three of them.

First, she needed to learn more about the man. How cliché could she be? Meet a man, have a fling and still know nothing about him. Of course, she knew that if her sister was here, Carmen would likely buy Harper a drink and toast to the fact Harper had finally let loose and had a good time…then she'd promptly follow that up with some very real advice on how to embrace this new role of becoming a mother.

Of the two sisters, Harper had definitely been the more responsible, the more structured one. Carmen had taken after their mother with a little more of a free-bird mentality. Harper had never let loose…ever. She'd been so structured—until she came here.

But now more than ever, she'd need that structured mind-set to get through the project and her pregnancy. She needed a timeline and some type of plan for the future. Raising a baby while trying to grow a business would be a challenge, she had no doubt. But she wasn't going to worry about that now. Millions of women worked and raised children. Harper had no doubt she could and would do just fine.

Harper slid open the door to the hallway and jumped.

"Ethan," she gasped. "What are you doing here? This area is closed off to guests."

If his wide eyes were any indication, he was just as surprised to see her.

"So why are you here?" he countered.

Harper chewed the inside of her cheek and considered how much to share. He'd find out everything at some point anyway, right? They'd well surpassed the fling stage.

"I was actually hired to revamp this resort," she confessed. "That's why I've been here so long—and will be for a while longer. I need to be part of each step and oversee the progress."

Ethan stared at her for another moment, his brows drawn in as if trying to figure something out. Silence settled between them, and she wondered what could be so interesting about what she'd just said.

"So you're an interior designer?" he asked.

"By default," she half joked. "My sister was the truly brilliant designer, but she always said I had a good eye. She opened Two Sisters Design a year ago and begged me to join her, so I did. And then… Well, you know she passed, so here I am."

Ethan remained silent as he shoved his hands in his pockets and rocked back on his heels. The quiet air seemed to crackle around them, and she hated this awkwardness that settled between them.

"And that's enough of my backstory for now."

She hated the tension that had slid between them. She had no clue how to act or what to say around him, which seemed rather odd considering they'd spent nearly every night together over the past month. Flings were messy, they were confusing, they were…

Harper mentally gave herself a slap in the face to wake up. She wasn't having a fling anymore. She was having a baby with a man she barely knew. Which raised the question of his presence here now. Had he followed her?

"What are you doing here?" she asked again.

Ethan shrugged. "Just wandering around."

"This whole area is closed off." The manager knew who she was and allowed her access to any part of the resort. "How did you get in here at all? The door to this whole portion is coded."

"Code?" he asked with a shake of his head. "The door was wide-open when I came through. I wasn't aware it was closed off."

Harper couldn't tell if he was lying or if the door had in fact been left open. He had no reason to lie that she knew of, but she was sure she hadn't left the door open. Something was off, but she couldn't exactly say if it was Ethan or not.

"So, you're revamping the entire resort?" he asked, glancing over her shoulder into the open ballroom. "That seems like quite the undertaking for one person."

"I'm up for the challenge. Besides, I have a team that will come in and do the physical work."

No need to tell him this was her first solo gig. She couldn't treat this as a rookie project. Now more than ever, Two Sisters needed her entire focus.

Ethan took a step toward her, and that focus tilted. How could a man wearing a pair of well-worn jeans and a T-shirt be so damn attractive? Oh, yeah. Because she knew every inch of muscle tone that lay beneath those clothes.

He slid the back of his knuckles across her cheek. Harper's breath caught in her throat as she closed her eyes and relished in his touch. When would she get over this? Would his touch always make her body tremble, her head foggy, her belly tingle?

"Ethan," she whispered as she focused back on his hungry gaze. "We need to stop this."

"That's impossible," he countered, bringing his other hand up and framing her face. "The attraction won't stop just because we say so. Is there a rule that I shouldn't want you just because you're pregnant? Because I want you now more than ever."

More than ever. In their month-long fling, she'd come to crave him more than anything, so she understood his need. They matched each other so perfectly in the bedroom. Never before had she experienced anything like Ethan Michaels…and the man was quite an experience.

"You can't say things like that." She was going for a scolding tone, but for reasons she ended up sounding breathless.

"Why? Because you're trying to lie to yourself and pretend you don't want me, too?"

She couldn't lie to him, and she shouldn't be lying to herself. She had to face every obstacle head-on.

"I just think…"

Harper shook her head and stepped away.

"I *can't* think when you're touching me and looking at me like that," she stated more firmly.

His lips quirked as he took another step toward her, then another until he'd backed her fully into the open ballroom. Without a word, he reached behind him and slid the doors closed, the smack of the wood echoing through the room.

"You love every second of my touching and looking."

That throaty tone sent shivers through her.

"We're having a baby," she stressed, as if he didn't already know. "You said yourself that changes things between us."

"It changes the timeline," he stated, reaching for a curl and wrapping it around his finger. "It means we'll be part of each other's lives forever. But it sure as hell doesn't change anything else."

Harper tipped her head and stared up into those bright eyes. She could get lost in them, and on several nights, she'd done just that. There was something so powerful and mysterious about Ethan that she'd never been able to put her finger on. She'd wondered what brought him here, what kept him here, and now she really wanted to satisfy her curiosity.

Before she could dig deeper into this man who'd swept into her world and turned it upside down, he eased down and captured her lips. Ethan slid one hand through her hair and the other hand over the small of her back, pressing her body into his.

The response was instantaneous as the familiar tingle swept through her. Harper gripped his biceps, just trying to hold on to some sort of stability. This kiss was no different than the others. Every one created an arousing sensation that slithered from her head to her toes and made her knees weak.

Ethan spun them until her back came in contact with the wall. Wedged between two rock-hard surfaces, Harper arched against Ethan's chest as his lips traveled from her mouth down the column of her throat. She tipped her head to the side, giving him more room to work even as a niggling voice in the back of her head kept telling her all the reasons she shouldn't be doing this.

Harper really wished that voice would shut up and just let her enjoy the moment. Ethan's hands bustled up the skirt of her maxidress. That voice grew louder, telling her to put an end to the madness.

"Need you now," he murmured against her ear. The warmth from his breath sent even more shivers coursing through her.

There was a clatter as something fell to the floor and tapped the side of her foot. She ignored it.

Then ringing sounded through the room. She ignored that, too, because Ethan's talented fingertips cruised along the edge of her panty line and silently promised delicious things.

The annoying ring persisted.

Her cell.

"Wait." Harper pressed her hands to Ethan's chest. "My phone."

"Leave it," he demanded.

She pressed a bit more until he muttered a curse and took a step back. Her dress fell back around her legs and she tapped her pockets, frantically searching for her cell before realizing it had fallen to the floor. Harper grabbed the phone and turned away from Ethan before she managed to control her shaky hands enough to look at the screen.

Of all times for this call.

"I have to take this," she stated over her shoulder.

Without another word, she walked toward the wall of windows and accepted the call. Her hands shook and her body still hadn't caught up with the fact there was nothing fabulous on the verge of happening right this minute.

"Hey," she answered, trying to catch her breath. "I've been wondering when I'd hear from you."

"I've been a bit busy," her father said. "But I just boarded my jet and wanted to touch base. My assistant mentioned you wanted to change some things from the original design."

"I do. In fact, I sent not only the new ideas but a new budget."

All correspondence for the renovations was supposed to go through her father's second in command. She didn't ask why—Harper was just glad to have the job.

"Good work," he praised. "I'll take a look at everything, but I trust your decisions. I'll have my assistant get with you about the new materials so you will be ready when your crew arrives. She mentioned next week sometime?"

"That's right," Harper confirmed. "I can't wait for you to see my vision."

Harper glanced over her shoulder, not surprised to see Ethan staring back at her. She turned her focus back toward the window.

"And when are you coming exactly?" she asked.

"Soon," he promised. "But I want you to go ahead and get started. Bring in however many people you need, and I'll okay the budget. I know I wanted to approve everything, but I simply don't have the time and I believe you'll do right by my resort."

A thrill shot through her at the idea of starting to bring her vision to life in a matter of days. After months of waiting, wondering if she could live up to her sister's vision and hopes, now was Harper's chance to prove to everyone, especially herself, that she was worthy of this position her sister had trusted her with.

"Everything else going smoothly?" he asked. "I trust your upgraded suite and the staff are nothing short of perfection."

"Oh, yeah. Everything is fine."

I'm just pregnant by a virtual stranger from a heated fling, but that shouldn't hinder my ability to choose paint swatches and lighting fixtures.

"I can't wait to see you," she said, smiling and wanting happiness and excitement to come through in her tone. "Hopefully soon."

"Hopefully," he repeated in a monotone voice. "I have to run. My assistant will be in touch."

He disconnected the call, and a little twinge of sadness clipped her heart. He didn't seem excited to actually see her, only concerned with the renovations. Granted, he'd gone over two decades without having a child, so she had to cut him some slack. Carmen had a different father and had actually had a relationship with him.

But Harper had been in Robert's life for several years now, and he still hadn't fully embraced fatherhood like she'd hoped.

Especially now, she wished he'd be a little more...

well, just a little more. Anything would give her hope they might eventually get to a loving relationship. Was he even capable of that?

She knew he'd been married years ago, but his wife had passed unexpectedly. Since then, Robert had remained single. Maybe that death had made him wary of further relationships. Maybe if she reached out to him in that regard, by listing their commonalities, perhaps then he'd open up a little more.

But since their first meeting, he'd been distant. They'd randomly meet up for dinners when he came to town or he'd call once a month to check in, but she usually got the impression he was doing so because he felt he should and not because he actually wanted to.

"Everything all right?"

Ethan's question pulled her from her thoughts. Harper spun around and forced a smile.

"Fine. That was just my father."

No need to mention her father owned the resort. Ethan didn't strike her as the type looking for money, but it was still best to keep some things to herself for now. Besides, it wasn't like she was some kind of heiress. She wasn't expecting anything from Robert—except for the chance to build some kind of emotional connection.

Another chime sounded through the room, and this time Ethan pulled his cell from his pocket. He glanced at the screen, sighed, then shook his head.

"I need to deal with this," he told her. "Come to my room tonight."

That potent stare from several feet away was no less

powerful than when he touched her bare skin with those big, strong hands. He always made her feel delicate... something she'd never felt before in her life.

"You already ordered me to be there," she reminded him, pretending like he didn't affect her. "If I'm free, I will come, but not because you say so."

Ethan chuckled as he started closing the distance between them. "You'll be there."

He stepped into her, laid his lips across hers and just as quickly stepped back.

"See you at seven."

"You said eight earlier," she reminded him.

He shot her a smile. "I want you sooner."

With a cocky whistle, Ethan turned and walked from the room, leaving her standing there irritated and completely turned on. Not that she'd ever let him know how much he affected her. Of course, someone as confident as Ethan probably already knew.

Well, she'd show him. She may be having his baby, but that didn't mean she had to jump at every command. She didn't know any other woman he'd had dealings with in the past, but Harper prided herself on being independent and unique.

Ethan Michaels might have finally met his match.

Four

"I guess he's held up in Barcelona," Ethan said, swirling the ice sphere in his bourbon. "The longer I wait, the more pissed off I get."

Granted, his edginess could have something to do with the fact he was still reeling from the bomb of impending fatherhood—and from the way that seven o'clock had come and gone over an hour ago without Harper arriving in his room.

He wasn't going to chase her down, and he wasn't going to beg. He'd never begged for a woman in his life, and he sure as hell wasn't going to start now...even if she carried his child.

"You're sounding a little edgier than usual," Dane stated.

His twin's statement pulled Ethan back. He set the

tumbler on the bar and flattened his hand on the counter. Ethan thrived on control, especially over his own damn life, but here he was watching it play out and all he could do was wait.

"I'm fine," he ground out.

"Trying to convince yourself?" Dane asked.

"I just want this to be over and for me to have my resort back," Ethan insisted. "That's all."

He wasn't ready to announce the pregnancy.

"As soon as you do, Stella and I want to get married," Dane moved on. "We don't feel it's right until all this is settled. Plus, it will give us another reason to celebrate."

Dane deserved the happiness. Hell, they both did. After nearly twenty years of planning, working their asses off to regain money and power after having it stolen, this reckoning was long overdue.

"You keeping out of trouble while you wait on your family reunion?" Dane asked.

"Nothing I can't handle."

Maybe a lie, but whatever.

"Do you even know her name?" Dane chuckled.

Oh, he knew her name. He'd moaned it enough times while he learned every inch of Harper's curvy body, and damn if he wasn't itching to touch her again. Hell, he was in trouble. Not just because of the pregnancy, but because he'd let himself get agitated by a woman. He'd let her under his skin just enough that he was getting cranky without her.

Sex muddled the mind. That had initially been the reason he'd used it. He'd wanted that foggy state to numb the pain; he'd wanted to disappear outside reality for a time.

But Ethan had never been in this type of situation, and he refused to lose control over his emotions or get swept up in some spiral of feelings.

"I'll take that as a no," Dane replied.

Ethan pulled himself from his thoughts and cleared his throat. "I'll keep you posted on Robert, but I'm expecting him very soon. Go ahead and make those wedding plans."

Just the words *wedding plans* sent a shiver of terror through Ethan. He supposed some people went for that type of lifestyle, but he was just fine without a binding piece of paper, thank you very much.

"Oh, Stella is all set as soon as I give her the go-ahead," Dane laughed.

Ethan couldn't recall the last time he'd heard his brother laugh. The foreign sound actually had Ethan smiling himself. They'd waited so long to claim their own happiness, their destiny.

The chime from the private elevator echoed through the open penthouse. There was only one visitor he was expecting, and she was overdue.

"I'll keep you posted," Ethan promised. "Give Stella my love."

He ended the call and slid the cell back into his pocket, trying to pretend he wasn't anxious to see Harper step through that sliding door.

She'd kept him waiting, likely out of spite. For reasons he couldn't explain, he found that sexy as hell.

Ethan remained by the bar, resting his elbow on it and forcing himself not to react when she came in.

Moments later, the elevator whooshed open, and there she was. All sexy in a little floral skirt that wrapped around her hips, paired with a bright blue tank. The simple yet skimpy outfit showcased those lush curves even better than the dress she'd had on earlier, and while he might not know her well, he knew she'd changed on purpose. The little minx.

She stared at him across the penthouse, silence filling the space. Finally, she broke eye contact and started across the room like she belonged here.

"Dinner is cold," he told her as she passed by the domed plates on the dining table.

Harper ignored the table and moved into the living area, where she took a seat on the white sofa. She sank down and propped her long, dark legs up on the glass table. Her red-polished toes brushed the edge of the floral arrangement that the cleaning staff frequently changed out.

"I already ate," she stated, crossing her ankles and meeting his gaze. "I hope you didn't wait. I got held up."

Likely waiting him out just to prove she could.

"I didn't wait," he lied.

He hadn't eaten a bite. He'd been frustrated by her absence, worried over the pregnancy news, irritated at Robert for being so damn late. Too many emotions and not enough space in his head to store them all had soured his appetite.

"I wasn't late on purpose." She flashed him a grin

as if she could read his mind, which only furthered his irritation. "I ran into a couple who couldn't find their restaurant, so I escorted them. Then when I left there, I ran into a little issue with a bellhop who was a little less than friendly, so I tried to smooth that over with the guests."

Ethan wouldn't put up with anything less than a loyal employee who respected each visitor that passed through their doors. He would make sure to keep an eye out and ears open for that subpar bellhop. He'd already been making mental notes of stellar employees he'd encountered. And the less-than-stellar ones.

"What made you intervene?" Ethan asked, taking his tumbler and crossing to the living area.

He rested his hip against the sofa across from where Harper sat. She stared up at him and shrugged.

"I think everyone should be treated with respect, and I figured the employee might be having a bad day. I was just trying to help."

Interesting.

"And did everything get worked out?" he asked.

A wide smile spread across her face. "Of course."

"So you design and you play referee." Ethan took a sip of his bourbon. "What other secrets do you keep?"

Harper laid a hand over her belly, and Ethan swallowed. No surprise there, but everything else about this woman was a mystery. He didn't know her, not in the ways a man should know a woman who was going to have his child.

"I think a few secrets are necessary, don't you?" she asked.

Considering he kept quiet about his true reason for being there, he would have to agree. But still, he didn't like not being in the know about everything that affected him. Shouldn't he know everything about the woman who was going to have his baby?

"I think there's more to you than what you show," he replied.

"That's a coping mechanism." She dropped her feet to the floor and crossed her legs, the move easing up the slit in her skirt. "Care to tell me what keeps your secrets bottled up?"

"Coping mechanism is a valid reason."

She'd completely nailed his reasoning for keeping his cards close to his chest. The little tidbits he uncovered kept revealing how their lives paralleled.

But right now, he wanted to intersect. Those legs all on display were tempting him to the point he was ready to unwrap that skirt and show her just how much he craved her.

"You've got that look in your eye," she murmured.

He gripped the tumbler. "And what look is that?"

Ignoring his question, Harper came to her feet, propped her hands on her hips and stared back without making a move toward him.

"You invited me here for sex," she said, crossing her arms and doing amazing things to her breasts in the process. "Dinner is a given."

"Well, you're here."

The corner of her mouth twitched, and he knew she wanted to smile. He had her. She couldn't dodge his advance, and she wasn't even trying. That wasn't vanity talking—it was the truth. And in all fairness, he was just as drawn to her...not that he'd admit any such thing.

"I'm here to discuss our child," she retorted. "We do have an obligation to make some sort of plan and keep our clothes on during the process."

"I'm well aware of what we need to do. When are you seeing a doctor?"

"Tomorrow," she told him. "Everything is set for this initial checkup. I'll have a few tests and an ultrasound, too."

Ethan started to close the distance between them. "Is there a problem?"

"Relax." Harper held up her hands and shook her head. "Routine testing. It's all perfectly normal during a pregnancy."

"How do you know so much already?" he asked.

Harper laughed, and he hated how he suddenly felt like an ill-prepared moron. How was he not on top of this and more in control? He'd have to do some research and read up on pregnancies and babies. He had a feeling he was about to get an education he'd never planned on in his life.

"For one thing, I'm a woman, and I've had pregnant friends," she started. "We like to discuss such things over fancy dinners. Another thing, when I called my doctor, the nurse went over month by month what to expect during the appointments. I took some notes, but I also remember what she said. There's a lot that they test for, just as a matter of routine—checking the boxes to make sure there are no surprises."

Routine. Okay, he could handle that.

What the hell would he do if something went wrong? He knew absolutely nothing about babies or pregnancies. When he got together with his friends, it was to discuss his nightclubs or a limited-edition bottle of bourbon they'd purchased. On occasion they'd discuss trading in their jet or their car for the next upgrade. But never, not once, had the topic of children come up.

"I want to be with you during the doctor's visit."

Harper stared at him for a moment, and he thought she was going to argue, but ultimately she nodded.

"I assumed as much," she said. "I wouldn't keep you out. No matter how all of this happened or how shocked we are, we're in this together if that's what you want."

"I want to be in my child's life." A ball of emotions rolled through him. "My mother passed when I was a teen, and I never knew my real father. There's no way I'd abandon you or this baby."

A soft smile spread across her face. She tipped her head, and he couldn't identify the look in her eyes.

"What?"

She took one step forward, then another. "You haven't shared much about your life. Just hearing you open up without me asking…it just means so much now."

There was no way to go through this with her and not get personal. As much as he kept his heart guarded, his life to himself, he couldn't be completely closed off to Harper. But he would have to decide how much to share and when to do so.

Once the resort reverted back to him, he wouldn't

mind telling her everything. Right now, though, he just needed to focus on Robert.

But he still wanted to get to know more about Harper—especially when it came to her connection to his resort.

"Did you get any more planning done today?" he asked. "When we parted, you were talking about the ballroom."

"I called in my team, and we're going to get started." She positively beamed when she spoke. Obviously decorating was her passion. "The ballroom won't be where we begin, though. I'd like to start with the lobby, because I want the first major impact to be the focal point of the resort. I want guests to believe they've stepped into another world when they arrive."

Could she be more perfect?

For the job and to be the mother of his child. Not for him. But the vision he'd gotten a glimpse of was exactly how he wanted to renovate his mother's dream. All of this was falling into place so perfectly. Robert would foot the bill for a grand redesign just in time for Ethan to take over.

Oh, the victory was going to be sweet.

"And what are your thoughts for the lobby?" he asked, crossing to take a seat next to her on the sofa.

She stared at how close he sat, hip to hip, but not reaching for her in any other way. Yeah, he was just as surprised by his restraint, but the talk of the resort trumped his desires…for now.

Harper's eyes darted back to his face. "You want to talk about my work?"

Ethan stretched his arm along the couch behind her and nodded. "Yeah, I do."

He didn't need to justify his reasons. She'd already mentioned she wanted to get to know more about him, and turnabout was fair play. Besides, he'd rather start with her...with Mirage.

Harper's dark eyes narrowed before she shook her head and eased back into the cushions. "I was thinking of a water wall, something tranquil and serene. I want the guests to immediately relax, and water is proven to do that. Decorating isn't just about what looks pretty—it's about making people feel good about an experience."

Ethan listened to her, watched how she spoke with those delicate hands. Her eyes shone in a way he hadn't noticed before. The more she discussed the style, the more he knew his mother would have loved everything this resort would become.

And that was ultimately what he wanted. Of course he deserved to have this place back in his name, but once he was in charge, he had every intention of paying tribute to the remarkable woman who'd started it all.

He remembered her favorite color being green. Somewhere, in some place, he had to incorporate that shade. Perhaps in the Caribbean-themed restaurant or the Italian one. Something classy with green and white, maybe a touch of gold.

"You've put quite a lot of thought into this," he told her when she stopped talking and he'd logged his thoughts for later. "You ran through nearly every detail and didn't once look at a note in your phone."

Harper's mouth spread into a wide smile—the action sent a sucker punch right to his gut. How the hell did a grin have his breath catching in his throat? She'd flashed a saucy smile at him before, but nothing like this. She genuinely beamed.

"Because I have a vision and it's all in my head," she explained. "Every aspect of what I want to do with this place is like a living piece, and there's no way I'll forget a single one of them."

"But...you do have everything documented. Right?"

Harper rolled her eyes and laughed. "My sister would come back and haunt me if I didn't have everything documented and backed up."

"Did you work long with your sister before she passed?"

Damn it. He hadn't meant to ask. That was too personal, and a question that would only lead to exposing vulnerability.

"Not long enough," she murmured, her smile instantly fading. "I believe everything happens for a reason, but I just can't fathom why she was taken at such a young age. I mean, surely there was so much more for her to accomplish. You just don't realize how fragile life is until someone intimately close to you is gone. That sounds clichéd, but it's true."

Ethan had experienced those very same thoughts for so long after his mother passed. He knew that pain, knew that aching void that nothing or no one could ever fill.

Ultimately, that's how he ended up living a reckless life, stumbling into owning and operating a string of profitable nightclubs and making billions. Yeah, everything happened for a reason, but he'd give it all back to have his mother.

"Then accomplish it for her," he finally stated.

Harper chewed her bottom lip for just a moment. Some women did that as a coy way to flirt, but he knew her well enough to know she wasn't playing some cutesy little game. Her thoughts were on her sister, on their business. Her loyalty and commitment were admirable traits, and as much as this whole baby news was still a shock, Harper had qualities he'd want his child to possess.

"I plan on doing just that," she confirmed. "Every job I take will be done in her honor. I won't fail, because I refuse to even allow the thought to enter my mind."

"Spoken like a true businesswoman."

Harper laughed and came to her feet. "I don't know about that. I never had my heart set on business, but I am creative and enjoy using my mind for work. I sort of just stumbled into the business part."

"That's how the best companies get started," he explained. "I never thought about going into business, either. Yet here I am."

Harper tipped her head to the side as her dark brows drew in. "And what are you, exactly? Jet-setting playboy tycoon?"

Ouch. That wasn't what he'd expected her to say. Clearly he hadn't made the best impression. Even though her description was dead on, he still didn't like the words coming out of her mouth.

Now he had to show the mother of his child—and prove to himself—that he was so much more. Because he was, damn it.

It was time for him to step up his game...and maybe open up that bank of emotions he'd kept on lockdown for nearly two decades.

Five

Maybe she shouldn't have thrown out such a label. From the pained expression on his face, she wasn't sure if he was reeling from the insult or trying to figure a way to defend himself.

"Ethan, I—"

"No." He held up a hand. "I'd say you're accurate. I work hard, I play hard. I won't apologize for the man I am. But at the same time, I'm not heartless and I'm not a bastard. I enjoy all aspects of my life, and sometimes I use coping mechanisms."

Sex. He used sex to cope…but what pain was he masking? Who had hurt him?

"Back to business," he said, circling around. "Because that's something where we can relate. I stumbled into my area as well, but after ten years, I'm damn good at what I do, and I couldn't imagine anything else."

"Nice dodge on your personal issues," she half joked.

With a mock nod, he smiled, and that gleaming grin had her nerves curling low in her belly. She had to remember even though he used sex as a line of defense, he still used it. She couldn't fall for his charms simply because he was irresistible and she carried his baby.

She'd done her fair share of using when it came to this fling...which was all the more reason to keep mentally reminding herself what this was and what it wasn't.

"So what is it that you do?" she prodded when he said nothing.

"I own nightclubs on both the East and the West Coasts. I'm acquiring a bistro in France, and I've been sniffing around a couple of pubs in Scotland. I plan to branch out globally and make a big impact."

Harper tried to hide her surprise. "Impressive résumé. I wouldn't have thought international business."

"Is this a job interview?" he asked with a quirk of his brow and a naughty grin.

"It wasn't, but since you're the father of my child, maybe we should dig deeper."

His smile slowly faded as the muscle in his jaw clenched. "My mother passed when I was a teenager, my stepfather was a bastard and stole my inheritance, and my twin brother is engaged. Oh, after the military I landed in a nightclub, got completely drunk for reasons that don't matter, and somehow that actually *did* turn into a job interview, which ultimately gave me my start as a business owner. And that brings us up to date."

Harper listened to the very abbreviated version of Ethan's life and figured he'd hit every highlight of what had caused him pain. But she opted to home in on the one area she hoped wasn't so crushing.

"You have a twin?"

Something in his dark features softened. "Dane. He lives in Montana on a ranch."

Harper laughed. "Quite the opposite of your beach-bum life."

"Quite the opposite of me," Ethan muttered in agreement. "He's kept to himself since Mom died, so the fact that he met someone who could penetrate that wall... She must be amazing."

"You don't know her?"

Ethan shook his head and came back to his feet. "We haven't met. Dane and I have been working on a project for a while that has kept us apart. We email or talk on the phone, but I haven't seen him for a few years."

There it was again. That pain.

Ethan paced to the wall of windows and stared out at the moonlight shining down onto the ocean. Harper knew she couldn't let this moment pass.

"You know, my sister has only been gone six months, and that void is unlike anything I've ever known."

Harper rose but didn't cross to him. She just felt like she should be on level field or be ready...for whatever.

"I don't know how I'll feel once years pass," she went on. "The thought of not seeing her is something I still can't fathom."

Ethan glanced over her shoulder. "It's not that I don't want to see him. I love my brother. But something shifted when our mom died. We dealt with the loss so differently. Then we were so set on trying to care for ourselves after our stepdad left us with nothing."

He turned back to the window, his shoulders rigid, his hands shoved in his pockets. Harper's eyes darted around the space, and she spotted the half-empty tumbler on the bar in the corner.

"Dane and I went into the army," he went on, his tone calm, yet broken. "We kept in contact, but it was so random and the interactions were spaced farther and farther apart. Then we banded together and decided to go after the bastard who stole from us."

Intrigued, Harper took one step, then another. Before she realized, she stood right behind him.

"Did you catch him?" she asked. "I hope you left him penniless and suffering. Stealing from kids after the loss of their mother is a new level of asshole."

With a mock laugh, Ethan turned to face her. "Oh, he's in his own league. But no. We haven't caught up with him yet. Soon. Very soon."

Harper knew Ethan would stop at nothing to seek revenge, and she honestly couldn't say she blamed him. He'd had years to let this anger fester and build.

"So is that what brings you here?" she asked, reaching up to smooth the frown lines between his brows.

Ethan gripped her wrist and pulled her arm behind her back, making her arch against him. "I'm done talking about him. There's only one person I want to focus on right now."

Harper's body responded—the tingling from head to toe had her closing her eyes and waiting on those lips to cover hers. Despite having told him no more sex, Harper wasn't sure she was strong enough to turn him away.

She was here, wasn't she?

But a moment later, Ethan released her, and she stumbled to keep herself upright. Harper opened her eyes and glanced around to see Ethan striding toward the kitchen. He removed dome lids from the plates on the long island. She hadn't even noticed the dishes there before.

"Sit down," he demanded. "You need to eat."

Harper remained in place, crossing her arms over her chest. "I ate dinner."

"Well, you're eating for two now."

She didn't even try to prevent the eye roll. "I always thought that saying was so silly. A tiny fetus doesn't need a large meal."

Ethan stared at her a moment before shrugging. "I don't know a damn thing about pregnancies, but I read that pregnant women might need frequent meals, and I thought you should eat."

Harper stared at the spread and realized he'd ordered all this food…for her. Well, for the baby, but the fact he truly cared and wasn't completely about ripping her clothes off was a little sweet.

But only a little. She couldn't blow his gestures out of proportion. That would mean she wanted him to be kind and do cutesy things.

Ugh. Her hormones were all over the place.

"I don't know what to do here," he admitted. "But if you could come eat some fruit or something. Hell, whatever."

Well, wasn't that adorable? Someone was insecure and fumbling over his words. Yet seconds ago he'd been more than in control when he'd had her arched against him and silently begging him for more.

The man likely wasn't used to being anything but in total control. Considering their current situation of being thrust into parenthood, she'd say that control would be a long time coming for both of them.

"Did you eat?" she asked, making her way to the wooden bar stool.

He nodded and pulled out a bottle of water from the fridge and set it in front of her.

"So you intend for all of this to be for me?" Harper laughed and selected a plump raspberry. "Have you ever seen me eat this much?"

She popped the piece of fruit into her mouth and welcomed the delicious burst of flavor. Maybe she was a little hungry, but she'd never admit as much.

"I wanted to make sure you had a good variety," he defended.

"There's enough variety here for the entire third floor."

Ethan's lips curved into another toe-curling grin. "I'll take that as a thanks for my gesture."

Harper grabbed a handful of blueberries. "And is that why you did this? So I'd be indebted to you and reward you as you see fit?"

"Talking dirty to me will get you everywhere."

"Do you think of anything besides sex?"

Ethan's intense stare stretched across the island, making her wish she could take those words back.

"My mind is typically on work," he finally answered. "But when I'm around you, those thoughts become a little muddled."

"Should I be flattered?"

Ethan circled the island and took a blueberry from her hand and held it up to her lips. "Flattered isn't what I want you to feel."

Her gaze dropped to that mouth that had caused her so much pleasure. When she shifted her focus back to his eyes, there was that passion, that desire she'd come to recognize from him.

"So we are back to sex," she murmured, taking the berry from between his fingertips. She might have bitten him lightly, but just so he knew who was in charge here.

"Even though you're carrying my child…" He stopped, shook his head and blew out a sigh. "*Especially* because you're carrying my child, I want you more than ever. Maybe we should cool it, maybe we should end this fling, but I keep asking myself why. We're adults who more than enjoy each other's company, and we both have outside issues that are put aside when we're together."

She'd been telling herself those same things. Granted, she'd also told herself she needed to keep her clothes on around Ethan from here on out, but suddenly everything he said made sense. Why shouldn't she seek this happiness, even if for only a few moments longer? There was no rule that just because he wasn't putting a ring on her finger, they couldn't continue their passionate nights until it was time for one of them to leave.

Right?

He took another blueberry and slid it back and forth across her lips. When she opened, he pulled the fruit away and covered her lips with his.

Harper fisted her hands in her lap to prevent herself from reaching for him. A woman had to maintain some sort of self-control. But the way he made love to her mouth only had her wondering if that was a promise of more to come. The man made a kiss a full-body assault, because there wasn't a spot on her that wasn't ready for more of his touch.

Ethan eased back; that smirk on his face and gleam in his eye had her gritting her teeth. He wanted her to beg, but she had more pride than that. This was still a fling, and she could walk away at any moment.

Without a word, he popped the berry into his mouth as he trailed his fingers up her bare arms. Oh, damn. She should've walked away before now. But she'd known what would happen when she came here. She was a glutton—there was no denying the fact she still wanted him. It wasn't smart, but she was human and had wants and needs she wouldn't deny herself.

Maybe one more time. She'd let this happen once more and then they'd start discussing the future and their child.

"You're thinking too hard," he murmured against her ear. "You're mentally arguing with yourself about being here."

"I couldn't stay away."

The truth slid from her lips before she could stop herself. It was almost like the man had cast some magical spell over her. She knew it was happening, and she simply didn't care.

"You made me wait," he scolded. "You did that on purpose."

"Maybe," she admitted.

His lips grazed the side of her neck, and Harper dropped her head to the side to allow him all the access he needed.

"I never thought a headstrong woman would appeal to me."

Huh? Did that mean he was attracted to her for more than a heated fling? No, that's not what he meant. It couldn't be.

For a split second, Harper thought about calling him on his statement, but those clever lips eased down to the scoop in her tank and the next thing she knew his hands were working the knot on her skirt.

Yes. This was what she ached for, what she needed. Just once more, right?

Ethan's hands seem to be all over her, and she couldn't escape the moan as he yanked the knot on her skirt and the material fell to either side of her hips. Ethan wasted no time in pulling her panties down her legs as his mouth worked over her breasts through the thin material of her tank top.

Harper reached for the hem and slid the shirt over her head and off to the side as she kicked away the panties around her ankles. Ethan's eyes devoured her the second he reached around and expertly flicked her bra open. In no time, that unwanted garment had been tossed carelessly away, as well.

Strong hands encircled her waist and lifted her onto the cold island. Harper let out a squeal of surprise but heated all over again when Ethan came to stand between her parted legs.

"You want me to stop?" he asked, his eyes holding hers.

"No," she whispered.

A flare of hunger flashed through his eyes before he dropped to his knees and gripped her inner thighs. Harper bit the inside of her cheek to keep from begging or crying out before he'd even done anything other than drive her mad from want.

She threaded her fingers through his hair as he dropped light kisses from her knee to the point where she ached most. Then he moved to the other leg, and Harper gripped harder.

With a chuckle, Ethan finally settled right where she wanted him. He held onto her hips and jerked her closer to the edge of the counter as he made love to her.

Bursts of euphoria spiraled through her. He'd never done this—nobody had ever done this. She'd never let anyone get that intimate with her. Insecurities and all that.

But Ethan wasn't just anybody.

There was no way to describe all of the delicious tingles coursing through her from his hands, his mouth. She didn't want this moment to end, didn't want to lose this perfect moment of euphoria.

After several minutes of the most exquisite pleasure, her entire body tightened as the experience became too much. Her fingers tightened in his hair, and there was no holding back the cries of pleasure.

Ethan nipped at her inner thigh when her trembling ceased.

"Harper?"

His husky tone broke through her haze, and she realized her eyes were squeezed shut. Coming back down from her high, Harper focused her attention on the man who now stood before her wearing a smile.

"You good?" he asked.

Good? That was such a mild, calm word for the storm that had just wrecked her in the most perfect, amazing way.

"I'll take speechlessness as a positive sign." He leaned forward and nipped at her earlobe. "Now, finish eating, since I distracted you."

Wait…what? Eat? He could think about food at a time like this?

Ethan turned and rounded the counter. Harper glanced over her shoulder, more than aware that one of them was totally naked while the other was fully dressed and picking out a cube of cheese.

"Are you serious?" she asked, easing down off the counter and rounding up her clothes.

He popped a piece of gouda into his mouth and stared across the space. "About food? Yeah. You barely ate."

Harper slid into her panties, then her skirt. Clutching her bra and tank, she pulled in a shaky breath.

"Are you playing a game?"

Ethan's brows narrowed. "Game?"

Harper didn't know if she was more confused or irritated. "Are we not going to finish what we started?"

"By my recollection, you finished—enthusiastically."

Yeah. Definitely irritated. She pulled on her bra and tank, needing the extra armor.

"You didn't."

Ethan shrugged. "I'll live. Are you complaining?"

No, that would make her a bitch.

"I've never met a man like you," she muttered.

Ethan let out a bark of laughter. "I'll take that as a compliment."

She continued to stare as he grabbed a small plate and started adding a variety of fruits and cheese, plus a small finger sandwich. Then he set it in front of the stool she'd been on before he blew her mind.

"Take a seat," he told her. "You can eat and tell me more about your renovation ideas."

She wasn't sure what his angle was by playing her and keeping her guessing, but she wasn't about to let her guard down. She was going to figure out Ethan Michaels one way or another…something she should've done before he permanently landed in her life.

Six

The next morning Ethan was still questioning who the hell he'd become. Since when did he have a willing woman—a sexy-as-hell willing woman—naked and ready for him, and not take full advantage of the situation?

With the time difference between California and France, Ethan had finally gotten out of bed at 4:00 a.m. after a restless night. He'd made yet another call to his Realtor to see where they stood on the final bid they'd put in on the waterfront bistro.

And yet it wasn't his latest quest that had his mind occupied or his sleep lacking. He knew he'd get the property, but he didn't know what the hell he was going to do with Harper.

She'd been naked, panting, sitting atop the island in

his kitchen. He'd given her an orgasm and what did he do next? Not take her to the bedroom or even take her right there on the floor.

No, he'd made her a charcuterie board and they'd chatted until midnight about water walls, open courtyards with lush plants, infinity pools and special couples' rooms for secret fetishes.

She'd thought of every aspect of this adults-only resort, and maybe that's what had him so distracted. He'd come here for the sole purpose of gaining back what should have been his. Hearing Harper talk about the future makeovers had him itching to get Mirage in his name sooner than ever.

So now he was sexually frustrated, confused at his own actions and not so patiently waiting to hear about his bid.

Ethan padded to his kitchen to make coffee, but his eyes landed on the island. As if he needed the reminder of how damn sexy she'd been, utterly bare, completely at his mercy and more than willing to give him more.

But something shifted after hearing her speak of her late sister and seeing the way Harper was so determined to complete her job despite having been dealt the bombshell of a pregnancy. The level of admiration he had for her now was something he hadn't expected, and he needed to sort it out before he made a fool of himself and she mistook his generosity for something more.

There could be no *more*. He was too busy, too devoted to his businesses. Not only had he had a mentor who had entrusted him with the nightclubs, but Ethan had branched out on his own. He'd made something of himself when everything had been stripped away. There was no way in hell he'd let anything or anyone sever the strings he'd so delicately forged to keep his life stable.

Not to mention the fact he and his twin were attempting to rebuild their relationship that had been upset when their mother passed. They'd each dealt with the loss in their own ways...opposite ways. Those ultimately pulled them in different directions.

So, no. Ethan didn't have the room in his life to add in more. While he would never, ever turn away his child and he fully intended on being a hands-on dad, he wasn't about to entertain the idea of a relationship with Harper.

Thankfully, she had her own agendas and felt the same about long-term commitments. They'd have to come to some common ground for co-parenting. He wouldn't give up any of his career, and he would never ask her to, either. They could work together to make everything work in the best interest of the three of them.

Ignoring the island as much as he could, Ethan brewed a cup of coffee and headed out onto his private balcony overlooking the Pacific Ocean. The view never grew old. Ever. Perhaps that's why he had been so willing to take over the nightclubs that were on the coasts. He needed that view, that freedom that came with staring out at the expanse of water and dreaming of bigger, better things. There was always another conquest to obtain, always another goal to reach.

He waited until he was halfway through his cup of coffee before he gave in and texted Harper. Last night they'd discussed breakfast but hadn't made any definite plans. He also knew she was a morning person, and the sun was up, so he figured so was she.

My place. Breakfast.

Ethan set his phone on the side table next to his patio chair and sipped his coffee. A second later the vibration caught his attention. He gave the screen a glance and smiled.

Already ordered room service. Should be there any minute.

And a second later, the chime on his intercom alerted him to a guest wanting to come up to his penthouse.

He'd never thought a take-charge woman would be attractive, mostly because he thrived on calling any and all shots. But something about Harper and her assertiveness turned him the hell on.

Within five minutes, his concierge had delivered quite the spread and had set it all up on the balcony. Ethan started to tip, but the young man said it had already been taken care of by Miss Williams.

He wasn't sure he'd ever had a woman a step ahead of him. Ethan wasn't quite sure what to make of that, but one thing was certain. He liked it.

Damn that woman for making him want her more than he ever should.

The elevator chimed once again, indicating a visitor. She had the pass code, so he didn't have to ring her up anymore.

The door slid open, and Harper stepped out. Her hair had been piled up on her head, stray curls tumbling down around her neck. She sported some red bathing suit cover-up with that damn red bikini beneath.

It was those tiny red scraps of material that had drawn him in to begin with. Was she purposely taunting him? Not that he needed any help in finding her desirable.

"I'd kill for a cup of coffee," she stated, marching through his penthouse and straight to the balcony.

He followed her out. "I'll make you a cup."

"No," she growled, shaking her head. "I'm trying to really be good because of the baby."

"You can't have coffee?" he asked, holding on to his own mug.

"Too much caffeine isn't good." She grabbed the pitcher of orange juice and poured a hearty glass. "I mean, I could have one cup, but I'd rather not."

He probably should figure out all the dos and don'ts regarding pregnancy.

"Are you feeling okay?" he asked, setting his mug down on the table and getting a glass of juice for himself.

"I'm starving and tired. And also a little nauseated, but I think I just need to eat."

She eyed his discarded mug. "You know, you can still drink that. I'm not offended."

With a shrug, Ethan reached for a plate. "I didn't

think you were offended, but I don't see any reason why I can't do this journey with you."

She stared another minute before shaking her head and muttering something he couldn't quite make out.

They made their plates in silence and settled into the corner at the table for two beneath a bright yellow umbrella.

The moment they sat down, Harper made a face and held on to her stomach.

"Maybe eggs weren't a good idea," she mumbled.

Ethan stilled. "Are you going to be sick?"

Harper closed her eyes and seemed to be taking some deep breaths. Without waiting for an answer, he took her plate away. If the eggs were the culprit, he'd throw them all out.

He took the plate and the dish of omelets into his kitchen.

When he came back out, Harper wasn't looking so ill.

"Sorry about that," she stated, glancing up to him when he approached the table. "I read that smells can affect you more strongly when you're pregnant, but I hadn't experienced that yet. So, eggs are definitely out. Well, unless they're in a cake. Then I'm sure they're fine."

Ethan laughed, thankful she was feeling better and still had her sense of humor.

His cell vibrated in the pocket of his shorts just as he sat. He spared her a glance as he pulled the phone out.

"Excuse me," he stated before glancing to the screen.

His investigator. Not a call he wanted to put off, since

his investigator wasn't one to call just to chat. There had to be a development where Robert was concerned.

"I need to take this," he told Harper.

"Oh, go ahead." She waved a hand in his direction. "I'm fine."

Another reason to be attracted to her. She didn't demand his undivided attention, and she understood the importance of work.

Ethan moved to the other side of the balcony and answered the call.

"Marcus. What's up?"

"Nothing dire, but something I found interesting in Robert's communication with his assistant."

Ethan gripped the phone as he stared out onto the calm ocean. "What was said?"

"Apparently Robert is making his way there, which you know, and he should be landing in the next day or so."

"And?" Ethan prompted.

"We know he has a daughter based on his background checks, but he's never mentioned her publicly. This is the first time since we've been tracking recently that he's actually going to see her in person. Apparently, she's staying at Mirage."

"She's here?" Ethan asked.

He didn't know anything about Robert's daughter except that she existed. He had no intention of involving an innocent in his quest for revenge. Everything going on was between him, Dane and their stepfather.

"I figure since you're there, maybe you could look her up."

"Give me her name."

It would be useful to at least know who she was so he could keep an eye on her for when her father showed. The old bastard might try to sneak in and out.

"Harper Williams."

Ethan stilled, his gaze jerking across the balcony to the woman in question.

"She's going to have dark curly hair, dark eyes. Her mother is Jamaican, and you know the father."

"I know exactly what she looks like," Ethan muttered.

Ethan disconnected the call without another word. Keeping an eye on Robert Anderson's daughter would be no problem at all...considering she was the mother of his child.

Seven

Harper smoothed a hand over her belly, which wasn't flat and never had been. But she couldn't wait to feel the baby bump, the little kicks—she'd even heard women discuss baby hiccups.

Despite being dealt the blow of a child when she wasn't even in a committed relationship, she wasn't sorry she was going to be a mother. Sure, the timing wasn't the best, but she couldn't help but wonder how Carmen would've reacted to the news of being an aunt.

Having a baby was exciting…this morning queasiness, not so much.

Ethan came back to the table, and she prayed her berries and croissant stayed down. She'd been feeling a little saucy this morning when she donned her bikini, but yacking all over the place would surely ruin her sassy vibe. Just when she was sort of getting the hang of this newfound confidence…

Every thought vanished when she saw Ethan's face.

"Everything okay?" she asked.

He hesitated a moment before grabbing his cloth napkin and placing it in his lap. With a forced smile, he nodded.

"Just some interesting developments with work. Nothing I can't handle."

"It's awfully early for work to already be catching you off guard."

"Time means nothing in my line of work," he informed her. "With things running on two coasts, plus my acquisition in France, I work all hours."

Harper smiled. "Then maybe you better get that coffee back, because you look like you need something stronger than juice."

His eyes raked over her, and she couldn't help but tremble.

"I'm sure it's nothing a sexy woman in a red bikini couldn't cure."

A wave of dizziness hit her that had nothing to do with his charming words. Harper closed her eyes and pulled in a slow breath, willing the moment to pass.

"Harper?"

His firm yet gentle grip on her arm had her shaking her head slightly.

"Give me just a minute."

He didn't say another word, but she heard his chair scrape against the concrete floor and the next instant she was swept up into his strong arms. Harper didn't protest as she laid her head on his shoulder, but she kept her eyes closed. The nausea seemed to be subsiding, but she wasn't so independent that she'd turn down the most romantic gesture known to woman.

When he laid her down, Harper lifted her lids and focused on his face, which was so, so close to hers.

"Okay?" he asked, obviously worried.

"It comes and goes," she stated, settling into the sofa cushions. "No need to worry. The doctor said this was normal. It's just annoying."

"You looking like you're ready to pass out isn't normal to me."

Aww. He cared. His instant reaction wasn't an act. She wasn't used to someone other than her sister showing concern for her, and as independent she was, there was no way she could deny that having someone care made her feel special.

"I assure you, I'm fine." She patted the side of his face. "But this is adorable."

Ethan's lips thinned, his brows drawing in as he eased back and stared down at her. "I'm not adorable," he grumbled.

Harper closed her eyes and rested her arm across her forehead. "Well, I think so. I'm feeling better, by the way. The dizzy spells just started yesterday, and they don't last long."

"I think you should stay here."

Harper lifted her arm slightly and opened one eye. "I'm here, aren't I?"

"You should stay in my suite for as long as we're

both at the resort," he amended. "It's ridiculous for us both to have a place, and mine is larger."

Harper listened to what he said but didn't say a word.

"With a better view," he added.

"I'm not just playing house with you while we're here." Harper let out a mock laugh. "You're not serious."

"Do I look like I'm joking?"

Ethan eased down to sit on the table in front of the sofa.

Harper shifted to look at him as his idea ran over and over in her mind. Why on earth would he suggest such a thing? He didn't want a relationship any more than she did.

"Is this because I wasn't feeling well?" she asked. "Because that's certainly no reason for me to move my suitcases up here."

"You're having my child, and I want to make sure you and our baby are taken care of. That's not too much to ask, is it?"

Not when he phrased it like that, but still. Why did she need a keeper? She'd gotten along this far in life without someone hovering over her. She and Carmen always looked out for each other, but that was different.

She and Ethan were obviously still attracted to each other, the baby threw out the whole "fling" thing and now they had to make some tougher decisions.

They were adults who wanted the same things: freedom, career and a good time. There wouldn't be any messy complications, even if the whole pregnancy thing would eventually make things a little tricky. They were both on board with no relationships.

Sex, though…she'd be a fool to turn down twenty-four-hour access to that body.

"I'll think about staying here with you," she informed him, unable to hide her smile.

"Sounds like a yes to me."

Harper started to sit up, but he placed his hands on her shoulders.

"No rush," he said, easing her back down. "I can bring in your breakfast."

"I think I'm done with food for the time being."

She settled deeper into the cushions and stared up at the white beams stretching across the ceiling. Her designer eye loved how the penthouse seemed to be its own private beach house. The cozy style of the beams and the openness to the ocean breeze. The wall of windows and balcony doors were elements she hoped to incorporate into more rooms. She definitely planned on upgrading all of the oceanfront suites to have more of an airy, relaxing feel.

"You're working."

Harper glanced to Ethan at his accusation. "Guilty."

"You had that look on your face," he said with a grin. "I know because I've seen it in the mirror."

"I just can't wait to dig in to this place. My team will be here next week, and I've spoken to the manager so we can hopefully have a nice, smooth transition from one area to the next and not disrupt the guests too much."

"Maybe adding in some perks would be the way to go," he suggested.

Now she did sit up—slowly, but she was feeling better. "What do you mean?" she asked.

"Nobody wants to be inconvenienced at all when they plan a getaway," he explained. "Maybe for the duration of the renovations, couple's massages could be free with a one-time limit per stay. Or one free room service meal. Just something so they know you're aware of their needs. People save and spend quite a bit to come here."

Harper listened to him, taking in his suggestion and fully intending to run it by her father's assistant.

"I wouldn't think someone like you would ever have a thought about saving money now that you have everything you want," she finally stated.

Ethan's face tightened, the muscle in his jaw clenched. "There was a time in my life where I watched every single dollar that came in and out. Just because I have a padded account now doesn't mean I'm not aware of other people's perspectives."

Never in her wildest dreams would she have guessed jet-setting playboy Ethan Michaels cared so deeply about how others lived. But everything he suggested sounded so perfect, she only wished she had thought of the idea before.

"You're a pretty smart businessman," she joked.

"I refused to be anything but smart when it comes to business."

His tone left no room for humor, and Harper had to admire him even more. There were so many layers to Ethan, and part of her wished she was at a point in her life where she could look for a husband. Eventually she did want a family and a loving man, but she had to devote her life to Two Sisters and to her child for now.

Part of her couldn't help but wonder if this baby was a special gift. Like maybe she was being given another chance at family after her sister's passing.

She'd never given much thought to faith or the idea of a grand plan before, but with her mother off gallivanting who knows where, her father not much of a hands-on guy and her sister gone, maybe this was just a blessing in disguise.

"I think I'll have the concierge bring my things up later this afternoon," she finally said, circling back to the offer. "If you're sure you won't get sick of me."

Ethan's smile widened, the naughty gleam in his eye stirring her body.

"Oh, I'm sure. In fact, I think we should get married."

Eight

"Married?" Harper screeched.

Ethan had to admit the words that had come out of his mouth had surprised the hell out of him, too. But he wasn't about to retract them. This was Robert Anderson's biological daughter. No way in hell could he let this prime opportunity pass him by.

Obviously he never would've mentioned marriage had she not been pregnant, but why not?

"I know we both agreed that we're not the marrying type of people," he started as the idea blossomed inside his head. "And I'm not saying I'm ready for the whole ordeal of marriage, but think about this for a minute. We are both driven in our careers, so we get each other. We both want what's best for this child."

Harper blinked, then shook her head. Yeah, the idea

was absurd, but the longer it was out in the open, the more he found himself wanting this to happen.

The reasons for his insane demand were mounting. His mother had been single, raising two boys on her own for quite some time before Robert had entered the picture. But his baby had a father who badly wanted to be part of its life. Given that, where was the logic in him living somewhere else and having to shuttle the kid back and forth between them? There was no way he'd want to give up any amount of custody of his own child. But the real reason he was pushing for marriage, if he were being completely honest, was that he wanted every single leg up on Robert Anderson he could get.

"That's it?" she asked. "Because we both like to work and we want a well-rounded kid, you think we should marry?"

Ethan shrugged, not backing down, but not about to beg. "People have been married for less."

"And divorced in no time when the marriage fails."

"I don't fail," he countered. "Ever."

Harper stared at him, but his gaze didn't waver. The more she pushed, the more he had to see this through. This was the riskiest, most asinine move he'd ever made, but the payoff would be everything.

Dane would have already called him a dumb ass and told him to think this through, but Ethan *had* thought it through...for a few seconds, anyway.

"I can't just marry you," she repeated.

"Think about it."

He came to his feet and started back toward the balcony. He could at least wheel the cart inside so he could finish his breakfast. Harper might pick around, too, if the food was in front of her.

"Think about it?" she mocked at his back. "You tell me to think about it and then walk away?"

He spared a glance over his shoulder. "I'm hungry."

By the time he had moved their breakfast and drinks back inside, Harper didn't look like she wanted to rip his head off anymore, but she still kept that questioning gaze locked on him.

"What changed?" she asked once he took a seat in the cushy white chair next to her. "You never wanted a relationship."

"I still don't," he explained. "This is nothing more than business. We both want what's best for our baby, and we're both workaholics. It's the perfect merger, really."

Harper stood and crossed to the cart, where she poured herself another glass of juice. "A merger."

"Are you going to keep repeating everything I say?"

She turned to face him with a smirk that made him wonder if he would get her to come around. He wouldn't have it any other way. Ethan never backed down from a challenge, and Harper, their baby and Robert Anderson were all part of his past, present and future. No challenge, no *payoff*, had ever been more important.

"Are you going to keep insisting this is a good idea?" she retorted.

Ethan crossed his ankle over his knee and leaned back in the chair. He didn't want to appear anxious or worried. He was neither of those. What he was, was determined, and that's precisely how he'd gotten this far.

"If you can move beyond the shock of my proposal—"

"Is that what that was?" she mocked, taking a seat back on the sofa and curling her legs to the side.

"Of sorts," he conceded.

Harper gripped her juice glass and stared down at the contents. Ethan waited, letting the kernel of an idea roll around in her head. She seemed skeptical, but she was still in discussion, so he wasn't discounting her just yet. He had a way of being persuasive.

"You can't just ask me to marry you as some sort of business plan," she argued, but her voice lacked the heat it once had. He was winning her over.

Dane had always said Ethan was the reckless one, the twin who jumped headfirst into things without thinking them through.

Well, here he was again. Wait until Dane heard about all of this.

"I figured you'd appreciate an honest, laid-out plan," he stated. "We marry, we raise our child together, we don't have to get our attorneys involved. We both can continue doing what we love and have someone who understands and is actually supportive at our sides while we share the parenting responsibilities."

Harper pursed her lips and leveled a stare at him. "And what happens when you want another woman or I see a guy I'm interested in?"

Ethan didn't hesitate to leap from his chair, circle the table and brace himself over her. With one hand on the arm of the sofa and the other on the back near her shoulder, he leaned down so there was no question about how serious he was on this topic.

"There will be no other men," he growled. "My wife will be in my bed and only my bed. I won't share."

Most people would be intimidated by his snarl and low tone, but Harper continued to stare, and she even had the nerve to pat his jaw and smile.

"Calm down there, sweetheart. Your proposal is getting less and less attractive." She narrowed her dark eyes and flattened her palm on his cheek. "There had better not be any other women, either. I also don't share."

A burst of accomplishment spread through him.

"Is that a yes?" he asked, inching closer.

When she didn't say a word, Ethan shifted to slide one hand over her bare thigh. He watched as her lids lowered for the briefest of seconds, her breath caught on a sharp inhale. Without taking his eyes off her face, Ethan trailed his fingertips over her stomach, straight up to the little knot tied between her breasts.

"I... I never said yes," she muttered.

"But you're thinking about it."

He gave the tie an expert yank, allowing the scraps of material to fall aside.

Harper closed her eyes and chewed on her lip. He had her...in every way he wanted her. She'd marry him; she'd be in his bed. He'd ultimately have his revenge on her father. He worried how she'd react, but he had to keep moving with this plan and take baby steps when it came to Harper. He had to choose his words, his actions, carefully so she didn't completely hate him at the end. He had to make her understand his side once everything was out in the open.

There was no way Robert Anderson deserved a

daughter like Harper, and the man sure as hell would have no part in the life of Ethan's child.

"I'm not thinking at all right now," she told him as he cupped her full breast in his palm.

Ethan eased his other hand behind her back, pulling her forward until she sprawled over his sofa. He wanted her on display before him. A body like Harper's was meant to be worshipped.

"Are you feeling better?" he asked, realizing he should've asked before now, but damn it, he couldn't resist her.

The health of her and the baby came above all else, though. Even his revenge against Robert would have to come second to Harper and the child.

"I'm feeling pretty good." Harper reached for him, her fingertips curling around his shoulders. "Don't stop, Ethan. And don't deny yourself like last night."

Oh, he fully planned on making sure they were both pleasured.

"You wore this on purpose," he accused, pulling her sheer cover-up off her shoulders. "Did you want to drive me crazy?"

Her delicate mouth tipped into a smile. "Maybe."

Ethan's body stirred at the little minx beneath him. That red material against her dark skin shouldn't be such a turn-on, but hell if it wasn't. Harper exuded sex and fantasies. Every time he had her, he wanted more. Now was no exception.

Harper wriggled out of the cover-up and the bikini top. He loved that a curvy woman had the confidence to wear something so sexy, so skimpy.

He hooked his thumbs in the waist of her little bottoms and eased them down her silky legs and flung the garment over his shoulder.

"You better take off those shorts fast," she warned. "Because I was cheated last night."

Ethan pulled his shorts off and laughed. "You were more than satisfied, so I'm not sure how you were cheated."

Her fingers ran over his abs, and his arousal spiked.

"Because I didn't get to see or touch you," she told him. "Not like I wanted."

"Then by all means." Ethan settled onto the sofa and eased back into the corner of the sectional. "Have your way."

Harper came to her feet. She tucked stray tendrils behind her ears as her eyes raked over his bare body. There was such a hunger, one that matched his own, staring back at him.

When her focus shifted to his eyes, Harper took a step forward and lifted a knee. She settled her legs on either side of his hips, perfectly straddling his lap. Her breasts came right in front of his face and Ethan wasted no time in reaching for her with both hands.

"If I marry you, there will be rules." She rested her hands on either side of his head and leaned down. "My rules."

"Yes, ma'am."

His body ached for her to join them and right now. He'd agree to anything she said. He'd never been at a woman's mercy before, but she was doing a damn good job of calling the shots now.

Harper leaned down and captured his lips beneath hers as she sank down onto him, finally joining their bodies.

She eased her hips back and forth, going much too slowly for his liking. Ethan took a firm grip of her hips, holding her in place while he set a new rhythm.

Harper let out a sharp cry, followed by a moan, so clearly she wasn't complaining. With her eyes shut, she tossed her head back and braced her palms on his chest. Her short nails bit into his skin, and he had to hold back his own groan at the delicious sting of pain.

Ethan held on to her hips, loving how she felt like a woman with all those luscious curves. They were so compatible, so in tune with each other.

Marrying her would be the best decision on both fronts.

Harper let out another cry of pleasure as her body tightened around his. She eased down onto his chest and claimed his lips once more as her climax hit her. He wasn't far behind.

Those lips of hers could make a man come undone all on their own. But it was her sweet little pants and cries that had him following her into oblivion.

Ethan fell into the moment and didn't worry about what would come next. She'd all but agreed to the marriage, and Ethan wanted this to happen fast. Before Robert arrived…and before he came to his senses.

Nine

"Say that again."

Ethan chuckled at his brother's response, but Dane wasn't joking. What the hell was his twin thinking?

"I said I'm getting married," Ethan repeated. "It's sudden, I know, but I promise you'll meet her."

"Are you out of your damn mind?" Dane growled, earning him a questioning stare from Stella across the room.

Dane gripped the cell and came to his feet, suddenly unable to sit still and listen to this nonsense.

"Who the hell is she?" Dane asked. "I just spoke to you a couple days ago, and you made no mention of any woman. Now suddenly you're getting married?"

Stella's eyes widened as he neared. Dane shrugged, because he couldn't make sense of this crazy notion of his brother's, either. Ethan had always been one to make rash decisions, but marriage at a time like this? What the hell? He'd never been serious about a woman, let alone mentioning he ever wanted that lifestyle.

"I'm marrying Robert's biological daughter."

Dane stilled. He reached for the back of the sofa and kept his gaze on his fiancée. She reached for his hand on the cushion and squeezed, offering him silent reassurance.

"Robert's daughter?" Dane repeated. "You're not seriously using a woman to get to—"

"No. I'm not a complete bastard," Ethan scoffed. "I had no idea who her father was when we started sleeping together. We were just a fling, and then she ended up pregnant and now I find out—"

"Pregnant?" Dane yelled.

Stella closed her eyes and shook her head. Yeah, that pretty much mimicked his internal reaction, as well.

"What the hell, man?"

"Obviously I didn't mean for that to happen," Ethan retorted. "Everything has snowballed here, and I'm doing the best with the situation I've been dealt."

"The best? You're calling this your best?" Dane slid his hand from beneath Stella's and reached up to rub his head, which suddenly started pounding. "You're bringing a child into this chaos? Are you even thinking of the goal we agreed on?"

"You think I'm not set out to take Robert down?" Ethan demanded. "That's all I've wanted since Mom died. We're so close, I'm not letting anything get in the way."

Dane blew out a sigh and reached for Stella's hand again. She always calmed him, always kept him focused on what was important. For nearly two decades, Dane and Ethan had wanted to get back at Robert for taking their legacy from them. Dane had reclaimed the resort in Montana, and now it was Ethan's turn. Then they planned on ruining Robert for good.

Yet now his reckless, playboy brother was veering off course, and Dane couldn't do much about the mess his twin was in.

"Listen," Ethan started in a calmer tone. "I had no clue who Harper was until this morning. She was just the woman I was having a fling with. I found out she was pregnant yesterday. Once my investigator told me who she was, I moved on that information. I'm not making apologies."

No, Ethan would never apologize. Not for this and not for closing in on himself when they lost their mother. Dane had needed his brother, had needed *someone* to seek comfort with during the hardest time in his life.

But Ethan hadn't been there. Not emotionally, anyway. Then Robert had stolen their financial stability and disappeared. Ethan had enlisted in the military, and Dane figured he might as well, too. Where else did he have to go? At least the military would provide a unit and stability.

"Now what?" Dane asked.

Stella wrapped her arms around him and laid her head on his shoulder. He loved this woman. He'd found her when he least expected to find anyone. He'd been so set on grabbing Mirage with both hands and never letting go.

But Stella had stepped into his path, and somehow he'd managed to get everything he hadn't even realized he wanted.

"Oh, wait." Dread hit Dane hard. "She doesn't know you hate her father, does she?"

"She's not aware of our history, no."

Dane let out a string of curses that had Stella smacking his chest.

"You know this not going to end well for you," Dane added.

"I'll get Mirage. That's what matters."

Dane snorted. "You don't mean that."

His brother sighed heavily on the other end. "No, I don't. I'm trying to keep my focus on the end result, but someone is going to get hurt, and now that all of this is in motion, all I can do is try to take the brunt of the blow when it happens."

Dane felt sorry for Ethan. For the first time in…well, ever, Ethan was feeling the ramifications of his actions, and Dane was truly worried.

Someone was going to get hurt, but Dane couldn't help but wonder if they were all going to feel the backlash from this series of events.

Harper stared over the various marble designs. All were in the same price point, all were equally stunning and all would make a killer impact in the lobby of Mirage.

But she couldn't decide.

She also couldn't stop thinking of Ethan's ridiculous half-assed proposal and her reply. What was she thinking? Sure, she could come up with some very necessary ground rules, but then what? Were they just going to play house and raise a baby like they were a happily married couple without having any kind of relationship beyond physical compatibility and a business agreement?

Sex could only take them so far. At some point, they'd have to actually do things together if they wanted this to succeed for the sake of the baby.

And how archaic did that sound? Was he just marrying her because of the baby? He'd made valid points of how they were both workaholics and they understood each other, but Harper had always envisioned marrying for love. Call her old-fashioned, but she truly believed there was a man out there for her.

Ignoring the marble slats on the desk, Harper pulled out her cell and brought up her texts.

Then she dropped her phone onto the desk and closed her eyes.

This wasn't the first time she'd started to message her sister for advice. In the past several months, Harper couldn't count how many times she'd started to call or text. How did she deprogram herself from that? Would there come a time when it would just click into place that this was her new normal? That there was no family to go to for advice?

Her mother had already stated that she'd raised her kids and now it was her turn to live. Her father was... well, not very loving.

Who did she have?

Harper truly hated this moment of self-pity, but she would like just one person to confide in. Someone she trusted to give her sound advice on what she should do.

Who knew when she came to Mirage over a month ago that she'd be in this situation? A baby, a proposal, a project of a lifetime. There was so much change, so much happening all at once, she didn't know where to direct her focus.

She flattened her hands on the desk, and the lighting caught the gold bracelet. At least she had that reminder of her sister. Little glimpses were warming, especially now when she needed to feel closer to Carmen.

The chime from her phone had Harper pulling from her thoughts and redirecting her attention to the new email. She quickly opened the message from her father's assistant.

The new budget was a go, and he'd even allotted an additional quarter of a million dollars. Well, that was certainly generous and shocking, but she didn't believe she'd go that far over.

Still, having a beautiful piece of property to renovate with virtually no top budget was a designer's dream come true. Carmen would have loved this.

This project meant so much for so many different reasons. Harper's giddiness rivaled that of a toddler on Christmas morning in a room full of unopened presents.

Harper shot off a quick reply and attached some of the files with her design sketches for the lobby, sample suites and dining areas. She doubted Robert would ever look at them, but she figured she'd show him anyway. He hadn't asked for an image yet.

Did he even care about the end result? Did he care she was here? She understood that he was a businessman first and a traveler second. She wasn't sure where father ranked in that list, but she hoped somewhere.

Every part of her wanted him to show up soon so they could maybe have a nice dinner and discuss goals and the future. This pregnancy was going to be a new chapter in her life, and she wanted him to be part of it. Harper just wasn't sure that he would want the same.

She was well aware of what Ethan wanted, though.

Marriage. A business marriage. How unromantic could a proposal get? Because she was pretty sure this one was up there on the sucky proposal chart.

Still, she might just be falling for the charmer. She'd never admit such things. He didn't want love, and she couldn't exactly say what she felt toward him, but the emotion was more than like and more than just sexual.

So where did that leave her? On the verge of saying "I do" to a man she knew very little about in the hopes that they could build some future together? Were futures really built on heated beach flings and accidental pregnancies?

Harper sank down into the leather office chair and stared back at the marble samples. She couldn't even choose a shade of rock—how in the hell was she going to make a final commitment for the rest of her life?

Ten

"What am I missing? There has to be a subtle blue undertone for the calming effect. But what if it's too much?"

Ethan crossed his arms over his chest and listened to Harper mutter to herself as she stood at the desk and stared down at samples. He couldn't help but smile. She hadn't even noticed him. When he'd been about to knock, he'd been struck by how stunning she was standing there.

Oh, the punch of lust at the sight of her was nothing new, but the way she'd tipped her head and chewed on the tip of the pen was downright attractive. He admired a woman who got swept into her work. He'd already established that she was devoted, but seeing her so hands-on, so committed, was something he couldn't dismiss.

Then she'd started chatting to her work, and he didn't want to cut in. Sometimes he was a total gentleman. But she was just so adorable that he was afraid he'd start laughing in a minute—which meant it was time to announce himself. If she looked up and saw him seemingly laughing at her, the conversation would not go well.

"Am I interrupting?" he asked, tapping his knuckles on the door frame.

Harper jerked her attention to him, then shook her head. "Just having a staff meeting."

Ethan laughed and stepped on into her makeshift office. She'd told him where it was, but this was the first time he'd actually made it down here. He'd had no reason to, really. Up until now, his days had been his, his nights had been hers, but they'd always been in his penthouse.

He took a glance around the small space that wasn't much bigger than a storage closet. Actually, this used to be a storage closet. Ethan recalled the many times he'd visit Mirage with his mother when he'd been younger and how he'd explored and learned every inch of it. She was so proud to show him the place that would one day be his. She'd done the same with Dane at Mirage in Montana.

Which was why he and Dane were stopping at nothing to make all of this right. Their mother had had a plan for the things she loved most in the world—her sons and her resorts. And just because she was taken from this earth all too soon didn't mean they shouldn't see her vision through.

Marble slats covered the old, narrow desk. She had a laptop open to a mock design of the lobby. Ethan whistled.

"That looks amazing," he stated, circling the desk to get a closer view. "This isn't your sister's design."

Harper came in beside him, her shoulder brushing against his. "How do you know?" she asked. "You never met Carmen."

"I don't know," he murmured, his eyes studying every last detail. "There's something about the blues here that make it seem like you're walking on water, but it's so subtle and calming. But then you throw in a subtle punch of red with the flowers and that's just so you."

"That's what I wanted."

"The lighting is magnificent," he went on. "You can't see the fixtures, but they're perfect. And that island of fresh flowers in all white…brilliant."

"The lobby is the first thing guests see when they check in," she stated. "I mean, I know they look online for every available picture, but once they step inside after traveling to get here, I want them to just let all the stress and exhaustion fade away. I want to transform them to another world where everyday problems cease to exist."

Ethan turned his attention to her as she spoke. Her eyes never wavered from the screen as she explained her reasoning behind such extravagance.

"You've managed to capture everything," he told her.

Harper blinked, turning her eyes to his. "Well, I don't know about that. I'm sure there will be stumbling

blocks, and issues will come to light that I'm not thinking of right now."

"That comes along with any business plan," he replied. "The important thing is to know how to handle
the hardships when they come along."

Harper pursed her lips. "I don't plan on failing."

"I have no doubt you'll make this a complete success."

She offered him a smile that did something unfamil-
iar to his...heart?

No. That was absurd. His heart wasn't involved in
any of this. Well, *part* of his heart was very involved
in all of this—the portion that belonged to his mother,
to her memories and legacy and the future she'd promised him.

"I think if I can get through losing my sister, I can
get through a bump in the road of this project," she
told him.

Ethan wanted her to remain focused on her reasons
for doing this, because ultimately, this remodel would
carry over into his ownership.

"Tell me more about Carmen," he commanded, easing his hip on the edge of her desk, meeting her eye
level.

Harper stared for a moment before she crossed her
arms over her chest. He wondered if she did this as a
coping mechanism to hold in the hurt. He'd had to break
himself of just that after his mother had passed.

"She was bright. Not only smart, but she just beamed
everywhere she went. It was impossible to see her and
not smile."

He could say the same exact thing about Harper, but he didn't interrupt.

"She had a big heart and an even bigger outgoing spirit." Harper let out an adorable laugh. "She was always dragging me to parties or out to dinner with her friends. She'd do anything to get me out of the house."

Ethan reached for her hands and gripped them on his lap. "You didn't get out much?"

Harper shrugged, glancing down to their joined hands. "Let's just say I didn't have the confidence my sister did."

She smiled and glanced back up to him. "I was always overweight and shy in school. My sister was the popular cheerleader and homecoming queen. I was so proud to be her sister, but I never felt like I measured up."

"That's absurd," he replied before thinking. "What does size have to do with anything at all?"

Harper tipped her head. "That's so easy for a man to say. Being a plus-size girl in high school is not the funnest of times. Changing for gym class while trying to hide that roll over your pants or going shopping for prom dresses when your friends are grabbing their size twos and fours while I'm over there whispering for an eighteen."

Ethan listened but didn't hear pain in her voice. He heard strength and bravery.

"And what made you see yourself differently?" he asked, tugging her farther to stand between his legs.

"I got out of school, where there was too much competition to be perfect," she told him. "My mother started traveling around the world, and my sister and I grew even closer. I realized I have one life, and spending each day questioning what other people thought wasn't the way I wanted to live."

Ethan released her hands and reached for her hips. "That's a pretty smart revelation."

"Well, I kept telling myself that, but it took a while before I started to actually believe the words." Harper rested her hands on his shoulders, the tips of her thumbs brushing along his neck. "My sister constantly urged me to get out more and more, so over the years I went when she asked. Coming here was strictly for work."

"You don't usually travel alone?" he asked. "Get away and just take vacations to treat yourself?"

"I never have. Carmen and I would go places, but this is the first time I've gone anywhere by myself. I was packing to come here and saw that skimpy red bikini." Harper laughed again and sighed. "Carmen bought me that last summer, and I refused to wear it. I tried it on, and she kept telling me how good I looked and told me not to hide a killer body."

"I like your sister."

Harper smacked his shoulder. "You like boobs, so don't act like it was the bikini."

"Why can't I appreciate both?" he asked.

"Anyway," she went on, rolling her eyes. "Circling back to my sister. She's the reason I've evolved so much, and she's the reason I'm here. She started this company and asked me to join her, having more faith in me than I did in myself."

"Sounds like she had faith in you about everything."

Harper nodded, biting her lower lip as her chin quivered just a touch. "She did. I guess I just feel lost without her. It's got me second-guessing my decisions here."

"She wouldn't want that."

"No," Harper agreed. "She wouldn't."

"So why are you doing this to yourself?"

With a shrug, she held his gaze. "Because I don't have anyone to tell me otherwise."

Ethan released her hips and framed her face. "Then consider me that someone. You're brilliant, you're talented and you're going to turn this resort into something magical."

Tears filled her eyes. "You sound so sure," she murmured.

Ethan was positive. There wasn't a doubt in his mind that she'd have Mirage on the bucket list of everyone from suburban housewives to A-list celebrities. Mirage of Sunset Cove would be the place everybody flocked to when they wanted to escape.

And it would be all his.

"I'm positive," he insisted, easing forward just enough to slide his lips over hers.

He couldn't resist her, wasn't even going to try. There was something here that pulled him closer and closer into her world. Not the baby and not the fact she was Robert's daughter. There was a storm brewing inside him.

And he was scared as hell.

Ethan nipped at her bottom lip and smoothed his thumb over the dampness as he eased back.

"Let me see what you're torn between here," he offered. "I know a thing or two about design."

Harper licked her lips, tempting him to clear this desk with one swoop and spread her out over it. But the businessman in him took over. He wanted to know about final decisions, and if he was careful, he might just be able to assist in achieving the end result he wanted.

Blowing out a breath, Harper stepped back and gestured to the samples beside his hip.

"I like them all," she stated. "I can envision each one of those in the lobby, and none of them are wrong."

Ethan came to stand and turned his attention toward the marble slats. He studied each one and then glanced to her screen, where the design layout was still pulled up.

"Which one do you think?" she asked after a bit.

Ethan shoved his hands in his pockets and shook his head. "I want to know your first instinct."

"I told you I love them all," she reiterated.

"No. When you look at them, if you're honest, you're drawn to one."

He watched as she glanced over them, her eyes lingering on the slat with a subtler swirl pattern—the exact option he would've chosen.

"This one was the first one I pulled when I initially asked for the samples," she said, smoothing her hand over the flawless piece.

"Don't doubt yourself," he told her. "You've got this. Not just the flooring, but the entire project. Do you think Carmen would've asked you to join her brainchild had she not had faith in your capabilities?"

Harper smiled. "You're scolding me like she used to."

"Well, maybe someone needs to move into her old spot," he declared. "Speaking of, you never gave me an actual answer to the proposal."

"No, I didn't."

Oh, she was such a tease. He loved every bit of her sass and knew they'd make a great team. He just needed her to officially say yes.

"How could a marriage between us work?" she asked.

"First of all, neither of us likes to fail or admit defeat, so we're already a determined pair."

Ethan moved around her, adjusted the desk chair and placed his hands on her shoulders, easing her down.

"What are you doing?" she asked as her butt hit the seat, her eyes wide as she stared up at him.

"You seem tired," he stated. "I didn't want you passing out on me."

"I seem tired?" she repeated. "Maybe it's because my nights are consumed with a man who has more stamina than a triple-crown racehorse."

Ethan let out a bark of laughter. "I don't know that I'm that active, but I'll take it as a compliment."

"You would," she murmured. "Anyway, I'm not passing out. I've never passed out in my life."

"You've never been pregnant before, either."

She pursed her lips, apparently irritated that she had no comeback.

"Good. Now, circling back around." Ethan rested his

hands on the arms of her chair, stared into those dark eyes and moved on. "The second reason we'd make this marriage work is because we both value family and would want the best for our baby."

"What if I want to marry for love?" she volleyed back.

Ethan jerked back. "Have you ever been in love?"

Harper seemed to roll the question through her head before she answered. "No."

"Can you think of a valid reason, other than love, not to marry me?"

She stared at him and smoothed a hand over her abdomen. "Well, we've only known each other just over a month. I'm not sure how stable our future can be since you started our fling based on a bikini."

"A move I don't regret, by the way."

She rolled her eyes as she went on. "I don't know where we'd live or how I'd carry on Two Sisters Design if I had to move."

"I'd never ask you to give up your life or your dreams," he told her. "Neither of us will have to give up anything. We can work together, we can live in your home or buy a new place. I'm flexible since I travel so much anyway, so our home can be anywhere that's good for your business."

"I can't believe I'm seriously considering this," she muttered.

"I can't believe you're taking so long to agree to what would be a perfect solution."

Harper moved farther away, which wasn't far since the room was so small. She continued to stare at him, and he could only imagine the war she was waging with herself. There wasn't a doubt in Ethan's mind that she'd agree. He *needed* her to agree. He liked things neat and tidy when it came to business, and whether he liked it or not, Harper was part of this scheme. Never in his life did he drop an innocent into his plans, but fate had other ideas for both of them now.

Trying to keep Harper safe from harm was impossible, but he planned on doing his best to protect her as much as he could. He wanted to be there for her once she found out the monster her father was. There was no way she could know already. Someone like Harper wouldn't associate with the likes of Robert Anderson if she didn't have to—her indignation on his behalf when he'd told her about his stepfather had made that clear.

And since she hadn't even connected with her biological father until she was in her early twenties, it was understandable that she didn't know him well enough to see past his respectable veneer. Ethan hated to be the one to have to reveal what a bastard Robert was.

It was best she found out now, though. Robert didn't deserve Harper, and he sure as hell didn't deserve a relationship with his grandchild.

"All right," Harper finally said. "I'll marry you."

Ethan released a sigh of relief. Everything was falling into place, and he was one more step closer to obtaining everything he wanted…and more.

Eleven

Harper's belly continued to roll, and she wasn't sure if it was morning sickness that had moved into the evening hours or if she was still reeling from agreeing to Ethan's marriage proposal yesterday.

Either way, she was out of her element with both new chapters in her life.

And her father was due here soon. Would he even take interest in the fact he was going to be a grandfather or have a son-in-law? He'd barely grasped the whole fatherhood role, so she highly doubted he'd be very interested in donning the other two hats.

Harper eased into the bright blue floor-length gown and wondered how much longer until her waistline expanded. She never thought she'd be excited about getting larger, but she was. She wanted to see that round belly, wanted to embrace the magical gift that only a woman could experience.

The shimmering material caught the light as she turned side to side in the mirror. This dress was going to make Ethan's eyes bug out of his head. Another magical spell women possessed. Men thought they were so tough, so strong, but in reality, a woman could render them speechless with such simple things...like a killer dress. Or a red bikini.

Tonight Mirage was hosting a mock casino night, and she wanted to go mingle with the guests, maybe even get a feel for what some of them thought about the resort. You could learn quite a bit just from small talk with people, and if she simply acted like any other guest, she might just discover the likes and dislikes the others felt toward Mirage.

While her plan for renovations was pretty well set, she could adjust if necessary...especially with that generous added budget.

She'd spent last night in his penthouse...their first night since agreeing to stay together. They were starting this new life since she'd agreed to marry him.

The words still felt so foreign running through her mind. But she didn't regret telling Ethan yes. Marriages were built on much less than what they had, as he'd pointed out.

Harper grabbed her small gold clutch from the dresser and slid her room key and red lip gloss inside. With a snap of the closure, she tucked the accessory beneath her arm and headed for the door.

The second she opened it, Harper let out a squeal and jumped back.

"Sorry." Ethan stood there, fist raised and ready to knock. "Perfect timing."

Harper put a hand to her chest and pulled in a shaky breath. "Perfect timing for a heart attack?"

Ethan's eyes raked over her from head to toe and back up again. Harper's heart beat fast for a totally new reason now. He stood before her in an all-black tux, looking both classy and dangerous. That messy hair had been calmed, but the stubble along his jaw lingered, as if he needed just that bit of scruff to remain true to himself.

"Have I told you today how sexy you are?" he murmured, taking a step forward and backing her into her suite.

"You don't say the words, no," she replied, suddenly feeling like prey...and she had to admit she didn't mind. "But I get the gist by how you look at me. And touch me."

Ethan took another step until he came within inches of her. His hands rested on her hips, and he tugged her pelvis to line up with his. The dress was clearly a hit.

"Let me rectify that," he growled. "You're the sexiest woman I've ever met. You're the sexiest fiancée I've ever had."

Harper laughed and flattened her hands against his chest. "Have there been other fiancées?"

Ethan eased closer, grazing his lips ever so softly against hers. "You're the only one."

Oh, how she wished he truly meant those words.

Was she naive and foolish to want more from him than a businesslike marriage?

"It still doesn't feel like a real engagement," she murmured. "I've never been engaged, though, so I'm not sure what it's supposed to feel like."

Ethan released her and smiled. "Something else I plan on fixing."

Confused, Harper stared at him as he reached into his pocket and pulled out a small box. Breath caught in her throat and her gaze went from the box to his cocky smile.

"I hope you like it." He slowly lifted the lid to reveal a bright emerald-cut ruby nestled in a simple gold band. "It's not a traditional diamond, but we don't exactly have a traditional relationship…if there is such a thing."

Harper couldn't believe the stunning ring he presented to her. Never in her life had she expected him to get an engagement ring. The thought hadn't crossed her mind.

"If you don't like it, we can get something else," he added. "This was my mother's ring. I just figured since family was important to both of us—"

"It's perfect, but how did you get it here so fast? I assume you don't travel with your mother's jewelry."

Ethan smiled and shook his head. "I pay my assistant extremely well to go above and beyond."

She reached for the ring, but he pulled back and took it out. Ethan grabbed her hand and slid the ring on her finger. Harper felt the familiar sting of tears, and she didn't even try to hold them back.

"Are you sure you want to waste this on me?" she

asked, admiring the ring and thankful it fit. "I mean, shouldn't you save this for someone... I don't know. Special?"

Ethan squeezed her hand. "You're the mother of my child. I'd say that makes you pretty damn special."

A tear slipped out, followed by another. Ethan swiped the pads of his thumbs across her cheeks and eased forward. Harper gripped his wrists as he framed her face and slid his lips over hers.

Ethan eased her backward, farther into the suite, all the while slowly making love to her mouth.

Harper's body tingled with anticipation. The silky lining of the gown caressed her bare skin like a lover's caress.

They weren't going to make it to the party downstairs...not while they were busy having their own private celebration.

Harper's dress hit the floor in seconds with a flitter of hands and lips working their way over her body. She stepped out of the puddled material as Ethan continued to walk her backward, leading her toward the bedroom.

But then he turned her in the hall and pressed her back against the wall. Harper wasn't about to have another repeat of the other night in the kitchen when she was bare and he remained clothed. She wanted him, all of him, and she wanted him now.

While his mouth continued trailing up her neck and back to her lips, Harper reached between them and slid his jacket off his broad shoulders. Then she went to work on each little button of his tuxedo shirt until she rid him of that garment, too.

Finally, she eased her fingertips over each taut muscle of his pecs and abs. Ethan growled and reached around to cup her backside as her hands ventured to the top of his pants. She hurriedly unfastened, unzipped and seesawed his pants down his hips.

Ethan took a step back, releasing her as he toed off his shoes and stepped from his pants and boxer briefs. Then he was on her again, gripping her waist and lifting her to meet him.

Instinctively, Harper wrapped her legs around him and was even more turned on by his strength, his hunger and his clear need to have her before they even reached the bedroom.

"Harper," he murmured in her ear as he joined their bodies.

She clung to his shoulders, dropping her head back against the wall. One of his hands rested beside her head while the other held on to her backside. His hips jerked, making Harper cry out. Every single time with Ethan was magnificent and unlike anything she'd ever experienced.

He whispered things to her, nothing she could make out, not when her entire mind and body were absorbing all of the tantalizing emotions.

The swirl of her climax spiraled through her, hitting her fast and hard. Harper bit down on her lip and shut her eyes, wanting to hold every single moment of this bliss inside her without allowing any to escape.

"Harper."

The demand had her jerking her attention to Ethan, whose face was a breath from hers. His body had stilled as hers ceased trembling. She'd shut her eyes, her lashes fanning over her cheeks.

"Look at me," he demanded.

Harper stared into those captivating eyes. Only the light from the main living area filtered down the hallway, leaving half of his face in the dark.

The intensity of his gaze had her wondering what his thoughts were. Was he feeling more for her than lust and camaraderie? Was he ready to take this beyond sex and a business-type marriage?

The flash of vulnerability and emotions vanished from his expression just as quickly as she'd seen them. Ethan started moving once again, but he kept his attention all on her.

Harper threaded her fingers through the hair at the nape of his neck and jerked him in for a kiss. She wanted every part of him he was willing to give…and more.

Ethan opened for her, inviting her lips, just as his body jerked and his hand on her tightened. She swallowed his cry of pleasure and gave a slight tug on his hair.

When he lifted his head, Harper watched as the wave of passion swept over his face. There was something so intimate, so bonding about holding the stare of someone during their most vulnerable moment.

Gradually, Ethan's grip on her lessened as he leaned forward and dropped his head onto her shoulder. The warm breath that hit her bare skin had her shivering and trailing her fingertips up and down his back.

If they could stay like this, maybe she could believe just for a moment that he cared for her the way she desired, the way she'd dreamed of someone loving her. Could he ever? Would he eventually want a deeper connection? She thought she'd seen a glimpse of something in his eyes earlier…but maybe it had just been wishful thinking.

Slowly, Ethan released her. Harper straightened out her legs and dropped them to the floor. Her muscles protested, and she held on to his biceps.

"Not too steady?" he asked.

Harper shook her head. "Give me a second."

Ethan scooped her up in his arms. "I've got you."

Harper wrapped her arms around his neck and rested her head on his shoulder. No matter how independent, how strong-willed any woman was, when a man pulled the ultimate romantic move, it was time to settle in and enjoy the ride.

She only hoped this would last longer and grow to mean more, because she couldn't have a one-sided relationship. She deserved more.

Twelve

"You look good wearing that ring."

Ethan crossed his arms behind his head and admired Harper as she walked bare, save for the ruby ring and the gold bracelet she always wore, into the adjoining bath.

"Do you think we missed the entire party?" she asked, grabbing a short red robe from the back of the door.

That woman made the color red look damn good.

Ethan laughed. "I'm pretty sure the party wound down a couple hours ago."

Harper pursed her lips as she knotted the tie at her waist. "Hmm… I was looking forward to the casino night. It sounded fun."

"There will be other fun theme nights," he assured

her. "I believe next week there will be a Mardi Gras party in the courtyard."

She adjusted the V on her robe and sighed. "I suppose I could order a mask to match my dress. It's a shame to let it go to waste."

"Oh, it wasn't wasted," he affirmed. "I thoroughly enjoyed you in it."

With hands propped on her hips and head tipped to the side, Harper offered him a wide grin that hit him straight in the heart.

But his heart couldn't get involved. He hadn't allowed his heart to get involved with anyone since he was a teenager. Whatever he was feeling had to do with the anticipation and anxiety surrounding the baby, the engagement and the reunion with Robert.

But there was a moment in the hallway, a sliver of a second when he'd nearly let his guard down. He couldn't risk letting Harper in completely. Not until this entire mess was sorted out and all the lies dealt with. She deserved better, and he would make damn sure she got it.

He only prayed she didn't want to completely leave him after this was all out in the open. Would she listen to his side? Would she understand why he'd gone to such great lengths for revenge and why he'd kept the truth from her once he realized who she was?

"Tell me about your mother."

Harper's demand pulled him straight from his thoughts. "What brought that up?"

With a shrug, she crossed to the side of the bed he lay on and eased down next to his hip. Ethan shifted and settled his hand on her lap.

"You mentioned her passing, and you're protective of me, of this baby. I just figure she must have been an amazing woman to raise such a caring son."

Ethan wasn't sure how to put into words how amazing his mother had been. There wasn't a day that went by that he didn't miss her or wish he had her back.

"She was a single mother who raised my brother, Dane, and me the best she could," he started. "She inherited a good chunk of money from her father, and she invested it into opening two businesses. Her ultimate goal was to pass those down, one for Dane and one for me."

"Sounds like a smart woman." Harper rested her hand over his. "So how did you end up with the nightclubs? That wasn't her business, was it?"

Looking back, his life was a complicated mess, and he couldn't divulge the entire truth right now. Guilt pumped through him. He wanted to tell her, though. He wanted Harper to know the man Robert was.

Ethan was still trying to wrap his mind around the fact Harper was involved at all—even if it was by default. He didn't like it, he wanted to somehow remove her from the equation, but that was impossible.

Robert would be here soon. He had to tell her.

It was still such a mind-boggling fact that Robert could produce anything good, yet here Harper was—the best thing that had happened to him in a long, long time.

"Ethan?" Harper patted his arm, pulling his thoughts back to the sexy woman at his side. "Are you going to tell me about your mysterious past?"

Which part did he start with? There were so many

layers to him, so much he hadn't divulged to anyone. But he was coming to realize that Harper was special. He hadn't lied when he'd told her as much. Something churned deep inside him. He couldn't put a label on the emotion and was terrified to even try.

"Like I told you before, after my mother passed, my stepfather stole our inheritance, and the businesses were transferred to his name by some slick, underhanded attorney. Dane and I had no idea until after all the legal paperwork had been signed."

"I still can't believe anyone would do that," she replied. "Especially to grieving kids."

If she only knew...

Damn it. He absolutely hated every bit of this. She was a victim, just as much as he had been. Harper was too innocent, too sweet to be wrapped up in this mess, and she had no clue the explosion that was on the verge of blowing up in her face.

Ethan didn't know how, but he'd do everything in his power to block the pain from reaching her.

"We were seniors in high school, so we were almost graduated," he went on. "We both ended up enlisting in the army. Something shifted with us when Mom died. I take the blame for that."

Harper turned and lifted her knee up onto the bed as she leaned toward him. "You can't take all the blame. Every failed relationship is two-sided."

"We didn't exactly fail," he amended. "But I closed in on myself. I didn't know how to handle all that grief, so I turned to liquor and sex as an easy escape. It hurt to look at my brother, because I didn't want to see that mirror image of pain."

Harper flatted her hand over his chest, the warmth of her tender touch giving him the courage to continue. Even nearly twenty years later, the ache of losing his mother and the tragic failure of his relationship with his brother all those years was almost unbearable.

"We drifted apart and I let it happen," he continued, swallowing the lump of emotion in his throat. "But as time passed, we agreed on one thing. We wanted to take down the bastard who stole everything from us when we were most vulnerable. It took time, it took patience, but we knew once we were powerful and wealthy enough, nothing would stand in our way."

"Good for you guys," Harper cheered. "He deserves to pay. But how did you come to be a nightclub owner?"

He let the conversation shift, but soon she would discover the truth…and it had to be him that revealed it to her. If she found out any other way, she'd hate him, and he couldn't stand the thought of Harper looking at him with anything other than infatuation and desire in her eyes.

"After the service, I was still lost. I had no clue what I was going to do with my life. I had little money, just what I'd saved from the army."

Harper's fingertips scrolled an invisible pattern over his chest, but her eyes remained locked on his. Did she even know she was silently reassuring him to go on? Did she have a clue that she was the balm he needed to rehash all of this?

"I was in San Diego and ended up at a bar." Ethan

slid his hand over the tie on her robe. "I'd been there before when I'd been home on leave. I've always loved that city. The bartender recognized me, we got to talking, sharing our veteran stories, and the next thing I knew, he was making me a partner in business. He had that bar and was looking to open another in LA and in Boston."

"That's rather lucky," she told him with a grin. "And you're trying to distract me."

She glanced down to her waist, where her robe had come apart. Ethan smiled as he slid the material even farther from her lush body.

"Did you ever think that you're the one who distracts me?" he retorted. "You have some power over me that I can't explain."

That was the truest thing he'd ever told her.

Ethan's hands grazed her belly, and the reality of a baby—*his baby*—being right there reminded him exactly what was at stake. Everything. His future was riding on Robert, on Harper, on himself.

"So are we done with story time?" she asked, easing up to straddle his lap.

"I'd say we've talked enough."

Because he still wasn't ready to tell her the last piece of the puzzle. Tomorrow. He would tell her tomorrow. He wanted one more night in this fantasy land where everything was all right and there was no outside force that could potentially ruin the way she looked at him.

Because something was happening between them that had nothing to do with the baby and nothing to do with sex. Now Ethan just needed to figure out what the

hell to do with that knowledge and how he should deal
with these raw feelings that could ultimately destroy
this good thing.

Ethan slid the crucial documents back into the safe
in the walk-in closet of his penthouse suite. He'd spent
last night in Harper's bed, but today she was moving
all of her things into his space.

Before that happened, he wanted to make sure everything was tucked away, out of her line of sight.

Ethan had several statements he planned on using
for blackmail against Robert should Robert not give
up the property willingly. There were papers regarding tax fraud and money laundering—just a sampling
of charges Ethan would threaten.

He sincerely hoped Robert would just man up and do
the right thing, but as that was highly unlikely, Ethan
had a foolproof backup plan. He wouldn't have come
here and wouldn't have collaborated with Dane if he
wasn't one hundred percent certain they were ready to
take down Robert.

Once the resort was rightfully signed over to Ethan,
he had every intention of turning Robert in to the authorities. There were two other copies of all of these
documents. Dane had a set and so did Ethan's attorney.

Robert should be arriving in the next few days.
Ethan wanted everything put away and not a trace of
the damning evidence for Harper to see. Not until he
had a chance to tell her everything.

Which would be today. He'd already told her he
wanted to meet her around lunchtime to discuss some-

thing important. He hated having to be the one to tell her that her father was a manipulating bastard, but if he didn't, she'd find out soon enough and likely the hard way...like when Robert duped her for his own selfish reasons.

The thought of Robert stealing anything from Harper was an added layer of motivation for Ethan to take full control over all of this and get ahead of the game.

Ethan punched in the code on the safe and stepped from the closet into his bedroom. He glanced at the time on his phone and blew out a sigh. He had about an hour to kill before meeting up with Harper.

There was nothing with his clubs or potential investment property in France that he could focus on right now. Nerves were getting the best of him, and he needed somewhere to channel all this restless energy.

He pulled up Dane's messages and shot off a text telling his brother that he was about to tell Harper the truth. He wasn't sure what sort of reply he was expecting from Dane, but Ethan wanted him to know what was going on. And he wished like hell his brother was here, but they would get together and celebrate once the deal was all done.

Once all of this was behind them, once the resorts were fully theirs and Robert was out of their lives for good, Ethan vowed to spend more time with his brother. If that meant flying to cold-as-a-polar-bear's-butt Montana, then so be it. He and Dane were both entering new chapters, important chapters, in their lives, and Ethan wanted them to grow together again. He wanted his child to know Dane. What better way to bridge their past and future relationships than with a fresh start and new life?

His cell vibrated in his hand, but when he glanced down, the screen showed a message from Harper.

Meet me in the lobby. I have a surprise.

A surprise? Well, if it was in the lobby then their clothes wouldn't be coming off. But what could she have for him? When did she have time to plan anything?

Something warmed inside him. He didn't know the last time anyone surprised him with anything. Certainly no woman. Harper was special, she was…

In the dark.

Ethan ignored the fear that crept up and threatened to strangle him. It was time to face her, and once she presented him with whatever surprise she had, he'd have to get her somewhere private and tell her the truth.

There was no more time.

Ethan made his way to his elevator, rehearsing in his head exactly how he'd break this news to her. Her reaction would likely be instant anger, but he needed to make her see his side of things. He needed to make her understand he'd truly had no clue who she was when he first approached her. But he should've, damn it. His investigators should've had Harper's name, age, address, hell, her favorite breakfast cereal in their research. But they'd given him nothing but the fact Robert had a daughter he rarely had dealings with.

A daughter Ethan was now engaged to and expecting a baby with.

Would she listen to him? Would she see the parallel between herself and his own mother and understand that he never wanted her to be hurt?

The elevator doors slid open, and Ethan was greeted by a bustling lobby. As he stepped out, he took in the well-dressed people he assumed belonged to a wedding party. The girls all wore pale pink dresses, and the men wore black pants and white button-down shirts. Ethan scanned a bit more until he spotted the beaming bride and groom near the fountain in the middle of the open lobby. The laughter and chatter were almost deafening to his ears.

His gaze traveled through the crowd as he made his way across the open lobby. The breeze from the ocean wafted in, but while the scent was typically a comforting one, given his love of the water and the beach, even that couldn't calm his nerves today.

Ethan circled the fountain, and there she was. Harper had on a beautiful white sundress that grazed the floor; her hair was down and all wild and curly. The juxtaposition of calm and chaos had his heart beating wildly.

This wasn't the first time she'd stolen his breath, but this might be the first time he couldn't ignore that niggle of something more stirring inside him. As much as he wanted to deny it, he was falling for her. How the hell had he let this happen?

She was talking to a man whose back was to Ethan, so he made his way over. Harper laughed at something, but then glanced over the man's shoulder and waved at Ethan.

The man turned around, and in that moment, Ethan's

world came to a crashing halt as Robert Anderson met his gaze.

Every noise, every person, every single thing happening around him ceased to exist.

Ethan's past and his future had just collided in front of his face like a ticking bomb, and there was nothing he could do to dodge the explosion.

He was out of time.

Thirteen

Ethan clenched his fists at his sides as Robert Anderson had the audacity to not only hold his stare with all the confidence in the world, but to smile like the underhanded, devious bastard he was.

What an arrogant jerk.

"Ethan, come here. I want you to meet someone."

Harper extended her hand, inviting him over, but Ethan couldn't take his eyes off the devil himself. Robert's evil grin never faltered. It was like the man didn't have a care in the world, and he didn't seem one bit surprised to see his stepson.

"Ethan, this is my dad, Robert," Harper introduced them, oblivious to the tension. "Robert, this is Ethan. My fiancé."

Robert's bushy brows rose up. "Fiancé? Well, let me shake your hand."

Oh, hell no. Ethan shifted out of reach and wrapped a protective arm around Harper's waist. He wasn't about to touch that bastard and play nice.

"I had no idea Harper was dating," Robert stated, dropping his hand.

Clearly stepdaddy was going to pretend like he didn't know Ethan. Fine by him...for now. Harper still deserved the truth, but since they were standing in a lobby full of people—including a wedding party snapping candid photos—this was neither the time nor the place.

"We've been seeing each other for a while," Ethan stated, daring Robert to say something crude toward Harper.

Ethan might have lied by omission to her, but there was no way he'd let anyone treat her with anything less than respect.

Damn it. He should've told her the truth before now. He had no clue how everything had spiraled out of control, but now that it had, there was no option for him other than to face the fallout.

He didn't deserve her forgiveness, but he would be asking for it later anyway. He'd never begged for a damn thing in his life, but Harper was the exception to all of his usual rules.

"Robert owns Mirage," Harper said, her voice full of pride. "That's why this renovation project has been so important to me."

"He owns the resort?" Ethan questioned, feigning surprise. He wasn't sure how else to act and being blind-sided didn't give him time to plan. "Well, that must be quite time-consuming." He finally turned to focus on Robert. "It's funny, though. I've been here over a month and this is the first I've seen you."

Robert's eyes narrowed slightly, just like Ethan recalled him doing when he'd gotten angry years ago. Like when Dane and Ethan had played harmless pranks that Robert never found humor in.

Apparently Robert wasn't amused now, either.

"I'm lucky that I'm free to come and go as I please," Robert finally replied.

Your luck is about to run out.

"I didn't know you would be here so soon," Harper told Robert. "I mean, I knew you were coming, but I thought you still had another few days with work."

Yeah, so did I.

Robert shrugged a shoulder. "Some things can wait. I wanted to see my daughter."

Ugh. The man dripped with a sliminess that Ethan didn't want near Harper or their child.

Robert hadn't aged well, which elated Ethan. The sixtysomething man had gotten pudgy around the middle, weathered in his face, with dark circles beneath his eyes. Apparently lying and deceiving people for a living didn't do good things for one's health. Shame that.

"Do you want to plan on dinner this evening?" Harper asked. "We have so much to catch up on, and I want you and Ethan to get to know each other."

Ethan literally had to bite back an instant refusal. A

patient man was a smart man. That's how he'd come so far in his line of work. He'd waited for the right opportunities for everything and let the payoff be his reward.

He would wait and see what Robert said, because there was nowhere Harper would go in this resort that Ethan wouldn't be right by her side now. No way would he let Robert be alone with her. There was no telling what lies the man would tell her.

"Dinner sounds fabulous." Robert's eyes drifted to Ethan. "You'll join us."

Ethan sneered. "Wouldn't miss it."

Harper let out a little squeal of excitement. "This is great. I'll show you around and you can get a better idea of my plans in person. The crew will start next week, so you're just in time. How long will you be here?"

Robert glanced between the two and quirked his lips. "Not sure yet. I'm open to sticking around awhile."

Not if Ethan had any say about it. Robert had better get his jet and pilot ready, because Ethan had every intention of getting this jerk out of here sooner rather than later.

If Robert wasn't ready to expose the fact they knew each other quite well, that might work to Ethan's benefit. He needed to talk to Harper without another opinion weighing in. His time had run out.

Every step from here on out would have to be more calculated than anything he'd ever done. Harper and this baby were his top priority, but he still had to get this resort.

Anything less than all of that was failure. And Ethan never failed.

* * *

"You were a little rude," Harper murmured as they stepped on to the elevator that would take them up to Ethan's penthouse. "I thought you'd be more excited about meeting my father."

Hadn't they discussed the importance of family? Surely he knew that she really wanted her family life to grow. She *needed* that comfort and stability in her life now more than ever.

"Was I?" Ethan questioned, lacing his hand in hers. "I wasn't trying to be. Maybe I was just caught off guard. I knew you were anxious for this project, but I didn't know your father was the owner."

The doors slid open to his penthouse…well, their penthouse, since her things were being moved in later today.

"I didn't want you to think I had this project simply because he took pity on me."

Ethan gripped her arm and pulled her to face him. Framing her face with his strong hands, he looked her directly in the eyes. A woman could so get lost in that dark gaze.

"I never would have thought that. Never," he repeated. "I've seen your samples. I've heard the passion in your voice when you discuss each detail. Maybe you had an advantage because he knew you, but if you weren't any good, you wouldn't be here. Robert wouldn't offer a pity job."

Harper rested her hands on his wrists at either side of her face. "You sound like you know him."

Ethan stared for a second before he shrugged. "I

know people like him. I'm a businessman myself. We don't hire out mega jobs just to make someone feel good."

"I didn't want you to think—"

Ethan's lips covered hers for the briefest of moments before he eased back. "Stop. I think you're amazing. Your work ethic, your ideas, everything. Be proud of what you're doing. Confidence will get you everywhere."

That sounded like something Carmen would say. Maybe Ethan coming into her life had happened for a reason. Maybe he was exactly what she needed, exactly when she needed it.

Maybe she was falling too hard for him when she wasn't completely sure if he could ever feel the same.

"I assume you didn't tell your dad about the baby."

Harper shook her head. "I thought I would wait. There was a lobby full of people, and it just didn't seem like the right time. I will at dinner."

She didn't know if her father would even care. She wanted him to take part in her child's life, especially considering he'd missed out on the first two decades of hers. But would he even want to? That was the question and one she feared the answer to.

"What's on your mind?" Ethan asked. "You have those worry lines between your brows."

"How do you know I'm worried? Those are just wrinkles."

Ethan kissed her forehead. "I know because they were there when you were looking at those marble samples and muttering to them."

Harper couldn't hold back her smile. "You think you know me so well."

His hands eased to her shoulders and gave a gentle squeeze. "I do know you. So, what are you worried about?"

"I just want him to be part of this baby's life," she admitted. "I didn't know who Robert was until I was twenty. I'd never met him. My mother was, and still is, quite the free spirit. She'd always told me my father wasn't interested in being a dad, so I let it drop. But then I just wanted to know. I wanted to give him the chance to see me for himself. So, Mom told me his name, and I looked him up. He didn't seem too thrilled to have a child when I met him, but we've been talking and getting together a few times a year ever since. I just wish…"

"You want a relationship."

Harper nodded. "I'm probably being foolish, I know. What grown woman begs a man for attention? I guess all the time we lost can't be made up, and I can't make him want to be a parent—much less a grandparent. Some people just aren't cut out for that job."

Ethan pulled her into his arms and wrapped her in his warmth, his strength. Harper rested her head against his chest, seeking his comfort, wanting so much more.

There was such a fine line between being hopeful and being realistic. She teetered on the brink of falling over into foolishness.

If Carmen were here, she'd be giving the best advice. Harper would give anything for one more conversation with her sister.

"I don't have the answers," he murmured against her ear. "But know that I'm here. This baby will know both parents love her."

Harper eased back, smirking, her brows raised. "Her?"

Ethan's mouth quirked into a grin. "I have a feeling the baby is a girl. I see her with your smile, your eyes. She's the most beautiful child."

Harper's heart swelled at hearing him talk about their child. He'd thought about the baby—he'd thought so much that he'd pictured her.

Stifling a yawn, Harper laid her head on his chest. Ethan's hands roamed up and down her back as he kissed her head.

"Go lie down," he urged. "I'll make sure you're not disturbed. That way you'll be refreshed for our dinner."

Harper smiled into his chest. "I don't know the last time I took a nap."

"Then I'd say you're long overdue." Ethan cupped her shoulders and pulled back. "Rest for as long as you want. You've got to stay healthy for our baby."

The baby. Yes. Maybe he only cared for her because of the baby. After all, that's the reason he proposed, right?

He placed another kiss on her forehead. "I have a few business things to tend to, but I'll make sure you're up in time to get ready for dinner."

Harper nodded. She was too tired to argue. These long nights were catching up to her, not to mention working during the day and the fatigue from pregnancy. Everything she'd read said that the first trimester was rough with nausea and the need to sleep all the time. Too bad she didn't have that luxury. Which was why she should take advantage of the opportunity to nap while she could.

"Wake me if you need me before," she told him.

"Don't worry about anything but getting some sleep."

As Ethan stepped back into the elevator and left her alone, part of her wondered if she should be completely open and honest with him. Should she tell him she was falling for him? If they were going to enter into marriage, she figured honesty was the best option.

After dinner, she vowed on another yawn as she crawled into Ethan's king-size canopy bed. Tonight would be one to remember with the two men in her life. She just wished she knew where she stood long term with both of them.

Fourteen

Ethan pounded on the wood door, clenching his other fist at his side.

A snick of the lock came a second before the door swung open to reveal a spacious ocean-view suite.

"Well, that took longer than I thought," Robert reprimanded. "I'm disappointed."

Ethan shoved his way into the suite. "I don't give a damn what you are. You're not staying here."

Robert closed the door and turned to face Ethan. He'd changed into some tacky tropical shirt and a pair of khaki pants. Just the sight of him made Ethan sick to his stomach, and it took every bit of his willpower not to punch that smug look off his face.

Spreading his arms out wide, Robert raised his brows. "Looks like I am."

Ethan had waited years for this moment. Years to make this bastard pay for everything he'd done—for destroying a legacy built by a single mother, for robbing two boys of their future.

But the dynamics had completely changed, and now so much more was at stake. Once again, Ethan's future and everything he'd come to care for were on the line.

"You're going to sign Mirage back to me." Ethan widened his stance, matched Robert's gaze and held his hands at his sides. "My attorney has the paperwork all drawn up. I have copies in my safe in my suite. I'll email a copy to whichever assistant of yours you want. But we're getting this deal done now. Today."

Silence settled heavy between them, but Robert made no move; he barely blinked. Ethan had no idea what reaction he'd expected. Perhaps mocking, arrogant laughter, but that's not the response he got. Robert continued to stare, and Ethan didn't know if the man was stunned speechless or weighing his attack.

Either way, Ethan was more than ready to tackle this beast.

"Is that why you're hanging all over my daughter?" Robert finally asked.

Ethan ground his teeth. "Don't act like you give a damn about her or anyone else. You care about yourself and your bank accounts, and that's it."

Ethan hoped to keep Harper out of this conversation as much as possible. Before Harper ever entered his life, Ethan had had one goal in mind. He hadn't lost sight of that—if anything he was more determined than ever to stake his claim and secure his mother's legacy so he could hand it down to his own child one day.

And Harper? She deserved to be rid of this piece of trash. She might not like that at first, because she had no clue who she was dealing with, but Ethan would protect her…at all costs.

"Why the interest in Harper?" Robert asked, quirking one silver brow. "Were you just passing the time? Waiting on me to arrive? If you're lying to her, deceiving her, that's no better than what you accuse me of."

Robert was trying to goad Ethan, but he wasn't having it. Guilt already laid a heavy blanket over him, and he was trying to make the right decisions from here on out. There were factors that were simply out of his control, much as he hated to admit it.

Now more than ever, he had people relying on him to make sure the right thing happened. This situation wasn't about him or Dane or even their mother right now. Harper and the baby were his future…his life.

Damn it. He couldn't lose her. He just…

He couldn't.

"You don't honestly think I'll just give you this property, do you?" Robert mocked with a sharp bark of laughter. "You're still a foolish kid. I did you and your brother a favor by taking these off your hands. What would kids have known about running a high-profile business like this?"

Ethan took a step forward, clenching his fists at his sides. "Our mother raised us in these resorts, and we knew every in and out of her work. We also would've trusted the managers she hired to work with us as we grew into our roles. But that's all in the past. Right here and now, I'm telling you that your time here is over. You're not keeping this place."

Robert studied him for a moment. "Is this because Dane has Mirage in Montana? Is that what this is about? You're jealous. You two were always in competition with each other."

Now it was Ethan's turn to laugh. "Now who's foolish? Dane and I have planned this for years. We're not in competition. We work together as a team, something you would never understand. We were never going to sit back and let you keep what belonged to us."

Robert's cheeks turned red as he puffed his chest with a big, deep breath. Every part of Ethan wanted to laugh at his stepfather trying to appear intimidating. That affect had come and gone years ago. Ethan couldn't wait to squash him and kick the bastard out of his life forever.

He only wished Dane were here to see all of this.

"And you think it's as easy as you just telling me what you want?" he retorted.

Before Ethan could reply, Robert circled him and went to the minibar to pour a drink.

"I'd offer you one, but you're not staying," Robert stated, tossing back the tumbler. "And as far as those documents, shove them up your—"

"Don't be so clichéd with your insults." Ethan shoved his hands in his pockets and glared across the room. "You've been laundering money and evading a good portion of your taxes for years. Well over a decade, actually."

Robert's eyes narrowed, but he remained silent…the one smart thing he'd done.

"I have proof, and with one word from me, I can have half a dozen law enforcement officials on you within minutes."

"You're bluffing," Robert accused. "You wouldn't do that to Harper."

No, he wouldn't purposely hurt Harper, but he wouldn't stop the inevitable, either. Everything that spiraled out of control now had been set in motion by Robert years ago.

Ethan took a step closer, then another, until the only thing between them was that narrow bar. "Is that a risk you're willing to take?"

The muscles in Robert's jaw clenched as his grip around his empty tumbler tightened and his knuckles turned white. Ethan waited for him to toss the glass across the room, but the raging fit never came.

"Does Harper know you're blackmailing her father?"

"Harper doesn't know, because I haven't let her in on what a bastard you truly are...yet," Ethan tossed back. "But if you want to show all your hands, go see whose side she takes."

This part actually was a bluff—Ethan had no idea if she'd take his side. She likely would hate them both. He couldn't fault her for hating him, but even if she never wanted to see him again, he'd use every trick in his arsenal to make sure Robert didn't stay in her life, either. She deserved better than his poison.

"Oh, you think she's going to cling to your side when you reveal that I'm some big, bad monster?" Robert tossed back. "Sex doesn't mean a damn thing. That girl thrives on family. She doesn't care about money, which is why she won't make it far in her career. But that means she'll choose me over you any day."

Oh, she'd make it far, because she had common sense and a heart for serving others. She'd make it because she was headstrong and resilient.

And she'd choose him because he was giving her a new family.

It was on the tip of his tongue to mention the baby, but Ethan wasn't going to reveal that bit of news. He had to keep his family protected.

The reality of the situation hit him hard. Dane wasn't the only one Ethan was fighting for. Harper and their child were every bit his family now…and he cared for them.

He cared for Harper. His heart had entered the equation when he wasn't looking. He'd been so focused on this takeover and his revenge, he'd had no clue that he was falling for the innocent in all of this.

He wouldn't lose her. He refused to imagine his world without everything he wanted. There didn't have to be an either-or decision. Ethan wanted it all.

"I'm done here," Ethan stated. "You can either sign the papers or you can face prison time. Your future is in my hands, but I'm kind enough to give you a say."

Robert jaw eased back and forth as he seemed to give his options some consideration. Finally, he glanced down to his empty glass and gave a curt nod.

"You win."

Two words had never sounded sweeter. All these years, all the times he'd wondered if he would ever see this day, the moment had finally come.

But Ethan knew not to let his guard down so fast. Robert was a shark—he was ruthless and never one to just give in out of the kindness of his black heart.

"I'll have dinner with you and Harper and explain I have to leave on business," Robert went on.

Ethan cocked his head. "And I'm supposed to just take your word for this? You agreed pretty fast."

With a shrug, Robert refilled his glass. "A smart businessman knows when to cut his losses."

Maybe Robert was legitimately worried about the legalities of the situation…as he should be. Perhaps there was some conscience in there after all, and he realized this place never should've been his to begin with.

Ethan wasn't asking—he didn't want to stick around for any more chatter than necessary. But that didn't mean he wouldn't keep his radar up. Robert would pose a threat until all documents were signed and filed properly…or until the man was behind bars.

Now, if he could keep all of the ugliness away from Harper, find some way to explain without hurting her so they could both just move on. They could marry, raise their child, go about their careers and…

Yeah, it was the *and* part that terrified him. Who knew what tricks or traps Robert had waiting for them? There was no way the old bastard would go down this easily.

Ethan turned from the suite and let himself out.

One hurdle at a time.

Harper settled her hand at the crook in Ethan's arm as he led her into the Italian dining room. The resort had several restaurants, but this one was her favorite. She didn't even care that she could pound an entire plate of homemade ravioli in mushroom sauce. She planned on not only having that mouthwatering dish, but also the fresh-baked bread that practically melted in your mouth.

Her baby was going to love carbs.

Good thing she wore a flowy dress so she could enjoy her dinner without straining any seams. Harper had pulled out her fun red maxidress with a halter top and pulled her hair up on top of her head to stay cool. And since this was a special occasion, she'd also donned the blingiest earrings she had packed. The gold and diamonds hung in an intricate pattern and swayed with each step she took. The ruby on her finger and the gold bracelet on her wrist completed her look, and she'd never felt better.

Maybe it was the nap, maybe it was the fact she was about to go into carb overload…or maybe her happiness had everything to do with the man at her side and seeing her father again.

A renewed sense of hope blossomed within her, and Harper truly believed she could forge successful relationships with these two men. She had every reason in the world to want to make this happen. This baby gave her a new purpose, a reason to really fight for a familial future.

This day was already amazing, and she hadn't even discussed business with Robert yet. She couldn't wait to actually walk him through the rooms and the grounds and let him visualize each detail from her plan.

Excitement burst through her at the prospect of her

ideas coming to life. The renovations would definitely take time, but in the end, the hard work would be worth it. Carmen would be proud, and that in and of itself was payment enough.

"I still say we should've stayed in the room and ordered room service," Ethan growled in her ear as they neared their table in the back. "I could show you how to properly eat Italian in bed."

Harper glanced his way. "Perhaps I'll let you do just that. Later," she vowed. "Right now, we're having dinner with my father. You already made me miss casino night because you couldn't leave the room."

He muttered something under his breath, but she couldn't make it out and she didn't get a chance to ask as they arrived at their table.

As soon as the hostess pulled out Harper's chair, Robert came through the restaurant, headed straight toward them.

He extended his arms toward Harper and kissed her cheek in a very robotic manner that lacked the affection she desperately craved from him.

"I was running late," he told her. "I was afraid you'd be waiting."

"We just got here," Ethan replied.

Robert eased back and gestured toward the table. "Please, let's take a seat. I'm anxious to talk to you both."

Harper smiled as she settled next to Ethan. The waiter came over to fill their water glasses and take their drink orders. Harper admired the stunning floral arrangement of whites and greens when Robert's voice pulled her back.

Ethan had mentioned green to her just last night. He thought it might be a nice clean yet classy color scheme for one of the restaurants. Harper hadn't put that in her plans, but her decorative mind could see it in this open room. Whites and various shades green would be something to set the Italian restaurant apart from the rest of the resort.

Ethan was quite the little decorative assistant and handy to have in her corner.

"No wine?" Robert asked. "Last time we met up, you raved about a cab that you loved. Wine is always a perfect accessory to Italian cuisine."

Harper bit her bottom lip and darted her gaze to Ethan. "Well, we're not only engaged, but we're also having a baby."

Robert's reaction was not one she'd thought she'd see. Granted, she wasn't sure what she'd expected, but maybe some semblance of happiness?

Instead, she was met with wide eyes, red cheeks, thin lips. Robert looked like he was about to explode. He jerked his eyes to Ethan and looked like he was about to leap over the table.

"A baby?" he finally gritted out. "Harper, you don't know what you're getting yourself into."

Well, that sounded a little…judgmental. Who was he to tell her anything about parenting, considering he hadn't known she was around until she was an adult? Even then, he had seemed to have little interest in playing daddy.

"Harper will be a wonderful mother," Ethan stated, coming to her defense.

Robert shifted his attention between Ethan and Harper. "I'm sure she will, but is she aware that the father of her child is a blackmailing bastard?"

Harper gripped the edge of the table. "Robert. What has gotten into you?" she demanded, stunned at his accusation and outburst.

"I think it's time for us to go." Ethan took her hand and started to come to his feet. "Clearly this was a bad idea."

"Oh, don't go yet," Robert demanded. "I was just getting to the good part."

Harper remained in her seat, her hand in Ethan's as he tried to nudge her up. She stared across the table at her father, waiting for some type of explanation.

"What are you talking about?" she asked.

"Let's go, Harper," Ethan tugged again.

Robert reached across the table and took her other hand. "Listen to what I have to say before you go."

Harper jerked her attention between the two men she was practically torn between. Both radiated anger and rage, and she'd never been more confused.

"Don't listen to him," Ethan pleaded. "Come with me, Harper."

Irritated, she pulled her hands from each of them and glanced around the restaurant. People were starting to stare, and that was the last thing she wanted.

Harper stared up at Ethan. "Sit down."

Robert remained the focus of Ethan. Harper had never seen such fury on anyone, let alone the man she'd fallen for. Nerves and fear pumped through her because whatever was going on had both men angry, and it seemed she was caught in the middle.

How could they already be feuding? They'd just met.

Unless they hadn't... Did they know each other? But they'd acted like strangers before. Was that a lie?

Ethan finally eased back down in his seat and retook Harper's hand, resting on the arm of her dining chair. But his eyes remained locked across the table.

"What are you talking about...this blackmail?" Harper demanded of her father. "I just introduced you and Ethan."

"Oh, I've known Ethan since he was about twelve." Robert shifted his focus. "Or was it thirteen?"

Harper glanced to Ethan. "Is that true?"

He remained silent, and Harper wasn't sure he was going to say a word, but he finally blinked and turned his attention to her. That rage that had been pouring off him seemed to vanish, replaced by something akin to guilt and remorse in his eyes.

Dread settled heavy in her gut. He'd been lying to her?

"Robert was my stepfather for five years," Ethan ultimately replied.

Those words hung in the air, and Harper attempted to process each one. There was no way this was true. Her biological father was the monster who'd stolen everything from Ethan? The man she wanted to build a relationship with, whose support and approval she'd wanted to gain, was scheming and deceitful?

Harper's breath caught in her throat as she stared back at Ethan. "You used me," she accused.

Ethan shook his head. "Never once," he murmured, his gaze holding hers, almost silently begging her to believe him. "When we met, I had no idea who your father was."

"I don't believe you. The timing is too perfect and you…"

Harper swallowed the lump in her throat and forced herself to keep her emotions under control. He'd admitted he was a jet-setting playboy. He'd discussed how relationships weren't his thing, yet he'd been the one to propose. Baby or no baby, she should've paid attention to that red flag waving around.

But she didn't have all of the information, from either side. She needed, no, *deserved*, to know the full truth before making any rash decisions. She just wasn't sure that she could believe anything she heard right now.

"Oh, now, don't be mad at Ethan," Robert chimed in. "He just wants to blackmail me into giving his resort back. I never stole it, by the way. He was underage and couldn't do anything with it at the time. I had every right to do as I saw fit. Same with the Montana resort, which I let go a few years ago. It's all business."

Ethan fisted his hands and slammed them onto the table. "I'll ruin you," he threatened. "Is that what you want?"

Robert narrowed his eyes. "You would've turned me in anyway," he accused. "And if I'm going down, I'm sure as hell taking you with me."

There were too many threats flying around based on things she knew nothing about. Her head spun, her heart ached and she couldn't stomach sitting at this table another second.

The two men she wanted most in her life had ruined every shred of happiness she'd built up just moments ago. She was sorely tempted to just get up and walk away from them both.

But she had questions and she wanted answers.

"You're turning him in?" she asked. "To the cops, I assume? For what?"

"The feds," Ethan confirmed. "Your father has been laundering money for years, and I'm sure the IRS would find his taxes more than interesting."

Her head started to spin, and her stomach felt queasy. Harper smoothed a hand over her abdomen and closed her eyes to gather her thoughts and will herself not to be sick after hearing all of this.

"What's wrong?" Ethan demanded, sliding his hand over hers. "The baby?"

Before she could answer, the waiter brought back their drinks and a basket of fresh bread, and suddenly Harper wasn't in the mood for food at all. She wanted out of here, but, unfortunately, she was owed the truth and had to wait so she could hear both men.

Granted, they were both probably still lying, but there was too much at stake for her to just storm out of here in a fit.

When the waiter asked about taking their orders, Harper forced a smile and asked for another few minutes.

Once they were alone again, she pushed Ethan's hand away.

"I'm fine," she stated. "Don't touch me."

"Are you seriously having his child?" Robert demanded in a low whisper. Apparently, her bout of queasiness was what it took to make the situation real to him.

"I am," she confirmed, but the idea of a liar being the father of her baby wasn't helping her worries.

How had she been such a bad judge of character?

Was it just because she'd wanted to believe, wanted to cling to the hope and dream of a family? Was that why she'd foolishly thought he cared for her?

"Do you just set out to ruin lives or is that a default setting?" Ethan growled.

Robert curled his hand around his stemless wine-glass. "I had no idea she was expecting your baby. That's hardly my fault."

"Would knowing she was pregnant have made a difference?" Ethan demanded. "You ruined my life once. I sure as hell won't let you do it again, and I won't let you touch Harper's or our child's lives."

"I can speak for myself," she ground out, then glanced to Robert. "Did you really do all of those awful things to Ethan and his brother when their mother died?"

"I did what I thought was best," Robert stated with confidence. "I have no regrets."

"Because you don't have a damn soul," Ethan threw out.

Harper had heard enough. Neither man denied lying, neither man apologized to her for being deceitful and she was tired of all the anger and hate surrounding her.

She slid her chair back and came to her feet. "I'm done here."

Ethan and Robert immediately stood, but she held up her hands. "I mean, I'm done here with the two of you. Stay, eat, threaten each other, whatever. Just do it without me."

She didn't wait to see how they reacted or what they would say. She didn't care. Right now all she cared about was getting away from them so she could be alone with her growing concerns and fears.

Harper hated to admit it, but the betrayal from Ethan hurt much worse than that of her father. She didn't know Robert well; they hadn't exactly forged a deep bond.

But Ethan…she'd gone and fallen in love with the man and thought they were going to build a future together. Yes, they'd only known each other a short time, but the things they'd shared were deep and meaningful. Had he lied about everything? Could she believe a word he said anymore?

She didn't want to think that she was naive enough to fall for nothing more than charm and sex appeal, but apparently that was the reality of the situation.

And now she was bringing an innocent baby into the mix. No matter how this played out with Robert and Ethan, Harper vowed to protect her baby at all costs. She knew what it was like to have a mother who put her own needs ahead of her children, and Harper was determined that she would be everything to her child that she'd needed in her own life.

As Harper made her way toward the private elevators, all she could think of was that she was glad she hadn't told Ethan she loved him. He didn't deserve to know, and he didn't deserve her honesty.

One day she'd find the man she was supposed to build a life with, but Ethan wasn't that man.

Fifteen

Ethan walked out on the disastrous dinner moments after Harper. He hadn't gone after her, though. She needed her space, and anything he said to her at this point would only make her angrier...if she even listened at all. He'd needed his own space to put his thoughts in order and figure out how the hell to fix this mess he'd been thrown into.

He also hadn't stuck around to say any more to Robert. The damage was done, and Robert was well aware of what would happen to him now. Ethan had already sent the text to Dane that he was turning Robert in.

He hadn't contacted his attorney yet. Ethan had pulled up his contact, more than ready to send the text that would set the ball into motion of getting the feds all over Robert. He'd waited years to break this news.

But Harper. At the end of every thought on revenge, he saw her face. Despite Robert being the monster Ethan wanted to destroy, he was still her father. Harper would be even more hurt if Ethan followed through… especially now.

He would have to seriously consider everything and talk to Dane.

This whole scenario was a complete and utter disaster, and all he could think of was how Harper likely felt alone and confused and betrayed.

Ethan hated Robert even more now than ever. He was pure evil, leaving a path of destruction in people's lives with absolutely no remorse. The man was a total bastard to have no emotional outpouring of affection toward his own daughter. Robert had been stunned about the baby, but he'd shown no joy at the news, and he'd never said he was sorry for dropping the bombshell about the blackmail that exploded in Harper's face.

Ethan shot another text off to Dane telling his brother he'd call later and explain everything in more detail and discuss further action.

He wasn't in the mood right now to rehash the evening's explosive events.

Once Ethan had left the table, he'd walked around the grounds until he'd covered every square inch. He saw his mother everywhere he went and would give anything to have her here for advice. There were many times over the years he'd had that very same wish.

Of course, if she were alive, Ethan wouldn't be in this position in the first place. But then he wouldn't have Harper.

There was no way he'd give up without a fight. He needed that woman, that baby…the future he hadn't even known he wanted.

Ethan made his way back into the lobby and down the hall toward the private elevator. He had no idea what to say to Harper, how to make her understand that he wasn't a heartless monster. How did he make her see that he truly cared for her? That he'd come to care for her more than he thought he was ever capable of. He hadn't wanted to develop feelings for her, but she'd made it impossible to ignore that pull.

When the door to his suite opened, Ethan stared straight ahead to the wall of windows and spotted Harper out on the balcony.

His heart pounded faster, harder. She'd come here and not to Robert. Did that mean she wanted to give him a chance to explain the situation?

With a renewed hope, Ethan crossed the spacious penthouse and opened the patio doors. Harper still wore that dress that had rendered him speechless earlier this evening.

Those dark curls had been released from her updo earlier and now those strands danced around her shoulders. He wanted to reach for her, but he didn't dare… not until he knew where they stood now. She might hate him even more now that she'd had some time to think, or she might have decided she didn't even want to hear his defense. But he wasn't leaving until he fought for the life he had within his grasp.

"I had nowhere else to go," Harper stated without turning around.

Her soft words traveled to him on the breeze and pierced his heart. She sounded so lost, so alone.

Ethan made his way to the set of chairs and took a seat across from her. She kept her gaze on the darkness over his shoulder, the sounds of the ocean enveloping them.

"All of my things were moved here, and my suite was given away," she went on. "I'll be sure to find something else tomorrow, but with the resort booked, I didn't have the energy to think of another plan tonight."

Of course. That's why she was here. It had nothing to do with wanting to talk or forgiving him or even being ready to hear his side.

"I'm sorry," he told her.

Now her eyes shot to his, and he didn't know what hurt him more, the pain or the anger glaring back. She'd definitely had time to think, and from the fury radiating from her, things were about to get worse.

"Sorry?" she mocked. "What exactly are you sorry for? That you used me? That you knew who my father was and never once said a word to me? That you thought I was foolish enough to marry you, raise this baby with you and never realize that you were trying to destroy my father? Exactly what part are you sorry about?"

Ethan pulled in a deep breath. "All of it," he admitted. "Except the part about using you. I never did that. Not for one second. If I could have spared you the pain, I would've. I never wanted you caught in the middle."

"Yet here I am," she fired back. "And you're not too sorry or you would've come to me the second you supposedly discovered the truth."

Ethan hated Robert. Damn it, he loathed that man with every fiber in his being.

But he had to admit he was angriest at himself. All of this couldn't be blamed on Robert. He was just the one who put everything into motion.

Ethan's cell chimed in his pocket, but he ignored it. A moment later, it chimed again.

"Better get that," she said with a sneer. "Might be your brother and you can celebrate your win. But please have the decency not to gloat around me."

Ethan's guilt spread. "There's nothing to celebrate."

Harper cocked her head, crossed her legs and smoothed her dress out. "Oh, really? You mean getting this resort, no matter the cost, doesn't merit popping open the champagne?"

He deserved her bitterness, her snark. He deserved so much more, and he was just waiting for the bomb to completely go off.

"Robert hasn't signed the papers," he informed her. "But that's the least of my worries now. I'm worried about you, about us."

Harper laughed and shook her head as she looked back to the starry sky over the ocean. Despite the calm, relaxing atmosphere, the storm enveloping them was raging out of control.

"Us," she muttered. "You say that like there was ever an us to begin with."

"We're engaged."

"We were," she corrected.

His heart sank as she started twisting off the ring he'd given her. When that had gone on her finger, he'd still been thinking of their relationship as brilliant and the best route to hold on to their careers and raise their child together.

But now? Well, now he wanted her to wear it because he liked seeing his mother's ring on Harper's hand. He liked knowing they were going to build a life together…a dynasty.

He foolishly had just started allowing himself to feel something, and now he could only feel pain—and guilt, since he only had himself to blame for ruining everything.

No, that wasn't true. Robert had done his share, but Ethan should've told Harper the second he discovered the truth. He couldn't blame her for not believing him now. The timing was just too perfect.

Still looking out at the water, Harper extended her arm and held the ring between her finger and thumb.

"Take it," she demanded softly. "I was naive enough to think something would happen between us. I let myself…"

Her voice caught on that last word, and Ethan felt her pain. His heart ached in a way he hadn't known for so long. This was why he kept himself closed off. Feelings and attachments always led to a hurt that couldn't be ignored.

Another reason why he hadn't seen through his plans of turning Robert in.

"I let myself fall for you," she whispered.

Her words were so soft, they were almost lost in the ocean breeze. But he'd heard them, and the raw honesty of her statement shredded his soul.

"I'm not a heartless jerk who took advantage," he stated, needing to plead his case, but not just to make himself look better. He wanted her to truly know he valued her.

"I know exactly how this looks," he went on. "But I swear to you that I didn't know who you were until a few days ago."

"A few days. Plenty of time for you to tell me, but you chose to deceive and lie and talk me into marriage."

Harper turned her attention back to him, and Ethan forced himself to look at her. He needed to take his penance; he needed to see her pain to drive home exactly how he'd damaged this innocent woman. All she'd wanted was to honor her sister's memory, to build her career, and he'd turned her life inside out.

And they were having a baby. There was no way to dodge that lifetime bond, and he didn't want to. He just hated the thought that they wouldn't be able to raise the child together, the way he'd wanted to. But he'd have to put that dream away now. All he could hope was that at some point, Harper came to see that even though his actions might have shown otherwise, he really did care for her.

Ethan reached out and took the ring, purposely brushing his fingers along hers. Harper snatched her hand back, and he knew in that instant that all was not lost here. She still cared, she still wanted him, but she was angry with herself…angry with him.

"I don't expect you to forgive me right now—"

"Or ever."

He nodded to acknowledge that he was actually listening to her, even if he didn't like what she was saying.

"Maybe once you have some time to think, you'll see where I was coming from," he went on. "More than anything, I need you to see that you weren't just a pawn in this. You were a victim, yes, but by the time I realized you were caught in the middle, there was nothing I could do about it. I swear to you—I wanted to protect you. I thought I could. I'm sorry I failed."

Harper came to her feet and crossed the balcony to the railing. She curled her fingers around the bar and glanced down to her hands.

The smart move would be for Ethan to remain in his seat and give her the space she clearly needed…but he'd already committed the ultimate sin of betrayal, so what if he added gluttony to the list?

He rose and came to stand at her side, ignoring the twinge of pain when she stiffened at his touch.

"No matter what happens, I'll make sure you're paid for your work on the resort," he vowed. "My attorneys will make sure this ends up in my name. It may take time, but I want you to move ahead just like you had planned."

Harper sighed. "I can't even think about that right now—but I don't really have a choice, do I? My team is due next week and I need this project. I've put too much time into it, and the future of Two Sisters is riding on a successful design. The snowball effect Mirage would have on future work is immeasurable."

That's why he wanted her to know he had her back where the resort redesign was concerned. She might be pissed at him for personal reasons, but she still had a career that she loved and wanted to nurture. She had a legacy to continue…one that tied right in with his own.

"I understand your need to do everything to honor your sister," he told her, reaching for her hand and sliding his thumb across the top of her knuckles. "That's just another thing we have in common. I came here to fulfill my mother's wishes. That's all. The only person I ever intended to hurt was Robert."

"My father," she murmured.

At least she hadn't jerked away from his hand, but he still didn't like the empty space on her ring finger.

"He's not a nice man, Harper." Surely she understood that. "You even said that he had been distant and not much of a father figure in your life. When I told you the story of my stepfather, you agreed he should be brought to justice. This is the same man we're talking about."

He stared at her profile, his heart clenching when her eyes glistened with unshed tears. She turned her head in the opposite direction, but Ethan was having none of that.

"Look at me." He reached around and cupped the side of her face, easing her back to focus on him. "Don't hide your feelings from me. I know you're hurting, and I know I caused a lot of that. I'm trying to fix this mess as best as I can."

"I don't think that's possible."

Wayward curls blew around, caressing his hand. He didn't realize how much he craved her touch until now…until he was faced with the possibility of never having it again.

"Anything is possible," he replied.

Then he did the most difficult thing he'd ever done. Ethan released her and took a step back.

"You stay here tonight," he told her. "I'll give you space and time to think."

Her eyes widened as she turned to face him. "Where are you going? There are no more rooms."

Like he'd be able to sleep or relax without her at his side? But the fact that she was concerned for him despite everything was only another added factor on the growing list of reasons he shouldn't just let her go. They both wanted to be together, but the damned outside forces were determined to pull them apart.

Ethan turned and left her on the balcony. The sniff and soft cry as he walked away gutted him. For all the time, the years, the money and everything else he and Dane had put into finding leverage they could use against Robert, Ethan was starting to wonder if any of this was worth it.

Because of his revenge quest, he might just lose the one woman he'd ever allowed himself to care for since his mother. And if he lost Harper and their baby, nothing could ever fill that void.

Sixteen

The elevator chimed, echoing through the empty penthouse.

Harper tightened the belt around her robe and set her glass of water on the kitchen island. After Ethan left a couple hours ago, she'd decided she was more than deserving of a nice hot bubble bath. But now that she was done, her problems were still there.

Apparently, Ethan wasn't done talking, or he'd forgotten something. Or maybe he'd just decided it was silly for him to leave when he had nowhere to go. She'd been shocked when he said he'd let her have the entire suite for the night.

First of all, the place was plenty big enough for both of them, considering it had other rooms: a den, a game room, a designated office. They could make it work. Second, this was his penthouse.

Damn him for being a gentleman and making her so confused. How could she hate him for just wanting to retain the place his mother had wanted him to have? How could she hate him when she'd looked into those dark eyes and seen a pain she'd never seen there before? And how could she hate him when he was the father of her baby?

But she did hate him. She hated him for making her feel, for making her want…for making her see a future that involved a family that she'd always wanted and then showing her that it was all a lie.

How could she turn back now? She settled a hand over her belly and fought back tears. It wasn't as if she could just erase Ethan from her life.

The elevator door slid open, and Harper pulled herself together, but it wasn't Ethan who stepped off.

"How did you get access up here?"

"I still own the place." Robert stepped into the penthouse and glanced around. "Your boyfriend here?"

Harper crossed her arms over her chest and willed herself to remain calm. Getting worked up wasn't good for her or the baby.

Besides, she'd heard Ethan's side, so she should listen to Robert.

Part of her didn't want to. She wanted to hide and ignore any of this was happening. Was that terrible? She was exhausted, and being fed more lies just didn't seem too appealing.

"What do you want?" she asked, ignoring the reference to Ethan.

Robert shifted his eyes back to her and came farther into the penthouse. "This suite is usually reserved for elite guests."

Harper said nothing as her father came closer and finally took a seat on a bar stool like he'd been welcomed in.

"Listen," he began, flattening his hands on the marble countertop. "I wasn't trying to hurt you."

"Funny how nobody was trying to hurt me, yet you both did," she retorted, anger bubbling back up to push ahead of the pain.

Harper reached for her glass of water and curled her hands around the base. The urge to toss the contents in his face seemed cliché, but the desire was there nonetheless.

"I'm aware I haven't been a great father," he went on. "That was something I had never intended on being. I'm too busy traveling and working. I've done what I could since I found out you existed. I gave you this job as an olive branch."

If what Ethan claimed was true, then Robert was busy traveling and breaking the law, but she remained silent and let him keep going.

And the olive branch? Did he really think that this was the way to build a relationship—by throwing money at her? As much as she wanted this project, she would've taken an invite during the holidays or maybe a few days' visit here and there. But he always rushed in their phone calls or emailed…anything to keep his distance and not get too involved.

"But I should warn you," he went on. "Ethan's out to get me at all costs. That includes using you, obviously."

Harper took a drink and weighed her words. "Whatever is going on with Ethan and me is really none of your concern. Did you come here to deliver a real apology or just to warn me away from your enemy? Because I won't be used as the ball you two volley back and forth."

Robert stared at her a minute before shaking his head. "I see he's corrupted you."

"He's done nothing of the sort," she argued. "I don't trust either one of you right now. But I do wonder why you were so cruel to those boys when their mother died."

Robert pursed his lips, and Harper assumed he was working on another lie—or perhaps he was debating whether or not to tell her anything at all.

"I've always been an opportunist," he stated, easing against the back of the stool. "When I married their mother, I thought I could help her run these resorts. I wasn't quite in the financial position I am now, and I needed a leg up."

Harper snorted. "So you took advantage of a single mother."

"Opportunist," he repeated. "When she passed away, I felt it my duty to take over. The boys weren't old enough to run anything. Hell, they were still in high school."

Harper listened to him justify his actions.

"Why did you hire me for this renovation project?"

she asked. "I mean, you barely know me. You toss a few hours of your time my way each year. Even though I'm always trying to reach out and forge a relationship. And don't say the olive branch. I don't believe it."

He stared at her another moment and sighed. "My assistant looked over the portfolio you sent, and she said your designs were fresh and new and exactly what Mirage needed. I agreed because you are my daughter."

Harper hated to ask, but she had to know. "Did you even look at what I sent? Do you even care, or were you just going to throw the money at me when I got done?"

"I didn't look at them," he confirmed. "But I trust the judgment of my assistant, otherwise she wouldn't work for me."

Harper's heart sank. She'd already known he hadn't hired her out of affection or a genuine wish to see her succeed in the business that meant so much to her. But now she realized he hadn't even hired her because he thought she was talented or because he loved her ideas. He hadn't even taken the time to look at a few images... images she'd painstakingly poured herself into for each space of this resort. She'd lost sleep, she'd shed tears, all because she wanted everything to be perfect for Robert and his property.

"Get out."

Robert jerked at her command, and she had to admit the steeliness to her tone shocked her, as well.

"You need tougher skin," he replied. "If every little thing hurts your feelings—"

"Little things?" she repeated. "Hurt feelings? You

don't know a damn thing about feelings, so don't attempt to lecture me on mine."

When he remained still, she jerked her finger toward the elevator. "Get. Out. We're done here."

Robert's lips thinned. "You won't make it in the business world if you keep those emotions on your sleeve."

"Yeah, well, from the sound of things you're not going to make it much longer, and you've had yours closed off for decades. So I'll take my chances and be human."

He stared another second, and she thought he'd toss out another nasty remark, but he ultimately turned on his heel and got on the elevator.

Once Harper was alone, she took two shaky steps to the nearest bar stool and slid up onto the metal. Crossing her arms on the bar top, he laid her head down and finally wept.

She couldn't hold the pain in any longer. She had no clue what move to make next. She had no clue how she would ever recover from this crushing blow.

All she knew was that her baby would need her to be strong, and Harper vowed to rise up from this setback and be stronger than ever.

And never let another man near her heart again.

"There you are."

Ethan jerked up from the desk in Harper's tiny office. He hadn't realized he'd fallen asleep, but he blinked and focused on the person in the doorway.

"Dane?"

His twin glanced around the room and shook his head. "Rough night?"

Scrubbing his hands over his face, Ethan leaned back in the leather chair and sighed. Rough night didn't cover it. He'd been tortured with his own thoughts, replaying his actions over and over, wondering at what point he could've prevented everything from falling apart, or if that had even been a possibility.

A woman stepped up from behind Dane and offered a sympathetic smile.

"You must be Stella," Ethan stated. "I'd offer you guys a seat, but…"

The office had no spare furniture—it barely had room for this desk.

"Don't worry about it," she said. "Is there something we can get you?"

Ethan's heart ached, but there was nothing anyone could do at this point, so he simply shook his head and focused back on his brother.

Dane wore his typical flannel and jeans, which looked extremely out of place at a tropical resort.

"You do know you're in Southern California, right?" Ethan asked.

"We hopped on my plane and came straight here," Dane growled. "I didn't take time for a wardrobe change because I was worried about my brother."

Ethan hadn't seen Dane in too long, and knowing he'd rushed here to see him during the most difficult time of his life had Ethan feeling so damn thankful. At least there was one relationship he hadn't destroyed completely.

"How did you know where I was?"

"I know my way around here, too," Dane replied. "But I overheard one of the staff members talking to a cleaning lady, and they said there was a man asleep in the back office. I figured it was you or another guy who was kicked out of his room."

Ethan rolled his eyes and pushed away from the desk to come to his feet. "I'm sorry I'm not making a better impression," he told Stella. "It's been a rough twenty-four hours."

That megawatt smile widened, and he could see how his brother fell so hard.

"No need to apologize," she told him.

Dane crossed his arms over his chest and leaned against the door. "So, where do things stand now?"

Ethan raked a hand through his hair and tried to organize his thoughts. "They stand in a mess."

"I'll put Robert aside for a second," his brother said. "How's Harper?"

Ethan swallowed and refused to be overcome by emotion. He would not break down, damn it. He certainly wouldn't lose it in front of Dane and Stella. He needed to get a grip, hold it together and focus on how to fix this disaster instead of wallowing in self-pity.

"I haven't spoken to her since last night."

Ethan had wanted to stay, he'd wanted to demand she hear him and understand, but he respected her enough to walk away. She was smart, and he could only pray she came to the conclusion that, despite his mistakes, he'd never meant to cause her pain.

"I told her to stay in the penthouse and I'd leave," he added. "There were no rooms, so I ended up here."

"Is she worth fighting for?" Dane asked.

"She's worth everything."

Ethan didn't even have to think of his response. Harper had come into his life like a whirlwind of freshness and had breathed new life into his heart, actually managing to fill that dark void.

"Then why are you down here sulking?" Dane demanded. "Go do something."

"I was giving her some space," Ethan muttered. "She doesn't want to see me right now."

"Then let's go deal with Robert." Dane cursed beneath his breath. "Not that I want to see the old bastard, but he deserves justice."

"You know I completely agree," Ethan replied. "But I haven't pressed on that just yet."

"Because of Harper," Dane guessed.

Ethan swallowed, but that lump of guilt hadn't moved since yesterday. He simply nodded, unable to go into more detail for fear of being too overcome with emotions. He didn't recall the last time he'd been so consumed by so many feelings.

"I'm going to let you two talk," Stella chimed in. "This is such a beautiful resort, and I haven't been to the beach in ages. I'm going to take a walk."

She went up on her toes and kissed Dane's cheek before slipping away. Dane stepped into the office and closed the door, leaning back against it.

"You need to pull yourself together and go talk to Harper," Dane repeated. "She's had all night to think. I know you screwed things up, but hell, I deceived Stella from the beginning and managed to make things work. You have to be honest and throw in a heavy dose of begging."

Ethan had already planned just that. Harper and their baby were worth putting pride aside and fighting for... no matter what he had to do.

"Where's Robert?" Dane asked, his voice hardened now.

"I'm sure he's still in his suite," Ethan stated. "You ready for a family reunion?"

Dane nodded. "The final one."

Seventeen

Harper zipped up her makeup case just as the chime on the elevator sounded through the penthouse. She stilled, her heart beating fast. She'd been trying to get out before Ethan came back, but when she'd gotten up earlier, her morning sickness had hit her full force.

She was getting a late start, but at least her queasiness had subsided somewhat. She didn't have much to gather since her things had just been sent up yesterday. She hadn't exactly unpacked.

Pulling herself together, Harper inhaled and counted to ten to calm her nerves. She'd just stepped from the master suite and into the living area when the elevator door whooshed open.

But her guest wasn't Ethan or even Robert.

"Hello?" she said in greeting to the striking woman who stepped into the penthouse.

"Hi, I'm Stella." The woman took a few steps in, clearly unsure if she should keep walking or remain still. "I'm Dane's fiancée."

Dane. The twin.

Harper clasped her hands together and nodded. They must've come after talking to Ethan.

As much as Harper would've appreciated another woman to talk to, she really wasn't in the mood to confide in a stranger—especially with one who was associated with Ethan…even by default.

"Did Ethan send you up?" Harper asked.

"No. He thinks I'm walking on the beach."

Harper studied the other woman. Long, silky hair. A simple green maxidress with a denim jacket and little booties. She was definitely not dressed for the beach.

"We hopped on Dane's jet as soon as Ethan texted him about the mess here," Stella stated, as if reading Harper's mind. "And there's no rooms available, so the desk graciously held our luggage. I haven't changed yet."

Harper softened and sighed. "I'm sorry. I'm being rude. Come in, please. Have a seat."

"No need to apologize," Stella replied as she moved into the living area. "From what I heard, you've had an explosive couple of days."

Harper followed and took a seat on the sofa. She smoothed her sundress over her thighs and crossed her legs.

Stella sank onto the edge of the opposite sofa and

rested her hands on her knees as she tilted her head, her face covered with concern. Clearly she had been filled in on the series of events that had taken place.

"I'm sorry for just coming up here," she started. "But I wanted to give the guys time to talk, and I thought you might need a female sounding board. Of course now that I'm here, I feel a little silly, since we're strangers."

Harper couldn't help but smile at Stella's obvious nerves.

"I'd like to think I know a little of what you're going through, though," she added. "I'm not sure how much you know about how Dane and I met."

Intrigued, Harper rested her arm on the edge of the couch. "I don't know anything other than the fact you two are engaged."

Stella beamed. "We are, but our road to happiness was not easy. The short version is Dane was an ass, but the longer version is, he had his reasons."

"Sounds familiar," Harper muttered.

Stella went on to explain that her father had won Mirage in Montana from Robert a few years ago. When Dane had come to Montana to get it back, he'd known full well who Stella was. He'd deceived her from the start. But then he fell in love, and Harper could see why.

Not only was Stella stunning with her dark skin, inky black hair and adorable accent, she seemed genuinely concerned, which really said something about her character. To come to the aid of a total stranger was something Carmen would've done. Harper felt an instant connection.

"Listen," Stella added. "I'm just saying that the Michaels boys might be a little hardheaded and have tunnel vision when it comes to their goals. Rightfully so, since their mother left this legacy for them."

Harper listened to all the reasons why she shouldn't be so infuriated with Ethan, but that didn't stop the pain from wrapping its talons around her heart and digging in.

"I just can't believe that he had no clue who I was at the start," Harper stated. "The timing…"

"I understand." Stella eased back on the sofa and crossed her leg. "And today is the first time I met Ethan, but I know Dane. First of all, they look so much alike, it's crazy. But second, I know those two boys have fought hard to get where they are. I truly believe Ethan had no ruthless intentions where you're concerned."

Common sense pushed through the pain, and Harper finally admitted to herself that she believed he hadn't approached her because of her father—but that didn't negate the fact he hadn't come to her when he did find out.

"Listen." Stella came to her feet and held out her hands. "What do you say I find somewhere to change my clothes and we take a walk on the beach or go grab something to eat?"

Harper's stomach rolled a little at the thought. "I'm still not up to the point of eating," she said, patting her stomach.

"Oh, I forgot! This is so exciting." Stella beamed. "I mean, *I* think it's exciting. Are you happy?"

Harper nodded. "I am. Despite everything, I'm really happy."

Stella smoothed her hair behind her ears and pulled in a breath. "Then let's take that walk, you can show me around and we'll talk babies."

"Are you…"

"Oh, no," Stella replied with a laugh. "But I can't wait until Dane and I start our own family."

"I'll call down and have your luggage brought up," Harper suggested. "There are plenty of bedrooms here, and I'm sure Ethan would insist anyway. I'm still in limbo, but you can change here and we can go out for a while."

"Sounds perfect." Stella pursed her lips. "You're re-designing the resort, aren't you?"

Harper nodded. "The design work is pretty much done, and I'm supposed to start the physical renovations next week. I'm not in a work mind-set right now, though."

"Would you be in the mood enough to give me a hint on what your plans are as we walk?" Stella urged.

Harper felt a spark of delight. "I think I could manage that."

"I'll tell Dane the plans."

Which meant he would tell Ethan, but that didn't matter. Harper wasn't asking his permission, and she wasn't going to be involved in the whole family thing now that his brother had arrived.

Harper might just have to go home and wait until her crew arrived. What once was the most important project of her life had been tainted by a dark cloud and had taken a back seat to the turmoil that had become her life.

* * *

Dane had waited so long for this moment. To finally come face-to-face with the bastard who had altered his future and stolen what belonged to him and Ethan.

His brother stood at his side at the closed door to Robert's suite. Dane knew the pain Ethan was feeling; he knew the confusion and angst. But Ethan would have to figure out the next steps with Harper on his own. There was only so much advice Dane could give. He would support Ethan no matter what, but that was one battle he'd have to fight alone.

Ethan rang the bell and took a step back.

"He's still just as much of an ass as ever," he muttered.

"Good to know some things never change."

The door swung open, and if Robert was surprised to see them, he didn't show it. The man had gotten pudgier, harsher. Good. Dane took joy in believing life hadn't been perfect and easy for his stepfather.

"I'm not surprised you're both here," Robert stated, blocking the door from letting them in. "I admit, I was hoping you wouldn't be so clichéd as to gang up on me."

"We're not ganging up," Dane offered. "Just letting you know how things are."

Robert crossed his arms over his chest but made no attempt to move or invite them in. Fine by Dane. He wanted this over with so he could put the black mark on his life behind him and move on with Stella and their life of happiness.

"I can't believe you don't have the authorities here yet," Robert scoffed.

"That's up to you," Ethan stated.

Dane fisted his hands at his sides. He wasn't sure what angle Ethan was taking, but Dane would wait this out. Since they were dealing with Harper's father, Ethan had final say on how they worked this. In the end, Robert would always be scum, but Harper and Ethan might be able to find happiness.

"Sign this resort over to me today, and I'll hold on to the damning evidence that would have you fighting for freedom for the rest of your life."

Robert narrowed his gaze at Ethan, then turned to Dane. "And you're just here for moral support? I heard you already got the Montana property."

"Don't worry about my business," Dane replied. "I'm here because Ethan and I are a team."

"Against me."

Dane shrugged and crossed his arms over his chest.

"Do you want to sign the papers or not?" Ethan asked. "Because this window is going to close soon."

"How kind," Robert murmured.

"I'm feeling generous."

Dane admired his brother for not completely going off on Robert—not just for their past, but also for treating the woman he loved so terribly. Their situations weren't so different. Stella's father was a complete jerk who had been using her to get his resort back up and running the way it should be. He'd promised her the entire resort all in her name, but had never intended on following through.

So, yeah, Dane understood just how much self-control Ethan was practicing right now. Dane couldn't stand the sight of Robert—seeing him again just dredged up all those memories of how much that man had destroyed.

Not physically, but emotionally. All those years ago, Dane and Ethan had already begun pulling apart because of the grief of losing their mother, but to have another blow had really blindsided them.

"How do I know you won't turn me in once I sign everything back over to you?" Robert asked, skepticism lacing his tone.

"You don't," Dane chimed in. "It's a risk you'll have to take."

"You're losing time," Ethan stated. "Do you want to sign or not? Either way, you're leaving the resort today. We need your room, and I'm sick of having you here near Harper."

"Don't act like all of this is on me." Robert dropped his hands and shook his head. "Whatever. Take Mirage, but you're paying for the renovations. I'm done with this place—it's not worth the headache."

Dane wasn't so quick to believe him, but he did sound frustrated and over it. Good. The sooner he was gone, the better for all of them.

"You should have the file in your in-box," Ethan replied.

Robert narrowed his gaze. "Awfully sure of yourself, aren't you?"

"I wasn't leaving here until you signed because I didn't want to put the feds on you. That would crush Harper, even more than you've already hurt her. There was no need to pile more on the burden she's already carrying."

"You have until lunch to sign," Dane added. "Ethan's nicer than I am, but I'm calling the authorities in three hours if Ethan doesn't have the final copy back."

Then if anything happened to Robert, that guilt would be off Ethan and onto Dane.

"They'll be signed," Robert grumbled. "I need to get back to Barcelona anyway. I have real work that needs my attention."

"Don't think we won't be keeping our eye on you," Ethan added. "If you cheat anyone out of investments, properties, money, I will not hesitate to make your life a living hell in ways the feds wouldn't dream of."

Robert let out a mock laugh. "You think I'm scared of what you could do to me?"

Ethan took a step toward Robert, and Dane waited, fully expecting to have to pry his brother off.

"Try me," Ethan said in a low, menacing voice. "I promise, you'll regret ever crossing me or my family."

Robert must've seen something in Ethan's eyes, because the older man nodded and took a step back.

"I'll pull up the documents now."

Without another word, he slammed the door, causing Ethan to jerk back. The echoing of the door sounded through the hallway, and Dane glanced each way, thankful nobody was around. Likely, they were all on the beach or still in bed.

"Do you believe him?" Dane asked as they turned toward the elevator.

Ethan nodded. "I do. He's too arrogant to let himself go to jail. If there's a loophole to save his ass, he'll take it."

Dane hoped that was true, for all of their sakes.

"I need to find Harper." Ethan punched the button on the elevator to close the doors. "I don't know what I'm going to say, but I can't stay away."

"She's with Stella right now."

Ethan jerked around. "What?"

Dane held up his hands. "Calm down. It was my idea. I thought Harper could use another woman to talk to, and Stella texted and said they were going to walk around the resort. Harper is showing her around and discussing new designs."

"And me," Ethan muttered, turning back to watch the numbers light up as they passed each floor.

"That goes without saying, but Stella is in your corner."

"She doesn't even know me."

"But she knows me," Dane countered. "Trust me on this. Stella might just tip the scales."

The elevator doors slid open, and Ethan stepped out first. The lobby had only a few people milling about, going in and out of the buffet area for a quick breakfast.

"I think I should change my clothes," Dane stated, glancing down to his attire. "Oh, Harper had our luggage taken to your penthouse."

"Did she now?" Ethan smirked, though it quickly faded. "I do have plenty of room. More if she's leaving."

"Then maybe you should give her a reason to stay."

Eighteen

"**Y**ou're a difficult woman to track down."

Harper glanced over her shoulder, and Ethan's heart clenched at the sight. She stood on the edge of the shore, the water lapping up over her bare feet. She held a dainty pair of sandals at her side, her other hand gathered up the skirt of her red dress and her curls tossed around in the wind. She was like something from a dream, something he could see, but not touch. Something that could vanish in a flash.

Her dark eyes locked with his a split second before she turned back to stare at the sunset.

"I haven't exactly been hiding," she said as he came to her side.

"I hear you spent some time with Stella."

"She's amazing."

Ethan had talked with Dane and Stella over dinner in the penthouse earlier. He'd hoped Harper would show back up—he'd even ordered enough dinner for four.

"She seems to think I should forgive you," Harper stated after a moment.

Ethan slid his hands into his pockets to keep from reaching for her. He wanted this too much to screw up by being selfish and thinking of his wants first. Harper was everything to him. Not just because of the baby, but because she made him feel so many things he'd never thought possible.

"And what do you think?" he asked.

Ethan studied her profile, trying to capture the proper words to describe the beauty she radiated.

"I don't know what to think," she murmured.

The gentle waves filled the silence, and he waited.

"Did you have my father arrested?"

Ethan pulled in a breath. "No, I didn't."

Harper's gaze shifted to his, her brows rising. "Why? That's all you've wanted."

"That *used* to be all I wanted," he corrected.

Unable to be this close and not touch her, he took a chance and reached for her hand, the one she clutched her skirt with.

The material fell down around her ankles as he raked his thumb over her knuckles.

She trembled.

"After my mother died, I shut down," he started. "Ask Dane. I even closed off from my own twin. I didn't want to feel anything for anyone. I wanted to crawl inside myself and never get hurt again."

Harper's chin quivered, but he kept going. He had her attention—this was the opening and the chance he'd been waiting on...he'd been praying for.

"Then Robert took the main part of my mother's legacy, and I didn't know what to do," he stated. "I know I was too young to run the place myself, but I would've listened to her managers. I would've done anything to make sure nothing severed that bond between my mother and me."

He drew in another shaky breath and squeezed her hand. "You know that I've been wanting revenge on my stepfather, and he deserves to have everything taken from him. But that all changed the second I realized you were his daughter."

"I don't know the man like you do," she supplied. "I met him when I was twenty, and we've had a handful of interactions since then. I believe you about the kind of man he is. What hurts is the fact you didn't tell me the moment you knew."

Ethan nodded in agreement. "I know I hurt you. Harper, you have to believe me. The second I found out, I started trying to find a way to make sure you were not involved in this backlash. I wanted to shield you and our baby from everything ugly about this. I know I should've come to you, but I wanted to handle it myself."

Emotion clogged his throat, and he swallowed back the lump as his eyes began to burn.

"I wasn't able to protect my mother," he choked out. "You're the only other woman I've ever loved, and I needed to make sure you—"

"What did you say?"

Ethan stopped and blinked. "What?"

"You said you loved me," she stated, tears swimming in her eyes.

A swell of warmth spread through him. He hadn't even realized he'd said the word, but now that it was out, he realized that's the exact word he'd been searching for to describe how he felt about Harper.

"Did you mean it?" she asked.

Ethan smiled for the first time in what felt like days. "Yeah, I did. I love you, Harper."

Tears spilled from her eyes, trailing down her cheeks. He released her hand and framed her face, swiping at the moisture with the pads of his thumbs.

"Sorry," she muttered. "People are probably looking."

"Of course they are. Who wouldn't, at the most beautiful woman in the world." Ethan took a step closer until his chest brushed hers. "And who cares? Don't be afraid to show who you are."

"I don't know who I am," she said. "I wanted to be the reckless woman having a heated affair with this hot stranger. Then I wanted to be the woman who was strong and could be a great mother. Then I thought maybe, just maybe, you and I could grow together and perhaps fall in love and raise our child as a family."

"You're all of those women," he told her.

Harper closed her eyes and licked her lips. "No, I'm not," she said, looking back up at him. "I'm the woman who is a poor judge of character."

"No, you aren't." He tipped her head so he could

focus on her and she had no choice but to hold his gaze. "You're the woman who is loving, trusting, caring, loyal. You demand those same things in return, which you should. You're not at fault here. But I do love you. I know you might not be ready for that yet, but I'm giving you all the time you need. Just…don't give up on us."

Harper smiled. "I love you, too."

Ethan had never heard sweeter words. He didn't deserve her affection or honest emotions, but that was his Harper. She didn't hide her thoughts or feelings.

"I want to try to make this work," she went on. "I feel like everything was so rushed. Maybe we could take our time, truly get to know each other more and dedicate each day to growing together."

Ethan couldn't hide his smile. "I'd love that."

Harper went up on her toes and wrapped her arms around his neck. "Don't hurt me again."

Smoothing his hands up and down her back, Ethan shook his head. "Never. I promise to always be honest with you, and we can face whatever obstacles the future holds together."

"That's all I ask," she told him. "I hope you don't care I invited your brother and Stella to stay in the penthouse. It wasn't technically mine, so…"

Ethan slid his lips over her mouth then eased back and rested his forehead against hers.

"I want you to share everything with me," he told her. "I can't wait for you to get to know Dane. We're all starting a new chapter."

"Does this mean we'll be going to Montana to visit?"

Ethan shuddered. "Cold weather? Maybe we could go in the summer."

Harper threaded her fingers through his hair and laughed. "I'd love to see it. I've never been there, and I hear it's gorgeous."

"In the summer," he repeated.

"Fine," she conceded. "A summer visit. Should we go back up to the room and visit with our guests?"

Ethan took a step back, took the sandals from her hand and laced his fingers in hers. "Is that what you want?"

Harper smiled and nodded.

They started up the near empty beach. It was getting later in the evening, and most people were at dinner or getting ready for the free entertainment in one of the resort's nightclubs or theater.

"I want that sense of family," she told him. "I feel like I'm getting a second chance at having a sister and the life I've always wanted."

"I'll give you anything you want," he told her as he guided her to the steps leading to the open lobby. "But I have one request."

She stopped and turned to face him. "What's that?"

Ethan slid his hand into his pocket and pulled out the ring. He'd never been so nervous, because he actually wanted this more than anything. He wasn't using the proposal as a ploy or any other reason than the fact he just wanted her in his life forever.

Harper's gaze landed on the ring, and Ethan wasted no time in dropping to one knee. He'd cheated her out of a real proposal before—he wasn't going to do that again. She deserved everything she'd ever dreamed of or desired.

"Harper, will you marry me?" he asked. "Have my children and grow empires with me?"

With tears in her eyes, Harper nodded her head yes and reached for the ring. "I know I said I wanted to take things slow, but I still want to marry you. I just want some time before we say 'I do.'"

Ethan came to his feet and wrapped his arms around her waist. He lifted her up and smacked a kiss on her lips.

"I don't care how long you want to wait," he told her. "Just say you'll always be mine and forgive me when I do stupid things."

"Done," she told him. "Now let's get upstairs and celebrate with your family."

"*Our* family."

"I like the sound of that."

Ethan covered her mouth with his, wanting to connect to her even more. He'd finally found a love he'd never thought possible with a woman he didn't deserve. She'd forgiven him, and he would never take her for granted again.

Now they were moving on to their new chapter, growing their family.

Seeking justice and revenge wasn't everything in life.

He had all he needed right here in his arms.

* * * * *

COMING SOON!

We really hope you enjoyed reading this book. If you're looking for more romance, be sure to head to the shops when new books are available on

Thursday 5th September

To see which titles are coming soon, please visit

millsandboon.co.uk/nextmonth

MILLS & BOON

LET'S TALK
Romance

For exclusive extracts, competitions and special offers, find us online:

- facebook.com/millsandboon
- @MillsandBoon
- @MillsandBoonUK

Get in touch on 01413 063232

For all the latest titles coming soon, visit
millsandboon.co.uk/nextmonth

MILLS & BOON

MODERN

Power and Passion

Prepare to be swept off your feet by sophisticated, sexy and seductive heroes, in some of the world's most glamourous and romantic locations, where power and passion collide.

MILLS & BOON
True Love

Romance from the Heart

Celebrate true love with tender stories of heartfelt romance, from the rush of falling in love to the joy a new baby can bring, and a focus on the emotional heart of a relationship.

MILLS & BOON
MEDICAL
Pulse-Racing Passion

Set your pulse racing with dedicated, delectable doctors in the high-pressure world of medicine, where emotions run high and passion, comfort and love are the best medicine.

MILLS & BOON
HISTORICAL

Awaken the romance of the past

Escape with historical heroes from time gone by. Whether your passion is for wicked Regency Rakes, muscled Viking warriors or rugged Highlanders, indulge your fantasies and awaken the romance of the past.

Six Historical stories published every month, find them all at:

millsandboon.co.uk/ Historical

JOIN US ON SOCIAL MEDIA!

Stay up to date with our latest releases, author news and gossip, special offers and discounts, and all the behind-the-scenes action from Mills & Boon...

 millsandboon

 millsandboonuk

 millsandboon

It might just be true love...